Heartbreak, Then Payne

Tracy Gray

A Shaydes of Gray Book

Also by Tracy Gray

Thug's Passion

Follow me on FaceBook at: *Tracy Gray*

Follow me on Twitter at: *@alwaystracygray*

Acknowledgements

El Shaddai: Thank you for your many blessings, your patience and your love for me. Thank you for the revelation that my gifts are not for me, but for others. Thank you for your peace, your joy, your favor and most importantly your faithfulness. There is none like you in all the earth. ~ I learned sooooo much about the industry, other people, and myself during the journey. Thank you for being merciful, and bestowing wisdom. Thank you for allowing me to be open, and adaptable.

Mike: Thank you for all of these years of marriage and companionship. I honestly could
 not have traveled on this journey of life with any other man, but you.

Kacie: Thank you for your support, your loyalty, and your faith in me. You are my ABSOLUTE most favorite daughter. (smile) I love you to life!!!!

Michael II: Thank you for being you. God brought you into my life with anticipation, and dramatics. It's been a wild ride since you arrived, but I'm so thankful for your presence. You're my baby boy, my joy, and my cuddle bug. You mean more than you could ever know to our family, and I love you to life!!

To my friends/readers: **Jackie Nichols, Brandy Means, Alma Friar, Angela Kent, Deana Clark-Anderson** (Dean), and **Gloria Pennick**. Thank you guys for reading, re-reading and offering the necessary feedback to make this the best novel it could possibly be. Special thanks to my bestie, **Barbara Hilton** for being my ABSOLUTE biggest cheerleader!!! You have probably read *Thug's Passion* more times than I have!!! LOL! You always, always have something positive to say about my books and writing ability. I just appreciate that soooo much. Special thanks to my girl, **Angela David**. I just love you, girly!! You're such a freaking hustler! LOL. Thank you for your offer, and please believe that I will definitely be taking you up on that!!!!

To my friend, **LaTricia "Shawn" Samson**: Thank you so much for your willingness to share the details and ins/outs of your son's medical diagnosis for use in this book.

To **Verlean Hollins-Singletary** – owner and operator of Da Book Joint: Thank you for all of your support. You hosted my first book signing, and were there for me every step of the way, when I was a new and clueless author. I appreciate you more than you probably know!

To **Christina Jones**: Thank you so much for your help, your expertise and your willingness to make my project a priority of yours. I'm so glad to have met you!!!!

To the lovers of *Thug's Passion*, my fans: Oh my goodness, I just love and appreciate you all sooooo much!! I would start naming people, but I know I would leave somebody out. Still, I would be remiss not to specifically mention the book lovers of

Chicago Transit Authority (CTA), who have embraced me, stayed on me to get another book out, sent messages to me, encouraged me, and waited (somewhat) patiently for this follow-up book. You ladies (and gentlemen) are the ABSOLUTE best!!! I wish I could wrap my arms around all of you and give you a great big hug. Your support means everything. You all are the reason that I do this…love this!

Look at what God can do with a little girl from the south side of Chicago. Watch out world, I'm back at ya!!!!!

Tracy Gray-Caruthers

Dedication

This book is dedicated to the memory of my mother-in-law,
Vera Caruthers
(March 29, 1953 – May 08, 2013)

Ms. Vera, thank you for birthing the only man who has ever been able to own my heart. Just, thank you! Thank you! Thank you! All those years ago, you turned him over to me, and I am so thankful. I love your son. He's the Godliest, most upright, loyal, hard-working, loving, sweet, funny and PATIENT man I've ever known. You did a wonderful job with him. He's definitely a keeper.

This book is also dedicated to the most important women in my life

My grandmother, **Dorothy G. Gray** ~ God only saw fit to bless me with one grandparent. I'm so thankful that He gave me the very best one. Words cannot express what it has meant to have the relationship with you that we share, Gammy. Thank you for everything.

My mother, **Lois R. (Barry) Bailey** ~ who could have raised a daughter like me, except a mother like you? We are such a perfect fit. I love you dearly, and thank you for every sacrifice, every tear, every iota of exercised patience, every time you had my back, every hug, every kiss, every word of encouragement, every correction…every prayer.

My aunts, **Gloria Gray** & **Vida Kent** ~ Aunt Gloria, thank you for being part-aunt, part-friend, and part-big sister. Thank you for all of the advice. I carry it in my heart, and I pass it along to "Miss Missy." Aunt Vida, thank you for being so freaking cool. You were the person I looked up to the most when I was a little girl. Your tiara will never tarnish in my eyes. I still think you're hot to death! Kisses & hugs to both of you.

My daughter, **Kacie Caruthers** ~ you are the greatest gift that God could have ever bestowed on me. I feel so lucky to be able to even know you, let alone mother you. I don't know what I ever did to be so blessed. God really is good. You're a joy and a pleasure. Even when you're being difficult, you're a joy and a pleasure. I love the young lady that you're growing up to be. The word "proud" doesn't even scratch the surface of how I feel. I love you. **You make life so good!!!!**

Prologue

Free Yourself

Joya

I floored the little white BMW 335i, as I cruised down Lake Shore Drive listening to Irreplaceable by Beyonce on the stereo system.

I sang along with Beyonce, because I felt like she recorded that song just for me and the crazy situation that I was in.

When I arrived at my destination, I made sure that my best friend, Chantelle Price was right behind me in her man's cherry red Chrysler 300. The two of us were checked in by security, and allowed to drive into the player's parking lot at the United Center.

I parked the car where I was sure dude would see it, turned off the ignition and waited. Chantelle parked nearby, got out of the Chrysler, and walked over to me.

"Where is this bastard?" She asked, as she leaned against the side of the gleaming BWM.

I looked over at her. The sun was so bright, that even with my sunglasses on I still had to shield my eyes. "He'll be out here. He said practice let out at 3:00." I checked my watch. It was 3:45. "Trust me, he'll be out here. He wants his stuff back."

"I can't believe you're givin' it back to him. If I was you, I would've told his dumb ass to kick rocks!" She sucked her teeth. "You know…"

Her thought was interrupted by the loud sound of the side door of the building swinging open. A few seconds later, he came into view. It had been almost six months since I had last laid eyes on Montez "Monte" Patterson. He looked exactly the same, though. Tall. Slim lower body. Muscular upper body. Dark brown skin. He was wearing the smirk that used to make my heart melt, but now only made my stomach queasy. He was followed by about four of his goon-ass teammates. He walked right up to the car. Having him in my face like that took me right back to the day we met.

***

Any flight from the east coast to the west coast was a long trip. It could last anywhere from six hours to eight hours, depending on delays. That was why I hated doing coast to coast trips. I usually tried to maintain my base in Chicago, and make sure that all of my return flights ended there. However, on that day in August, I got stuck doing a trip from Miami to San Francisco.

I was working first-class, which I liked. So, that was a plus. The flight was a routine one. No problem passengers, no turbulence in the sky, no delays. I disembarked the plane at San Francisco International, and was so caught up my own thoughts, that I didn't even notice dude until he fell into step with me.

He said a few words, flashed his bright smile, and gave me a peek at his upbeat personality. I was reluctant about giving Monte any rhythm at first, because when he introduced himself to me, he made sure to mention that he was Montez Patterson, and that he played (at the time) for the Indiana Pacers. His boastfulness rubbed me the wrong way, but I decided to overlook it. I thought he seemed genuine.

We had drinks at his hotel, The Mandarin Oriental. The bar closed early and he insisted that he wasn't through talking to me. So, he took me to a bar in a nice little area called SoMa, and talked to me until I almost fell asleep on him. That was all it took. We exchanged numbers, and no matter how hard I tried, I never could shake Monte after that.

We did the long distance thing for about eleven months. Anytime Monte wasn't playing basketball, he was laid up under me in my Hyde Park condominium. Any time I wasn't flying for work, I was hopping on planes, jetting to whatever city he was playing in just to be close to him. The relationship was bananas, in a good way. I lived and breathed that boy. I was so in love with him, that I couldn't remember what not being in love with him even felt like. I didn't remember a time when he wasn't a part of my life. I was gone over Monte, and happy about it.

About a year into the relationship, I came out of my love-induced fog and realized that the relationship I thought I was in wasn't the relationship I was really in. It happened very abruptly.

Monte's teammate had a birthday party. Monte didn't formally invite me to the party. The wife of another teammate mentioned it to me in passing. Since I usually attended team functions on Monte's arm, I didn't see why that party would be any different. I figured it slipped his mind. He just forgot to mention it to me. The night of the party, I made myself beautiful, jumped in my car and made the two hour (plus) drive from Chicago to Indianapolis.

To say that the sight of Monte hugged up with some chicken-head in the V.I.P shocked me, would be the understatement of the century. You could have knocked me over with a feather. I really didn't even know how to react...at first.

But after a few seconds of watching them cuddle and whisper to one another, the ghetto paid a visit, and I went buck-wild. I turned that V.I.P section out. I ran up to Monte and his "date" and commenced to beating the hell out of both of them. I was just swinging. I didn't really care who I connected with. I just made sure that every punch that I threw, connected! A couple of Monte's teammates finally restrained me.

Monte didn't utter one word, but he looked at me with hatred in his eyes. I could read his thoughts. I knew he was thinking that he was the man on that team. The franchise player. And his girl was up at a nightclub showing her ass. I knew he thought my behavior reflected badly on him, but my pain and anger were too raw. I couldn't care about his thoughts or his image.

"Get her outta here." He said to his teammates, like I was a groupie or something.

"And take her where?" The rookie questioned. He was the low man on the totem pole. He understood that I was his problem.

"I don't give a shit." Monte said dismissively.

The rookie walked me to the exit of the club. "Listen..." he started.

I cut on top of him. "You listen. I don't need you to 'get me outta here'. I got it."

I left the club, and drove back to Chicago. God's hand had to be on me that night, because I could barely see the road for all of my tears. I was weaving from lane to lane, doing no less the 85mph all the way. When I made it to my apartment, I drank an entire bottle of Cristal, fell into bed fully dressed (shoes and all), and cried myself to sleep.

I was awakened by loud ranting and raving a few hours later. Stupidly, I had given Monte a key to my spot, and he chose that night to use it. He walked into the bedroom, flipped on the lights, and let me have it. We got into a fist fight. I was still drunk, but that didn't diminish the pain from the blows he was landing all over my body. When the ten rounds were over, it was easy to see who won the fight. I was swollen and bruised all over my body. I hid from my family and friends for over a week.

After that incident, Monte stopped bothering to hide his indiscretions, and fist fighting became a way of life.

***

"You bring my shit?" He asked, in a no-nonsense tone. That was his idea of a greeting.

I hit him with the screw face. "Who are you talking to like that?" The days of him talking garbage to me were long gone.

"Did you bring my stuff?"

"Yeah, I brought your stuff."

His face was a grimace. "So, give it to me. I wanna get outta here."

"The feeling's mutual." I assured him as I slowly opened the car door, and even more slowly climbed out of the supple, leather interior. I was glad that it was an unseasonably warm day in May, because typically, I would've frozen my butt off trying to show off like I was doing. My upper body was encased in a breasts hugging halter top. My lower body was poured into the tightest, shortest pair of shorts that I could find. I wanted Monte and his entourage to see exactly what he would never get to fall into again. And I knew he was watching me, because he was on some sex addict type stuff.

I walked to the back of the car, hit the button on the remote, and pulled Monte's bag of belongings from the trunk. I moved back to the front of the car, making sure to put an extra bounce in every step. I held the bag out to him.

A second or two passed before he took the bag from my hand, because he was too busy looking me up and down. When he finally did grab the bag from me, he shook his head and spoke. "You're too damn big to be wearing those shorts. You look like Precious or somebody with them fat ass thighs."

I flipped him off with my freshly manicured middle finger. "If I remember correctly, I couldn't pull your head out from between my *fat ass thighs* for two years straight, Bastard!"

His teammates started to snicker behind him.

"Bitch, please." He was embarrassed.

"You're the bitch, Monte. Just take your stuff, and go."

"You're showin' off." He accused me.

"Oh, I'm showing off? The way I remember it, you were always showing off for your men. You were showing off when you were cheating on me. And when you got that chick in New Orleans pregnant…and when you caught that rape charge in Phoenix."

"Those charges…"

I didn't let him finish his thought. I kept right on talking. "You were showing off when you smacked me up in front of Culpepper and Stallworth and when you blacked my eye at

14

Davis' house, in front of everybody. And remember that time we had that fight in the 40/40 Club in New York? You know, when I hit you over the head with that bottle of Hypnotiq? Weren't you showing off then, too?"

"What you gotta bring that up for? Miss me with that usual bullshit, Joya. All I want is my stuff. Your big ass can get in the wind."

I let the third comment about my weight ride, even though it did bother me. It pissed me off that dude could stand there talking tough, like he wasn't down on his knees seven months earlier begging me to stay with him. Like him crying in my face and promising to change had never happened.

"Gimme my car keys." He demanded.

I tossed them towards his face; hoping one of the keys would poke him in the eye and render his dumb ass blind. Unfortunately, as a professional athlete, his eye-to-hand coordination was top notch. He caught them in mid-air. "That's right." He said, closing his fist around the keys. "I'm havin' it shipped to S.C. in the morning."

Monte played for the NBA's newest expansion team, the Columbia Cougars, out of Columbia, South Carolina. He was the franchise player. The big name that made bells ring all over the NBA. And he had the over-inflated ego to prove it. "I hope you gotta drive around on ya feet." He continued.

"Don't worry about what I do." I started walking towards the Chrysler. "Let's go, Chan."

Monte peeked inside the bag I had given him and threatened me. "If anything is missin', I'm at you, Joya."

I gave him the finger, again and kept it moving towards Chantelle's car.

Chantelle's voice was soft and soothing as we drove out of the player's parking lot. "You okay?"

15

I shrugged my shoulders. "I'm cool." It was true. I was cool about the entire situation. I had given the relationship with Monte my time, my energy, my effort, my heart, my tears, and my anger. I didn't have anything left to give to it. I was over the whole thing. "I'm just glad that it's done. Now, he has his stuff. I don't have to worry about him calling me, sweating me about his car, or any of the other gifts he bought me."

"I still can't believe you gave back the gifts. You gotta be crazy. There's no way in hell I woulda gave back the gifts."

I sighed. "To be honest with you, Chan...I really don't want anything around me that reminds me of him. So, he can have the gifts. He already lost the best gift he's ever had...me."

She smiled. "You're so crazy. But you're right. You were too good for him. Hopefully, you'll meet somebody who appreciates you."

"I'm not trying to meet anybody. After everything I went through with Monte, all I wanna do is be by myself for a minute."

We rode in silence for a while, both caught up in our own thoughts.

"What're you doin' tonight?" She questioned.

"Probably chilling. I have to fly out Monday night. I'm doing a west coast swing. Chicago to L.A., then L.A. to Portland. Portland to Seattle. Seattle to Denver, then back home. I'mma be tired as hell if I don't get some rest."

"So, rest tomorrow. Tonight I want you to come by the house. It's wifey weekend..."

"Wifey weekend? What is that?" I twisted my face.

"It's somethin' Izz made up." She explained happily. Izz was her man, Israel Allen. "One weekend outta the month, he agrees to give the streets a rest, and kick it with me. He stays home for the whole weekend. I love it!"

Izz agreed to stay home with her one weekend out of the month? What part of the game was that? Weren't there like four or five weekends in a month? What was he doing for the other weekends? Playing "wifey weekend" with his side chicks? I didn't get it. "Uhm." I said, noncommittally.

"Anyway, we're partying at the house tonight. Izz and his guys are playin' poker. You should come through, instead of moping around your spot, thinkin' about Monte taking your car."

"That did hurt." I admitted.

"I know it did. You loved that car. You treated it better than some folks treat their kids." She teased.

"Whatever."

"So, you coming through or what?"

"I don't know. I'll think about it." I told her. "What time is everything going down?"

"Uhm, around 10:00...10:30."

"Chan, I'mma be sleep around 10:00. I work a job. Your man, and his guys don't know nothing about that. They fall outta bed and hit the block at whatever time they feel like it. 10:00 in the morning, 10:00 at night, it's all the same to them. People who work real jobs need rest."

"We're twenty-four years old, Joya. Quit acting sixty-four. We're gonna have fun. Plus, it's gonna be nothin' but dudes there. Come meet somebody. Let him help take your mind off your BMW."

I semi-smiled at the thought of a guy taking my mind off of my problems. It had been a minute since I made time with a dude. And even longer than that since I had spent time hanging out. After my break up with Monte, I threw myself into work. It seemed like every time I looked up, I was racing to Midway Airport to fly out. I was picking up extra trips like crazy. Flight attendants that I didn't even know would call me to work their hours, and I would make it happen. My paychecks were fat as hell, but jetting around the U.S. six days a week was tiring.

"If nothing else, come hang out with me and Bubbles." She suggested.

Bubbles, Chantelle's younger sister, was a live-wire, who was as full of energy as her nickname implied.

"Okay." I relented. "I'll come through. Look for me around 10:30."

Chapter One
Big Pimpin'

Payne

My eyes darted over to the clock on the dashboard of Justus Calhoun's Chevy Tahoe, as we rode to our destination. Justus and I didn't speak to one another. Subconsciously, I bobbed my head rhythmically to the sound of Nas' *New York State of Mind,* as it reverberated through the truck stereo on "repeat." Justus pulled to a stop in front of the house. There was moderate activity on the block. I figured that was to be expected, since it was 3:47 on a Friday afternoon. Israel's Navigator was parked a few feet from us. Israel Allen, Dex Robertson and Patience Black exited the vehicle. Justus and I followed suit.

The five of us walked up to the porch carrying the tools that we would need to remove all of the windows, so that they could be replaced. Israel unlocked the front door, and we walked inside.

Justus tapped me on the arm. "Ay Payne, you wanna start in the bedrooms?"

I really didn't care where we started. I was more-so looking forward to finishing. It was Friday. I wanted to spend my night chilling, not working my ass off. "Cool." I responded.

"Me and Dex got the living room." Israel told us. "Patience, you wanna get the kitchen?"

Patience shrugged his slim shoulders. "Yeah." He agreed easily.

The five of us split up, and got down to the business we had come to handle.

We were former dope boys turned real estate investors. We played both ends of the real estate business. We bought and flipped houses for a profit, and we rehabbed spots and turned them into rental units. When the dope game went sour, the need to get that paper didn't stop. We had to adjust our hustle.

When we bought our first piece of property, me, Justus, Israel, Patience and Dex really believed that we were trading in our hood ways to go straight. Little did we know that we would need our "D-boy" mentalities more in the real estate business than we did on the block. Motherfuckas did not want to see five, young, black men get rich legally. Everything was dog-eat-dog. But as it turned out, me and my mens…we liked the taste of dogs. So we ate all the dogs we had to eat in order to get to where we wanted to be. Our company, *Exit Strategy, LLC*, was mad successful. We had completed over forty-five flips, and rehabbed and rented out countless apartments and houses in less than two years.

Justus and I made quick work of the windows in the three bedrooms, and moved on to other areas of the house. By a little after 5pm the only thing left to do was to remove the front and back doors from their hinges. Israel and I had just finished with the front door when we spotted our renter, Elliott Pettigrew coming up the walkway.

"Look at this nigga." Israel said to me.

"He looks surprised to see us." I commented jokingly.

Israel chuckled, then turned his attention to the renter. "What good, *Elliott*? You just comin' from work?"

Elliott nodded hesitantly. "Uh, yeah." He looked from me to Israel. "What're you doin' here?"

"Taking care of some maintenance work." I replied.

Justus, Patience and Dex entered the foyer where Israel and I were standing with Elliott.

Dex gave Elliott a bright smile. "Ay, I hope you like what we did to the spot, Nigga."

Elliott watched in confusion as they walked away with the door in their hands. "Where are they goin' with my front door?"

"Oh that? Yeah, we're replacin' your front door. Back door, too." Israel informed him.

"And the windows." I added.

"Damn, I almost forgot. The windows, too. But what's messed up, is that we can't get your new windows or replacement doors until next Friday."

It took a second for the realization of what Israel was telling him to sink in, but when it did, Elliott's face fell.

"Dog, in this neighborhood, I don't know how I would feel about leaving my stuff in the crib with no windows or doors." I instigated.

He nodded his agreement. "So, what am I supposed to do? How am I supposed to live here for a week with no windows or doors?"

"Motherfucka, you ain't paid rent in this bitch since January. You think we give a fuck?" Israel asked.

"Take it light." I told him.

"Deadbeat ass nigga." Israel added, before the two of us blew the spot.

We had been in the game long enough to know that rental laws gave way too much power to the tenant. We knew that it took forever to go through all of the channels that the court system had set up to evict tenants, so the five of us had developed our own way of encouraging deadbeat tenants to vacate our shit. It worked wonderfully.

***

After the episode with deadbeat-ass tenant, Justus, Patience and I ended up at the *Exit Strategy* office going over a business deal. Patience told us that one of the sellers was trying to strong arm us into a bad deal. It was a six-unit building over on 69th and Crandon. We were looking to rehab the flat and fill it up with renters as quickly as possible.

It seemed like dude had zeroed in on the weakest link, and had decided to run his bullshit through Patience. Of the five of us, only Patience had a problem with confrontation. It wasn't his thing. He was laid-back and mellow, like his name implied. Not that he was soft. He wasn't. He just wasn't good with confrontation. He was the type who was unpredictable when pissed off. When he was twelve years old, he shot and killed his mother's boyfriend after he got tired of watching dude beat on his moms. His mother never completely forgave him for killing her man. Soon after the murder, she gave up her parental rights and remanded Patience over to the state of Illinois. Eventually, an aunt got custody of him, but Patience was never the same. Because of his history, the rest of us tended to look out for Patience whenever a confrontational situation arose. Somebody else always seemed to step up and take care of business on his behalf.

Anyway, the seller decided that he wanted to accept a higher offer from another buyer. So, dude was doing everything he could to kill our deal. Every minor detail somehow had major importance. That was some bullshit. Dude had accepted our offer. The contract was signed. He was going to run the deal the way we wanted it ran. There wasn't any other option. Once the three of us had come to a consensus on how we were going to handle the renegade seller, it was time for my weekend to begin.

As the three of us walked out of the office that night, Justus got a text from Israel. Izz wanted the three of us to come through his crib and hang out. He was hemmed up at the house with his girl on some bullshit he'd created called "wifey weekend." He had suggested to his girl that he would spend one weekend a month holed up in the crib, if she stopped nagging him about the amount of time he spent in the streets. She went for it, so he was stuck. He wanted us to come through and be *stuck* with him.

I already had plans to stop through Tashera's spot. Tashera was a dip that I hit from time to time. I decided to blow her off. I wasn't too pressed to get to her spot anyway. She was the type of chick who never wanted to let me leave when I rolled through. After the sex, she always wanted me to hang around on some "pillow talk" type garbage, like we were in a relationship or something.

***

I made a quick stop at my crib to change clothes before I headed over to Israel's. As soon as I pulled to a stop in front of his house, my cell phone vibrated. I knew it was Tashera without even checking the screen. Sometimes, I felt like old girl had a tracking device on my dick. Her GPS system must've alerted her that I had made a detour, and wasn't on my way to her spot. I let her call go to voicemail, while I parked my Denali. I jumped out, hit the switch on the alarm, then made my way up the front walk. I walked up the concrete steps, rang the doorbell and waited.

Israel answered the door for me. Izz was a tall, dark skinned, over-weight brother, who put everybody who came in contact with him in the mind of Notorious B.I.G. And like Biggie, Israel was a cool dude, who despite his questionable looks and large body size, never seemed to lack female companionship. "What's good, Son?" He asked, slapping me dap, and briefly embracing me.

"Not much, Izz. What's good with you?" I replied, slipping the Cincinnati Reds cap off of my head. Not because Israel expected me to, but because my grandmother had me trained to always take off my hat when I came in from outside.

"Chillin'."

"You heard from Elliott?" I asked, trying not to chuckle.

"Man."

"Yeah, he blew the damn phone up at the office."

"Fuck that nigga." He was dismissive. "He wasn't blowin' up the damn phone when he wasn't payin' his rent. We're back here playin' cards. Come on."

I followed him down the long hallway, and into his dining room. It looked like I was the last of the crew to arrive. Justus, and Dex were already seated at the table. Patience was posted up against the back wall.

I walked over, and greeted J with dap. As I went to greet Patience, Chantelle appeared in the room carrying two bottles of beer. She handed one to me, and the other to Patience. Chantelle was Izz's girl. She was a toffee colored shorty, with a pretty face and crazy body. I liked Chantelle and the way she handled her business. She was on some old-fashioned type shit. She knew how to make a guest feel welcomed. She understood what Izz expected from her, and she made it happen. She pimped her role as wifey.

"Thanks Ma." I told her.

She grinned at me. "You're welcome."

"Thanks Chantelle. Good lookin'." Patience cheesed at her.

"You're welcome, Patience."

I hit Dex with dap. Chantelle's younger sister, Bubbles had her chair pulled up close to Dex's. I tried not to smirk as I gave her a quick hug. I had noticed a few weeks earlier that

Bubbles had been giving Dex a lot of "attention." She was making it *real* obvious that she wanted to give him the ass. I kinda wished that he would go ahead and hit that, so Bubbles could stop playing herself. It was sort of sickening to watch.

The front doorbell rang. Chantelle walked away to answer it, as I made my way back over towards Patience.

"What's good, P? You straight?" I asked him.

Before he could respond, my phone vibrated. I checked the screen. Tashera. I sent her to voicemail.

"I'm good. I just got a lot on my mind." He told me.

I nodded slowly, and took a swallow of beer. Chantelle walked back into the dining room followed by the sexiest redbone I had seen in a minute. My eyes swept over her quickly. She was sporting a short skirt, a tiny top, and high heeled sandals. Shorty was thicker than a motherfucker, with thighs that looked edible.

Chantelle was whispering in her girl's ear, and it looked to me like they were talking about my man, Patience. But every now and again, Shorty Redbone would cut her eyes at me. I wondered if she liked what she saw as much as I did.

"Ay Chan, run out to my truck and grab some more beer." Israel said, reaching into his pants pocket, and pulling out the keys to his Navigator.

"Chan," Dex said, holding up his empty beer bottle. "Grab me a refill."

"Joy, can you get Dex a beer, while I run out to Izz's truck?" Chantelle asked Shorty Redbone.

Shorty hit Chantelle with the screw face. I could tell she wasn't used to waiting on dudes like Chantelle was.

"Please Joy." Chantelle begged.

"Yeah, okay." Pretty Girl finally relented.

She had a sexy voice. Real feminine. I watched each sway of her hips as she left the room to get Dex's beer. She returned a few seconds later. "Who needed another beer?" She asked.

"Me." Dex took a pull from the tree he was blowing, and tried to hand his empty beer bottle to Pretty Girl.

She ignored the empty bottle and sat the new beer in front of him. "Uhm, I'm not Chan and I'm not the maid. You're gonna need to throw your own empty bottle away, Bruh."

He looked up at her and grinned. Of the five of us that crewed together, Dex swore he was the biggest mack. He was a medium-height cat, who thanks to his white moms and black pops had the "pretty boy" look that only a mulatto could have.

"Come on, Ma." He said, and lightly ran his hand up the inside of Shorty Redbone's bare thigh.

I don't know what he did that for. Shorty Redbone went bananas.

"Are you crazy?" She asked in disbelief as she rained punches down on his back and shoulders.

"Whoa! Whoa!" Israel interjected, jumping up from his chair and attempting to reign Shorty in. "Calm down, Joy."

"Yeah, calm down, Little Mama." Dex drawled, still trying to win her with his grin. "I ain't mean no harm."

"Then you shoulda kept your hands to yourself!" She responded, pulling away from Izz's grasp. "You don't know me."

I tried not to laugh out loud. I liked Shorty's style.

"Exactly. And that's what I'm tryin' to do. Get to know you." Dex said, eternally macking.

"Wrong answer, Bastard." Her face was still balled up into a mean frown.

"What the hell is wrong with you, Shorty?" He was starting to lose his cool, which wasn't out of character at all. Dex was a hot-headed individual who would snap-off at a moment's notice. "Why is your attitude so fuckin' stank?"

Before Ma could respond, Israel spoke up. "Come on, Man. You know that was disrespectful. How do you expect her to react? That's Chan's friend. Look at her. You can't tell she's on some stuck-up shit?"

Pretty Girl gave Israel the finger.

"Am I lyin'?" He teased, still trying to lighten the mood as he took his seat.

"Dumb bastard." Shorty Redbone hissed at Dex, then walked out of the room.

I saw my opportunity to slide in, so I followed her. I found her in the empty living room. "Ay Ma, you straight?" I asked walking towards her. Her back was to me, and even from behind, Baby Girl looked like sex personified. I could tell that she was still mad, though. It was in her body language.

She turned around and looked over at me. Her light brown eyes landed on my green ones. *Damn!* I thought to myself. Not only was she sexy, she was beautiful, too. She had hazel eyes, and long brown hair. Her pink lips were full, and shiny. She had lip gloss on them. Not lipstick. I noticed stuff like that, because lips were my thing. I was a sucker for full lips.

She gave me a small smile. "Yeah, I'm cool."

My phone vibrated, again. Tashera was a pro at making a pest out of herself. I looped my phone, sent all the calls straight to voicemail. "What's your name?"

"Joya." She responded easily. "What's yours?"

"Payne."

"Pain?" She repeated. "As in heartache?"

"Somethin' like that." I responded with a smirk.

"What, they call you that because you go around inflicting it?"

"Nah, they call me that, because it's my last name." I clarified.

"So, what's your first name?"

"Nasir."

Her facial muscles relaxed and she gave me a real smile. She had a little dimple embedded in her right cheek. Her smile was beautiful.

"Why're you smilin' like that?" I wanted to know.

"No reason, really. It's just a coincidence. Nas is my favorite rapper. I've never personally met anybody with that name." She paused. "I like that name."

"I like your smile." I shot back.

"Nasir." She sounded like a mother who was about to scold her child.

My name sounded good as hell as it came from between her lips. "What's up?"

"Joy!" Chantelle burst into the room. "Did you beat the hell out of Dex? You should've gave his ass a mouth-shot, for real. I can't believe he put his hands on you."

"Me either. Nasty bastard."

Chantelle looked more pissed than her girl did. "I can't stand him. He's so damn ignorant. Come on, let's go upstairs for a minute."

As Chantelle led her out of the room, Joya turned back to me and gave me a small wave. "See you later, Nasir."

"Later." I had to force myself not to follow her a second time.

***

Later that night, I ended up at my original destination. Tashera's crib. Tashera was a pretty girl with smooth skin the color of midnight. I had met her a year earlier. I was leaving the office as she was coming out of *Platinum Plus Hair and Nail Salon,* which was right next door. We checked each other out as we walked to our respective rides. Right before I climbed into my wheels, she got up the balls to holler. She stopped me on some bullshit. Asked me if I had a minute to show her how to put some windshield wiper fluid in her car. I had a minute, so I did that for her. Later that night, I sexed her. She lost her mind behind it, too.

After the hit, I couldn't shake her. She would hit up my phone every other week or so, and beg me to stop by and bang the bottom out. If I wasn't doing anything else, I would stop through and beat it up. The problem was, I only wanted to sex. She wanted…more. Knowing that she was looking to tie a brother down should've been reason enough for me to leave her alone. But for some reason, I was still hitting that.

That night, she was ready and waiting when I got to her spot. She answered the door wearing a tank top and booty shorts. I pulled her into my arms, and gave her a hug. While I was hugging her, I whispered in her ear. "I'm not staying long." Then, I grabbed a handful of her ass, and released her.

She looked up at me with her doe eyes. "Why not, Payne? I've been waitin' all day for you."

I shrugged my shoulders and repeated myself. "I'm not staying long." I watched her body language, ready to blow the spot if she looked like she wasn't down. "You cool?"

She folded her arms across her chest and sighed. "I guess so."

"If you're not cool, say it now, Tashera. I'll leave and holla back later in the week."

"You're here. I might as well enjoy you while I have you." She took my hand, and led me to her bedroom. She had candles blazing, and massage oil on the night stand. "You look tired."

"I am tired." I assured her. "You gonna give me a massage?"

"I'm gonna give you anything you want. Let Tashera take care of you."

I liked the way that sounded. I watched while she laid a towel on top of the bed sheets.

"You need to be naked to get the most out of the

massage." She pretended to be professional. "Please remove your clothing."

I quickly divested myself of everything I was wearing. Apparently she needed to be naked as well, because she removed her clothing, too.

"You seem so tense, Payne." She said in a baby voice. "Lie down and let me relax you."

I laid face down on the towel she had spread out. She straddled my back and poured some oil into her hands. Tashera's hands were small, but strong. She worked the oil into my skin and massaged muscles that I didn't even know were sore.

"Turn over, Baby." She murmured.

The massage had me feeling so relaxed that I almost missed her command. I turned over slowly. She straddled me again, her hot box to my stomach, and started to massage my chest.

I moaned lightly, as she made her way down the front of my body. It wasn't too long before she had my dick in her hands, massaging him. I moaned again. That seemed to encourage her to continue. She took my dick into her mouth and sucked me, while her hands continued their massaging action on my balls. I held her head to my pelvis, as she slowly relaxed the muscles in her throat and took all of me inside her hot, wet mouth. She deep-throated me, while I tugged on her hair like I was trying to rip out every strand. I held her face steady, while I did whatever it took for me to get the most pleasure out of the act. The tip of my dick tickled her tonsils, as she increased the pressure of her suction. Tashera was the Prime Minister of head-bangers. She ruled the hell out of the kingdom, too. Before long, loads of hot semen were rushing down her throat, and Tashera swallowed every drop.

That was probably the main reason I was still hitting her.

***

The following Friday night, I was in the studio trying to put the finishing touches on a track that I was producing. Music was my thing. The real estate game was only a means to an end. The money I made flipping cribs financed my dreams. It paid for studio time, and other overhead issues.

The chick in the booth was local talent.

I looked over at Justus and Israel who both happened to be in the studio with me. "What do you think?" I asked them.

The girl was murdering the hook of the song, and not in a good way.

"It's not that she can't sing. Her voice just ain't right for this track." Justus replied.

Justus' opinion carried weight with me, because he was like a brother to me. Closer than a brother to me. We had grown up together, from the pacifier to the blunt. He was my best friend.

"She's fine as hell, though." Israel said. "I'm sayin', she's thick…look at them thighs…"

"Dude," I interrupted, "come on, this is B.I. You can knock broads later. I need to get this handled. Trey's talking about putting this track on his mix tape. It needs to be ready by Monday."

Trey was a local artist who was starting to do big things and make major noise in Chicago. I was trying to get him to cop one of my tracks for his mix tape.

"You wouldn't have to wait on Trey to blow up, if you would go 'head and let Rook bust over one of your tracks." Israel informed me.

Rook was Israel's younger brother. We had all grown up on the block together, from little homies to wanna be gangstas. Initially, the six of us were as close as homeboys could be, then the whole thing switched.

I would never forget that day during the last week of June in 1999. It was the year that Justus and I turned 14. Israel and Dex were 16. Patience and Rook were 13. It was the hottest day of the year. The only people really out that day were the fiends, and kids. Everybody else was posted up inside, trying to suck up some air conditioning. It was the first full week of summer vacation from school, so we were hugging the block like madmen, trying to get that paper. We exchanged rocks for handshakes all up and down Brandon Avenue, on the southeast side of the city.

We were professional little cats, so we knew the police who worked our neighborhood and we had stash spots all up and down the block, just in case a patrol car from a neighboring district eased down the Ave. We had the spot straight popping, and we felt untouchable…until that day.

The block had been particularly hot that week, and the cat we worked for, Big Al, had warned us to watch how we conducted biz, until things calmed down. We thought we had it covered, though. Monday through Thursday, there hadn't been any incidents or even close calls. Maybe we got lax. Maybe we got too careless. Friday afternoon, the cops showed up outta nowhere. Before I even knew what was happening, I was being thrown on the ground, and handcuffed. I can't lie. As a shorty, being arrested had me shook. Then, I looked to the left and saw Izz. He looked more pissed off than scared. He looked like if those cops let him off the ground, he was gonna make it rain. So, I swallowed my fear and let the cops lead me silently to the squad car with the rest of my comrades. It wasn't until they put us in the back of their whip that I realized Rook wasn't with us. Later I found out that he had gone in the crib to "take a leak", mere seconds before the cops pounced.

Justus, Dex, Patience and I got three months in juvenile detention behind that incident. Izz got six, because he already had a record. I always felt like Rook got away clean, because he saw the cops roll up. I always felt in my heart that he saw those cops and didn't tell us. Izz wasn't trying to hear that, though. He couldn't allow himself to believe that his little brother would let him go out like that. He chose to accept Rook's story, about luckily having to pee at that same time we were getting tossed by the cops. Dex didn't allow himself to meditate on it at all. He felt like he did the crime, he did the time. The whole thing was whatever to him. But me, Justus and Patience knew what it was. We knew that Rook was on some snake shit. From that day forward, I would kick it with Rook and keep the peace, but I didn't trust dude for nothing on earth.

Now, Rook was trying to do his thing in the music industry. Israel was financing Rook's hip hop career. He paid for studio time, beats for mix tapes, trips to New York, Miami, Atlanta, L.A. - wherever. He made sure that Rook stayed dressing fly, attended the right events, mixed and mingled with the right crowds, and was able to keep a party going by popping unlimited bottles. Izz was basically buying

Rook's success. It was costing him a stack, but he felt like Rook was worth it.

Rook was making a few waves. Nothing major, but a few waves. You couldn't tell him that, though. Let Rook tell it, he *was* the industry. Listen to him, and he was out there killing it. Personally, I wouldn't have cared if Rook's name made bells ring from NYC to L.A., there was no way in hell that I was getting mine by eating off of his table. I didn't want to owe him a damn thing. I didn't fuck with Rook.

"Rook's straight." I mumbled.

"This broad ain't working, Payne." Justus said, bringing me back to the present with a change of subject. "Hit the switch. I don't wanna hear no more. She's giving me a headache."

He was right, it did sound like she was wailing over my beats. "Ay Ma, come on out." I told her.

She grinned at me like she was the hotness, took the headphones off, and came out of the booth. "Did you get what you were looking for?"

"Nah, Shorty." I was honest with her. "I didn't get the sound that I'm looking for on this joint."

Her face fell. "I could do it again." She suggested. "I could go back in the booth and try it a few different ways."

"Hell naw!" Israel protested.

Justus laughed out loud. I chuckled.

"Go to hell!" She told Israel. "Payne, let me know if you change your mind."

"I will, Ma." I couldn't even remember Baby's name. But I smiled at her, like she had actually impressed me.

"He ain't gonna change his mind. You sound bad." Israel taunted.

Baby Girl flipped him off, and exited the studio.

Israel and Justus continued to laugh. I didn't. I had the studio for a couple more hours, and no artist to utilize it. It was money down the drain. "Damn." I said. "I need to find a singer...like yesterday."

"Buy some airtime on one of the radio stations. Have an open call." Justus suggested.

It was a good idea, and it probably would've worked if I had done it a few weeks earlier, but it was basically too late. My back was against the wall. I didn't have time to be on no American Idol shit.

"Ay Son, check this out." Israel said.

"What's up?" I asked, half-listening. I was racking my brain, trying to see if I could come up with a singer.

"Chan's homegirl, Joya...that broad can blow."

I hoped Israel didn't notice that I froze for like a milli-second when he mentioned old girl's name. For six days, I had alternated between grinding, producing, sexing, and working out, all in an effort to get and keep old girl off of my brain. Nothing worked. Every time I looked up, I was reminiscing about the beautiful chick that cursed Dex out and tried to lay him flat. I couldn't stop thinking about her honey brown eyes, or her pink lips, or her big tits, or her phat ass. "Who're you talking about?" I fronted. "That redbone broad who wanted to beat the hell outta Dex?"

"Yeah, she can sing."

I was doubtful, and I didn't want to take a chance on having her in my space if she wasn't gonna work out. She was already hanging around in my mind, which was unusual. Chicks didn't usually stay on my mind…even the ones with good sex. But this chick had knocked me off my square. I didn't like that feeling. "I'm looking for a real singer, Izz."

"What you think, Son? That I'm lyin' to you or something?"

I gave him the eye. "I don't know, Dog. You have been known to bring a female by here, talking about how she can sing, when really you're trying to knock that."

He chuckled guiltily. "Yeah, I have. But I ain't tryin' to knock Joya." He paused. "Not that I wouldn't, she's thick than a motherfucka. Fine as hell, too…"

"Dude." Justus said, interrupting Israel.

"Damn, sorry. Yeah, Shorty can sing."

I sighed heavily before I gave in. "You think she can get up here tonight?"

"Let me get at Chan."

***

An hour later, Chantelle and Joya filled up the studio with their presence.

Chantelle was all smiles as she greeted us with hugs. "Hey Justus. What's up, Payne?"

"I see you, Chan." I responded. Then I made eye contact with Joya. Her expression was serious. And even with that frown on her face, she was still gorgeous. "How're you feeling, Miss Joya?"

"I'm good. What about you, Nasir?" She replied, never letting her facial muscles relax.

"Cooling. You wanna go in the booth?"

"Can I hear the track first?"

"When you get in the booth, I'll give it to you through the headphones." I said in exhaustion. It wasn't personal, I was just ready to be finished with the track.

"Okay, dang." She said, then pranced into the booth.

I couldn't help it. I watched her ass as she went. The way the trousers she wore accentuated her lower half was criminal. Even though I was under the crunch of a major deadline, I sort of hoped that things wouldn't work out with

Joya. I wasn't sure that I could work with her in the studio and not be distracted by wanting to fuck.

I played the track for her.

Justus stood up. "I'm outta here, Son. I gotta make moves."

"The Pancake House. Tomorrow. 8:45." I called to him before he left.

He threw his fist in the air to let me know he heard me.

"We're in the wind, too, Dog." Israel informed me.

"Joy hasn't even started recording." Chantelle protested.

"She don't need us here for that. Payne got it." Israel replied.

"Yeah, but how is she supposed to get home? I drove her."

"You got Joya, right man?" Asked Israel.

I hit the switch to the booth, so Joya could hear the conversation. "You need to clear that with her."

"What are we talking about?" Joya asked.

"We're talking about how you're getting home." Chantelle filled her in. "Izz is ready to blow. Are you straight with Payne droppin' you off?"

She seemed to think about it. "Yeah." She finally agreed.

Chantelle turned to me. "Make sure my girl gets home safely, Payne."

I nodded ever so slightly.

"One hundred, Dude." Israel said, then he and Chantelle disappeared.

I turned my attention back to the booth. Joya was warming up her voice. I watched her lips move, and the motion of her opening and closing her mouth so sensually, took my brain to the dark side, on the real. "Ay," I interrupted her, "I know you're trying to get into your 'artist vibe' and everything, but I only have this studio for two more hours. If I go over, I gotta pay time and a half. You ready to make it happen or what?" I was all business with her.

She cut her eyes at me. I could tell she noticed that I was showing her shade, but she played it through. "Yeah, I'm ready to make it happen."

"Do your thing." I said, and dropped the track for her.

She started humming along with the music. After a few beats, she was doing riffs, runs and adlibs on top of Trey's vocals. Each time she did it, she did it differently. Straight. Bouncy. Jazzy. Raunchy. Innocent. Breathy. After about eight times, she took off the headphones. I flipped the switch so we could talk.

"Did you like any of those, Nasir?" She asked sincerely.

I had to fight to keep my composure, so I didn't come off like I was star-struck or something. "I liked all of them, Ma.

Real talk, you sound like a straight star in there." Israel had come through big time on Joya. She had talent.

She smiled at me. Her smile messed with my concentration.

"Which one did you like best?" She questioned.

"The last one." I told her.

She was breathy on the last take. Sounded liked she was getting straight sexed. She made Trey sound like the man as she moaned and hummed over his vocals.

She smiled at me, again. I wished she would stop doing that.

"I figured you would like that one."

"Take it from the top, and watch those adlibs, Joya. Control your diction. Don't let the words run into each other like that." I instructed.

"Okay." She nodded and went through the song again.

I ran the track back and played a section for her. "You hear that part, right after he comes outta the bridge, I need you to say 'yeah', right there. Put something on it, Ma."

Joya was easy to coach, it didn't take a lot. She was done with the entire track in a little more than an hour. I was actually proud of Shorty.

"Damn Baby." I said when she came out of the booth. "You did ya thing." I pulled her into a hug. She felt good wrapped up in my arms. Natural. I quickly released her. "You got talent."

"Thank you." She was humble.

"Damn, I never thought I was gonna get that track done." I shook my head in disbelief, then glanced over at Joya. "Ay, so you gotta price list or somethin'? Tell me how much I owe you."

"You're straight." She assured me. "Consider it a favor."

"You ain't getting real far in this industry giving away your talent for free."

She threw me a wink. "Then, I guess it's a good thing that I'm not trying to go far in this industry, huh?"

"Ma, I'm feeling something like I'm robbing you. You gotta let me do something."

She hit me with the side eye, so I figured she thought I was feeding her bullshit, trying to get next to her, but I wasn't. I was being straight-up.

"Let me think about it." She finally relented.

"Cool."

***

"So, who is dude rhyming on the track I worked on?" She asked, as we made the trek from the studio on the north side, to her spot in Hyde Park, on the south side.

"His name's Trey Whisper. He's a small time artist, trying to become big time."

She smiled her beautiful smile. "He might be on his way. That track is hot. How long have you been producing?"

"I've been making beats since I was a shorty. I started laying tracks in the studio about six and a half years ago."

"Have you sold any?"

I cocked my eyebrow. "You're kinda nosy, aren't you, Beautiful?"

She looked guilty for being all in mine. "I was just wondering. I'm saying, you're good at what you do in the studio."

"Thanks."

"You're welcome."

"What do you do, Joya? I mean, like for a livin'?"

"I'm a flight attendant."

"Real talk? Cool." I paused. "You think I can…"

"No, you cannot get hooked up on no free plane tickets. So, don't even ask."

I laughed out loud. "Damn. You shut me down quick as hell on that one, didn't you?"

She laughed, too. "Yeah. I already knew where you were going. People are always coming at me about free plane tickets, so I let 'em know off the bat. There are no free plane tickets. I gotta fill out paperwork, and make arrangements to get free plane tickets for myself. I definitely don't have no *extras* to give away."

"Okay. Okay. Hold your head, Beautiful. I get it."

"Okay." She pretended to calm herself down. "As long as you understand."

"I get it. No free plane tickets." We drove in silence for a few minutes before I spoke again. "Ay, I'm bugging. You don't do nothing with your music? You got talent. Straight up, you could be killing the music industry. You can sing, you're beautiful, and you got body. They would eat you up."

"Singing is cool." She responded. "I'm saying, I love music, but that's not where my heart is. It's just a hobby. I love to travel. I've been places and seen things that a lot of people can only dream about. Being a flight attendant suits me perfectly."

I noticed the way she was smiling and grinning when she talked about traveling. She was too damn beautiful. I could do some serious damage with a female like little Miss Joya on my team.

***

"You ready to go in?" I questioned when we pulled to a stop in front of her building. I couldn't help being me. I wanted to see if she was down for letting me knock.

She glanced at her cheap, little watch. Baby really needed to get her jewelry game upgraded. Her watch was trash, she didn't have on any earrings or bracelets, and the only thing on her fingers was her class ring.

"Yeah, it's late." She answered.

I cut my eyes at her. "You sure?"

"Positive." She knew what I was on, I could tell. She couldn't stop chuckling. "And you really need to stop it."

"What?" I played dumb.

"Stop trying to set me up for the hit, Nasir."

I could tell by her body language that she wasn't going, so I didn't press the issue. "Thanks for making that track hot, Little Mama. I really appreciate you."

"No problem."

"So, are you gonna let me hold your number or what?"

"Uhm, I don't think that's a good idea. I'm saying, I'm really not looking for a man right now. I got…"

I cut her off. "Stay in your lane, Ma. I'm not trying to be your man. I was thinking you might want me to let you know if Trey likes what you did on the track."

The look on her face was classic. I had to fight hard not to laugh at her. She was so cocky, acting like l was sweating her to link up. I *had* to put her in her place. I *had* to.

"Oh yeah, that's cool." She agreed, trying to regain her composure. Then she recited her phone number, while I entered it into my cell.

Once her digits were safely stored, I put my phone away. "You take care, Joya."

"You too, Nasir."

I watched her let herself into her building. My feelings were crossed up about Pretty Girl. She was sexy as hell, and gorgeous, too. She was kinda stuck-up, though. She probably thought a cat like me was beneath her.

***

The next morning, Justus and I linked at The Pancake House for breakfast.

"You look tired, Playboy." He told me, as we waited for the waitress to bring our food.

"I am, Dude. It was a late night."

He raised his eyebrows. "What? You must've been up all night hittin' that red bone."

"Nah, I tried for a minute, but she wasn't going. So, it was whatever." I said dismissively.

"She looked too young for you, anyway."

"She's legal." I paused. "You look tired, too. What? Nia keep you up?"

50

Nia was his wifey.

"I wish. I was up fuckin' around with Dex. You know he agreed to play them lottery numbers for Patience."

That was code talk. Dex agreed to holler at the owner of the six-unit for Patience.

"Number came in last night, and I had to help Dex collect." He continued.

I hit him with the screw face. "What kinda help did he need collecting?"

"You know Dex likes to be trying to intimidate niggas and shit."

That definitely sounded like Dex to me.

"Me and Izz ended up riding through the spot, helping him handle things."

"So, what it look like now?" I questioned.

"Looks like everything is fallin' into place."

I nodded my head. I was glad to hear that. I just wanted to get into the building and do what we needed to do to make money off of it.

He changed the subject "Ay, how you love Shorty that came through the studio last night? If I wasn't with Nia, I might've had to take your ass to the mat over that one." He joked. "She had body and a pretty face."

"Yeah. She's cold. Kinda snooty, though."

"Yeah, I could tell by the way she tried to beat the hell outta Dex for rubbin' her thigh."

"Yo, I can't blame him, though. Had she been standing that close to me, I probably woulda rubbed it, too." I admitted.

"And she woulda beat the hell outta you, just like she did him. Shorty's straight gangsta."

I chuckled at the memory and nodded in agreement.

"Could she sing?" He asked.

"Man, Baby Girl can blow. Her vocals are crazy."

"Good. Good. That means this track is basically a wrap?"

"Pretty much."

The waitress brought out our food and sat it down on the table. "Enjoy it, fellas." She said.

"Ay, I'm outta here next week." He told me, as he shook black pepper on his eggs. "I gotta go to Miami to shoot a video."

He was trying to act like he wasn't excited, but I knew Justus well enough to know when he was fronting. He was excited.

Justus and I both had big dreams. I wanted to be a music producer, and he wanted to direct music videos. He was closer to realizing his dream than I was. He had already shot three videos, and now he was on his way to Miami to shoot another one. I was happy as hell for my guy. If anybody deserved success, Justus deserved it.

"Who's the video for?"

"Licks Harlow."

Alixandra "Licks" Harlow was a raunchy, sexually explicit, female rapper. Most of the people who listened to her music thought of her as a hoe and a tramp, based on the lyrical content of her records. The way she presented herself in her videos, and in the public arena didn't help matters. Yet, most of the people in the industry realized that Licks was a regular chick, trying to get her hustle on by pimping a sellable image.

"Straight up?" I was impressed. She was a major talent. "How'd you swing it?"

"I met her at this club, *Crave*, a couple of weeks ago when I was in New York. I was in the right place at the right time. She came in and plopped down next to me at the bar. She was sitting there complaining to her homegirls about how she hates all of her videos except for one. She says that no matter how she explains her concept to the director, she never gets what she wants outta videos. She was going on and on. Finally, I cut on top of her whining ass and told her that I was a new director outta Chicago. Her eyes got all big, and she started blasting me with all these questions." He shrugged his shoulders. "I must've answered right. Next thing I knew, she was telling me her concept for the video. We chopped it up for a minute, and she said she would have her people contact me." He paused. "Yesterday, her people hollered at me."

"Damn, that's what's up!" I gave him dap across the table.

He nodded slowly. "Yeah, this right here could be major. I mean *major* for me."

"No doubt." I agreed. "When are you leaving?"

"Next Wednesday. The record label is giving me two days to make it happen."

"Don't even sweat it, Bruh. You was born to do this. You got it." I assured him. "So, what're you getting into today?"

"I'm headed to the crib. I gotta holla at Licks, so we can discuss exactly what her concept for this video is. I'm trying to lay this video flat. I wanna kill it. I'm trying to make my name ring bells all over the industry. Ya'mean?"

"I feel you, Son."

"What about you? What time is Trey coming through the studio?"

"Later. Right now, I'm about to shoot through Grandma's spot and check on her."

He smiled at the mention of my grandmother. She was his surrogate grandmother, too. "Tell Grandma that I said, what's up."

"I will." I said, taking enough money from my wallet to cover my breakfast.

Justus held up his hand to stop me. "I got this, Dude. I'm sayin', I'm about to get on, and you're not."

"Oh, so now that you're doing this Licks video, you're the shit, and I'm nothing?"

"That's right. Holla back…scrub."

"Fuck you, Dawg." I chuckled all the way to my wheels.

***

I left the restaurant, and headed west. My grandmother stayed on 73rd and Eberhart. Me and my grandmother, Dorothy Jane, had a special relationship. She was the mother in my life. She was my heart.

When I was six years old, and my younger sister, Yasmeen was three, some real tragic stuff went down in our lives. My biological mother, Nicki, was pregnant with my baby sister, Torri at the time. She was dabbling in drugs and running around with a couple of scumbag type dudes.

Apparently Nicki took a dump too close to where she laid her head, because one of her men, Vincent showed up at our spot early one Saturday morning on a mission. He greeted me as I opened the door for him, and waved to Yasmeen as she laid in the middle of the living room floor, watching cartoons and munching on Apple Jacks. Then, he made his way straight to Nicki's bedroom. Unfortunately for Nicki, she was laid up in the bed sexing the next man.

Next thing we knew, commotion started coming from the back of the house. Me and Yasmeen, being the type of nosy kids that we were, went to find out what the deal was. I would never forget watching a grown man cry over the fact that the woman he thought was his lady, was fucking around on him. Vincent was ranting, raving, and crying like a baby.

Nicki tried to reason with dude, as she fought to untangle the blanket and hide her nakedness from all of the spectators. She tried to talk slick, while Isaac (old boy who had been getting some ass) tried to gather his clothes as inconspicuously as possible. It seemed like Vincent came out of nowhere with the burner. He pumped about three shots into Isaac, before anybody could react. Isaac went down in slow motion. Then the room was eerily silent…except for Nicki's whimpers. A second later, the gun was pointed at Nicki. I think the only thing that stopped Vincent from killing her, was Yasmeen's voice.

"Daddy. Daddy, what's the matter with that man?"

Hearing his daughter's voice seemed to snap Vincent out of the trance. He turned around and let his eyes sweep quickly over me and Yasmeen, as we stood there in up our pajamas watching. Then, he quietly left the room, and the apartment.

Both of my sisters lost their fathers that day. Torri's was killed in cold blood. Yasmeen's was captured and sentenced to eleven years in jail for manslaughter. He was murdered in prison after serving four and a half months.

The fallout from that day straight wreaked havoc on my family. The stress and the strain immediately sent Nicki into premature labor. The doctors held off the arrival of Torri as long as they could, because Nicki was barely seven months pregnant. But Torri would only stay inside Nicki's tormented womb for an additional two days.

The doctors didn't think Torri would make it. She was tiny and sickly. Torri was a fighter, though. Unlike her pops. Sometimes, I would think to myself that maybe if Isaac had the balls to go 'head up' with Vincent, he would've lived to see another day. If Isaac had pounced, before Vincent had a chance to pull the burner, instead of trying to sneak outta the room like a punk, maybe he could've prevented the whole shit. Then I would think…who knows? Maybe Vincent still would've whipped out the pistol and me or Yasmeen would've caught a stray bullet instead.

Whatever the case, Torri lived…and Nicki, the Nicki that I knew, died. After she was released from the hospital, she went from dabbling in drugs to dabbling in sobriety. After that, I rarely saw my mother without a heroine needle or a belt to tie off in her hand.

She was gone…hopelessly strung out in a matter of months. She couldn't take care of three kids, especially not when one of them was a premature, newborn baby. Torri's constant cries put the neighbors on to the fact that something was wrong in our crib. Eventually, DCFS (social services) showed up at the spot. Next thing I knew, the three of us were moving from 50th and Federal to 73rd and Eberhart.

My grandmother took us in, loved us, and raised us. Nicki was never completely off the scene, though. She showed up at my grandmother's every so often, begging for money. She never asked about us. She never tried to get clean so that she could get us back. She never tried to get clean, period. Nicki was quite content being strung out, bouncing in and out of jail and going from one homeless shelter to the next. She probably would've been dead long ago, if my grandmother hadn't spent so much time on her knees begging God to bring her oldest daughter back to her. My grandmother had already buried one daughter; she could barely stand the thought of possibly having to bury another one.

About five years ago, Nicki got picked up for a parole violation, and the judge must've been tired of seeing her dope-fiend ass. The lady judge sentenced her to two years in jail. That was when Nicki finally got clean for good.

I didn't hold it against my biological mother that she had problems with drugs. After what she witnessed that day in her bedroom, it would've have been hard for anybody not to snap. So, I gave her that one. I treated her cordially whenever I ran into her. Kinda like a distant relative, or a cool neighbor.

All I knew was that seeing Torri's father get murked in that bedroom left an indelible mark on my young mind. It taught me from a young age not to play with people's feelings. I saw first-hand what happened when you played with the wrong motherfucker.

I made it my business to let females know from the jump exactly where they stood with me. I never uttered the word "love"…never pretended that a chick meant more to me than she did. Any time a female showed me that she couldn't handle my honesty, I hit the bricks. The last thing I wanted to do was meet up with some chick that I had played out, on the wrong end of her burner. I knew for a fact that sometimes people ended up dead behind ass or dick. And I didn't care how juicy, hot, deep, or tight some ass was. I wasn't dying behind it.

I used my key and let myself into the Chicago-style bungalow. "Ay Gorgeous, where you at?" I called, as I walked through the living room and into the dining room.

"I'm in the kitchen, boy." She called back.

I made my way to her recently remodeled kitchen. She was sitting at the island with my biological mother. I was shocked to see Nicki, but I tried not to let the reaction show on my face. I walked around the island and pulled my grandmother into my arms. I gave her a firm squeeze. "What's really good, Grandma?"

"Life, Baby. Being on top of God's earth, and not under it." She told me. "Do you see your mother sitting there? You're not speaking to her, today?"

"Yeah, I'm speaking to her." I turned to the woman who gave me life. "What's up, Nicki? How're you doing today?"

She nodded her head. "Good. Good."

"Ay Grandma, I didn't come by here to stay. I stopped through to check on you. See if you needed anything." I kissed her cheek. "You straight? You need anything, old lady?"

She chuckled, like she always did when I called her an old lady. "Yeah, I need something. Let me talk to you in the front room. Nicole, you pour yourself something to drink, Sugar."

"Okay." Nicki answered.

I followed my grandmother into the living room. "What's up, Grandma?"

She looked me in the eye. "What have I told you about calling your mother by her given name?"

I sighed. Even though she knew that Nicki had only mothered me for six years, my grandmother still expected me to act like Nicki was mother-of-the-year, or some shit like that. "What do you want me to call her?"

She pinched me lightly on the arm. When I was a shorty, she used to pinch it for real, and I could still remember the pain. I smirked at her.

"You know what I want you to call her." She told me.

My grandmother was my heart. I loved her more than I loved myself. There was nothing that she could ever need or want that I wouldn't make happen for her. I wasn't used to denying my grandmother anything she asked for, but she was asking for a lot. "We'll see." I said vaguely, and turned to walk out of the room.

She caught my arm. "There's another thing."

"What's up?"

"Your mother needs your help, and she's scared to ask you."

"She ought to be scared to ask me." I responded before I thought to edit myself.

Dorothy Jane gave me another pinch. It was noticeably harder than the first one.

"Cool out." I said, twisting my face.

"Don't talk about your mother that way. I'm your grandmother, Nasir. That's your mother sitting in my kitchen. You have to learn to love her the same way you love me."

I cocked my head to the side. "Are you serious? She's at a twenty year deficit."

"It's never too late, Baby. And you have to start somewhere." She sighed. "One day, the good Lord is gonna call me home…"

I interrupted her. I hated it when she talked like that. "What does she want, Grandma?"

"She's short on her rent money."

When isn't she short on her rent money? I thought to myself. Out loud I asked, "by how much?"

She looked down at the floor. "A lot. Now, I could take the money out of my bank account and help her. Because you know I have it."

I knew she had it, because I stacked cash in her bank account on the first of every month.

"But it should come from you, Son. Directly from you." She concluded.

"How much are we talking?"

"Seven hundred dollars."

"I don't have that kind of cash on me right now. Let her know that I'll drop some money off at her spot tomorrow afternoon."

She looked at me like I was crazy. "Since when did you start telling me what to do? Do I look like your foot soldier? You better tell it to her yourself."

"Come on, Dorothy Jane." I teased.

She rolled her eyes and shook her head. "You better come on yourself, boy."

I walked back into the kitchen. "Ay Nicki."

She turned around and looked at me. "Yeah?"

"I, uh, talked to Grandma and she told me about your little situation." I took a deep breath. "You gonna be home tomorrow afternoon? I got some stuff to do out your way, and I was thinking that I could stop through your spot for a minute. Drop off a little package."

I saw her breathe a sigh of relief. "Yeah, I'll be home."

"I'm outta here." I kissed my grandmother on the cheek again, and gave her another hug.

"Give your mother a hug, Baby." She commanded.

I was hesitant about hugging Nicki. I mean, I hadn't physically touched her in a loving way since I was a kid. I took a deep breath, and pulled her into my arms. Surprisingly, she was soft. It never occurred to me that her skin would be soft.

Chapter Two
Mama Said Knock You Out

Joya

Saturday night, Chantelle called and asked me to go out with her. Club hopping wasn't normally my scene. I had spent more time than I could remember partying at clubs when I was with my ex-boyfriend Monte Patterson. Once I gave him the boot, I felt like I closed the door on that chapter of my life. But Chantelle acted like she was really pressed to go out, so I agreed to hang with her. While I was parking, Bubbles pulled into the spot behind me.

"What's up, Bubbles?" I asked, adjusting my lilac colored wrap-dress as I exited my wheels.

"Hey Joy." She responded, making the alarm on her Jeep chirp. "I see Chan got you to agree to go out with her tonight, too."

"Yeah." I admitted.

Bubbles and I walked up the front stairs together. She rang the doorbell of the two-story, brick home. Chantelle greeted us a few seconds later, wearing cream colored suede booty shorts, and a matching bustier that had her breasts lifted to the ceiling. When I saw the outfit, I was speechless.

Bubbles? Not so much.

"What the hell did Izz do to you?" She asked her sister. "Do I have to beat his ass?"

Chantelle turned and walked away from the door. The view from the back was even more heinous than the view from the front. All I saw was booty cheeks hanging out the back of the short-shorts.

"What makes you think Izz did somethin' to me?" She asked Bubbles.

"The way you're dressed, Hoe."

"If Izz sees you looking like that, he's gonna flip." I added.

"He's not gonna flip, he's gonna whip that ass." Bubbles corrected.

"Izz ain't gonna do shit." Chan disagreed.

"Famous last words." Bubbles shook her head. "Do you know how many broads have said that exact same thing, right before they got smacked-up?"

I silently agreed with Bubbles. Israel was gonna have a fit if he saw Chantelle dressed like that.

Chantelle blew her sister off with a dismissive wave of her hand.

"Where are we going?" I asked, thinking that I was probably under-dressed. Chantelle was decked-out in the video-hoe look, and Bubbles was on her way to turn a few tricks on the track in a skin tight, black mini dress with "cut-out" sides.

Chantelle handed me the plugger to a club.

I unfolded it and read it out loud. "*Blaze the Mic* night at *Kacey's*." I looked over at her. "What's *Kacey's*?"

"It's over in the south Loop. On 19th and Indiana." Bubbles supplied, snatching the plugger from my hand. "It's a club. Nice spot with a stage. They have live music every Friday and Sunday night."

"Well tonight, they're havin' '*Blaze the Mic*', and Izz entered Rook in the contest." Chantelle said.

"Who is Rook?" I questioned.

"Israel's whack-ass baby brother. He's a wanna-be MC." Chantelle shook her head in disgust. "Izz didn't even tell me about this thing at *Kacey's*. That means that he's takin' one of his hoes. I swear, I get so sick of this nigga. It's like no matter how much I do for him, he gotta keep disrespecting me, running around with these bitches."

"If you don't like the way the nigga's treatin' you, leave his ass alone." Bubbles suggested.

I silently agreed.

Chantelle gave her younger sister the side-eye, but didn't respond. Clearly, her leaving Israel wasn't open for discussion.

***

It took us a minute to find parking in the south Loop. But luckily, the "*Blaze the Mic*" contest hadn't started by the time we got inside in the club. The place was packed, and I didn't think we were gonna be able to find a table, but Bubbles found us one.

We followed her through the crowd, stopping every few seconds as some random dude grabbed either her hand or Chantelle's and tried to holler. We finally arrived at the table that was meant for two, but had four chairs squeezed around it. No sooner than we sat down was the waitress on top of us.

"There's a two drink minimum tonight, Ladies." She informed us. "Can I get y'all started?"

"Amaretto sour." Chantelle ordered.

"Tequila Sunrise." I told her.

"Cranberry vodka."

The waitress gave us a pasted on smile. "Be right back."

As soon as she was gone, we started scanning the club for Israel.

"There he is." Bubbles said pointing.

I followed the direction of her manicured finger. I saw Israel posted up at the table closest to the stage. He wasn't alone. The same guys from the card party were with him, along with several females.

67

"I knew he was gonna be with a bitch!" Chantelle said. "I knew it."

I didn't respond. I was too busy peeping out the fact that Nasir was posted up with a chick, too. I wished we were closer so I could get a good look at old girl's face.

"We oughtta go down there and bust a bottle of champagne over his head…Biggie Smalls looking ass." Bubbles fumed.

Chantelle was silent.

"Do you wanna go down there, and make somethin' happen?" Bubbles pressed.

Before Chantelle could respond, a short man, wearing a bright red suit took the stage. The lights in the club went down, and the man in the red suit began to speak. "What's up, Chicago?!?" He yelled.

The crowd yelled back.

"I say, we go down there and beat the hell outta Izz. Once we dust him, we can beat the hoe's ass. Then we bounce." Bubbles said over the volume of the crowd.

Chantelle didn't say anything. She sat there looking like her world was crumbling around her.

"Chan!" Bubbles called, snapping her fingers in front of her sister's face. "Chan!"

"Fall back, Bubbles." I said. "Let her get her thoughts together."

I could tell that Bubbles wasn't down with my suggestion to chill. She was the type who was about making things happen. Surprisingly though, she rode and left Chantelle alone.

After four of the eight acts had performed, the lights in the club went up and the contest went into an intermission.

"Let's go down there." Chantelle finally spoke. "Let's do this."

It didn't take much to prompt Bubbles. She was a high-drama female. Bubbles loved theatrics. She quickly jumped up from the table and was half-way across the club before Chan and I were even out of our chairs.

The three of us cut through the crowd, and came to a stop on the left side of the table that was closest to the stage. We were directly facing Israel. He held a glass of amber-colored liquor in his left hand, and cradled some random chick with his right arm.

"What's good, *Izz*?" Chantelle asked in a calm voice.

If he was surprised to see us there, he definitely didn't let it show on his face. His facial expression and demeanor remained unchanged. I chuckled to myself at his swagger. I had to give it up for his gangster.

"What's up, *Chan*?" He asked, sarcasm dripping from his voice.

"Who is this?" She gestured toward the chick chilling up

under his arm.

Before Israel could respond, some sweating cat who didn't fully check out the situation, tried to step to Chantelle. I figured that all he caught was the view of her ass cheeks from behind, and that was enough for him.

"Ay Ma," he said, interrupting the staring contest Chantelle was having with Izz, "you need a seat?"

Chantelle turned around, and gave him a sweet smile. "Nah, I'm good. Thanks."

Dude wasn't about to give up that easily. "You sure?"

Israel pushed old girl out from under his arm roughly and stood up. "Motherfucka, walk away." He commanded dude.

"Tell that bitch to walk away." Chantelle said loudly.

"That's right." Bubbles co-signed. "Make that bitch walk away."

The sweating dude finally read the situation for what it was and disappeared, while the fight raged on.

Chantelle let her eyes fall on the chick making time with Izz. "Bitch, if you wanna be able to walk outta here, then I suggest you get up right now."

Old girl looked up at Chantelle slowly. "Fuck you."

Chantelle picked up the drink closest to where she was standing, and threw the contents of the glass at the chick. Liquor and ice went everywhere, including on Patience, who was seated next to old girl.

"Whoa." He said, as he stood up from his chair.

The second that Patience stood up, Chantelle moved like a cheetah. She reached across the table and grabbed a fist full of old girl's hair in one hand. She used the other hand to repeatedly punch the chick in the face. She caught us all off guard, and for a second or two, everybody at the table just stood there watching.

"Sittin' here chillin' with my fuckin' man!" Chantelle said, bashing the helpless girl's face into the table.

Israel just sat there like it wasn't a thing to him. He didn't try to assist old girl, or stop Chantelle from putting the ass whipping down.

Apparently Justus had seen enough, though. He stood up and started to pry Chantelle's hands off of the chick. "Stop tripping, Chan. You're gonna fuck around and draw security over here!"

The threat of being booted from the club convinced Chantelle to let Justus kill the madness.

"You straight, Sharon?" Israel asked old girl.

"Karen." She corrected, mean-mugging Chantelle.

"How the hell are you gonna ask that bitch if she's okay?" Chantelle yelled, still enraged. "What about me? What about me, Izz?"

"Chan, you need to calm the hell down. You that damn threatened by the next bitch?"

"Bitch?" The girl repeated in a stunned tone.

"Oh hell no. He just called you a bitch." Bubbles instigated.

"Make her get her busted ass up from this table!" Chantelle shouted, stomping her foot like a two year old.

"Ay, why don't you go get yourself a drink?" Israel finally told the female. "I'll get back in a minute."

"No, the hell you won't." Chantelle assured him. "No he won't. Beat it, Bitch. And don't come back…unless you want some more."

Sharon/Karen pulled herself up from the table.

Once she had disappeared, Israel was up from the table and in Chantelle's face. "What the fuck is wrong with you, Chan? You lost your mind, or what?" Before she responded, Israel took a good look at her outfit, and changed his entire line of questioning. "What the hell do you have on?"

"Who was that bitch you were hemmed up with?" She asked, trying to keep him on the topic.

I shook my head. I knew it was about to go down.

Israel looked like he was ready to bust Chantelle in the face. "I asked you a question, Chan. What the hell is this you have on?"

Security finally appeared on the scene. "Ay, is there a problem?"

Israel took a deep breath. "Nah, we're straight."

"We're trying to start the show back up. Y'all need to settle down, for real." The security dude looked at Chantelle, Bubbles and me, who were standing and continued. "You ladies need to go back to your table."

"I ain't goin' nowhere until you tell me who that bitch was." Chantelle said, folding her arms across her chest.

The security cat looked exhausted as he addressed Izz. "Ay, Dude."

"Quit fuckin' showing off. You tryin' to embarrass me?" Israel asked through gritted teeth.

"You embarrassed me." She replied.

Israel grabbed Chan by the arm roughly. "Ay, we'll be back." He said and led Chantelle away from the table.

I hoped that he wasn't about to take her somewhere and smack her up. I started to follow them, but since Bubbles didn't seem concerned, I decided to let Izz ride.

Bubbles immediately went and sat in Israel's seat. "Y'all can start the show." She told the security guard, with a bright smile.

He grinned back at Bubbles, then turned to me with a frown. "You need to find a seat."

Nasir's date saved the day. "Here's a seat." She offered me the seat between her and Justus.

I tried not to sigh out loud, but the last thing I wanted to do was sit beside Nasir and his date. It didn't help that she happened to be some Victoria's Secret model-looking Latin chick.

"Thanks." I said, and sat down.

"Hey Dex." Bubbles said from across the table. "You're not speaking today?"

Dex looked over at her. "Yeah, Shorty. I see you. Hell, I can't miss you in that dress. What's good?"

"You, noticing my outfit." She flirted.

Luckily, the next act took the stage before Bubbles' desperation made me throw up. Two acts later, Israel and Chantelle returned to the group.

"That's Rook." Chantelle informed me as she pulled up a chair from a neighboring table.

I watched as a slim, six feet tall, penny brown cat took the stage. When he opened his mouth to rap, he was confident and had a fair amount of stage presence, but his performance didn't win me over. The whack beat he rhymed over was distracting. I wondered if it was one of Nasir's tracks.

You wouldn't have known that Rook's performance was lackluster from Israel's response. He was going bananas for Rook. He was acting like Rook was…Nas or somebody.

The last act of the night was a dude called KJ Jamison. He ripped the spot. When he finished rhyming, he tossed the mic to the floor. Dude was a future star. I could tell from that one performance. When the winner of the contest was announced, Rook took second place, and KJ Jamison came out on top.

"Fuck him, Man." Israel said dismissively. "It wasn't your night. The next time we run up on dude, we'll make sure you lay his ass flat."

"Start with ya production." Nasir suggested. "That beat was trash."

I silently agreed.

"That beat was cold." Rook insisted. "This is just KJ's spot. If the contest had been anywhere else...I woulda buried him."

Whatever. I thought to myself. Dude was in denial.

"Whatever, Man." Nasir told him, like he had read my mind.

"Let's blow. I got eats and drinks back at my spot." Israel announced.

I saw Nasir's date lean in close to him and whisper something in his ear. He nodded. She stood up, grabbed her purse and walked away from the table. I figured she was going to the ladies room. The moment she was out of earshot, Nasir slid into her chair.

He picked up my right hand and held it in his as he spoke to me. "Ay, why're we pretending that we don't know each other?"

"We're not." I insisted.

"So, why you ain't speak to me?"

"You didn't speak to me, either." I reminded him.

He smiled at me, and showed me the deep dimples that were etched into his smooth, peanut butter brown skin. I wanted to reach out and touch them. I wondered if his skin was really as creamy as it looked. Nasir was so handsome. I could have done some major things with him, but after the garbage I had been through with my last guy, I really didn't trust my own judgment when it came to men. Each time I looked at a man, all I saw was a future heartbreaker.

"You're right. My bad." He said bringing me out of my daydream. "What's good, Miss Joya. How're you doing tonight?"

I couldn't help smiling back at him. He was too gorgeous. "I'm good. How're you, Nasir?"

"Cooling."

"What'd you think of KJ Jamison?" I asked him, just to make conversation.

"Awww, dude murked Rook. He outlined Rook in chalk, rolled out the yellow police tape and called the time of death."

"That's what you think, huh?" I teased.

"I think," he said lowering his voice, so that I had to lean closer to hear him, "all dude needed was you up there blowing that hook."

"I thought he did a good job on the hook."

"You coulda made it better." He assured me.

I stared into his green eyes, feeling mesmerized by their uniqueness.

"Uhm, I'm ready, Boo." Spanish Barbie said returning to the table.

I released Nasir's hand quickly, and turned around to face her. I could tell by the expression on her face that she did not like the look of what she walked up on.

I stood up from my chair. "Well, take care, Nasir." I turned my attention to his date and gave her the type of fake grin that chicks give to each other. "Nice meeting you." I lied.

"You too." She lied back.

"Yo, you ain't coming through Izz's spot?" Nasir asked me.

Spanish Barbie turned her head in his direction so quickly, that I just knew she gave herself whiplash.

"Nah, I'm straight." I responded.

"Not even for a minute?" He pressed.

Baby Girl's mocha-latte colored skin began to turn red. She was getting heated. "If she don't wanna come, why're you trying to force her, Payne?"

"It's late. I'm flying out in the morning. Gotta do that east coast swing." I joked to lighten the mood. "Take care."

"Later." Nasir told me.

"Bye." The date said happily waving me away.

***

I walked back to my car with Chantelle and Bubbles.

"Chan, I can't believe what you did to old girl." I teased.

"Psshhttt." She said dismissively. "She's lucky that's all she got. Sittin' at the table chillin' with my man. Then, had the nerve to say, 'fuck me'? That bitch must've had her brain in backwards. She got off easy. If I woulda had my way, she wouldn't have been able to walk away from the table. The paramedics woulda been carryin' her ass outta there."

"I wonder where she disappeared to." I mused.

"Who cares? All I know is she better stay the hell away from Izz."

"What happened with you and Izz when he dragged you away from the table?" I questioned.

"You know how they do." She sucked her teeth. "He was grabbin' all on me, and pushin' me up against the wall."

"I told you that he was gonna beat the hell outta you." Bubbles reminded her.

"Whatever. I know he better not let me catch him with no other hoes, or I'mma beat the hell outta him."

"Slow down, y'all." Bubbles lowered the speed of her pace.

"Why?" Chantelle asked her younger sister.

"I'm trying to see if Dex is coming back to the house with us."

"Why?" Chantelle repeated. "So, you can be swingin' from his balls, like you were the other day?"

Bubbles gave her sister the finger.

"Now, you just saw what happened to the last chick that said, 'fuck me'." Chantelle joked.

"Whatever, Man." Bubbles said. "I know you don't like Dex, but he's sexy to me. I'm trying to tap that."

I stumbled on my silver Stuart Weitzman sling backs, but kept my mouth shut. Not Chantelle, though. She wasn't about to let that comment ride.

"Why would you wanna sleep with Dex's pretty ass? He'll probably make you get on top, so he doesn't have to bust a sweat." She shook her head. "Dude don't even look like he's good in bed."

"Whatever." Bubbles disagreed. "Just looking at dude, I can tell how he puts it down. He's got too much pride to let his skills be half-assed. I betcha he be laying chicks flat all over the city."

"I don't see it." Chantelle insisted.

Silently, I agreed with Chantelle. There was nothing about Dex that would ever make me want to give him a shot at the big time, but I wasn't Bubbles.

"What about Patience, Bub?" Chantelle suggested. "He's so sweet. Why don't you try to link with him?"

I laughed, because Chantelle had tried to set me up with Patience, too. "What is this obsession you have with match-making for Patience? Why are you always trying to set somebody up with Patience?"

"Word." Bubbles agreed. "Especially since you know that Patience gotta thing for *you*."

"What're you talkin' about? Patience ain't got no thing for me."

"I guess you don't notice the way he acts around you. All nervous and shy." Bubbles schooled.

"He's nervous and shy all the time." Chantelle insisted.

"Maybe, but he's way more shy around you, Chan. I can't see how you haven't noticed. It's so obvious that he's feeling you."

"I don't think so." Chantelle shook her head.

"Dude is weird." I commented.

Chantelle gave me a look of disbelief. "Weird? Why would you say that? Patience is the boy."

"The weird boy." I stated. "I don't know. Something about him makes me think he doesn't have it all."

"I'll give you that. Izz told me that Patience killed somebody when they were shorties. He's been a little messed up ever since, but I still think he's cool."

"Whatever, enough about Patience." Bubbles said, dropping the subject. She bumped me lightly. "What's up with you and Payne?"

"Nothing." I was nonchalant.

"Sure ain't look like that to me. Looked like you was digging what you saw."

"What female wouldn't dig Payne? Dude got mad swag, he's fine and he's paid." Chantelle said. "Now, that's who you should be tryin' to get with, Bubbles."

"Stop trying to hook me up! I already told you who I'm trying to get with. Anyway, your girl is feeling Payne. I could tell by the way she was watching him all night."

Was I watching him? I asked myself, while I tried to keep the expression on my face as blank as possible.

"When we get to Izz's crib, I'll distract Jennifer Lopez, while you do your thing." She offered.

"I'm not going over Izz's." I told them.

Chantelle stopped walking. "Why not?"

"You're not going over Izz's?" Bubbles asked at the same time.

"Nah, I'm kinda tired."

"Uuhhh." Chantelle threw her hands up in frustration. "What's wrong with you, Joy? Ever since you and Monte broke up, you've been so…" she searched for the right word, "boring! All you wanna do is sit around your apartment watching the second hand move around the clock. We're too young for you to never wanna kick it. You're coming back to the house with us."

"Not tonight, Chan. I'm flying out at 6:35 in the morning. I'm going home. But y'all have fun. I'll call you later."

Chapter Three
Miss Independent

Payne

I gave Joya a call the following Sunday night. Trey and I had been in the studio all day, and he was wilding over the track with her vocals on it.

It took her so long to answer her phone, that I was about to hang up.

"Hello." She said finally.

"Ay Ma. What's the deal?"

She didn't respond for a second.

"What's up, you don't know who this is?" I teased to mess with her.

"Nah, and I'm hesitant about saying the wrong name." She admitted. "I don't wanna offend you."

"Yo, I won't put you out there like that, Beautiful…"

She cut on top of me. "I thought it was you, but I wasn't sure I caught your voice, *Nasir*. You calling me at this time of night? What's up?"

My eyes moved to the clock on my dashboard. It was a little after ten. "Is it too late for you? I ain't catch you at a bad time, did I?"

"Not really. I'm just chilling on my couch."

"You feel like hanging out? I wanna come scoop you. Take you out to have a celebratory drink."

"What're we celebrating?"

"Your track. I just came from the studio. Trey was bugging over it."

"You gotta be lying." She said in disbelief.

"Nah, that's my word." I assured her.

"He actually liked the version with me on it?"

I wasn't sure if Shorty was fishing for compliments or what. "Come on, Ma. You know your voice is bananas."

"But my voice on a track? That's crazy."

"Trust me, it's the most natural thing in the world. Do you wanna kick it or not?"

"Yeah, I wanna celebrate getting on my first track. I'm putting my shoes on right now."

I smiled to myself. "I'm on my way, Beautiful."

***

I took Joya to my uncle's club, *Classified.* The club was located on the south side of the city, just west of 87th and Stony Island. The lounge catered to an older and more upscale clientele than 'shake your booty' clubs did. It was decorated in muted tones of tan, camel and sand. The chairs, bar stools, and chaises were plush leather and suede. The imported bar was made of Koa wood from the Hawaiian Islands. My uncle only served top shelf liquor, and he kept the music mellow. Mostly jazz. People didn't come to *Classified* to jump and wiggle. They came for an experience. It was my uncle's showpiece.

"Wow." Joya said, as we stepped inside the lounge. "This is really nice."

"Yeah, my uncle and his wife decorated it."

"This is your uncle's club?"

"Yep. Come on." I took her hand and led her to the bar. "What's good, Joe?" I asked the bartender.

"Life, Youngster." He said. "Who's the beauty, and does she know who she's runnin' around with?"

I laughed. My very first legitimate job had been at my uncle's lounge as a stock boy. My grandmother insisted that Justus and I start working there the year we both turned eighteen. Joe was our manager. He was one of a very few people who could get away with teasing me like that. "This is Joya. Joya, this old ass cat…"

Joe and I both fell out laughing.

"Nah," I said regaining my composure, "this is Joe. He's cool people."

"How're you doin', Miss Lady? What can I get you to drink?"

"I'm fine. May I have a Tequila Sunrise?"

"Tequila Sunrise, heavy on the sunrise." He commented. Then he looked from Joya to me. "Do I need to card the beauty, Youngster?"

I cracked a grin. "What're you trying to say, Man?"

"I'm sayin', the beauty looks young."

"Everybody looks young to you, Grandpa. But she's legal."

"You sure?"

Joya whipped out her license. "Here you go."

Joe's eyes quickly scanned the piece of identification. He looked into Joya's face as he handed her back the ID. "You gotta single grandmother at home that looks anything like you?"

Joya blushed and shook her head. "Sorry."

"A day late and a dollar short. Story of my life." He joked. "What're you drinkin', Youngster?"

"Heineken. We'll be in the game room." I took Joya's hand, again. I led her through the club and into the game room which was in the very back.

The game room offered patrons the opportunity to shoot pool, throw darts, or play video games. The room was empty except for my uncle. I was surprised to see him in there, shooting pool alone.

"What's good, Unc?" I asked.

He looked up after he sank three balls. "I thought that was your truck I saw pull into the parking lot. I was watching the security camera, and I said to myself, 'that looks like Nephew's truck'."

I walked over to him, and gave him dap and a hug. "How's the family? How're Lynne and Passion?" I always asked about his wife and daughter.

"Good. Good. How's Dorothy Jane?"

I smiled at the mention of my grandmother. "She's cool. Doing good."

"And Nicki?"

"I saw her about a week ago at Grandma's house. She's maintaining. Still clean."

"Good." He nodded.

The uncle that I was talking to was my uncle by marriage. Once upon a time, he had been married to my Aunt Angel. He was also the best friend of my father, Khalil.

Both my father and my aunt were killed in drug related shootings when I was a shorty. But even after they were gone, Unc remained close to my family.

"Excuse my rudeness, Darling." Unc said turning his attention to Joya. "How are you?"

"I'm fine. Thank you. How're you?"

"I'm good. I'm Chad, and you are?"

"Joya."

"It's nice to meet you, Joya."

"You, too." She told him.

One of the waitresses, Marilyn came in with our drinks. Unc looked over at me.

"We're here celebrating. I sold a track today."

He shook my hand firmly. "Congratulations, Nephew. Who bought it?"

"This new cat, Trey. He's putting it on his mix tape. Joya did some vocals on it."

Unc looked back over at her. "Beautiful and you can sing? Imagine that."

Joya blushed up a storm.

"I'mma get outta here. I need to wrap up a few things before I leave for the night. If you need anything, holla at me. I'm in the office."

As he left the room, I called out to him. "Ay Unc, this is a private party. Can I have the room for a minute?"

He nodded slightly. "Sixty minutes, Nephew. Then, I open it back up to my paying customers."

"Cool. Thanks."

He closed the partition, and cut us off from the rest of the lounge.

"You ever play pool?" I asked Joya, as I took a drink from my bottle of beer.

"A couple of times as a kid, at The Boys and Girls Club,

but I'm not good at it."

I racked the balls, picked up my favorite pool stick, then beckoned to her. "Come here."

She came over to me.

"Get a stick. I'll let you break."

"So, we're about to play pool?"

"We're about to play pool." I assured her.

"You can shoot first. If you run the table, then you run the table." She said dejectedly.

"What's the problem?" I took a few seconds to chalk my stick.

"There's no problem. I just don't know how to play pool, and I definitely don't know how to break."

"Stand in yours, Beautiful. It's a friendly game of pool. If you mess up…you mess up. I'm not gonna blast you on Twitter. Besides, if you never *try* to play pool, you're never gonna *learn* to play pool."

The two of us walked back over to the pool table. Joya sat her drink down, and did a horrendous job on the break.

"You want solids or stripes?" I asked, neglecting to comment on her jacked-up break.

"Stripes."

"Do your thing. The table is yours."

"Okay." She said tentatively. She leaned over the table awkwardly.

"Beautiful. Beautiful." I stopped her, before she hurt herself. "Here, let me show you." I sat my beer down, and stood behind her. I positioned the pool stick in her arms, and held her body close to mine.

She started to giggle.

"What's up? What's funny?" I wanted to know.

"Somehow, I knew we would end up here."

I bent down and put my face in the crook of her neck. She smelled edible, like fresh fruit. "So, is this a problem?"

"Not really. I just don't want you to get the wrong impression."

"And what's the wrong impression, Joya?" I asked, feeling little Nasir wanting to make his presence known.

"That you're getting some tonight."

Little Nasir retracted himself. I backed off of her. "Make it funky, Shorty. Do you really think I'm sweating you for some ass?"

She put the pool stick down, but didn't respond.

I kept it moving. "You're beautiful and sexy, that's a true story. But I don't sweat chicks for ass. Don't need to…got too many options for making it happen."

"Uhm."

I sat my pool stick down, and picked back up my beer. "And since I'm giving you real talk, I'll tell you what…I would be reluctant to put my hands on you at all, Ma."

"Straight up?" Her head was cocked to the side, like she didn't believe a word that I was saying.

"Straight up." I replied.

"Okay, why wouldn't you put your hands on me, Nasir?"

"Because you seem like the type that would need to be in a *relationship* before you would be comfortable letting me touch you, and tease you the way I would want to. I'm saying, if I hit that and didn't call you the next day, you're the type who would probably blow my phone up, going off. "

"You think you got me all figured out?"

"I wouldn't say that, but I know your type. And I know me. I don't do relationships. I do…mutually beneficial agreements." I said. "I agree to give your body as much pleasure as it can possibly stand, and you agree to do the same for me."

"I don't negotiate with my body." She told me.

I left her by the pool table while I went to chalk my pool stick, again. I needed a second or two to evaluate what she said. Initially, I thought Shorty was trying to flex. A lot of females liked to pretend that they weren't gonna give up the ass. But it never failed that by the end of the night, I was rocking those same chicks out. Joya seemed serious, though. The idea of that was intriguing. I hadn't met a chick who wasn't willing to give up the ass since high school.

I changed my tactic, as I walked back over to the pool table. "What kinda things do you do with your body, Beautiful?"

She rolled her eyes to the ceiling. "I think it's your turn to shoot."

I went over to her. Backed her up against the pool table and wrapped my arms around her waist. "Why're you so selfish?"

"Why're you so greedy?" She inquired, but I noticed that she let me remain pressed up on her, with my hands on her waist, and my pelvis against her stomach.

I laughed out loud at that one. "I'm not greedy."

"Yeah, you are. You just told me that you have options when it comes to getting some. Now, you wanna add me to this list, too? That doesn't sound greedy to you?"

I released her, but didn't reply.

"It's your turn to shoot." She informed me.

"Nah, it's your turn to shoot. Don't hurt yourself." I watched her walk over to her pool stick, pick it up, and lean across the table in the tight ass pants she was wearing.

She acted so innocent that I could almost believe she was a virgin, but one glance at those curvy hips and that phat ass, and I knew she was sexing. I didn't care how much cornbread and fried chicken a virgin ate, she would never be built like Little Mama. Some dude had put in major work helping to make Joya's body as shapely as it was.

I sighed heavily. Shorty really expected a cat to jump through hoops to sample that. I wasn't sure if I was up to the challenge. My days of chasing chicks and wearing them down ended in grade school.

But there was something about her. Of course she was showstopping. Her face was angelic. And her body was bananas. Thick and curvy in all the right places. I could only imagine how juicy the middle was. But there was something more than her physical beauty that kept drawing me to her like a magnet. I couldn't figure out what would make me even consider pursuing her.

I mean, I knew she was a headache. I figured that out the first day I saw her snap-off on Dex at Israel's spot. Still, against my better judgment, something in me wanted her.

She shot, badly. Balls went around the table, but she didn't sink anything.

I sat my drink down, picked up my cue stick, and quickly sank two balls.

"Show off." She taunted, with a shake of her head.

"How about, if I sink the next one, you gimme a kiss?"

Her eyes glinted with amusement and her cheeks grew pink with a blush. "I don't know."

"I'll call the shot." I offered.

"Okay." She agreed finally.

"4 ball in the right corner pocket." I threw her a wink, then sunk the ball.

"Uhm." She said, like she was disappointed, but the half-smile on her face gave her away.

I walked over to her. She leaned in and gave me a feather-soft kiss on the cheek. I hit her with the screw face. "Damn Ma, at least let me get the lips."

She leaned in a second time, and let her luscious, lip gloss covered mouth brush against mine. Before she could break contact, I stuck out my tongue and licked her lips. She reflexively licked her own lips after I did. I knew it was a subconscious move, but it was sexy.

"Ill! You taste like beer. Why'd you do that?"

"Ay, I couldn't help it. Your mouth was calling me."

"Whatever." She chuckled.

"Wanna go for double or nothing?"

"Nah, no thanks. I can see that you're some type of pool shark. You're not about to get all my kisses."

"Please." I pleaded, with the sad face.

She laughed out loud. "Nasir, you're too much, Boo. What do these regular chicks do with you?"

"Gimme what I ask for." I replied honestly.

"I'll bet."

I ran the rest of the table while she watched in silence. When I was finished, I put both of our sticks away. "You wanna get something to eat? Chill for a minute?"

She looked down at her garbage watch. I hated that damn thing. If we ever got to the point where I started dropping dollars on her, a new watch was the first thing I was copping. "It's late."

"Do you have to fly out tomorrow?"

"No, but I'm tired."

I gave in. "I'mma stall you out…this time. But the next time I scoop you, be ready to hang."

"Okay." She agreed easily.

I pulled her into my arms, and hugged her. She hugged me back. She felt so good in my arms that I didn't really wanna let her go.

Chapter Four
Falling

Joya

Two weeks later, I headed to Israel's house to watch the NBA Finals. The Bulls had been knocked out in the first round, so I really didn't know who was playing. I was only going over Israel's, because I didn't wanna spend the night stuck in the crib. Plus, I couldn't lie to myself. I was hoping that Nasir would be there. I wanted to see him. I hadn't laid eyes on him, or heard from him since the night he took me to play pool.

Since, I wanted Nasir to see what he was missing, without being obvious about it, I made sure that my outfit was casually cute, but not over the top. I slid into a pair of ass-accentuating Tori Burch denim capris and a halter top that made my size D breasts look like melons. On my feet were flat, Gucci thong sandals. My hair was brushed back and secured in place with a suede headband that was the same color as my shirt and sandals. My eyes were lined with brown eyeliner and my lips were covered lightly with gloss. When I peered into the mirror, I had to admit that I looked good.

Since I was dressed down in casual-wear, I decided to add some sparkle into my life with a pair of platinum, diamond encrusted hoops from Tiffany & Co. While I was at it, I decided to rock the bezel-set platinum bracelet that matched them. The jewelry was the one gift from Monte that I had conveniently chosen not to return to his bastard ass, when we broke up.

I loaded my purse, grabbed my car keys, and hit the streets.

***

When I fell into Israel's family room, the game was well into the first quarter, and it seemed like I was the last person to arrive. I let my eyes rest briefly on each of the guest. I couldn't really say that I was surprised to see Nasir there with a female, but I was woman enough to admit to myself that it bothered me…a lot.

I discreetly checked her out. She was a cute girl, if not somewhat tomboyish. She was fair-skinned like me. Her hair was covered by a navy blue, fitted baseball cap and her sandy brown ponytail made its exit through the hole in the back. She was dressed like one of the boys, rocking baggy jogging pants, an oversized Carolina Cougars jersey, and Jordan's.

Nasir caught me peeping her. I held his gaze for a few

seconds longer than was necessary, then averted my eyes. I looked around for someplace to sit down, since most of the chairs were unavailable.

"Ay Joya, I saved you a seat!" Dex called to me, as he patted his lap.

Everybody in the room laughed, including me. I still didn't like him, but funny was funny. I let his joke ride.

"Yeah, and when you finish with him, I'll take a lap dance, too." The stranger seated next to Dex told me, as he flashed what looked like a twenty dollar bill.

I looked at dude like he was an escapee from the mental institution, but otherwise ignored him.

"Don't pay him no mind." The dude I recognized as Rook said to me. "That's Ant. He's like…my hype-man."

"Uhm." I said, and sat down on the nutmeg colored, suede sectional sofa beside Rook.

"Ay, I'm Rook." He told me.

"Yeah, I saw you at *'Blaze the Mic'*. I'm Joya."

"You smell good, Joya." He leaned in, pulled me to him and sniffed almost too close to my neck. "Girl, don't fuck around and make me write a rhyme about you."

It seemed like everybody in Izz's crew was cocky. I pulled away from Rook's grasp. "Go 'head and kick me a few bars." I encouraged, jokingly.

"Kick out a few dollars, Shorty." Ant told me. "Rook

don't drop 16s for free…especially not for bird ass chicks."

"What is wrong with you, Dude?" Justus asked him.

"Yeah, you basically need to shut up talking to me." I started. I was sidetracked from saying more when Rook started rhyming.

"*Ay Miss Joya let me tell you how I feel,*

  Let me really keep it real,

  So that you can know the deal." He free-styled.

"Uuhh." I said in total surprise. "I didn't think you were really gonna do that."

"Ay, it's who I am." He winked at me and was ready to add some more bars to the lyrics, when Israel cut him off.

"Quit showin' off, Motherfucka. This is the NBA Finals, not amateur night at The Apollo."

"I ain't no amateur." Rook informed his older brother.

"That's right, Nigga. Rook got the microphone on straight lock." Ant chimed in.

Rook looked at his guy and shook his head. "Fall back, Ant."

"Dude, are you tryin' to pop shit to me, in my own crib?" Israel asked him, getting up from the recliner where he was chilling.

"Come on, Izz," Justus said easily, "stall dude out."

"Please Izz." Chantelle added.

Israel's response was cut short by the action on the large

television screen. I didn't know which team scored, but Nasir's date cheered, and celebrated in her chair.

"Who's playing?" I asked Rook, knowing I sounded like a typical female. I was kinda pissed with myself, because I loved B-Ball and usually kept up with each series. However, I had been flying so much that I lost track of what was happening after the Bulls got knocked out.

"South Carolina and The Lakers."

I froze. Monte played for South Carolina. He was their franchise player. The big name on the team that made bells ring all through the NBA. The last thing I wanted to do was watch my ex and his basketball team play for the championship.

Chantelle's voice interrupted my thoughts. "Joy, come help me get the rest of this food."

My phone vibrated in my pants pocket. It tickled my thigh while alerting me to the fact that I had a text message. I leaned towards Rook as I fished it out of my pocket. While I was leaning, my shoulder rubbed gently against his arm. He put his dark brown eyes on mine.

"What're you doin', Shorty? You tryin' to get got, up in here? Lean on me like that again and see what happens."

I couldn't help laughing at his bravado. "You're crazy." I declared, as I quickly read the text from a fellow flight attendant asking me if I could pick up her flight on Tuesday.

"That's not your man texting you, is it?" Rook was bold enough to ask me.

"I don't have a man." I assured him, as I stood.

"Keep doin' what you're doin' and you might before the night is through."

Nasir gave me the eye. I ignored him, and instead gave my attention to Rook. "Yeah, all right, Super Star."

***

Chantelle pounced on me the second I stepped foot into the kitchen. "Joy, what are you doin'?" She asked me quietly.

"I'm about to beat the hell outta Rook's boy if he says one more outta pocket thing to me." I assured her.

"That's not what I'm talkin' about."

"What are you talking about?"

"Let me break it down for you. Why are you stuntin' in whack-ass Rook's face when Payne is sittin' there? Do you think that's makin' you look more desirable to him or something?"

I cocked my head to the side. "First of all, I wasn't stunting in Rook's face. Second of all, I'm not trying to look desirable to Nasir. Ain't that him sitting over there with a *date*? You think he's checking for me with her sitting

101

there?"

"Yeah, he is. He's watchin' every move you make."

"Good. He needs to be watching every move I make, while he sits over there with his boyish woman."

"All I'm sayin' is that there's a thin line between being receptive to Rook's flirtation, and playin' ya'self. Your toe's on the line, Chica."

"Whatever." I said dismissively.

A pretty, dark skinned, model-type female joined the two of us in the kitchen. I was about to give her the mad-face for being bold enough to walk up and join what she had to know was a private conversation (being that Chan and I were practically whispering). But she threw us a smile that was both friendly and disarming, and I felt my attitude start to subside.

"What are y'all in here whispering about?" Little Naomi Campbell asked, leaning against the granite counter.

Chantelle cut her eyes towards the family room.

"Uhm." Little Naomi said, like she wasn't surprised.

"Joy, this is Nia. She's Justus' girl. Nia, this is my best friend, Joy."

"Hey, how're you doing'?" I asked, giving her a smile.

She smiled right back at me, but the smile quickly faded and was replaced with a look of suspicion. "You aren't the female that has my brother all crossed up, are you?"

She got hit with the screw-face. "I don't even know your brother."

"She's talkin' about Payne. He's her play brother." Chantelle explained.

"Payne?" I repeated, looking at Chantelle. I turned my glance back to Nia. "If that's who you're talking about, then nah. I'm definitely not that female."

The suspicious look remained. "You're not the female who laced the track for him?"

"Yeah, that's her." Chantelle said, barely concealing her smirk.

"I laced the track, but I don't have dude crossed up at all. Maybe you're thinking of old girl sitting next to him on the couch."

Her eyes got big. "Who? Donyae? Hell-to-the-no. If that broad misses one more 'girl's night out', her ass will be a man. It's probably you. You seem like the type. Like you think Prince wrote *Diamonds and Pearls* about your coochie."

"Uh." I couldn't believe she said that.

Chantelle practically fell over with laughter. "Yep, that's definitely Joya."

I lifted my perfectly French manicured middle finger and flipped Chantelle off. "Go to hell, Chantelle." I paused. "You too, Nia."

"Don't get mad." Chantelle teased. "The truth is the truth."

"Just because I don't set my coochie out every time a cat says, 'what's good, Ma', doesn't mean I think I'm sitting on blood diamonds."

Chantelle tried to hug me. "I'm just playin' with you, Joy."

I pushed her away.

"For real, for real. I didn't mean any harm." Nia told me. "I was kidding. Sometimes, I overhear conversations between J and Payne. I heard Payne say that the other day, and personally I thought it was hilarious. I was…"

Chantelle cut her off. "You overhear conversations? Heifer please, you mean you be eavesdropping."

"Whatever." Nia waved her hands like it was unimportant. "Overhearing…eavesdropping, all I know is I hear stuff. And that's what I heard. J was like, 'Dawg, go on and call the broad. You know you want to."

Broad? I thought to myself.

"And Payne was like, 'I ain't calling her ass. What am I supposed to do with a chick who acts like Prince wrote *Diamonds and Pearls* about her…'p' word?" She relayed. "And I was tripping, cuz I couldn't believe some chick had knocked Payne off his square enough to have him over J's house whining about whether to call her or not. What did you do to my brother?"

My need to reply was cancelled out by Israel's booming voice. "What the hell is y'all hens over there cackling about? Chan, you better not be starting no bullshit in my kitchen. Quit yakkin' and bring the food out! We ready to eat in this piece!"

***

When I got back to my seat in the family room, Rook was still on my tip. "You ever been to New York?"

"Yeah. I love New York." My phone sang, alerting me to yet another text.

He gave me the mad-face. "Damn, who keeps blowin' you up?"

I held my tongue, to keep from checking him. Instead of giving him a verbal lashing, I played it smooth and gave him a small poke with my elbow. "Ill," I said easily, "get out my business."

He was patient while I read the message, but the second I put my phone away, he wanted my attention again. "What you know about New York?" He asked me.

"Boy, you act like New York is on Mars or something. What kinda chicks are you used to? Chicks that never see more than the four corners of their own block?" I cracked. "I do my thing. New York is one of my favorite places to shop."

"Is that where you got the caked-up ass bracelet that's lacin' your wrist?"

"I meant to mention that." Chantelle said jumping into the conversation. "Is that the jewelry you got from...?"

"Yeah." I cut her off, before she could mention my ex-bastard's name. I gestured towards the television. "That's his team playing."

Her eyes got wide. "For real?"

I nodded.

She gave me the sad face. "Well, I hope him and his busted ass team loses."

"Me too." I agreed with a smile.

"Anyway, I'm loving those earrings. They're too nice."

"Yes, they are." Nia co-signed. "Whenever you get tired of them, please make sure to pass them over here."

"And I'll take that bracelet." Donyae teased, getting in on the joke.

Rook picked up my wrist and studied the bracelet more closely. He let out a low whistle. "VS diamonds set in platinum...some brother broke his pockets for this joint." He lifted his eyes, so that they met mine. "He must've really loved your ass."

I didn't respond. I wasn't trying to open up that can of

worms.

"What is it about you that could make a cat fall like that?"

It came out so sincere, that I almost tried to find an answer to his question.

"Awww." Nia said. She was caught up, too.

"Bullshit." Justus said, pretending to cough.

All of the men in the room laughed.

"Dude, you're playin' yourself." Ant spoke up. "The music industry's killin' ya gangster. Get off that bitch's tip."

Bitch? I thought to myself. But before I could reply, the big dummy kept talking.

"You know what made that nigga come up off the paper. Look at her. She thick, curvy, got ass, tits like a motherfucka…she was lettin' dude hold somethin' on the regular. He was probably beatin' that pus…"

Before I even thought about what I was doing, I leaned across Rook and mushed old boy dead in his ugly face. "Now, who's the bitch?" I asked him.

Apparently in his mind I still was, because he reached across Rook and tried to slap me. Luckily Rook's reflexes were on point. He caught dude's hand and pushed it down. "Chill, dude."

"Hell no!" Ant stood to his feet. "I'mma kill that bitch!"

From the corner of my eye, I saw Nasir get up from the

sofa. I didn't pay him much attention. Instead, I prepared to protect myself. As I went to stand up, Ant pushed me back on the couch. I caught his arm on the way down, gave it a quick, but painful twist, then kicked him dead in his balls.

Unfortunately, I didn't kick him hard enough. He didn't go down the way I wanted him to. He was bent over, but still on his feet. I stood up and got in my boxer's stance. I knew his type. I knew he was coming back for me. He was pissed that a female had gotten the best of him.

Once the initial pain in his nuts subsided, he was ready to go another round with me. I was ready for another round, too. And the next time, I would make sure to put more force behind my blows.

He came towards me, and pistols starting clicking. I looked behind me, and burners were pointing at old boy from every corner of the room. Nasir was at point blank range. The only ones not holding were Israel, Patience and Rook.

Israel approached dude.

"Ay…" Ant began.

Israel didn't let him get anymore else out. He busted dude in the chops with a left hook. Ant was so shook by all of the guns trained on him that he didn't know whether to fight back or just take the ass whipping. He didn't have a chance to really consider either option, because Israel was right back at him with two vicious rights and about eight quick body blows. When Ant moved to protect his body, Israel went in for the kill. He was known for his hand game. It was nothing for him to lay a cat out with his fist, rather than with his heat. He did just that, laid Ant out with an upper cut and two more vicious rights.

"Get this motherfucka outta here." He commanded to no one in particular.

Nasir put his heat back in its hiding place, and returned to where his date was still seated.

A couple of guys that I didn't know hustled to the middle of the floor, picked Ant up and carried him out of the family room.

"Party's over." Israel announced. "Roll out."

"Thanks for bringing the asshole who ruined the whole shit, Rook." Dex joked sarcastically.

"My bad." Rook stated regretfully.

Chantelle walked over to me. She was grinning. "Dudes always think they can do whatever they wanna do to a chick. He ain't know what you was holdin'." She teased.

"It's been a long time since I had to use my powers for evil." I joked. "I just wish I woulda kicked him harder. If I had laid him flat with the kick to the nuts, Izz wouldn't have had to knock him out."

"Girl, Please. You know Izz don't care nothin' about

knockin' no lame cats out. That's like…his hobby."

We both laughed.

Around us, people were getting up from chairs.

Nia walked over, and gave both Chantelle and me quick hugs. "It was nice meeting you, Joy. I'll call you, Chan."

"Nice meeting you, too." I told her.

"Later, Girl" Chantelle said.

"Holla ladies."

"Bye Justus." We responded in unison.

Nasir gave us a slight nod of his head. His date gave us a small wave. We returned both gestures.

Then Chantelle peeped Izz getting his car keys from off the mantle. "Israel," she said with annoyance, "where're you goin'?"

"B.I., Shorty. Hold your head. Rook, let's make moves."

Rook reluctantly stood up from the couch.

"Bye Rook." I said to him.

He walked over, and pulled me into a hug. "Later, Love."

Once he had walked away, I turned back to Chantelle. "Oh well, guess I'm headed home."

"Don't go. Hang out for a little bit."

***

I stayed with Chan for an additional hour, then made my way home. No sooner than I had exchanged my sandals for slippers, did my doorbell ring. I walked over to the intercom. "Who is it?" I wasn't expecting anybody.

"Payne."

Payne? Did I hear him right? "Who is it?"

"Nasir." He reiterated.

What does he want? I thought as I buzzed him up. But I knew what he wanted. He saw the way Rook was all in my grill, and that bothered him. I stood in the hallway, with the door to my condo closed as he walked up to the first floor landing. "What's up?"

"Nothing. How ya feeling?"

"I'm good. Where's ya girl?"

He grinned at me. "In her skin."

"You ain't funny."

"Whatever, Man. You gonna keep me in the hallway or what?"

"Were you trying to come in?" I asked, head cocked to the side.

"For a minute."

He was too fine. Looking into those green eyes, it was mad hard to deny him. I opened the door to my refuge and allowed him to step inside. I led him into the living room. It was painted a color called "crisp linen" that fell somewhere between off white, and a very pale tan. My furniture and accents were varying shades of tans, browns, creams, yellows, and corals. Pictures of my life were displayed all around the room.

Nasir acted like he had been to my place before. He walked around like an invited guest. I laid in the cut and watched as he made himself at home. He picked up a picture of Chantelle and me that was taken on prom night and studied it. He sat that one down, and picked up a picture of me in my dorm room at Gilbert Hall. I had spent four years at Northern Illinois University, earning a degree in elementary education that I had yet to put to use. He sat that picture down and picked up a picture of me and Monte at the All-Star game in Oakland. I walked over, took the photo out of his hand, and put it back in its rightful place. I vividly remembered taking that picture, pretending to be happy when actually I was miserable. The only reason I even kept it on display was because I looked so cute in it.

He walked over to the couch and sat down. I followed behind, and sat across from him on the loveseat.

"Real talk, why'd you do dude like that?" He was barely able to contain his grin. "You on some gangsta-glamour type shit or what? You made Izz beat dude's ass in front of everybody. That wasn't right."

"I didn't *make* Izz beat dude down. One of y'all coulda just as easily shot him." I teased.

"You're like…a big contradiction. What's up, Joya? You a gangsta girl, or a princess, cuz I can't tell?"

"I'm a princess with a little bit of gangsta in her." I joked.

"Yeah well, ya gangsta got dude smashed."

"I would feel bad about it, but I ain't appreciate the way he was coming outta his mouth at me all night." I said honestly. "I mean, from the minute I got there, he was tripping. He popped off one too many times, and he got what he came for."

"I don't think he came to get kicked in the dick." Nasir told me, and both of us laughed.

"Too bad, then." I said, once my laughter had subsided. We were both silent. I decided to speak. "So Nasir, why haven't I heard from you?"

He shook his head. "Right now, you're showing me that I called it the day we played pool. I'm saying, I ain't even tapped that and you're questioning me about why I ain't called."

"You're the one who showed up at my spot…uninvited. Since you're here, I figured that I might as well ask."

"Are we cool, Joya? You consider us friends?"

"We're cool." I conceded with a nod of my head.

"Where I'm from, friends don't need to be on no 'rules of

engagement' type shit. I'll always call you when I wanna talk to you. If you don't hear from me, then I'm cooling."

"Is that what you tell your women? And they fall for that mess? Yeah, we definitely need to remain *friends*, because if you came at me with some mess like that, I'd key your wheels." I teased.

"First of all, I don't have *women*. I have friends. Second of all, they don't fall for nothing, because I don't spit lines. I keep it a hundred. They know what it is from day one. Third of all, if you ever feel sporting enough to key my whip, you better hire 24 hour security. I ain't Ant."

"And I ain't Donyae. So, if you wanna maintain a friendship with me…you're gonna need to call me sometime…and don't just be showing up at my spot, like we're on it like that."

"Yo, what cat have you been messing with that let you get away with popping off like that? I wanna meet dude, cuz he gotta have a problem, on the real. Your mouth is too slick."

"Maybe that's why I'm single."

He hit me with the screw face. "You think? If you wanna maintain a friendship with me, you need to reign in your mouthpiece. I can't stand that shit. I can't stand a flip-mouthed female."

I didn't reply.

"But I saw what your problem is at Izz's spot."

"So, I have a problem?"

"You think you're tough."

"I don't think I'm tough, but I'm not about to sit there and be disrespected. You're a man. I wouldn't expect you to understand. But it's hard to get these brothers to treat you decently out here. There are so many females in the hood, willing to sex, suck, trick, crack…whatever they gotta do for cash. They got the brothers thinking that we're all like that. In order to show them that you're different, you basically hafta present yourself like a nun. And I *always* present myself like class. So, I don't want nobody treating me with less than the amount of respect that I feel I deserve."

"I guess game *doesn't* always recognize game, huh?"

"What're you talking about?"

"You couldn't see that dude was feeling you? A young-minded cat like that
, he probably didn't know how to express it. Like you said, you present yourself as class. You probably intimidated him. Then, he saw his guy stepping up to the bat, and it really made him tight."

"Well, he played himself, then. I don't give rhythm to cats that come at me like that."

Nasir twisted his lips. "You wouldn't have given dude rhythm no matter how he came at you."

"True." I giggled. He had me on that one.

"Especially not with me in the room."

The giggle died on my lips. I waited for him to tell me that he was joking, or crack a smile. After a few seconds, while he was still looking at me with a straight face, I spoke. "Are you serious?"

"Don't I look like I'm serious?"

"Yeah, you do, but you gotta be playing. You are not this conceited."

"I'm not trying to be conceited. This is real talk. You weren't gonna try to holla at no cat in front of me. We dig each other. You know that."

"Well, if I didn't before, I definitely knew once I heard that you were over Justus' house discussing me." I said with a smirk.

He chuckled a little bit. "That right there, was totally unnecessary. But just so you know, all those whispered conversation you be having with Chan…they come back to me, too."

I wasn't surprised by that. I figured that Israel had overheard Chantelle and me talking and reported back to Nasir. Even though fellas tried to act like they weren't into gossip, they told everything they knew as quickly as women did.

Neither of us spoke for a minute.

"Come here, Joya." He said finally, and beckoned to me with his finger.

I fought my nature, which told me to ask him why, and went and sat next to him on the couch. My butt had barely hit the cushions of the sofa, before he was pulling me to him. He gently touched his lips to mine.

I put my hand on his chest, to hold him off. "Uh, you're not trying to kiss me with the same lips you were kissing old girl with, are you?" I was feeling Nasir, but there were some things that I couldn't abide.

"Nah. I didn't kiss her."

He kissed my lips, again. The tenderness of the act made butterflies hit the runway and take-off inside my stomach. He pulled my bottom lip into his mouth and sucked it. I wanted to melt from the way he was making me feel. My mouth opened for his invasion and he kissed me deeply. Passionately. Held my face to his. I liked the feeling of being in his arms. We kissed again and again. He barely let me have time to catch my breath.

When he finally released me, I scooted back from him, like he might start the assault on my mouth again. "What's up?" I looked into his eyes.

"I'm trying to see something."

"Something like what?"

"Like what it is about you that's knocking me off my

square like this. I'm saying, what is it?"

"I told you that I'm a princess. Ask about me." I joked.

"You're stuck-up. I know that much."

"I am not stuck-up. I was playing with you." I shook my head. "I can't believe you called me stuck-up."

"You're not stuck-up…maybe a little siddity, but it's cool."

Neither of us spoke for a minute.

"Chop it up with me for a minute. What's your story, *Joya*?"

I loved the way he said my name. He made it sound like the sexiest name ever uttered. "I don't have a story."

"Quit tripping. Everybody gotta story."

I sighed. "I was born and raised here, in Chicago. Single mother, older brother. You can guess the rest."

"You're a pain in the ass." He told me.

I laughed.

"You won't let me hold something until we know each other. How am I supposed to get to know you, if you won't tell me nothing?"

I couldn't believe him. "So, you wanna get to know me, so you can hold something?"

"Check it out, I'm not into trickery, running game and shit like that. I know most chicks are used to fast-talking cats, spittin' that, '*Ma, you know you got me open. Ma, you know you my wifey'*." He mimicked the sweet-talking young boys. "I'm not for that. You'll always know where you stand with me, because I'm honest from the jump. So, honestly…I wanna put my hands on everything you're holding."

I hated myself for it, but my stupid cheeks started glowing red with the tell-tale signal of a blush rising.

He continued talking. "But I wanna know more about you, too."

"Dang, how bad do you wanna put your hands on what I'm holding?" I teased.

"You and that mouth." He told me, then changed the subject. "Dude in the picture over there. That's not old boy from the NBA…what's his name? Patterson? Monte Patterson? That ain't him, is it?"

"Yeah, that's him." I admitted reluctantly.

"Y'all used to deal?"

"Yeah." I repeated.

"Is he the one that lit you up with the bracelet and earrings?"

I nodded my head. "You know he's in the NBA, so the money wasn't a thing."

"What happened?"

"We don't need to get into all of that."

He watched me. "He fucked up bad with you, huh?"

"He tried to wreck me."

"How?"

"Ooh, I really don't wanna talk about that." I said.

"That's cool." He stood up from my sofa. "It's time for me to blow, anyway."

I didn't try to dissuade him from leaving. I stood up, too. "Okay."

"Walk me to the door."

I followed him to the front door. Once we were there, he pulled me into his arms. He sucked my bottom lip lightly, then kissed me deeply while his hands were placed firmly on the cheeks of my ass. Being in his arms felt way too natural. I was starting to like his kisses more than I wanted to like them.

"Man," he said when he released me, "you gotta nice ass."

I shook my head in disbelief, but I couldn't help grinning at him.

He cocked an eyebrow. "You sure I can't hit, before I leave?"

I unlocked my front door. "I'm positive." I was trying to act normal. Like my lower-region wasn't throbbing from having him kiss me. "Bye Nasir. Talk to you later."

"Yeah, okay." He made his way towards the hallway. Right before his feet crossed the threshold, he pulled me to him again and kissed me once more. "We'll talk later,

Beautiful."

***

A few days later, Chantelle asked me to rush the mall with her. We browsed side by side at *The Pleasure Principle*. *The Pleasure Principle* was the lingerie store that Nia owned. It sold everything a girl could ever need to properly seduce her man. It was a cross between *Victoria's Secret*, *Frederick's of Hollywood*, *Lovers Lane* and a kinky sex-shop.

I picked up a pair of lavender panties that featured a picture of a rhinestone encrusted cat on them. Over the cat, in a dark purple script was the word, "Platinum", underneath the cat was the word, "pussy". As much as I hated, and found the 'p' word vulgar, I had to laugh.

"If I can find a matching bra, I'm getting these." I handed the panties to Chantelle, so she could get a laugh.

She glanced at them and handed them right back. "Joy please, get your life. How 'bout you get them in a thong?"

I sucked my teeth. "Some people actually like their asses covered up. Is that okay?"

"Panties can be sexy." Nia said entering the conversation. "Plus, they leave a little bit more to the imagination."

"Uhm, you won't catch me in no panties. All of this,"

Chantelle spanked her own butt, "needs to be free. So, point me to the thongs."

"How's Payne doing?" Nia asked casually.

I continued to peruse the panties. "He's good."

Chantelle looked over at me. "When did you talk to him?"

"Yesterday." I added a pair of green panties to my growing pile. They featured a velvet turtle and the words, "snaps back."

Chantelle shook her head. "What brother has time to read words?"

Before I could respond, Nia spoke. "You and Izz aren't into foreplay? What? He just rips the thongs off you, and takes the coochie?"

I chuckled.

"Whatever." Chantelle said dismissively.

"Rough sex can cause urinary tract infections, Chan. Make him slow down, sometimes." Nia suggested.

"Yeah, maybe that can be your 'wifey weekend' gift." I joked.

"Forget you, Heifer. At least I'm gettin' some on the regular." She told me. "What are you and Justus doin' this weekend, Nia?"

"We're going to see Jill Scott over at The Star Plaza in Merrillville."

"That sounds like fun." I commented.

"The fun starts after the concert, when I get my man up to that hotel room, Chica. I don't own a sex shop for nothing." She smirked. "I'mma do some illegal stuff to J's sexy ass. I'm breaking' out all the toys. I got my crystal encrusted hand cuffs…"

"I want some of those." Chantelle interrupted.

"I got my motion lotion, my Ben WA balls, my…" Nia continued.

"We get it, Girl." I told her.

"Yeah well, I have everything I need." She finished.

"Don't let me leave without gettin' some of those handcuffs." Chantelle repeated.

"I won't. What are you and Israel doing?"

"Girl, you know Izz is about them streets. I might not even see him this weekend."

"How do you live with somebody and not see them?" Nia asked, perplexed.

"Move in with Justus, and you'll know exactly how it happens." Chantelle suggested.

"Chan, Please. You know I'm not having that stupid shit from J that you put up with from Izz. I don't live with J and I see him *every* day. Let him go an entire day without seeing me. He'd turn up missing. You'd be reading about him in the newspaper."

"Izz ain't Justus. Justus is a good dude."

"He wasn't always. He used to be just like Izz, and Dex and them. But I let him know off bat that if he wanted to be with Nia, then he needed to step his game up. Otherwise, he needed to kick rocks."

"Like I said, Izz ain't Justus." Chantelle repeated, and I could tell she was getting defensive about the conversation.

Nia must've caught Chan's attitude, because she changed the subject. "You in town this weekend, Miss Flight Attendant?"

"Nah, I'm outta here Friday night. I'm not back until Sunday night."

"Well, just in case you see Payne before you fly out on Friday, I'm having a sale on flavored massage oil. They're two for $10.00." She paused. "And I know for a fact that Payne really likes strawberries."

"Shut up, Nia." I said, but couldn't help blushing at the thought of Nasir licking strawberry flavored oil off of my body.

***

Sunday night's plane was delayed. It was supposed to get in at 7:10. It didn't end up getting in until 8:05. By the time I made it home, it was after 9:00. All I wanted to do was take a shower, put on my night clothes and fall into bed. I dropped my luggage and purse on the floor right in front of my closet. I kicked off the Eastern Airlines regulation high heels that I was required to wear, and started stripping out of the restrictive uniform.

I was down to my panties and bra when my cell phone started to sing, alerting me that I had a text message. I grabbed my cell from my purse and read the message.

Holla when you touch down, Ma. Let me know you're cool.

I smiled at the message from Nasir. He was concerned about me.

I took a shower, made myself a sandwich, and called him. "Hey you." I said when he answered the phone.

"Hey yourself. What's good?"

"You, texting me, because you were concerned." I teased.

He chuckled. "Yeah, I'mma hard rock, but I guess I gotta soft spot for you."

"I guess so. You in the streets? It's kinda quiet."

"Nah, I'm at the crib. I've been posted up in here all day. I don't know what's wrong with me. Maybe it's sinuses or something. My head's pounding."

"Have you been taking anything?"

"Nah, I ain't have nothing at the crib. I've been laying down all day. I fell asleep a few times, but whenever I wake up, this pain is still crashing my brain."

"Gimme me about an hour. I'mma come by your spot and bring you some painkillers."

"You don't have to do that." He insisted.

"I know I don't." I assured him.

"Ay, since you're stopping through, bring me something to eat, too. A brother ain't ate all day."

He gave me his address, and I ended the call.

***

I arrived at his apartment about forty minutes later carrying pain killers, orange juice, a turkey sandwich from Subway, and a bag of chips.

Nasir answered the door for me wearing baggy jeans, a bright white wife-beater, and whiter than white socks on his feet. It was the first time I had seen his naked arms. A tattoo was etched into the peanut butter brown skin of his muscular right bicep. The tat featured an intricately designed cross, flanked by angel's wings, and surrounded by clouds. The longer of the two bands showed the name ANGELICA. At the letter 'E', Angelica's name was intersected with the word FOREVER.

I wondered who Angelica was. "Hey." I said, as he invited me into his space.

"What's hood, Beautiful?" He gave me a quick hug.

"Nothing. I brought you some medicine and some food."

"Good looking out." He grinned at me. Showed me his deep dimples. "It's like you're looking for ways to make sure that I never get back on my square."

"Whatever." I blew off his joke. "Uhm, can I get that together for you?"

"Nah, I got it. Have a seat."

I sat down on his distressed leather couch. I looked around Nasir's apartment. I had never been there before. He had a nice place. All of the walls were painted a stark white, but he had at least taken the time to decorate the spot nicely. His sofa, loveseat, and recliner were all made of the same expensive looking, distressed brown leather. His cocktail table and end tables were a combination of walnut wood and glass. His furniture sat atop a deliciously lush looking, colorfully patterned rug. He had lamps, pictures, and other accents strategically placed around the room. And his place smelled good. It smelled like candles. If I hadn't known any better, I would've said that his apartment had a woman's touch to it.

"Come sit in the dining room, Joy. Keep me company." He called.

I walked into the next room. His dining room was decorated in strong colors. Lots of wrought iron, dark wood, glass and chrome filled that space. I sat down with him at his table, which was a modern piece, that featured a square glass top, and legs made of cappuccino wood. Again, the hardwood floor was covered with a beautiful rug.

"Where'd you get these rugs?"

"My baby sister designed 'em." He responded between bites of his sandwich.

"You gotta be lying."

He cocked his head to the side. "Why do you always say that? I ain't lying. My sister's in design school. Got crazy talent. She designed this table, too. Actually, she designed almost all of my furniture."

I looked at the unique and modern furniture, again. "You think she can make something happen for me?"

"You looking for a hook-up?" He teased.

"I'm not looking for a hook-up."

"You better not be looking for no hook-up, after you wouldn't let me get hooked-up with the free plane tickets."

I laughed. "For real, Nasir. I'll pay your sister's price. I'm just looking for a few things for my place."

"I'll get at her about you. Put y'all in touch." He looked around his apartment. "Torri does her thing. She decorated my apartment for me."

That explained why it had a woman's touch to it. "You just have the one younger sister?"

"Nah, I got two little sisters. Torri is the baby. My other sister, Yasmeen, she does event planning. Owns her own business."

I was impressed. "Dang, your moms must be mad proud of them."

"I don't think my moms cares too much. But my grandmother, she wilds out over practically anything they do."

I didn't reply.

"My grandmother raised us," he explained, "from the time we were little."

"Was your mom sick or something?" I didn't want to come right out and ask him if his moms was on drugs, but that was the vibe I was getting.

"You could say that. She was strung-out." He was honest. "She was never completely off the scene, but none of us have like, a real relationship with her. My grandmother raised us. She basically raised Justus, too. His moms was always working, so he was practically lived at my crib."

We sat in silence as he finished off his food.

"You feel any better?"

"I think the medicine is kicking in." He stood up from the table. "I really need to lie down, though."

I stood up as well. "That's cool. I'll get outta here and let you rest."

He walked over to me and caught my hand in his. "Come lay down with me." He nodded his head in the direction that I figured his bedroom was in.

"Nasir." I whined. He was putting me in an uncomfortable position.

"It ain't like that, Beautiful. My head is bangin', straight up. I couldn't knock you if I wanted to. Lay down with me for a minute. Keep me company. Can you do that for me?"

I thought about it for a few seconds. It sounded innocent, and I trusted that Nasir wasn't a rapist. "Okay." I agreed, and let him lead me into his bedroom.

One look at his bedroom furniture and I could tell that it, too, had been designed by his sister Torri. The styling and the lines of the furniture was modern with a funky flair. His bed was simple, and classic, minus the frills. It was designed in the same black wood as the dining room table, and was covered with hunter green linens. A fifty inch flat screen television was bolted to the wall across from it. A black leather chair, a dresser with a mirror, a chest of drawers, and two nightstands in the same dark wood as the bed completed the décor. His bedroom was nice.

"I thought you said you've been laying down all day."

"I have."

"So, why is your bed made up all spiffy?" I asked suspiciously. "Were you expecting me to come in here all along?"

He gave me a guilty smirk. "I won't say I was expecting it, but you never know."

"Whatever, Nasir."

"Don't start wildin', Ma. You know I got this headache."

"Any old excuse." I mumbled, as I slid out of my gym shoes, and started to climb into his bed.

He stopped me with a shake of his head.

"What's up?" I asked.

"You can't get in my bed with your street clothes on."

I gave him my "nucca, please!" look. "What does that mean? You think I'm about to get in your bed naked?" I wanted to ask him if he was puffing that same stuff that had his moms out there like that, but of course I didn't take it there. Instead, I started putting my shoes back on. "All right, then."

"Joy. Joy. Joy. Come on, Joy." He quickly caught my wrist, before I could make like Ludacris and the homies, and ROLLOUT. "Come on, Girl. Stop bugging. I'mma give you something to wear."

"Something like what?" I asked, calming down a little.

"You want a jersey, some jogging pants? Whatever you want...I got you."

A few minutes later, I was in Nasir's bed, and he was posted up behind me. I hugged the Miami Heat jersey that featured Dwyane Wade's number to me. It smelled like fabric softener and dryer sheets. A thug that understood the importance of fabric softener when doing laundry. That was interesting to me… right up until I started wondering if some chick was doing his laundry for him.

Nasir distracted me from thinking those kinds of thoughts by letting his hand glide down my body, and land on my hip. I didn't say anything. It had been too long since a man held me in his arms. It felt good to be held again. Nasir moved closer to me. His chest was pressed against my back. He lifted my hair with his hand, and started to kiss the back of my neck softly. Slowly. I fought the urge to moan. He kissed my neck, again.

"Nasir." I sighed. "Come on, now. I thought you said your head hurt too bad to be trying to get freaky."

"I'm saying, Girl. How am I supposed to have you lying in my bed like this and not get none?"

I turned around and faced him. "This was your idea!"

"I know." He admitted, sounding like a kid. "It was a bad one."

"Definitely."

"If we can't get it in, what're we supposed to do?"

"Let's talk." I suggested, turning back around so that my back was to him.

He sighed heavily.

I laughed out loud. What dude wanted to have a conversation? Especially if it wasn't going to lead to or end with sex.

"Talk? I gotta headache."

"We can talk softly." I promised.

"Whatever." He sighed again. "Do your thing."

"Who's Angelica?"

"Angelica?"

"Yeah, the tattoo on your arm." I reminded him.

"Oh, that's my aunt, Angel. She was killed when I was a shorty." He semi-chuckled. "Who'd you think it was?"

"I didn't know. That's why I asked. But you do have a lot of women."

"This is like, my fifth time telling you this. I don't have women. I have friends, and I damn sure wouldn't get any of them tatted on me."

"But they're good enough to sex when the mood hits?"

"Ssshhh." He whispered. "My head hurts."

I elbowed him lightly in the ribs. "Whatever, Man."

He tickled me in the stomach. I laughed, and pushed his hand away.

After a few minutes of silence, he spoke. "What happened with you and the cat from the NBA?" His fingers were lightly playing in my hair, brushing against my scalp, and sending shockwaves through my entire body.

"He dogged me."

"Say more."

"I don't wanna talk about it."

"I don't remember asking if you wanted to talk about it. Stand in yours. Address what went down. You ain't the first chick to get dogged. You won't be the last. And you ain't gotta be embarrassed in front of me."

"I'm not embarrassed. It happened, I learned from it. What's to be embarrassed about?"

"Well, if that's the case, put it out there."

He acted like he wasn't gonna give up on finding out about the hell Monte had taken me through, so it was whatever. I decided to tell him some of the things that had happened. "I met him at San Francisco International Airport. He was a passenger on my flight. We had drinks at his hotel bar, and everything popped off from there. When we first got together, it was all love. It was your typical long-distance relationship. Hour long telephone conversations, flowers and gifts, sexy text messages, game tickets. He played for Indianapolis at the time, so either I was there, or he was in Chicago. I was so sprung." I shook my head at the memory. "He was like, my everything. I loved him more than life."

"Yo, apparently something went to the left, or you would still be with him."

"Yeah, things definitely went to the left." I told Nasir about the first time I caught Monte out at a club with his side-chick. How I showed my ass in front of his teammates, and set it off in the club. How he made the team rookie put me in my car and send me back home with a broken heart and a broken spirit. I told him how Monte came to my spot hours later and beat me up. "That was the end of the 'good times'. Everything went down-hill from there. He stopped trying to hide the cheating. He would do whatever he wanted to do, and I would ride. I swallowed it. Everything."

I rested silently in Nasir's arms for a minute or so. Then, the words started spilling out, again. "Do you know that I stood by him through two paternity suits, despite the fact that he was beating the hell outta me on the daily?"

"Nah, I didn't know that." He said quietly. "Did you ever think about leaving him alone?"

"Not really." I admitted. "I mean, I had given the relationship a year of my life. I loved him, and in spite of the cheating, and the paternity cases and the fighting, I had convinced myself that he loved me, too. He could be really sweet when he wanted to be. Sometimes, he would treat me like a princess. He would tell me how he wanted to wife me. How he couldn't imagine himself with anybody, but me."

I picked up Nasir's hand and laced my fingers through his. He kissed me on the shoulder. "You believed him, huh?"

"I had to. I wanted to stay in the relationship. As long as I let myself believe that he loved me, and that he would marry me, I could justify the craziness."

He hugged me tightly, like he wanted to take the bad memories away. Sometimes when I thought about the way Monte had played me, I had to admit that I was more upset with myself for being so damn dumb, than I was at him for being so damn grimy.

"Ma..."

"Don't say it." I whispered.

We laid in silence for a few seconds.

"When did you decide to leave him?" He asked.

"Eastern Airlines does this thing called *Eastern Cares*. It's a community service project. That year, the theme was battered women and children. They took staff members to battered women's shelters all over the country. It was like, every time the women would start telling their stories, they were telling my story."

"Damn." He said softly.

"I started to accept the fact that the way Monte and I were living wasn't normal. I started to think, 'I'm a battered woman.' But I still wanted the relationship." I chuckled at the stupidity of that thought. "I thought, if I could get him to stop putting his hands on me, the relationship could get back on track." I paused. "Notice that I didn't bother to address the fact that he cheated on me constantly. Or the fact that he got some broad in New Orleans pregnant. I kept thinking that I needed to deal with one problem at a time, and the most important issue was that he was beating the hell outta me."

"How'd you get him to stop fighting you?"

"It wasn't like he would smack me up and I would let him. I'm from the block. I grew up fighting. So, when we got into it, I tried to give as good as I got, but he was stronger than me, so he always came out on top. I got my licks in where I could, though."

"So, little mama was a boxer? That's cool, Shorty. How did you get him to stop fighting you? You need to talk fast, cuz listening to this shit is pissing me off to the point where I wanna fly to South Carolina, find dude, and body him."

"I did two things. The first thing was I enrolled in this real crazy self-defense class. After about twenty-five lessons, I knew how to stop dude from putting his hands on me."

"What kinda class was this?"

"It's called Krav Maga. It's an Israeli combat technique. While I was learning that, this pilot that had a thing for me, started talking to me all of the time about guns. I thought I was hiding the fact that Monte was killing me at the crib, but everybody knew. My friends knew. My co-workers knew.

My family knew. I guess the big sunglasses, and liquid concealer weren't enough to cover my black eyes and bruises. Anyway, this pilot told me that during his off time, he liked to go to the gun range. He started taking me with him. I've been in gun ranges all over the United States."

"Straight up?" He sounded shocked.

"Yep. I'm a good shot, too. If you ever need pointers on how to hit that target, let me know." I teased.

"Nah Ma. You got that. I have *excellent* aim. I never miss." He told me. "What kinda heat you good with?"

"I gotta small little 9 millimeter. Bubbles was messing with this crazy hustler at the time. He had the handle covered in lavender mother-of-pearl for me, and had a silencer put on it. It's a pretty little gun. Just the right size. It fits perfectly in the inside pocket of my favorite purse."

"You own a burner?"

"Yep. And I'm legal with mine…which you wouldn't know nothing about." I joked. "It's registered and everything."

"You're right. I don't know a damn thing about registering no gun."

I chuckled.

"What ended up happening with you and the NBA punk?"

"I talked to him about leaving the violence on the basketball court, and he agreed. Everything was all good for about three weeks. Then, one day he got pissed with me, and he went to smack me up. I hit him with the Krav Maga. He went down like a ton of bricks. The first time I had to use self-defense techniques on Monte, I knew I was never gonna marry him. The first time I had to pull out on him, I knew the relationship was over. One of us was gonna end up dying, and I honestly believed that it would be him. I couldn't see myself serving jail time over him, so I ended things."

"Why'd you have to pull out on him?"

"Because after about two shots of Krav Maga, he stopped putting his hands on me. And once he stopped, I knew I couldn't go back to fighting him, again. Well, one time he got pissed, and we got into it. I was hitting him with all of my techniques. Throat chop; a shot to the nose that made him bleed, all of that. But it was like dude was possessed or something. He was still coming for me. So, finally as a last resort I went to kick him in the balls, and he had on his cup. He actually had on his athletic cup. He thought I was done. He was coming at me like he was about to break me in two or something. Luckily, my purse was close by, so I pulled out on him. I told him that I would shoot him before I would take another ass-whipping from him."

"He think you were bullshitting?"

"Not at all. I think he was shocked to see that 9 milli pointed at his face. He backed right down. I think he realized that he underestimated me. He was kinda scared of me after that. He was never sure what to expect."

"Fuckin' coward."

"Bastard." I agreed. "When we broke up, he made me give back everything he ever bought for me. Jewelry, purses, fur coats, a car. Everything. He taught me a valuable lesson, though. Now, I don't take gifts from men. Anything that Joya can't get for herself, she most likely won't have. That's why I stay working overtime. I keep my own bank account fat and buy my own stuff."

"Check you out." He said.

I lay there silently. I was waiting for Nasir to assure me that he would never play me like Monte had played me. I waited for him to make the promises that dudes made to women when they wanted to sex. He surprised me when he finally spoke.

"I appreciate you telling me the deal."

"You're welcome."

"Krav Maga? That's what you were using when you got that cat off of you at Izz's crib?"

"Yeah, but I hadn't used it in a while, so I didn't kick him with enough force to knock him down."

"And the NBA dude took all of your jewelry?"

"Except for those two pieces that I wore to Israel's house that day."

"That's why you don't wear any jewelry." He stated.

"I wear jewelry." I insisted.

"Ma, your jewel game is cracked. All I've seen you sporting is your class ring, and that garbage ass watch you love to wear."

"Stop talking about my jewelry. I'm doing the best I can."

"Don't tell nobody else that." He teased.

We laughed together.

A little while later, I fell asleep in Nasir's bed, wearing his jersey, wrapped in his arms.

Chapter Six
Mo Money Mo Problems

Payne

The last Wednesday in June started off like any other day, but that didn't last long. As I was headed towards the office, Justus hit me on my cell.

"What's good?" I asked, when I answered.

His response was a heavy sigh.

I knew I wasn't going to like what he was about to tell me.

"The house out in Riverdale, burned to the ground early this morning." He said, barely managing to control the anger behind the words.

"Elliott's house?" I questioned, even though I knew that was exactly the house he was talking about.

"Yeah."

"Is anything salvageable?" I asked.

"Hell no. Even the fuckin' grass is a wrap."

"Damn." I muttered. "Did we have anything on the house for fire?"

"Yeah, *Exit Strategy* has it covered. It's just fucked up."

"No doubt." I agreed. "So, what are things looking like?"

"Preliminary investigation says that it looks like arson. But hell, I could've told them that, without even looking at the scene. Me and Izz are about to head out that way."

"Cool, let me know what's up, after you find out the deal."

Three days after that, a house we had on 83rd and Wood got blazed. Two weeks later, the building on 69th and Crandon went up in smoke. That was when I knew that Elliott was living his last days.

***

About ten days after the 69th and Crandon property burned down, I went in the studio with Trey. He had copped another track from me, and I was definitely with it.

He had asked me to get Joya in the studio. He was feeling her vocals and wanted her to do the hook on the new track. She was about forty-five minutes late, and I was kinda starting to wonder where she was. As I was about to call her phone, she fell into the spot followed by Rook, Bubbles, Dex, Israel, Chantelle, Justus, and Nia.

As they came through the door, Rook had his arm draped around Joya's shoulder. He was whispering in her ear. She didn't look like she was digging it, but I noticed that she hadn't removed his arm from her shoulder, either. It sort of got next to me that dude was hugged up with her. When Joya's eyes fell on mine, she easily pushed Rook's arm off and made her way over to me.

"Sorry it took so long." She apologized, hugging me. "I mentioned to Chan that I was coming to the studio, and somehow the studio became the place to be. Sorry."

"You're straight." I told her. "What is Rook doing with his arm all draped across you?"

"You know how Rook is. He thinks he's the King of Chicago or something." She winked at me. "You know he's feeling me."

She was joking around, and didn't realize that I was serious. "Keep playing, and get your man fucked up if you want to." I warned.

She twisted her face, as she leaned against the board. "Come on, Nasir. You know what it is. Rook can't even see me. Stop tripping."

"He can't even see you, huh?" I repeated.

"No, he can't."

"Watch that…for real."

She grinned at me, like that made everything cool. And basically she was right, it did.

Trey walked over to where Joya and I were lounging. "Ay, what's up? Are you Miss Lady that made my track hot as hell?"

"Are you Trey?"

"Yeah."

"Hey, I'm Joya. It's nice to meet you."

"Damn Ma, gimme a hug." He pulled her into his arms. "Your vocals are straight bananas. I couldn't believe it when Payne played the track for me. I was like, 'who is that?' You sounded like a straight angel, Girl. I was like, 'Dawg, I want her on every track.' Payne'll tell ya."

Joya blushed and grinned while Trey complimented her. "Thank you. I'm glad you liked it."

"Liked it? Maybe I'm not expressing myself properly. I more than liked it, Shorty. I'm ready to see how I can connect with you on a more permanent level."

Joya glanced at me. I gave her a blank stare. I didn't know what the hell Trey was talking about, but I knew he needed to talk fast, telling my girl that he wanted to get at her on a more permanent level.

My girl? I thought to myself. *Did I call Joya my girl?*

"What do you mean?" She asked him.

"I'm sayin', it's *Freestyle Friday*, over at *Club Potion* week after next. First prize is $2000.00. I'm thinking about going over there, and laying the rest of those cats flat." He paused, and tapped her lightly on the hand. "You roll through there with me, kill the hook, and I give you $500.00 off top."

"You gotta be lying" She told him.

I shook my head, and smirked to myself. That was Joya's favorite expression. She was always accusing somebody of lying to her.

Trey looked surprised that she questioned his sincerity. "Hell naw, I'm not lying. This is real talk. I've been around the industry for a while now, and there's nobody out there that has your sound. With you blazing the hook, I know we're gonna walk away with that dough. You down?"

"Friday after next? I gotta check my schedule, but if I'm free, I'm down. Can I hear the song you want me to sing on?"

"I'mma lay the track in a minute." He turned his head and looked behind him at the crew that had come into the studio behind Joya. "I gotta wait for some of these *people* to clear outta here."

I figured he was referring to Rook.

"Is it one of Nasir's tracks?" She asked Trey.

He looked confused.

"It's one of Payne's tracks?" She corrected herself.

"Yeah." He responded. He looked at her quizzically. "What'd you call him?"

"Nothing. Don't even worry about it."

He looked at us suspiciously. "Yo anyway, I'm looking forward to seeing what you can do with this hook."

Rook moved over to where we were. He gave both Trey and me dap before he spoke. "What's the deal, Payne? What's good, Trey?"

"What's up?"

Rook glanced from me to Trey. "You came through to cop another track from Payne?"

"Maybe." Trey was vague.

"I guess as long as you keep tryin' to break into the industry, Payne'll always have at least *one* customer coppin' tracks from him." Rook stated.

That was a shot at both me and Trey.

"I guess so." Trey agreed. "I heard you cop your tracks from Diamond Diego."

"That's right." Rook nodded his head, proudly. "That nigga is the next Kanye."

"Straight up? I heard that last track you copped from him was straight garbage. I heard KJ Jamison ate you up a few weeks ago, over at *Kacey's*."

"Fuck you, Dude." Rook said between clenched teeth.

Trey laughed at him.

"On that note, I'm going in the booth to warm up." Joya said, and both men put their attention on her.

"You're goin' in the booth?" Rook asked. "For what?"

Joya rolled her eyes. "To warm up."

"You can sing?" He was surprised. It was evident by his

expression.

"I do a little something."

"And you're doin' *a little somethin'* on this track Trey copped from Payne?"

"Yep."

Rook turned to me. "Payne, you kept Little Mama's skills quiet, then you linked her with Trey? What type of shit is that? I know we go back way farther than you and dude."

"You need to be beefin' with your brother about that, Son. Izz is the one who put me up on the fact that Joya had skills."

"So, why you ain't on one of my tracks?" He asked Joya.

"You never asked me." She replied with a shrug.

"Well, I want you on one of my joints…if you sound hot. I gotta hear you for myself, though."

"I don't blame you."

"Go 'head and blow for me. Just sing a few bars of whatever song you think you sound good singin'."

She gave him the screw face. "Uh Rook, first of all, I'm not on your payroll. Second of all, I'm not a trained parakeet. I don't sing on command."

While I couldn't stand it when she popped off at the mouth to me, it kinda made me laugh when she did it to Rook.

"How am I gonna know if you can blow or not?"

"I really don't know." She shrugged her shoulders, then headed into the booth.

Trey walked away, and I was left standing there with Rook. We both watched Joya put the headphones on, and prepare to sing.

"I swear, as fine as that bitch is, if she can sing, too…I'm fuckin' her tonight." He promised me.

"How're you gonna make that happen?"

He looked at me like I was crazy. "I'm Rook the Crook, Son. I knock hoes by the dozens."

"Dude, you really need to let the blunt miss you the next time it comes around. You're ridiculous."

He sucked his teeth. "Go to hell, Payne. You just mad, cuz you could never hit a chick like that."

"Word?"

"If that tomboy hoe you brought to Izz's crib for the NBA Finals was an indication of what you can pull, you're hurtin', Dawg."

"And who did you bring to the party, again? What was dude's name…Ant?" I watched as realization washed over his face.

His chest puffed up. "What're you tryin' to say dude?"

"I'm saying, you're dissing my female, but you ain't even have a girl with you."

"I was…"

He was cut short by Joya's crystal clear voice. It was like the entire room went silent as she lit the atmosphere with her God-given gift.

"That's my girl!" Chantelle said loudly, then took a hit of the weed she and Israel brought with them.

Justus made his way over to the board, with a blunt hanging precariously from his lips. "Your girl got talent." He took a deep hit, and then offered me one.

I declined with a shake of my head. "I told you, Son. Izz called it on this one."

"He did. She can sing."

"She's makin' my dick hard. I'm fuckin' this broad tonight." Rook stated, then walked away from us.

"What's wrong with dude?" Justus asked me.

I shrugged my shoulders. "He's an idiot."

"Does he know that you and shorty…"

I shook my head, before Justus could even finish the statement. "Nope, and he doesn't need to. Let him do his thing. Joy'll shoot him down."

About twenty minutes later, Trey approached me. "Ay Payne, I'm ready to go 'head and do my thing. You think you can get the rest of these people outta here, so we can start?"

"Fo' sho'." I assured him.

I was about to call out to my peoples and tell them to hit

the bricks, when I was distracted by Joya. Trey had gone into the booth, and the two of them were going over the lyrics he had written for her. She laughed, and ran her fingers through her long hair. I remembered the last time I had put my hands on her. We were at my spot. She fell asleep in my bed, wrapped up in my arms like she belonged there. I watched her sleep and wondered about dude who had played her out. He had to be on some whole other shit, because as far as I could tell, Joya was the business. Smart, beautiful, sexy, motivated. Dude must've been intimidated by her gangsta or something.

When she was in my bed half-naked, it was hard as hell for me to keep my hands to myself. Especially with the way my jersey kept riding up and showing me the creamy, yellow skin on her healthy ass thighs. Instead, I had gotten up and chilled on the couch in the living room for a few hours. I made my way back to the bedroom about fifteen minutes before Joya woke up. The sweet smile Shorty gave me when she saw me sitting at the foot of the bed watching her, made me feel some kinda way about her.

I regained my focus on the matter at hand and started encouraging my people to kick rocks. "Ay, we're about to start recording, so I'mma need y'all to bounce out." I told them.

Chantelle was still on ten, blowing trees and talking

garbage to Izz, Bubbles and Dex. Nia and Justus were on the sofa. Nia was asleep with her head on Justus' shoulder. Justus was staring off into space. To everybody else in the room he probably looked straight blunted-out and sky-high. But I knew that look. I knew that he was probably imagining video concepts, mentally staging and blocking how each shot would go down. I did the same thing with beats. I could sit in a room full of chaos, zone out and hear beats talking to me, telling me exactly how they should sound.

Joya had come out of the booth, and was sitting at the boards. She was humming and bobbing her head to music that only she could hear. That caught Rook's attention and he made his way over to her. I figured his plan to sex her that night was still in full-effect. I paid it no mind.

"Ay man, don't forget we're working out in the morning." Justus said, standing up from the couch.

Nia stood up after him and stretched. Her arms went into the air, and her shirt rose up a little giving me a clear shot of her flat, chocolate covered belly.

"I got you." I assured Justus. Then, I nudged Israel. "You should come, too. You know you could use a workout." I gave him a light punch in his large gut.

"Eat me, you green eyed bastard." He said, grabbing his dick. "As long as my girl ain't complainin', I ain't got no problem with my size. And you ain't complainin', is you

Chan?"

"Hell naw, Big Daddy." Chantelle responded, wrapping her arms around Israel's rotund frame as best she could.

"I'm out, Dawg." Dex said, moving towards the studio door.

Bubbles followed behind him. She waved at me, and flashed me her million-dollar smile.

"Later, Dex." I said, then sweetened my voice. "Later Bubbles."

"See you, Payne." Nia said, as she followed close behind them.

"One, Nia. I'll hit you up in the a.m." I told Justus.

"Do that."

"Ay Rook, if you tryin' to get shuttled back to the crib, you need to come on." Israel called to his younger brother.

Rook looked over, and waved Israel off.

"I think Rook is trying to hit." I explained to Izz.

Chantelle heard me. "Tryin' to hit who with what? I know you're not talkin' about Joya."

I didn't respond, neither did Israel.

"Why aren't you tellin' Rook what's up, Payne? Aren't you and Joy…"

"We're cool." I said shortly.

"Aren't you two more than *cool*?" She pressed. "Aren't you feelin' her?"

"Who Joya decides to let hit that is her business."

She gave me her 'nigga please' look. "It's mad easy for you to say that, when both of us know that Joy ain't givin' up no booty."

I remained silent.

"Whatever." She gave me the hand, then turned her attention to her girl. "Joy, I'm exhausted. We're about to go. See you later."

Joya walked over to us, and hugged her girl. "See you, Chan. I'll call you. Bye Izz."

"Later, Shorty."

"Let's go, Rook!" Chantelle demanded.

"I'm talkin' to Joya."

"Uhm, I'm about to get in this booth. You might wanna make sure they don't leave you." Joya told him.

"I can't believe you're doin' vocals for Trey's lame-ass, and ain't doin' nothin' for me." He shook his head.

"Get a good track, Rook. Not like that garbage track you had at '*Blaze the Mic*', then make me an offer." She suggested. "If your price is right, I can do something for you."

"Get a good track?" He repeated. "What does that mean? Get one from Payne?"

"He is good at what he does."

Rook eyed her suspiciously. "You fuckin' Payne?"

Joya looked at him in disbelief. "Bye Rook." She walked away, leaving him standing there.

He turned to me. "You fuckin' Shorty?"

"I can't hit a chick like that. Remember?"

He continued to watch me suspiciously.

"Rook, 100 hundred, Dude." I told him.

"Yeah, whatever." He said, finally leaving the studio.

I turned my attention to Trey, and Joya.

***

Once the recording session was finished, and Joya and I were the only ones still in the studio, I pulled her into my arms. I leaned against the boards, and pulled her in between my legs. I brought her so close to me that her pelvis rested against mine. She didn't stop me, or move away.

"You did your thing."

She smiled at me. "Thank you."

"I think Trey's gotta crush on you."

"He needs to get in line, then." She joked.

I shook my head. "You are so vain."

"You like it." She stated sassily.

I more than like it, Ma. I thought to myself. Out loud I said, "no doubt."

I was horny as hell for Joya. Something about being in

her presence always made me wanna sex. I leaned towards her, until we made contact. I took her bottom lip into my mouth, and sucked it greedily. That lip was fat and juicy. I let my hands travel down to her ass, and pulled her even closer to me. After a few seconds of sucking her lip, I plunged my tongue into her sugary mouth and kissed her deeply. I hadn't really kissed a chick since high school. That was around the time when I realized exactly how grimy and nasty females could really be. That was when I stopped trusting women. But I liked kissing Joya. Her mouth was so sweet. We kissed like that for a minute. My hands were all over her. On her ass. On her breasts. On her waist. On her thighs.

I finally released her mouth to ask her a question. "You coming home with me tonight?" As far as I was concerned, she had held out long enough. I got the fact that she was a "good girl." It was time for her to let me fall inside.

She looked regretful, and I had my answer. I tried not to be pissed.

"I don't think that's a good idea, Nah Nah." She called me by the nickname she made up to soften the blow.

"Why is it not a good idea?" I asked, freaking her neck with my mouth. It only took one lick for me to realize that she was crazy sensitive on her neck. I intensified my game. I was competitive like that. I played to win, and I was trying to win her panties that night.

"Because," she started. She couldn't finish, because she was distracted by the things I was doing to her neck. It didn't help that my hands were cupping her breasts, and easily stroking her growing nipples. She tried again. "Because, I'm not ready yet, Nah Nah."

"Come on, Ma. What is there to get ready for? I'm diggin' you, you're diggin' me…let's do this." She had me pleading. I hated that shit. I wasn't the type to plead for ass, but I didn't know how else to get her to give in.

"Sex means a lot to me." She said. "I'm not into…"

That was when I tuned out. I backed up off of her neck, and discontinued my assault on her nipples. Joya was giving me flashbacks of high school, when females whined excuses about why I couldn't hit. I didn't wanna hear that. Either she was down, or she wasn't. I didn't need an explanation as to why I couldn't get it.

When she was finished talking, she hit me with the sad face. "You mad?"

I shrugged my shoulders and was honest with Shorty. "Nah. I'm disappointed."

"Trust, when I do let you hit it, you'll forget all about your disappointment." She pressed her pelvis into mine, and wiggled her hips.

"You better be telling the truth, Man." I said, gently

pushing her off of me, and standing up from the board.

Her mouth fell open. "You doubting my skills?"

"Yeah, I am. And they're gonna stay in doubt, until you let me test 'em out."

"I can't believe you."

"And you better not be the type that just lays there, either." I continued.

Her cocky attitude returned. "Definitely not. Believe that!"

I twisted my lips. "That's what they all say."

She stood there watching me in silence for a few seconds, like she was gonna take up the challenge. Then, she relaxed her posture. "When it's time, I'll show and prove. Until then, dream about me, Bruh."

Dream about her? What part of the game was that?

***

After I made sure that Joya got home safely, I headed towards the crib. My forward motion was halted by a text from Dex. He wanted me to slide through 94th and Yale. One of the chicks he messed around with had a crib on that block. So, I made a left on 55th Street, and headed west towards the Dan Ryan Expressway.

Justus, Patience, and Israel were chilling in the living

room when I arrived.

"Ay, what's the word?" I asked, plopping down on the sofa next to Justus.

"Elliott's a dead man." Israel replied.

"You gotta plan? Or are we just supposed to ride through the city looking for him, waiting to blast his ass on sight?" Justus joked.

"Who gives a fuck how it happens, as long as this nigga gets dealt with?" Asked Dex.

"I give a fuck." I spoke up.

"Yo, I give a fuck, too." Justus seconded. "The shit needs to be done seamlessly."

"It'll be neat and quick." Israel promised. "And most importantly, it'll be discreet."

"Ladies!" Dex called loudly.

I wasn't surprised when Bubbles and her best friends, Shaniece and Midori walked into the living room. Israel was a fan of using females whenever he planned a lick.

"What's up?" Bubbles asked Israel.

"We gotta job for you. And I need it handled right."

"Why do you always lean on me when you have a lick? Chan ain't no damn square. I'm sure she could handle it."

"This type of hustle ain't for her. Chan is wifey material. Stay in your lane, Shorty."

"And what am I good for, Israel?" Bubbles asked, hands

on hips and attitude written all over her pretty face.

He winked at her. "Pullin' licks."

"Fuck you." She said, then turned on her heel to leave the room.

"Come on, Bubbles. You know I'm just playin' with you."

She sighed heavily. "What is this 'job'?"

"I need you need to give me this motherfucka." He handed her his cell phone, so she could see the picture of Elliott. "Patience did all of the initial recon. He can tell you where dude hangs, who he kicks it with…all that. I just need you to get close to dude. Infiltrate his circle…if you can. Every move dude makes, I wanna know about it.

Bubbles studied the picture on the screen, then handed the phone to Midori. "How long do you want me to stay on him?"

"How much time do you need?" Dex responded.

Bubbles glanced over at Midori and Shaniece.

"Four weeks." Shaniece said, nonchalantly shrugging her slim shoulders and making the gum in her mouth pop. Shaniece was Dex's jump-off. She was a cinnamon colored beauty.

Midori shook her head. She was a beautiful half black, half Japanese chick. She was the only person on earth, besides Beyonce whose physical beauty could give Joya a run for her money. Midori had a thing for me, too. She made it real obvious that any time I wanted to hit, she would make the ass available to me. "Two weeks. Two and a half, tops." She disagreed.

"Two weeks." Bubbles seconded.

"Do it the usual way, Bub." Israel warned. "I don't need no brand new shit on this one. Find out how he moves. What kinda heat he carries. How many cats ride with him? Everything we need to know to bring him down quickly and quietly. Got it?"

"Nigga, please." Bubbles said. "You know I got it. That's why you keep bringin' the business to me…cuz I got it."

***

A few weeks later, I was in the office that I shared with Justus at *Exit Strategy, Inc.*

I was moving money between accounts online, when my phone rang. "Yeah." I answered.

"Hey Payne." Came the sweet sounding female's voice. "Did I catch you at a bad time?"

"You're straight. What's up?"

"This is Tashera." She clarified.

"Yeah, I know that." Females were always on something.

"Uhm, I wanted to be sure that you knew it was me, and

161

not Donyae or whatever new hoe has your nose open right now."

Chicks could always smell each other. How the hell did she know somebody new was on the scene? "Did you call to talk shit, or to actually say something?"

"I'm sayin', I haven't seen you. I'm over here horny and shit, and you been playin' me. I've been puttin' so much wear and tear on my 'boy toy', that it's about to blow a fuse."

I laughed out loud at that one. "You gotta slow down, Little Mama."

"You gotta hit me off, Big Daddy." She retorted.

"I don't know, Tashera, man." I was trying to wean myself off the tricks and concentrate solely on Joya. "I'm on something today."

"On somethin'…or on somebody, Payne?" She sighed. "Tell the truth, Nigga. I know you're fuckin' around with some new broad. It's whatever. But just because you found a new toy to play with, doesn't mean you should neglect the old ones. You might get bored with the new toy, and wanna come back to the old ones. They might be too busy for you…if ya know what I mean."

"Ay, if any old toys wanna find new owners, they should do what they do." I stated flatly. She should've known better than to try to flex with me.

"I'm not sayin' that."

"What are you saying?"

"I'm sayin'…I give the best head-bangers in all the Midwest. Make sure that when you trade me in, you're tradin' up and not playin' ya'self."

She wasn't lying about her head game. She gave the best head-banger I had ever gotten. But even that didn't make her irreplaceable.

"So, you comin' through tonight?" She continued.

"Doubtful, but we'll see."

"Payne, you know…"

"Later." I cut on top of her, then ended the call.

Justus walked into the office as I ended the call. He sat down at his desk, and turned on his computer. "What's on your brain?" He asked, never taking his eyes off of the monitor.

"Not much." I lied.

"Why're you lying, Son?"

"What made you decide to wife Nia?" I knew I had probably asked him that before, but I didn't remember his answer.

I couldn't lie though, just looking at Nia gave me an idea about why my guy wifed her. She was beautiful. Her physical reminded me of Gabrielle Union. She was pretty, but still approachable. Her chocolaty complexion was smooth and creamy. She was slim, with long legs, a nice ass, and sizable breasts. Her attitude was all Lauren London. Nia was "no nonsense." She didn't take trash. Plus, she was a go-getter. She owned her own home and that lingerie store before she linked with Justus. Females from our neck of the woods didn't always have that type of drive.

He shrugged his shoulders. Justus was a small dude. Typical pretty-boy. Short, buffed, and light-skinned. Physically, he and Nia were polar opposites.

"She was different. She wasn't pressed to catch my attention." He chuckled at the memory. "And at first, that kinda fucked me up. I was like, 'does she know who the hell I am? I'm Justus Calhoun, dammit. I'm a good looking cat. I got that paper.' I couldn't understand why she was acting like she was doing me a favor by spending a little time with me."

I shook my head slightly. That sounded just like Joya.

"But the more time she let me spend with her, the more I realized that she was doing me a favor. I'm saying, Payne, I'm from the gutter. You know this. I never had a plan for my life. My main goal was, 'stay my ass outta prison.' Since I've been with Nia, it's like…she showed me a whole 'nother side to life. Ya heard?"

I nodded. I heard him.

"This about Joya?"

"Somewhat."

"You thinking about cutting your other shorties loose, and just doing her?" He was surprised.

I understood why. He had known me forever, so he knew that I had never been tied to one female in my entire life. I blamed it on seeing Vincent murk Isaac in that bedroom all of those years ago. I liked keeping chicks at a respectable distance. They were cool to sex and chop it up with occasionally, but commit to? That shit was suspect to me. Committing to a female could lead to love. I never wanted to love a broad. Love was what led Vincent to do what he did. Love was why he ended up in the slammer. Love was why he was laid flat in prison. I really didn't think commitment and love were for me, but Joya was making me reconsider my stance.

"It's the only way she's gonna let me hold that." I tried to explain.

He raised an eyebrow. "How bad do you wanna hold that?"

"You sound like her."

"I hear you talking, but on the real, I think there's more to it than that. I think this chick put something on your brain."

"I think she put some roots on me." I joked.

We both laughed.

"From what I can see, Joya seems like a good girl. She

might be the one to get you to change your wicked ways."

"I doubt that, Playboy. Plus, she ain't fucking me. As long as she ain't giving it up, I don't see how I can be serious about switching my style." I said honestly. "Where's the benefit?"

"I feel ya, Dog. Nia wasn't letting me hit at first, neither."

"How'd you deal with it?"

He cut his dark brown eyes at me, ran his hand over his freshly trimmed goatee and finally spoke. "I got it in on the side." He kept talking, before I could respond. "Getting ass was what I knew. I felt like if I wasn't getting it in, then I was missing out. So, I kept hitting my regular chicks."

That was exactly what I was leaning towards doing. I was leaning towards getting a shot from Tashera to tide me over until Joya hit me.

He turned in his black leather chair, so that we were facing each other head on. "Payne, real talk, if I had it to do over again, I wouldn't do it that way. I would wait on Nia. These other females out here can't touch her. They can't even see my girl." He semi-smiled at the thought of his woman. "When I look back on it, it fucks me up that I could've gotten caught. I jeopardized my baby, for some ass."

***

That was exactly what I was thinking while I was running up in Tashera later that night. That I was jeopardizing a possible future with Joya, for some ass. But Tashera felt good. I couldn't lie. She didn't have the best sex, but she was freaky and energetic. That was exactly what I needed at the moment.

She was on all fours, taking backshots like a stallion. "Payne." She grunted.

I pulled her hips back to me with force. My left hand was wrapped up in her weave, pulling steadily, because I knew she was crazy sensitive on her scalp. My right hand was placed firmly on her side, controlling the tempo. Both of our bodies were glistening with sweat, and she was groaning loudly. I stroked her out for about twenty more minutes. She pressed her body into mine roughly, and I knew she was doing her thing. When she was satisfied, she fell off to the side. I laid next to her, on my back. I was mentally tripping that I couldn't get off. I knew for a fact that I was backed up as hell.

"What's the matter?" She asked, when she finally caught her breath.

"Nothing." I lied. "I got a lot on my mind."

She sat up on her elbow, looked me in the eyes, and spoke to me in a baby voice. "You didn't get yours? That ain't right. Let Tashera take care of you."

It was like magic watching Lil Nasir disappear between her luscious lips. She did her thing for a good long while. Still, I didn't get my rocks off.

A few hours later, I woke up to Tashera hitting me off with a "second try" head-banger. She gave me everything she had. And after about fifteen minutes of her intense spitting; sucking; squeezing; licking; and massaging, I gave her everything I had. It felt mad good, too. Relaxation washed over my tired body. Then, Tashera killed the buzz.

"Payne, I wanna see you more often, Daddy."

"Don't start that bullshit, Man."

"Why is how I feel, bullshit? I wanna spend more time with you. I don't see why that's a problem."

My need to respond was cut off by the ringing of my cell phone. I was glad as hell for the distraction. Dex's number was displayed across the screen. I knew what it was before I even answered. "What's up?"

I was greeted by the sound of Tupac's *Me and My Girlfriend*. "Where you at, Cous?" Dex asked over the volume of the music.

"81st Street."

"Ay, the movie just let out."

Code talk. The hit had happened.

"Why y'all ain't hit me up?" I wanted to know.

"You already saw this flick. Yo, come through the spot."

"Where?"

"The Golden Gate Bridge." That was how Dex referred to the apartment he kept on 62nd and Francisco.

"One." I said, and ended the call.

Tashera sucked her teeth loudly. "Don't tell me…you gotta go."

"You know it." I reached for my drawers. I pulled them on quickly, and followed that up by pulling on my jeans.

"I'm sick of this shit, Payne. I'm sick of you stoppin' by my house, gettin' your shot, then runnin' out the door. How do you expect me to feel?"

"Man, you can miss me all day with that shit. Don't start acting like you ain't know what it was."

"I'm just sayin'. How would you feel…"

That was when I started walking out of her bedroom. I wasn't trying to hear that. I had more important matters on my mind.

***

They were partying at Dex's. Loud music, the smell of weed and the sound of clinking beer bottles greeted me at the door. I gave dap to my guys and looked around the spot for Bubbles. I wanted to get the details on how the lick went down from her. I finally found her in the back bedroom by herself. She was sitting cross-legged on the queen sized bed. She was staring at the television screen, but nothing looked like it was really registering with her.

"What's good, Bubble-licious?" I joked.

She semi-smiled at me. "Hey Payne."

"What's wrong, Ma? You straight? Everything go okay with the lick?" I wasn't used to seeing Bubbles look depressed.

"Payne, you ever been in love with somebody that didn't love you back?"

I sat next to her on the bed. "You talking about Dex?"

She cut her eyes at me. "Hell naw, I ain't talkin' about Dex. I don't want Dex. I was using him."

"Using him? For what?"

"You ever been in love with somebody that didn't love you back?" She repeated. "You ever loved somebody that would fuck you over and leave you for dead?"

"Nah, Little Mama. I've never been in that situation."

Tears started to form in her eyes. "It hurts so bad, Payne. It really hurts." She cried.

Bubbles wasn't a crybaby, so the tears caught me off guard. The Bubbles I knew was a down ass chick, who could pull off a lick better than most cats. She used to move dope for us from state to state and never blinked an eye. I had known her for over five years, and never once had I seen her cry. I pulled her into my arms, held her close, and whispered in her ear. "Ay, any dude that can't appreciate what you bring to the table doesn't deserve you."

Israel walked into the room, took in the scene of me holding Bubbles and raised his eyebrow quizzically. "What's up?"

"She's upset." I responded.

The words were barely out of my mouth before Bubbles broke the embrace, wiped her tear-stained face, and stood up from the bed. "I'm outta here. Bye Payne."

Izz and I watched her leave the room.

He shook his head. "That broad is crazy."

"Nah, she's goin' through somethin'." I told him.

"Whatever." He said dismissively. "She needs to leave that shit at the door."

"What happened tonight?"

He grinned at me. "It was lovely, Son. Elliott's dumb ass let Midori seduce him. He was fuckin' gone over her. So, he didn't think nothin' of it when she hooked his partner up with Shaniece. It was like taking candy from a baby." He gloated. "A few dates, and Midori and Shaniece were in. They knew everything they needed to know. Bubbles got the info to me and Dex about where it was going down, and we crept up on the scene. We caught them niggas with their dicks out…literally. Midori and Shaniece were giving 'em hand jobs. I came up so smooth and easy, that dude ain't even realize I was on him until Midori took her hands off his dick. He looked up. I know he was about to ask her why she stopped. And *pap*. *Pap*. I had him. Two to the dome. Ain't no comin' back from that." He paused. "Dex was all sloppy with his. Damn near let the kid get the drop on him. Shaniece had to pull out. She shot dude in the shoulder, then slow ass Dex gave dude about five blasts to the chest. I never seen nobody who was always so ready to shoot somebody, be so slow on the draw."

I agreed. Dex was not the cat you wanted with you in a situation where gun play was fast and furious.

"Is Shaniece straight?" I asked.

"You know Shaniece is heartless as hell. She ain't care. She probably woulda put one in dude's dome if she had to. She only shot the shoulder to keep dude from gettin' his burner out and killin' Dex's dumb ass."

Chapter Seven
Take a Bow

Joya

The Tuesday before *Freestyle Friday*, I went to *Platinum Plus Hair and Nail Salon* to get my nails done. After Celeste finished my nails, I made my way over to Bubbles' styling station to say hello. She didn't have a client, so I made myself comfortable in her styling chair, while she was getting something from the storage room.

"Hey Bubbles." I said when she returned.

She grinned at me. "Hey, Joy. What's up? We didn't have an appointment, did we?" She grabbed her book to figure out if she had forgotten about me.

"Nah, not at all. Celeste just did my nails." I held up my hands and let her see my freshly manicured fingers. "I'll be in to see you on Friday morning."

"Since you're sittin' in my chair, let me bump your ends before you go."

"Okay." I agreed.

She picked up a few strands of my hair and looked at them critically. "When is the last time I clipped your ends, Joya? These things look really bad."

"I know." I admitted.

"Hey Keena." A female called Bubbles by her government name as she approached the styling station. "What's the deal?"

"That's my next client. Let me give her to the shampoo girl, and I'll take care of those ends. Sit in Jainelle's chair." She told me, as she pointed to the station next to hers. "She won't be in until 3:00 today."

I moved to the station next to Bubbles' and took a seat in the styling chair.

Bubbles greeted the client. "Hey Tashera. Have a seat." The short girl sat down, and Bubbles wrapped a mauve colored smock around her neck. "What's goin' on, Girly?"

"Nothin'." The girl sighed. "You know I'm pissed with your boy, Payne."

My ears perked right up.

Bubbles cut her eyes at me, and quickly looked away. "I know how that goes. How's work?"

"It's cool." The client said, then went back to her favorite subject. Payne. "I'm gettin' sick of his ass. Always wanna be comin' to my house, gettin' his shot, then runnin' out on a bitch. Nigga lay in the coochie for hours, but as soon as he bust, he can't get his shoes on fast enough."

"Girl, you know how these cats are." Bubbles mumbled.

"I know, Keena. But I think some new hoe got his nose

open. This last time he came over, I had barely swallowed the nut before somebody called him, and he had to blow. I know it's a new bitch on the scene. I know it is."

She continued talking, but I zoned out. I was too busy texting Nasir. *Hey, where are you?* I sent.

The office. He replied.

I'm next door at the salon. I left my wallet at home. Can you spot me some nail money?

I got you.

Can you bring it over here?

Gimme five. He wrote back.

Yeah, I'll give you five minutes, Bastard! I thought to myself. In my mind, I could hear R. Kelly's whiny voice singing, "Same girl. Same girl."

About ten minutes later, Nasir walked into *Platinum Plus*. The receptionist directed him to Bubbles' station.

"Hey." I said grinning at him like everything was cool.

He hugged me. I let him.

"How'd you leave your wallet at the crib, Ma?"

"I don't know." I told him.

The entire time I was talking to him, I could see Bubbles trying to give him the 'high-sign' with her eyes that it was a set-up. He didn't catch her signal, though. So, when the shampoo girl brought Tashera back over to the station, he was caught with his drawers down.

"Payne?" Tashera asked in surprise.

He ignored her.

"You know him?" I asked.

"Hell yeah, I know him." She told me.

"You know, when she kept talkin' about a cat named Payne who was coming through her spot to bang her out, I hoped it wasn't you." I shook my head. "I hoped it wasn't you. But deep down inside, I knew it was."

"Joya."

"I'll see you Friday, Bubbles." I turned to Tashera. "I guess he can spend more time with you, now."

"That's the new bitch?" She asked Nasir.

I walked away from the three of them.

Nasir followed me. "Joy! Joy!"

I kept walking, until I got to my car. Finally, I turned around and faced him. "What Nasir? What? What can you possibly have to say, when you know what I've been through? You know how Monte played me. Then, you turn around and do the same thing?"

"I wasn't trying to do you dirty…"

I cut him off. "Seriously?"

"Joy."

"Bye Nasir." I said, then climbed into my wheels.

Chapter Eight
If I

Payne

"I fucked up." I said, downing my sixth shot of Courvoisier.

I was riding the bar at *Classified*, later that night. Justus was on the barstool next to mine.

"This whole thing is so ironic." He gloated, taking a swallow of his Corona. "Seeing as how I *just* told you not to get it in on the side. I *just* gave you the benefit of my experience. You pissed on it…now look at you. Sick, and trying to get drunk enough to forget."

"Damn! How could I forget that her and Tashera go to the same hair salon? I met Tashera coming outta *Platinum Plus*. And Bubbles is Chan's sister. Why wouldn't Joya go to her to get her hair done?"

"Try buying her something." Justus suggested.

"I don't know, Man. I can't see that working. She doesn't take gifts from men."

"What're your other options?"

"You tell me."

"I don't know. If you can't hit her off with a little gift,

some diamond earrings or something, then my hands are tied."

"What would you do if it was Nia?" I asked.

"First of all, I wouldn't get it in on Nia…especially not with a rat like Tashera. But if I messed up with Nia? I would beg. On my knees. Let a couple of tears fall, if I had to. But Nia's my baby. I can't breathe without that girl. How far are you willing to go for Joya?"

"Not that far." I assured him. There was no way in hell that I was getting on my knees for no chick. I didn't care who she was. I waved Joe over, and ordered another shot.

"Last one, Youngster." He told me.

"Come on, Old Man. Don't be like that."

He looked at Justus. "What the hell is wrong with Youngster 1, Youngster 2?"

"Man, his girl caught him up." Justus tricked.

Joe raised an eyebrow. "You done messed up with the beauty this quick? I knew you weren't ready for her."

"Whatchu mean by that?" I questioned. "Ain't a broad alive that I ain't ready for."

"That's your main problem, *Youngster*." Joe said, pointing a slim finger at me. "You don't treat Courvoisier like Night Train. You don't treat Cristal like Boone's Farm. So, why would you think you can treat a lady like a broad? It's a wonder that you young cats ever get any ass. Y'all don't know shit about women."

Unc joined us at the bar. When he took in the visual of me downing shots, he twisted his face. He placed his hand on my shoulder. "What's going on, Nephew?"

"Nothing." I said, slamming the shot glass down on the bar.

"What's good, Unc?" Justus asked, extending his hand.

Unc shook it. "What's wrong with your partner in crime, Nephew?"

"Female drama." Justus replied.

"Grab your drinks, let's talk in my office." He suggested.

Justus picked up his beer, and got off the barstool.

"Hit me up." I told Joe.

He took my shot glass off the bar, but didn't replace it. "Didn't I tell you that was your last one?"

"Come on, Man." I pleaded.

"Get your ass up off that bar stool, and go find out what your Uncle has to say. I'm not giving you nothing else to drink."

Anger washed over me at that thought that Joe would deny my request. "Fuck you. I'm a grown ass man…"

"Youngster, I will beat your grown ass." Joe said, reaching back to where I knew he kept a Louisville Slugger.

"Nephew," Unc admonished in a calm voice, "I know you aren't getting outta pocket with Joe."

"Ay, I'm sayin'…"

He cut me off. "It's clear that this situation with your girl has you twisted, and you've had too much to drink. Now, apologize to Joe. He's old enough to be your grandfather. He doesn't have to take no shit from you. If he loves you enough to pull your coattail, be grateful. Everybody won't do that. Act like the grown ass man you claim to be, and accept the fact that you were wrong."

Everybody waited for me to stop acting like an ass.

"Sorry Joe. My bad. I got a lot on my mind." I reached cross the bar to give him dap.

Joe, being the mean bastard that he was at times, let my hand hang out there for a few seconds before he took it and shook it. "Better not happen again, Youngster."

"It won't." I said

"It won't." Unc assured him.

Justus and I followed Unc into his office. He gestured for us to sit down in the chairs facing his desk, while he sat down behind it.

"This is about the young lady you brought by here the other day, huh?" Unc asked.

Justus cut his eyes at me, because he didn't know anything about me bringing Joya to the lounge.

"Yeah." I admitted.

"I knew you were gonna have problems with that one."

He shook his head.

"Why do you say that?"

"Because your nature is in direct conflict with hers. She's commitment oriented. And you're a whorish little dude, Nephew."

"Whorish?" I repeated.

Justus tried to choke back his laughter.

"You gotta lot of Khalil in you, Young Blood. And Khalil's major problem was that he loved sex. He loved it. It was one of his few weaknesses. He lost his mind over new ass. Always wanted to be falling between the next pretty young thing's thighs. I watch you and I can see that same desire for women. I know that getting women has never been a problem for you, Nephew. You got Khalil's over-confident, pretty-boy swagger and Dorothy Jane's killer green eyes."

I smiled a little bit.

Unc caught the move. I wasn't surprised. Not too much got passed him. "Your daddy's swagger, and his big head. That's the main reason Khalil and Nicki couldn't stay together. Khalil felt like he was doing females a disservice if he denied them the pleasure of being with him. He never took the time to realize what he had in Nicki, until it was too late. By the time he recognized what he had, she had linked up with that dickhead, Vincent. Stop being so much like your father, Nephew. I know some of it is genetics, but some of it is choice. Be smarter than him. Better than him. That's what he wanted for you. For you to do better than he did."

I nodded in agreement.

"You know what Joe used to tell us? He used to say, be careful who you give your time to, cuz that's the one thing you can't get back once it's gone. You can get more money. You can get more women. You can get more houses, cars, jewelry…whatever. But you can never get more time. So, be careful about which of these chickenheads you choose to spend your time with."

"Joe got something to say on every subject." I said.

"Joe has experience in every subject." Unc replied. "And he called it on you and your young lady. He told me that you weren't ready for a woman like her."

I didn't respond.

"What happened?"

"She ran into this jump-off chick I hit from time to time."

"You couldn't talk yourself out of it?"

"Nah, I walked into an ambush. And what's really fucked up is this last cat she was with…he dogged her, beat her up, cheated on her, everything. She got like, zero tolerance for bullshit. And first time at bat, here I come with my bullshit."

"You know any jewelers? Cuz if you don't, I can recommend one."

"Same thing I said." Justus commented, finishing his beer.

"I can't come like that. She doesn't take gifts from men. Says she prefers to buy her own stuff."

Unc placed his hands together and created a steeple with the tips of his fingers. "You cool with any of her girlfriends? Cool enough where the girlfriend would be willing to put something in your ear?"

"Maybe." I said. My thoughts went to Chantelle.

"Talk to her girl. Ask her what's up. She'll know exactly what you need to do to get back in."

"Damn, Unc!" Justus said. "Where were you when I was sweating these hoes in the streets? I could've used this knowledge."

"Justus, you're cut from a different cloth than Nasir. You always had it in you to be a stand-up cat. Your father was a good dude. James was a hardworking, honest man. He loved your mother, and took better care of her than anybody in the neighborhood took of their wives. Every broad on the block envied your mother. And every man on the block respected your pops. We all mourned with Elizabeth when your pops was killed. The game lost one of its best that day."

"What're you saying, Unc? You saying that J is a good dude, and I'm a bastard?"

He chuckled. "I'm saying that Justus is always gonna

recognize gold when it glitters, and you're too distracted by rhinestones and cubic zirconium. Keep your head in the game, Nephew. And not the little one, Man." He stood up, signaling that the conversation was over.

Justus gave him dap, and a one-armed hug. "All right, Unc."

"All right, Nephew."

I followed suit, and gave him dap, and a one-armed hug. "Thanks Unc. Good looking."

"Call your girl's friend. Find out the deal, and make it happen…if you're serious." His eyes searched mine.

"I'm serious." I promised.

"I'm straight up, Nephew. If you're not serious, then you need to leave her alone. This girl is different. She has a light in her eyes. She's gonna do big things. The first time I saw her, I saw that same glint in her eyes that I used to see in Angel's. As much as I love Lynne, I would walk away from her in a heartbeat for one more week with Angel. Recognize gold, Nephew."

***

Chantelle, Nia and Bubbles caught me up at the front door the next day when I stepped into Izz's house.

"I heard the whole story." Chantelle told me. Then she

took my arm and pulled me into the living room. "I'mma be honest with you, Payne. You messed up bad."

I nodded, because I figured that was the case.

"Joy took so much garbage off of Monte, that she's not about to let this incident ride."

I nodded, again.

"Damn, Payne." Bubble said. "I was tryin' to give you the 'high-sign' that it was a set-up. I kept tryin' to catch your eye, so I could let you know the deal."

I winked at her. "Good looking. I appreciate that."

"I just hate to see you mess up with Joya over Tashera. Especially when I know you don't want Tashera."

"Have you called her?" Nia asked me.

"Nah." I remembered Unc's words. "Whatchu think Chan? You think I should call her?"

She considered it. "She's probably not gonna answer, but yeah, you need to call her."

"Repeatedly." Nia chimed.

"And I'll strike your name up whenever I can. Keep you on her mind." Chantelle assured me. "I'll let her know that you're a good cat, who made a bad decision."

"Yeah." Bubbles agreed.

Nia swatted me in the back of the head. "But in the meantime…keep it in your pants, Payne. Leave these hoes alone."

Chapter Nine
Can't Leave 'em Alone

Joya

The night of *Freestyle Friday*, Chantelle, Bubbles and Nia came to my house to help me get ready.

"I brought you a few things from my closet to try on, because I know you aren't gonna have nothin'." Chantelle told me, as they came through the door.

Chantelle was a size seven, and I was clearly an eleven. I wondered how she thought I was supposed to fit in anything from her closet.

"Uh, don't you think something from your closet might be too small for me?" I questioned.

"That's the point." She explained to me. "You're gonna be singin' at a club. You need to wear somethin' short and tight."

"You shoulda brought that outfit you wore to '*Blaze the Mic*', Chan." Bubbles told her sister. "That woulda been perfect."

"Those little suede shorts that had most of her booty hanging out?" I inquired, shaking my head. "I don't think so!"

"Holla!" Chantelle said happily, as she pulled the outfit out of the bag she had with her.

"That's what's up!" Bubbles co-signed. "That's what you should wear, Joy!"

"What is it?" Nia asked, taking it from Chantelle's hand.

"It's a pair of panties that are masquerading as shorts, and a bra that's masquerading as a bustier." I responded.

"It's not panties." Chantelle disagreed. "It's shorts."

Nia held it up. "It does look like panties." She said. "And I own a lingerie store, so you know I know what panties look like."

"Thank you." I sighed. "Chan, I'm not wearing that outfit. Let me see what else you brought."

She showed me the rest of the pieces that were in the bag. Everything she brought with her was overly hoochie. I was willing to go a little hoochie, but Chan acted like she was trying to get me on the stripper pole.

"Okay." I said, once I had seen everything she brought with her. "We're gonna have to find something outta my closet."

We went through my clothes, and finally decided on a pair of black shorts, a black crocheted halter top (that I usually wore as a sweater, over another shirt), black fishnets, and black Michael Kors stilettos.

***

I knew I made the right decision on the outfit when Trey saw me at *Club Potion*.

"Damn!" He said staring at me with no shame. "You trying to make sure I win this dough, huh? Ay, try not to distract the judges from my rhyming."

"Leave her alone." Chantelle told him. "Don't make her self-conscious. You don't know how Joya is."

"You gotta minute before we hit the stage." Trey told me. "We're number six. The last ones to perform."

For the first time that night, I started to get nervous. A huge pit started to form in the center of my stomach.

Chantelle looked over at me and noticed the expression on my face. "Calm down, Joy." She said gently rubbing my back. "You got this."

"You definitely got this." Bubbles agreed. "I don't know anybody with a voice that can touch yours. You got that flow like them old school chicks. Like from when singers could actually sing."

I was still freaking out, I just wasn't letting them know it. On the outside, I probably looked like I was calming down, but on the inside I was losing it. It wasn't that I was worried about my voice. I knew I could blow the hook. I had been practicing for two weeks. I just wondered if I could concentrate on blowing the hook, when I was so damn uncomfortable. I did not like the outfit I was wearing. I felt like everything I owned was on display.

Chantelle's cell phone went off. She took it from her purse and checked the screen. "That's Izz textin' me. They just got here."

"Do you need Payne?" Nia asked with concern. "You want me to get him?"

"Ain't nobody thinking about Payne." I told her with a sigh. For the last two days, every other word out of Chantelle's mouth had been something about Payne. Now, Nia was starting with the same garbage.

I barely got the words out, before Nasir was approaching us. "Ma, you straight? You look nervous." He put his hand on my shoulder.

My skin grew warm under his touch. I moved away from him and gave him a fake smile. "I'm cool." I lied.

"Good. Good." He looked me up and down, taking in my outfit. "This is what you're wearing?"

I hoped he hated it. I hoped it bothered him to see so much of my body on display like that. "Yep."

He nodded slowly. "I like it. You look sexy as hell. The crowd is gonna go bananas over you."

"Uhm." I said, disinterested. I wanted him to leave me alone and stop talking to me.

He chuckled and shook his head. "Okay, Beautiful. Do your thing." He finally walked away.

"Joy, why're you treatin' Payne like that?" Chantelle asked once he was out of earshot.

I looked at her like she was crazy. "How would you be treating him, if you were me?" I asked. "Oh yeah, I forgot how you act when you catch your man cheating. You beat the hell outta the chick and let Izz smack *you* around."

She took a deep breath. "I almost said somethin' about whose been gettin' smacked around. Cuz the way I remember it, I'm not the only one who took a few ass whippings. But it's your night. So, I'mma let you ride on this one." She started to walk away.

"Chan!" I called, putting my ego to the side.

She turned around.

"I'm sorry." I apologized.

"I'm sorry, too." She walked back over to the group.

"Good, y'all made up." Nia said, putting an arm around each of us. "Y'all don't need to be fighting."

"Right." I agreed. "Especially not over Nasir. I just want you to stop shoving him down my throat."

"And I want you to stop actin' like he's Monte. He's not, Joy."

"Then, he should stop doing the stuff that Monte did." I held up my hand before she could speak again. "Please

Chan, leave it alone. I need to concentrate on this performance. Not Nasir."

"You're right." She said. "Where's that special 'throat tea' that you brought to lubricate your vocal cords?"

"My cup's right there." I pointed at my pink travel cup.

"Well, get it and start sipping."

I smirked at her.

She hugged me. "You got this, Girl. Easiest $500.00 you ever made."

***

By watching the rest of the competitors from backstage, it was easy to see that there were more heavy-hitters in this contest, than there had been in the *'Blaze the Mic'* contest. KJ Jamison was back. He was number three. He did his thing and once again ripped the stage with his skills, his confidence and his showmanship. He did the same song that he had done at *Kacey's*, but it didn't even matter, because he killed it.

Trey came up to me when the fifth performer was in the middle of his set. "You ready to do this? You ready to make this money?"

I tugged at my short-shorts, and adjusted the see-through top I was wearing. "Yeah, I'm ready."

"Do it like we practiced it. I'mma go out first, and I'mma hype the crowd. As soon as you hear that beat drop, you need to rush the stage and you need to be on fire."

I nodded. "I got you."

The fifth performer left the stage, and the M.C. introduced Trey. Like he promised he would, Trey ran out on the stage and started hyping the crowd. Before I knew it, the first beat of Nasir's track dropped. I had to hustle from behind the curtain and onto the stage.

"*When you touch me, daddy, you know one thing's for sure.*

When you touch me baby, I'mma want some more.

When your eyes meet mine, I get all sexy, soft.

I lose my mind, and all my clothes come off."

I repeated the hook twice, then Trey took over spitting lyrics like he was on a mission. While he rhymed, I moved around the stage. I hummed and moaned adlibs over his verses. Eventually, I forgot about the fact that I was half-dressed in front of a room filled with men. I got so caught up in the excitement and vibe of the moment that when the track ended, I was kinda disappointed.

At the table, Rook was all on Trey's jock.

"Y'all know y'all got this one." Rook told him.

Trey was humble. "I don't know, Man. KJ does his thing. You never know."

"His ass ain't all that." Rook disagreed. "Niggas be actin' like dude is untouchable. He ain't untouchable."

"Well, you can't seem to touch him." Bubbles reminded him.

Everybody at the table laughed, except for Rook and Israel.

"Fuck you." Rook said.

"Fuck you right back, you nasty Bastard." Fire and anger blazed in Bubbles' eyes.

"Let's get some drinks." Nia suggested to ease the tension.

"Yeah," Justus agreed, "get some bottles popping. Trey and Joy just killed the spot, with my dude's track. I got the first round. Ay Payne, you killed 'em with that track."

"That track *was* hot as hell." Bubbles agreed.

"That track was more than hot." Justus said. "That track was bananas! Can't nobody do it on the boards like my guy."

"No doubt." Patience agreed, giving Nasir dap.

"Rook, why don't get your tracks from Payne?" Chantelle asked.

The entire table went silent.

Chantelle was confused. "What?"

Nia waved a passing waitress over. "What are we drinking?" She asked Justus, breaking the uncomfortable silence that had settled over the group.

"Hpnotiq for the table." Justus told the waitress.

"Ay, while you're back there," Dex told the waitress, "grab a bottle of Patron for table. Second round on me."

The Hpnotiq was a distant memory, and the Patron was half gone when the M.C. of the contest took the stage to announce who would walk away $2000.00 richer.

Rook called it, Trey took first place. We celebrated at the club for a while longer.

"I gotta go to the bathroom." I told Chantelle, as we prepared to leave the club.

"Me too."

The two of us went to the ladies room. On our way back to the table, we were accosted by KJ Jamison, and a guy that I didn't recognize.

KJ took in every inch of my body before speaking. "What's good?"

"Hey." Chantelle responded.

I wished that I had on more clothes. Since I didn't, I had to get my gangsta up and act like I felt comfortable in the tiny shorts and knitted top. "What's up?"

"Your voice, Shorty Songbird." The guy that I didn't recognize told me.

"Yeah." KJ Jamison agreed. "You know you won it for dude. Otherwise, that dough would've been in my pocket."

"Thanks." I said humbly. "But Trey won it for us. I just added a little glamour to his gangsta."

The stranger let his eyes move slowly over my frame. "Ma, you added a whole lot more than a *little* glamour."

"What's good, Northern?" Nasir asked, appearing out of nowhere. "I know you're not trying to get at my girl…right in front of my face."

His girl? I thought to myself indignantly, but I kept my mouth shut.

"Aw Payne, don't trip. I ain't even know this was you."

Nasir draped his arm across my shoulder. I only let him do that, so he wouldn't be embarrassed in front of KJ Jamison and his friend. "Now you know. Joya, this is Northern McKinley. He's a producer. Northern, this is Joya. She's the hottest thing to come off the south side since Kanye and Common."

"She's definitely better looking than both of them cats." Northern complemented.

Nasir shrugged his shoulders. "Get fucked up if you want to, Northern."

"You know I'm just messing with you, Man." Northern insisted.

"Whatever." Nasir replied.

"She signed to you exclusively?"

Nasir hit him with the screw face. "You really do wanna

get fucked up, don't you?"

"Come on, Dude. This is business. No disrespect. We all want the best. I just wanna know if she's available."

"Yeah, cuz I would love to have your vocals on my next track. You could make it hot as hell." KJ said to me.

"Sorry." I told him. "Right now, I'm unavailable."

"Well, if you ever become available..."

"She won't." Nasir cut him off.

"But if you do," KJ said to me, "get at a brother."

"Bye." I said waving at them. Then I turned around and walked away.

Nasir walked right beside me. "Did you bring some extra clothes? I think it's time for you to go change. You're gonna fuck around and make me murder somebody."

"Uh," I got ready to say something really flip.

Chantelle grabbed my arm.

I looked over at her.

"Joya, shut up." She mouthed.

I shut up.

**

Even though I rode to *Club Potion* in Chantelle's Honda CRV with her, Bubbles and Nia, I ended up riding home with Nasir. Only he wasn't driving towards my building, he was driving towards his.

"Where are you taking me?" I asked. My eyes were half-closed and I was barely awake. I was so sleepy, that all I wanted to do was fall into bed and get some rest.

"We need to talk. You gotta problem with that?"

"Not tonight, Nasir. I'm too tired to do this. I've flown every day this week, except Tuesday and today. I can't even keep my eyes open."

"You're straight. I gotta bed and pillows at my spot. You can take a nap there. When you wake up, we need to talk."

Chapter Ten
Say Yes

Payne

"Ay, do you need to lay down?" I asked Joya, as we stepped into my apartment.

"Nah. Since you feel like we need to talk, let's have this talk."

I threw my house and truck keys on the glass top of my dining room table and kept walking. "Do you need something to drink? You hungry?"

"No, I just wanna have this talk. I wanna hear what you have to say." She pranced over to the sofa. I tried not to let her catch me watching her ass as she went.

I grabbed myself a bottle of water from the refrigerator, then joined her on the couch. "Ay Beautiful, I know I fucked up..."

She interrupted me. "Well, I'm glad you know it."

"Yeah, I know it. And like I told you that day, I wasn't trying to do you dirty. I'm not dude from the NBA and this situation ain't the same."

"First of all, if you stop actin' like dude from the NBA, then I won't treat you like I treated dude from the NBA.

Second of all, how is this situation different from that one? You aren't beating my ass?"

Little Mama and that flip mouth. I had to chuckle. "Come on, Beautiful."

"You come on, Nasir. What's really real? You told me that you keep it one hundred. You told me you aren't into trickery. So, what's up? Are you trying to date me, or are you trying to add me to the list of jump-offs?"

"You know you ain't jump-off material."

"Stop kicking game and be real with me, *Payne*."

I didn't miss the fact that she called me by my last name. That was something she hadn't done since I had known her.

"I don't wanna hear the playboy bullshit you tell the hoes." She continued. "Let's talk straight up."

"I'm being straight up. Think about it, Joy. If I wanted you as a dip and you ain't sexed me in all this time, don't you think I woulda been left ya ass alone? You think I would give a jump-off two months to decide if she was with it?"

"Why couldn't you just wait on me? Why'd you hafta go sleeping with old girl?" She asked me.

"Real talk? I ain't used to waiting for ass."

"Ppssshhht." She acted like I was popping garbage.

"That's my word. Usually the chicks that wanna save it, they get left where they're standing."

"So, why am I here? Why didn't you leave me where I

was standing?"

"I really don't know. There's something about you, Ma."
I shrugged my shoulders.

"Yeah, well there must be something about you, too.
Because under normal circumstances, I'm not into second
and third and fourth chances. Especially not after everything
I went through with dude."

"I got you." I assured her.

"I'm being so serious with you, Nasir. I've already had
my heart ripped out and torn to shreds. I'm not going
through that, again. I'm not gonna let no other dude dog me
out."

"I'm not trying to dog you out."

"Then you need to show me that. You need to let the bird
chick from the salon, the tomboy chick from the NBA Finals
party and the Barbie Doll chick from *Kacey's* know that it's
a wrap."

"Not a problem." I agreed easily.

She looked over at me. "I'm serious, Nasir."

"I know, Joya."

"Don't pull this crap, again."

"Ma, I said I got you."

We sat on my sofa in silence, watching the television. We
must've both been sleepy, because the next thing I knew, I
was waking up. I looked into Joya's angelic face, as she

slept in my arms. I had never held a chick in my life who felt so right to me. Joya made my heart-rate slow down. She took my mind off of everything but her. I didn't know if that was good or bad, but I liked it. I kissed her on the cheek. Then, I checked the clock on my cable box. 4:01am.

I shook her slightly. "Let's go get in the bed, Beautiful."

She opened her eyes slowly.

"Let's go get in the bed." I repeated.

"Okay." She stood up from the sofa and stretched.

When she made that move, the little see-through shirt she had on raised up, exposing a small slice of her stomach. Since I had a thing for women's stomachs, my gaze was glued there. My eyes had to be playing tricks on me, though. I thought I saw colors on her stomach. "Do that again." I instructed.

"What?"

"Lift your arms up."

"Why?" She asked, suspiciously.

"What's on your stomach?" I moved closer to her.

"Oh," she stated with realization, "you're talking about Pretty Kitty." She lifted her blouse, lowered the waistband of her shorts and revealed the tattoo of a fluffy white cat, with one paw raised in the air. It was sporting what looked like a diamond encrusted necklace as a collar, and a diamond encrusted tiara on its head. It was located between her belly button and her pubic hair.

I didn't say anything. I just stared. Little Mama kept shocking me. First the gun, now the tattoo.

"That's what I call my…you know…vagina." She confided in a whisper, like we weren't the only two people in my spot.

"So, you not only named your vagina, you got a tattoo for it, too?"

"Hey." She shrugged her shoulders, lifted her hands, and apparently felt no shame.

The tattoo and it's placement on her body was enticing as hell. "Damn, that's sexy." I pulled her to me. "You're making it hard as hell for me not to put my hands on you, Girl."

She broke the embrace, looked me in the eye and spoke with a straight face. "You're gonna need to work harder, Partner. Cuz won't be no hand putting, tonight. I barely forgive you, Nasir. You gotta know that you're not getting none." She walked away, and left me standing there watching her.

She's a lie. I thought to myself as I followed her into my bedroom.

"You got something for me to wear?" She asked, when I made it to the room.

"Get your jersey off the chair."

"Oh, it's my jersey, now?" She asked sarcastically.

"Go 'head on, Joya." I told her, as I started taking off my shirt.

"I need socks."

I directed her to the dresser drawer where I kept my socks, and stripped out of my jeans while she grabbed a pair.

"Be right back."

"Joy," I called stopping her, "you ain't gotta go outta the room to change."

"I know. But I'll be right back."

"Innocent ass." I mumbled to myself.

She came back into the bedroom a few minutes later in my Heat jersey and socks. Her long hair cascaded down around her shoulders. She looked innocent and erotic at the same time. My dick started to harden. She sat her clothes in my armchair, and climbed in the bed next to me.

"Can I see that tattoo, again?"

"Stop trying to get something started. I already told you that you aren't getting any." She chastised.

Her eyes were telling me that she wasn't bothered at all by my request. So, I pressed on. "Straight up. Let me see it."

She lifted the jersey, revealing her panties along the way. Purple bikinis with the words, 'platinum pussy' on them. I laughed out loud at that one.

"Man Girl, I ain't never met a female who thought so

highly of her…"

"Kitty cat." She cut me off, before I could spout the 'p' word.

"Yeah. You gotta lot of kitty cat-confidence. What you holding down there?" I teased.

She winked at me, then kicked Craig Mack. "Here comes the brand new flavor in ya ear. Time for new flavor in ya ear." She sang. "I'm kickin' new flavor in ya ear. Joya's the brand new flavor in ya ear."

"What you know about Craig Mack?" She caught me totally off guard with that one. I couldn't believe she spit "Flava in ya ear."

"Come on, Nasir. I know you do music, but I do music, too. I'm an undercover hip hop head. My secret is out." She joked. "Yeah, I love hip hop. Even the old school stuff. I love it."

"So, you're about to be the new flavor in my ear?"

"Maybe."

I kissed her lips. "Ay, let me see that tattoo." I slid down the bed. My face was level with her pelvis.

She slowly lifted my jersey over her hips and exposed the little white kitten.

"And you call this tattoo what?"

"Pretty Kitty."

"Why is that?" I asked, looking up at her.

She made eye contact with me. "One guess."

"I don't know which one I like better, the panties or the tat."

"Well, I hope the tat, since its permanent."

"Yeah, I think so." I started tongue-kissing her belly button. "Can I take your panties off?"

"Did you think you would just slip that in?" She asked, and I could tell she was trying not to moan.

I slowed my roll and made my way back up to the top of the bed.

"Nasir, for real...please don't ever hurt me. I mean it. I really don't wanna get hurt, again."

"The last thing I would ever wanna do is hurt you, Joy. I'm digging everything about you." I confided.

"Mutual." She responded, placing her manicured hand on my chest.

I lifted it to my mouth and kissed it. I let my hand glide across her cheek, through her hair and behind her head, then I pulled her face to mine. I pulled her bottom lip into my mouth and sucked hungrily, before I dipped my tongue inside. Her mouth was warm and sweet. She wrapped her arms around me, and pulled me closer. Testosterone started guiding my actions. I rolled on top of her and got between her legs. I kept the pressure from my tongue consistent in her mouth, while I pressed my pelvis into hers. I wanted her to feel what the nearness of her was doing to me. I held her face to mine with one hand, and rubbed rhythmically on her ass with the other hand. I grinded her like her panties and my drawers weren't preventing us from having actual physical contact.

She moaned in my mouth.

Damn. I thought to myself, as my dick stood up even straighter.

The softness and curviness of Joya's body was fucking my head up. Plus, she was moaning up a storm. I wanted to kiss every inch of her skin. My dick was struggling to get free.

I helped her take off the jersey, then tossed it on the floor. I let my eyes move over her beautiful frame. I couldn't believe I finally had Joya in my bed wearing nothing but her panties. My dick throbbed with anticipation. I captured her right breast in my mouth. It wasn't enough. I needed all of her.

"Beautiful," I whispered like I was cool and collected, when really I wanted to do outrageous things to her sexy ass body. "Can I take your panties off?"

"You got condoms, right?"

"Yeah." I promised, as I started moving her panties over her hips.

I couldn't believe the way she was knocking me off my square. I hadn't been so pressed to get inside a female since high school. But I wanted Joya. I was dying to bury myself deep inside her.

When her panties were finally off, I easily inserted one finger into her waterfall. She gave me the sexiest groan I had ever heard. I covered her mouth with mine again, and kissed her. Slow and tender.

"The condom, Nasir." She reminded me.

She was wiggling, and moving so much underneath me that I knew she was fiending for a shot of me just as badly as I was fiending to give it to her. I rolled the condom on, then moved over her body, tasting her skin along various points. When she couldn't take it anymore, when her moans got too strong for me to ignore, I slid inside. She wrapped her arms around me, lifted her hips and sighed softly.

She was so tight, that I knew it had been a minute since she last let somebody hit it. Her walls gripped me. I settled on an easy stroke. Let my dick hit every nook and cranny. I took the time to get to know her body. I listened for the sounds that escaped her mouth. Tried to pin point what she liked and what drove her crazy. She matched my rhythm after a while and gave me back every stroke with the same intensity that I was giving it to her. Then, she switched it up. She started to move her hips slow and sexy. When she did that, I had to catch myself to keep from getting buck with her. She arched her back and ran her fingernails along my arms. I grinded my middle against hers and kissed her lips.

"Open your eyes, Joy." I commanded.

She opened them.

I stared into her pretty face. I could see the passion and pleasure she was getting from what I was doing to her body. She was caught up. I could tell. Her eyes were like flames. Her body was blazing. The heat that was coming from her core was setting my body on fire. My skin was tingling. Every nerve in my body was active. I really wanted to snatch off my condom and dig her out raw-dog. I wanted to feel the heat skin to skin, but I couldn't. We weren't there yet. Instead, I increased the tempo of the strokes. Soft sounds came out of her mouth, and she picked up the speed of her counter-strokes.

"Oooh!" She said in the middle of her thunderstorm.

Another one bites the dust. I thought to myself. Then I devoured her mouth with hot kisses.

A few minutes later, I started getting caught up, too. Everything around me, the bed, the bedroom, the apartment, the world ceased to exist. It was me and Joya.

I had my fingers in her hair, pulling. My pace quickened, deepened. I felt myself on the verge of exploding. But I wanted her to go first. I held back. Then, she started whining and moaning. I knew she was right there. I kept putting in work a few minutes longer. I pushed deep inside of her and held her hostage under the weight of my body while I experienced my eruption.

When I was back in control of myself, I kissed her lips. "Ay, what was that thing you were doin' with your hips?" I had to know. It felt too good.

"The figure eight?"

"The figure eight?" I repeated.

"Yeah. I learned it in this belly dancing class I took."

"The figure eight, huh?"

She rolled her eyes. "I see you like that."

I didn't respond. I was storing that information in my mental rolodex.

She curled into a ball, right next to me. I laid there thinking about how good she felt, and about how I was feeling things for her that I didn't know how to define. I looked down at her, snuggled up under my right arm. She was sound asleep.

Contentment washed over me. Little Mama was the whole package. She was beautiful, smart, classy, motivated, hard-working, and she could sex. For the first time in my life, I felt like I could actually settle down with a female. The one thing I knew without a doubt, was that I damn sure wasn't about to let the next cat get his hands on her.

***

If I thought that Joya had knocked me off my square before, I never should've dipped inside. Linking up with that girl sexually had my mind straight gone. The things I was feeling and thinking had me wondering if I was in love. I was tripping on levels that I never thought I would. Justus noticed how much I was flipping the next time we handled business.

We were in the office and I was cutting earnest money checks from the business account for houses we were in the process of buying. I handed the first check to Justus and was about to write the next one, when he spoke.

"Son, what are you doing?" He sounded alarmed.

I hit him with the screw face, and wondered why he was raising his voice at me. "Whatchu mean?"

"Who did you write this check out to, Payne?"

"Angela David and Associates Realty."

He tossed the check on the edge of my desk. "Then why is it made payable to Joya Bingham?"

I looked down at the check and sure enough Joya's name was on the first line. What the hell was I doing? That was a pussy-whipped move. "Damn." I couldn't help laughing at myself, even though Justus was straight mean-mugging me.

"Where's your head, Payne?"

"My bad. I don't know." I lied. In actuality, I was thinking about Joya, and the sex she had given me the night before. It was like she was trying to make up for lost time, when she wasn't getting dick. We were getting it in like rabbits. I wasn't complaining. I loved getting it in with her. She was just killing my gangster. I couldn't even concentrate on the business at hand for thinking about licking her in some unseen place.

"I think that bitch got your mind blown." He spat.

"Dude, watch your mouth." I warned.

In all the time that Justus and I had been friends, we had never come to blows. We had never even had words, because we usually respected each other's flow so tough, that it was never an issue. But he was tripping.

He shot daggers at me with his eyes.

I took a deep breath, before things went too far to the left. "J, you my man, twenty-grand. I don't wanna fight with you. I know I messed up with the check. I'll rewrite it. But what's your real problem? Cuz I know it ain't the check and I know for sure that it ain't Joya."

His facial muscles finally relaxed. "Me and Nia had it out."

"You had it out with your oxygen? Thought you said you couldn't breathe without your girl." I joked.

He looked at me like I was crazy. "Dude, I know you ain't joking nobody about being gone off a female. You done dipped in Joya what? Twice? And you're over here writing checks out to her? Shut your ass up! Don't say nothing until Joya gives you your brain back."

By that time, both of us were rolling with laughter.

"Fuck you, Man." I told him between chuckles.

"Nah, fuck your girl. Better yet, don't. You can't seem to handle what Little Mama is putting down."

"Whatever. You know me better than that."

Justus got serious. "Payne, come on, Son. I've known you since before we were getting it in. And with all the broads you done hit, I've never seen you act this goofy. Cous, you act like you love shorty."

"Nah." I said quickly.

Justus watched me closely. "Don't speak so fast. If you love her, you love her. It's cool. Ay, I love Nia...even when she's pissing me off."

"What'd y'all get into it over?" I asked, changing the subject.

"She got pissed, cuz I re-upped on my spot. I signed the lease for another year on my apartment yesterday."

"What does she want you to do? Move into her spot?"

Nia owned a two-flat over on 72nd and Constance. It was in South Shore, an area that had been on the come-up due to gentrification, but was sitting idle since the housing bubble had burst.

"Yeah."

"You ain't getting it in on the side. Why don't you wanna move in with her?"

"I've told her a million times, I ain't moving in her spot. That cat she used to mess with gave her the down payment for that joint. Does she really think I'm about to crib in a spot the next cat helped her pay for? She done lost her mind."

"Why not put her spot on the market and cop a new spot? It ain't like you ain't got the paper."

"I'm two steps ahead of you." He confided. "She loves Bronzeville. So, I had Angela draw up a contract on a vacant lot over there. I'mma let Nia custom design the spot. She can pimp it out anyway she wants to. That'll be her engagement present."

"Her engagement present? You planning on marrying Nia?"

"I'm giving her the ring when we get home from the premier of the video I directed for Licks."

"Straight up?" I was surprised. I knew that my guy loved his girl, but he hadn't mentioned to me that he was planning to propose.

"Straight up. Ay, the only reason I ain't tell you, was

because I kept going back and forth about it with myself. I kept saying that I wasn't gonna wife Nia until I got my music thing off the ground. With this Licks video…what can I say? I'm doing big things. It's time. My girl's been patient."

"You got the ring?"

"I had Torri holla at a friend of hers who makes custom jewelry."

"Torri knew, but you couldn't tell me? What part of the game is that, Son?" I wasn't serious. I was messing with him.

"My bad. I've been meaning to tell you, but my shit's been in overdrive lately. Between making deals on property and flying back and forth to New York about his video, everything's been bananas."

"Flying back and forth to New York?" I questioned. I didn't know he had been out of town. "Where was I?"

"Where were you, Payne? I don't know. I think you was somewhere cradling ya girl."

I didn't respond.

He cocked his head to the side. "You in love, Bruh?"

"What?" I fronted.

"Did somebody get close enough to Payne to pierce his heart?" He teased.

"Hell naw, Man. Ain't nobody pierced my heart, and if

they did they'd be disappointed. My heart pumps ice water, Son. Love don't live here."

"I've been outta town four times in the last two weeks or so, and you didn't even know. What's up with that? We watched the Cubs beat the hell outta the Indians last night at Izz's crib. Where were you, Payne?" He asked me.

Before I could respond, he spoke again.

"Last weekend me, Izz, Patience, and Dex played pool at *Classified*. Where were you, Payne?"

"I was…"

"Posted up with Joya. Probably giving her a foot massage or something. Now, tell me that 'love don't live here' bullshit again." He taunted.

Justus knew me too well for me to keep trying to lie to him. So, I put the truth out there. "On the real, I'm digging her. I'm not gonna say its love, but I'm definitely digging her. This female got me twisted. I cut out all the side action. I don't fuck around with Tashera, Sonia or Donyae no more. They call me up, they get straight forwarded to voicemail. No vocals. They can't touch Joya. I'm saying, I go to sleep thinking about this female. I wake up thinking about this female. Every time I turn around, I'm thinking about this female." I exhaled loudly.

"My son, you are a man." Justus joked, patting me on the shoulder. "Nah, for real, I know you never wanted to fall in love. I know you been spooked about that ever since we were shorties, but it happens."

"It's crazy, though." I admitted. "I'm not cool with some of the thoughts that I be thinking, Man. I don't wanna look up one day and find myself putting four in somebody's dome over this girl."

"You ain't Vincent, Payne."

"Vincent wasn't Vincent, 'til he caught Isaac knocking his woman." I reminded him.

Chapter Eleven
No Guarantee

Joya

Nasir and his guys flipped their fiftieth house in the middle of August. To celebrate the accomplishment, the fellas put together a little impromptu gathering at the *Exit Strategy* office. There was music, food, liquor, and even a few blunts.

Chantelle was the center of attention, in the middle of the crowd out-dancing everybody. My girl had real talent when it came to dancing.

Nia approached me. "Hey Girl."

"Hey Nia." I gave her a quick hug.

"You see Chan out there on the dance floor?"

"Yeah. I'm surprised Bubbles isn't out there with her." I joked.

"I haven't seen Bubbles. I don't think she's here, yet." She took a sip of her drink "You ready for Vegas?"

We were all headed to Las Vegas in a few weeks, to celebrate Justus. The video he directed for Licks Harlow was premiering at the opening of a new club out there called *Opulence*.

"Yeah, I'm excited. I couldn't believe it when Nasir told me that we were going."

"I'm excited, too." She admitted.

I smirked at her. "I'm sure you are. Your man is about to be all *Hollywood* and stuff. You're about to be rubbing shoulders with the rich and famous, Girl."

"I know, right? I need to be dusting off my boxing gloves. Cuz you know when Justus goes Hollywood, the industry hoes are gonna be right there."

"Of course they are." I knew all about industry hoes from my time with Monte.

"I heard Payne booked y'all a room at Mandalay Bay." She changed the subject.

"Yeah. Where are you all staying?"

"Lick's label, *Spot Check Records* is putting Justus up. They booked him a room at The Bellagio."

"Check that out." I teased.

She pretended to model. "That's right. Check me."

"You are so crazy, Nia."

"Anyway, if you're gonna need any *special accompaniments,* to really get things cracking in Vegas make sure you come and see me."

I gave her a playful push. "Why do you always think that somebody wants sex toys?"

"Who said you have to buy toys? I have costumes, edible

body creams, bondage materials, body jewelry…stimulators. I sell a lot more than just toys."

"You are so nasty."

She shrugged her shoulders. "Show me the dude who doesn't appreciate a little nasty in his
woman, and I'll show you a homosexual, Ma."

I laughed out loud. But my laughter was cut short by a recognizable sound that I couldn't place.

Pap! Pap! Pap!

I finally recognized it. Gun shots.

"Get down! Get down!" Voices were shouting.

Chaos ensued as the plate glass window that proudly displayed the business's name shattered into thousands of pieces and rained down on the floor. The gun shots continued.

"Nia! Joya! Get in the office!" That was Justus.

I had no idea where the office was, but luckily Nia started leading the way. I turned around, still on all fours and looked for Nasir. I didn't see him. Reluctantly, I followed Nia.

Once we made it to the safety of the office that Nasir and Justus shared, I stood up and brushed off my kneecaps. "What just happened?" I asked Nia.

She didn't respond. Instead, she turned her back to me and started to silently pray.

I watched in silence for a few seconds, then started

saying prayers of my own. I didn't know where Nasir or Chantelle was. I prayed that both of them were okay. About a minute later, Nia and I were joined in the office by Chantelle, Dex's baby's mother, and Patience's date for the evening.

"What's going on out there?" I asked Chantelle.

"Madness. Pure madness. They're out there trying to get everybody to calm down."

"Did anybody get hurt?"

She shook her head. "Nah."

"So, everybody's cool?"

"You know the type of people they hang out with are used to this kinda stuff. I do think their lawyer and their real estate agent were kinda shook, though. Especially the lawyer."

"Did you see Nasir out there?" I tried to be nonchalant, but Chan knew me well enough to know that I was worried.

"Yeah, I saw him. He's cool." She assured me.

I breathed a sigh of relief.

"Chan!" We heard a female yelling. "Chan!"

She looked at me. "Is that Bubbles?"

"I don't know."

The office door burst open and Bubbles stood there. "Chan! What the hell? What happened? What happened?" She ran over to Chantelle and threw her arms around her sister's neck. "The police are out there. The front window is gone. Glass is everywhere."

"Somebody shot up the spot." Chantelle replied.

Bubbles' eyes got wide. "Are you serious?"

"Yeah, I'm serious. You couldn't tell with all the broken glass and whatnot?"

"I didn't know what happened."

"Well, somebody shot up the spot."

"If the police are out there, I guess that means we can leave." Nia said.

"I guess so." Chantelle agreed.

"Did anybody get hurt?" Bubbles questioned.

"Nope." Chantelle shook her head.

"Damn, I can't believe somebody blasted *Exit Strategy*." Bubbles repeated in disbelief.

***

I kept cutting my eyes at Nasir as he drove me home that night.

"What's up, Beautiful?" He asked finally.

"Tell me the truth, Nasir. That *Exit Strategy* building isn't a cover for your dope operation, is it?"

"Nah, not at all. I don't do dope, Shorty. I left that game alone before I even met you."

"You all might not do dope, but you do dirt." I stated.

"True." He agreed, with a slow nod of his head.

"Is some dirt coming back to find you?"

He sighed. "You never can say. Things like that can be random, or things like that can be orchestrated. We won't know until we know."

"How're you gonna find out?"

"We've got eyes and ears everywhere, Beautiful." He rested his warm palm on my thigh. "What's up? You spooked?"

"Not really. I'm just wondering if I need to start carrying 'Thriller Killer' when I hang out with you."

"Thriller Killer? What's that?"

"That's what I call my burner."

He chuckled. "You got a name for everything, Ma. Gangsta Kitty. Thriller Killer."

"Okay, my vagina's name is Pretty Kitty. Not Gangsta Kitty."

"Nah, that's Gangsta Kitty, cuz that kitty cat is bound to knock the fight right out of a brotha."

I pushed his shoulder. "Shut up! You like it."

"I more than like it, Joya." He assured me as he pulled into the first available parking spot on my block. We exited the Denali, and walked to my building.

"You're coming upstairs, huh?" I questioned, as I

unlocked the downstairs door.

"Yeah, I'm coming upstairs."

I cut my eyes at him. "All that drama tonight got you horny?" I teased.

He grabbed me around the waist and pulled me close to him. "You got me horny."

"Imagine that."

***

On the third Wednesday in September, Eastern Airlines flight #1208 touched down at McCarran Airport in Las Vegas at 7:45pm, Pacific Time. Nasir and I checked into the room he reserved at Thehotel, in the Mandalay Bay about an hour later.

Nasir was ready to hit the streets as soon as we got our bags up to the room, but I wasn't trying to leave. I had never seen a hotel room that looked anything like the one I was standing in. The place was bananas. The space was humungous and the way it was decorated was total lavishness. I was in love from the moment I stepped inside.

"Ooh Nasir, it's so beautiful." I told him.

The living room was insane. The color palette was decadent. Chocolate brown and black accented with dark purple and cream. The artwork on the walls and the extra-large flat screen television added a classic touch to the luxuriousness of the room.

I made my way into the bedroom. It was all about romance and intimacy. The décor was similar to the décor in the living room, but in the bedroom setting, all of that chocolate brown, cream, black, and dark purple was fantasy inducing. I looked around and admitted to myself that it was exactly the type of room that I would love to get sexed in. I could just imagine laying in the middle of that big old bed while Nasir put in work.

"Ay, you ready?" He asked, walking up behind me.

I turned around and faced him. "Don't you wanna bless me right quick, before we go?"

"Shorty, I always wanna bless you. But I gotta get this monkey off my back first. It's too much free money out there. I need to put my hands on some of it."

I climbed on top of the bed, and the little denim mini skirt that I was wearing rode up my healthy thigh. "Wouldn't you rather put your hands on me?"

He looked at me for a few seconds, like my seduction technique was working, but the draw of the loot must have been stronger. "Trust me, I'mma put more than my hands on you later. But for now, let's ride." He held his hand out to me.

I got out of the bed, crossed the room, and took it.

We linked up with the rest of our crew at the casino in The Bellagio. While everybody else did their things, Justus, Nia, Nasir and I were at the craps table. I laid in the cut and watched the action unfold as Nasir traded his cash for chips. When the dealer gave him his allotted chips, he made a large bet.

"Let me find out you're as lucky as I think you are." He teased me.

"I am." I assured him with a sassy smirk.

Justus picked up the dice, and rolled them. Craps was a fast moving game. It was like…put your money out there, roll the dice, and collect. I couldn't really follow how to play, or what was going on. All I knew was that Justus was killing the table. Everybody around us was screaming, clapping and yelling. Justus' hand was hot for a nice little while. He finally crapped out and the dealer handed the dice to Nasir.

He slid another stack of chips towards the dealer. "Put that out there for me. Let me roll a hard eight, and all that belongs to my girl." He winked at me.

I winked back, with no expectation. I didn't even really understand how the game was played, let alone understand what a hard eight was.

Two rolls later, Nasir rolled that eight the hard way. His four hundred dollar bet turned into thirty-six hundred dollars worth of chips for me. I was too excited when the dealer pushed all of those chips towards Nasir. I quickly became my man's number one cheerleader.

Nasir's hand was killing the casino. He stayed on that table so long, that I thought we would never leave. The other gamblers were loving him, too. He was getting everybody's pockets fat. We were there for at least two hours and Nasir was winning for most of them.

After the casino, we caught a corny comedy show over at The Luxor; grabbed some food at an all-night restaurant; then Nasir and I headed back to our room.

Chapter Twelve
No More Pain

Payne

Thursday night the crew and our women climbed out of the stretch Navigator limo like celebrities. When we stepped inside the club, I understood why it was called *Opulence*. The décor was designed to make every patron feel rich. The walls were covered in light brown suede, and the booths were covered in dark brown leather. The table tops, the bar and the floor were made of glass. Several huge fish tanks were embedded in the walls. The tables were spaced far enough apart, so conversations could remain private. The lighting was intimate, and in the middle of the room was a waterfall that dumped perfectly blue water into a stream, that ran underneath the floor, giving you the impression that you were literally standing on water.

The joint was closed to the public for its grand opening and the premier of Licks' new video, but it was still packed. Heavy-Hitters from every branch of the entertainment industry were in the spot.

"Come on. *Spot Check* has the V.I.P. That's where we're at." Justus said, leading the way.

The ten of us were in the banquette for less than five minutes, when Cameron Chambers, the president of *Spot Check Records* sent over two bottles of Cristal Gold Label.

When we looked over at the table where Cameron was posted up with his people, he hit us with a head nod and a raise of his glass. Justus returned the gesture.

"Damn," Dex's date exclaimed, "that nigga is rich, rich, rich! I can smell the loot from over here!"

She got hit with the screw face by the nine of us.

"What did you say?" Dex asked her.

"Hold that down, Dude." I said, before drama could erupt. It was my guy's night. I didn't want Dex's drama with his woman overshadowing Justus' accomplishment.

Dex ignored me. "What the hell did you say?"

"Ay Dex, stall her out." Justus said. "This ain't the time or the place."

"It's definitely not the time or the place." Nia seconded.

"I'm sorry." The date apologized. "I was thinkin' out loud. I thought it was classy of Cameron Chambers to send over the champagne."

"I brought your ass on an all-expense paid trip to Vegas and you're ready to jump on that nigga's dick, cuz he sent over some drinks?"

"Why don't y'all take that to the parkin' lot?" Chantelle suggested. "Justus is here on business. He doesn't need y'all acting all ghetto, like you've never been anywhere before."

"Exactly." Nia seconded. "This is Justus' future right here. Y'all are not about to ruin it for him."

"I'm sorry." The date repeated.

"Sorry my ass." Dex told her. "I will…"

Dex's rant was cut short by the appearance of Licks Harlow at our table. She grinned happily as she greeted Justus. "Hey J."

He quickly climbed out of the banquette and gave her a friendly hug. "What's the deal, Licks? You're killing that dress, Little Mama."

"Thanks." She said, still grinning.

"You ready to do this?"

"Hell yeah. Are you? Once this video drops, your name is gonna be ringing bells all through the industry. Everybody's gonna be looking to work with you."

"That's what's up. I'm definitely ready." He replied. "Ay, I want you to meet a couple of people. This is my girl, Nia."

Nia waved. "Hey. How're you doing?"

"What's up?" Licks asked her.

"And this is my guy, the hot producer I was putting you on to, Payne. He owns Payne Killer Productions."

Licks gave me a bright smile. "What's good, Green Eyes? You're a producer, huh?"

"Most definitely. You looking for tracks?"

"Hell, if I wasn't…I am now." She flirted, giving me the eye. "J, make sure that Big Mike gets Green Eyes' information. We can definitely do something together."

One of Cameron Chambers' security men came up to the table and whispered a few words into Licks' ear.

"Gotta go. Business is calling me. Make sure you rush the stage during the video, J. When it's over, I wanna introduce you to everybody."

***

We partied like rock stars until the sun came up. Justus was the new shit in the music industry when it came to directing videos. The video he did for Licks was insanity. It was the hottest video I had seen in a minute. The imagery was crazy and Licks looked like a sex goddess from the planet, Bend Me Over, in every shot.

One of the things that made Justus my closest road dog, was his loyalty. As Licks took him around to meet industry heavies, he pulled me right up front and center with him. He introduced me as the hottest producer out of Chicago to everybody he met. I went back to the hotel room with a pants pocket full of business cards from music execs who wanted to hear samples of what I could do. Plus, Licks practically had her manager book me before we left the club.

It was early (or late depending on how you looked at things) and I had been up for about eighteen hours straight, but I was still on ten. Joya was feeling the same excitement. The second I put the latch on the hotel room door, she was at me.

"Can I bless a future superstar before he gets too large?"

"Hell yeah." I assured her.

We stripped naked and dropped into the king-sized bed. I kissed Joya deeply, while I slid my body between her parted legs. I teased her with the tip of my joint and sucked on her bottom lip. After a minute, she didn't need any more foreplay. I could feel the honey her sweet spot was releasing. She was ready. She pressed her hips up towards me, so I would know that she wanted me inside.

My lips curved into a smirk. I didn't make her wait. I gave her what she wanted.

"Nasir." She whined, as I buried myself deep within her confines.

I stroked her slowly, until we were a perfect fit. Then, I increased my pace. Deepened the stroke. She moaned my name.

"Put your legs up." I whispered.

She lifted her legs. I held them up for her. She ran her fingernails down my back. And I pumped her. I gave it to her like I knew she belonged to me. Like I had papers on her.

She whimpered and closed her eyes tight. "You feel so good."

I didn't appreciate the fact that she could still make words. I picked up my rhythm. Arched my back, and pulled the strokes up from Mississippi. That shut her up. She was incoherent. I kissed her mouth. She lifted her hips. We rode like that for what seemed like forever. Me in her space. Giving her the physical version of what was in my heart for her.

I made my thrusts slow and methodical. About fifteen minutes of strokes like that, and she was right there. I could feel her pleasure intensifying. I could hear it, too. Joya was a vocal lover. She wasn't raunchy. She was sweet and sexy. Her demeanor made me keep the beast inside me contained whenever we got down. I wanted to love her gently. Not blow her back out.

I kept my tempo steady as she went over the edge. I held back. Let her get hers all the way out, then I went. I hid myself in her as deeply as I could, while my body jerked involuntarily.

"I love you, Nasir." She said, when we finally came down from our mutual highs.

"I love you, too, Ma." I admitted for the first time, shocking the shit out of myself. I didn't know if it was the high of meeting and conversing with so many top dogs from the music industry, or what. All I knew was that I loved Joya, and I wanted her to know it.

My plan was to drift off into a peaceful sleep, after blessing my girl. But she seemed to have other plans. As soon as my eyes closed, she started touching me. Doing things to me. Playing with me. Since it was all about her, her every wish had to be my desire. I pulled from my reserves and serviced her every need. She was like the energizer bunny. Every time I thought it was over, she came back for more. When it was finally all said and done, my balls ached from all the nuts I busted.

***

Joya and I stayed in Las Vegas a day longer than the rest of the crew. That wasn't the initial plan, but she claimed she was having so much fun that she wanted to stay. I knew what she really wanted was more time to shop.

She put those pretty hazel eyes on me and hit me with the puppy dog face. Next thing I knew, I had agreed to stay the additional day. It was cool, though. I liked seeing Joya happy. And the way I saw it, staying one more day was a small price to pay to make my girl happy. Our flight left Vegas at 8:00 Sunday night. We landed at O'Hare Airport around 1:30 the following morning.

Both of us were dog-tired, as we got our luggage from the baggage claim and drove to Joya's spot.

"You staying at my place?" She asked when I pulled on to her block.

"I'mma take a nap at your spot, then I'm going home." I was exhausted. Between the late nights and the time change, I was feeling something like a zombie.

I dropped Joya's luggage down in front of her closet just as my cell phone rang. *Who the hell is calling me?* I thought to myself. It was almost three in the morning. I knew that only bad news and wrong numbers came at three in the morning. If it was bad news, I needed to know what was up. I checked the screen. Izz's cell phone number was displayed. I felt a pit start to form in my stomach. I knew for sure that it was bad news. "What's up?" I asked.

"Payne?" His voice sounded strange.

"Yeah, it's me, Dude. What's up?" I repeated.

"Payne, you need to get ya ass back to Chicago. ASAP,

Nigga."

I heard what sounded like shrieking in the background. *Damn*! I thought to myself. "I'm in Chicago. What happened? What's going on?"

"J and Dex…they got blasted tonight."

"What? When? What happened?"

Joya walked into the room.

"I don't know. You need to get to the hospital, Man. Like yesterday. Get here, Dude."

I had to ask the question that I hated to ask. "Are they dead, Izz?"

He hesitated for a second, but it seemed like hours to me.

"Are they dead?" I repeated, growing frustrated.

"Is who dead?" Joya asked. Her voice was filled with concern.

"Justus or Dex." I responded.

She left the room. I didn't pay her any attention, because Israel finally responded to my question

"Dex is outta here. He was gone at the scene. J? That nigga holdin' on…but you need to get here."

"Damn!" I said. "What hospital are y'all at?"

"Northwestern." Israel told me, then hung up.

I ended the call. I sat on the arm of Joya's sofa for a few seconds trying to get my mind right. I slowed my breathing down to take some of the rush off my heartbeat. I knew I needed to get control of my emotions. I didn't wanna wild out.

Joya walked back into the living room. She had changed her clothes, fixed her hair and rather than looking sleepy, she looked ready to handle business. She took the keys to the Denali from my hand. "What hospital are they at? I'm driving."

***

The scene at the hospital was surreal. The first person I spotted was Nia. She was seated in a chair in the emergency room waiting area. Patience was sitting next to her, with his arm wrapped around her shoulder, but her eyes were vacant. I doubted she noticed he was there. She was slumped down in the chair and every stitch of clothing she had on was splattered with blood. The pit returned to my stomach. I walked over to her, with Joya following hot on my heels.

"Nia." My voice was barely above a whisper.

She looked up at me, and tears began to pour from her chocolate brown eyes.

From out of nowhere, Chantelle appeared at my side. "Payne." She said sadly. "They're both gone."

Her words registered, but at the same time they didn't. "What?"

236

"They're both gone. Dex died at the scene. Justus died on the table before they could even start the operation." She confirmed.

Israel joined the group.

I hit him with the ice grill. "You said J wasn't dead, Motherfucka."

"I ain't wanna tell you over the phone. I ain't want it to be true. I ain't wanna…" His voice started cracking.

The most heartless cat I knew was trying not to break down in front of me. Pain started replacing the pit in my stomach. A feeling of hopelessness washed over me. I felt like I was about to bust a blood vessel.

"Where's J?" I needed to see him. Not that I didn't care about Dex. Not that I wasn't torn up over losing him, but it was different with Justus. Justus was my brother. Closer than a brother.

Nia finally spoke. "I'll take you to see him."

Nia found a nurse who allowed us access to Justus' room. He looked like he was asleep laying on the gurney. He looked peaceful, even though there seemed to be over one hundred tubes attached to him.

"There only keeping him in this room until his mom can get here. Then, they're gonna put my baby in the morgue. He's dead, Payne. He's dead." She started wailing hysterically.

I put my arm around her and held her close to me. She cried on my shoulder until my shirt was damp. It didn't bother me. I was in shock. My closest dog. My brother. Gone.

I would never talk to him, again. Never hear his laughter. Never get the benefit of his advice. We would never pull another lick together. Kill the music industry together. Make it big together. Raise our shorties together. Grow old together.

I walked over to the bed slowly. Nia hung back, but didn't leave the room. "What's the deal, Son?" I put my hand on Justus' forearm. "Ay, I'm sorry. I'm so sorry." I fought back the tears that were threatening to spill. "If I had known that this was gonna happen, I never woulda stayed outta town. I woulda been here. I swear, I woulda been here. Yo, you know I would trade places with you in a minute, Dude. Damn! What happened, Man? What happened?"

Nia finally joined me by the bed. She was still bawling, but she wasn't hysterical. "What happened, Payne? How the hell did we get here?"

"I was tricking off when I should've been handling my business." I responded softly, then exited the room. Nia followed me.

When I walked back into the waiting area and spotted Joya, I felt rage start to overtake me. Thoughts started crashing my brain. I was pissed as hell that I let her keep me in Vegas when my guy needed me at the crib. She needed to stay an extra day to shop. Selfish ass bitch! I was in Vegas fucking around with her, when I should've had my ass in Chicago. The more I thought about it, the more I wanted to mush her fucking face in.

"Did you see who shot J?" I asked Nia.

She shook her head, still whimpering. "Uh urn. Everything happened so fast. Me; Justus; Dex; Izz and Patience all came outta the club together. Chantelle and Bubbles went back inside, cuz Bubbles thought she left phone on the table. As soon as we walked out, a black truck pulled up slow. I wasn't paying any attention. I was messing around with J. Next thing I knew, he threw me on the ground. And I wondered why he did that, until I heard the gun shots. There were so many shots Payne. I mean, like…so many."

I pulled her into my arms, as she started to cry, again.

"J got on top of me. He covered my body with his. He traded his life for mine. He took all the bullets. He took all the bullets. I…" She was too upset to continue.

I held her more tightly. There were questions that I wanted answers to. Like why did Justus and Dex get it, but Patience and Israel didn't? How many shooters were there? Did it have anything to do with the altercation at *Exit*

Strategy? But I couldn't ask Nia. She wasn't in any shape to be interrogated. She was too upset. So, I swallowed my curiosity for the moment and tried to comfort my friend.

***

The ride back to Joya's condo was a silent one. Finally, I pulled to a stop in front of her building.

"You're not coming upstairs with me?" She asked.

Forever selfish. I thought to myself. "Nah." I paused and took a deep breath. I knew what I needed to do. "I'm an honest type cat, Joya. Always have been. So, I'mma be honest with you. I really ain't feeling you right now."

Her mouth fell open.

I wanted to bust her in it. "Straight up. I just saw my closest guy stretched out on a fuckin' gurney. Dead. Because you wanted to stay in Vegas and *shop*."

"Nasir, us staying in Vegas an extra day didn't have anything to do with Justus and Dex getting shot."

"If I had been here, instead of there, maybe I could've kept my dog from catching some slugs. I don't know. I'll never know. I was too busy tricking off when business needed to be handled."

"Tricking off?" She repeated, like she was in disbelief.

"Yeah, tricking off." I shook my head in disgust. "Man, blow the spot." I popped the locks on the truck. "I can't fuck with you right now. I feel like I might snap out and..."

"What? Whoop my ass?"

"Shake the spot, Joya. On the real." My patience was waning.

She opened the door of the truck slowly. Once she had her right leg out, she turned around and looked at me. "Nasir, I am so sorry about what happen to Justus and Dex. I am so sorry. But you gotta know that this doesn't have anything to do with me, or with us staying in Vegas. If we had been here, that might've been you stretched out on the gurney."

"Kick rocks, Shorty." All that talking was pissing me off even more.

She sighed heavily. "Whatever, *Payne*."

I pulled off before she even made it to the curb.

Chapter Thirteen
Crying Overtime

Joya

I was so hurt by the way Nasir played me, but the main thought going through my mind was, *"Never let 'em see you sweat."* So, I gathered up my gangster, and made it into my apartment without letting so much as one teardrop fall from my amber colored eyes. Once I was inside the privacy of my condo, I stripped out of my clothes, threw myself on the bed and cried buckets of tears. Some were for Justus and Dex. Some were for Nia, and the loss she had suffered. But most of them were because of Nasir.

***

Dex's family pulled his funeral together in a matter of three days. I flew that day and was able to avoid going to the services for him. That was cool, because I wasn't ready to face everything attending that funeral meant I would have to face. When Justus' home-going service came around two days later, Chantelle wouldn't let me off the hook. She volunteered me as the soloist.

Justus' funeral was heart-wrenching. His friends and loved ones were racked with grief. Nia; Izz; Patience; and Nasir were like zombies. Bubbles was inconsolable. And Justus' mother was practically comatose. The spirit of misery was so strong in the church that I didn't think I would be able to get through my solo. Especially since Justus' mom, Mrs. Calhoun had requested that I sing "The Battle is the Lord's."

When it was time for me to sing, I walked over to the microphone slowly. I could hear the quiet whimpers, and soft cries as the pianist played the opening notes of the song.

"There is no pain Jesus can't feel

No hurt He can not heal

All things work according to His perfect will

No matter what you're going through

Remember God is using You

For the battle is not yours

It's the Lord's." I sang.

Soft weeping became loud wails. That was the thing that I hated most about singing at funerals. It broke my heart to see so many people in so much pain.

***

After the funeral, I met up with Chantelle and Bubbles in the lobby of Oakdale Covenant Church.

"You killed that solo, Chica." Bubbles said giving me a hug. "You sounded so good up there."

"You did." Chantelle agreed.

"Thank you." I replied humbly. Sounding good was really the last thing on my mind. I just wanted to pay Justus the proper respect he deserved.

"You wanna ride to *Classified* with me?" Chantelle asked her sister.

Classified was where the repast was being held.

Bubbles blew her nose loudly and wiped her bloodshot eyes. I wasn't there to see how she handled Dex's funeral, but I could tell that she was taking Justus' death hard.

"I'm not goin' to the repast. I can't do it, Chan." She shook her head violently. "This whole thing with Justus got my mind straight twisted."

Chantelle nodded her understanding. "You want me to come with you? Keep you company?"

"Nah, you're straight. I'm hookin' up with some friends later."

"What friends?"

"Midori and Shaniece. You don't know 'em." Bubbles assured her. "I need to be around some people who don't know y'all. Some people who aren't in mourning right now. Y'all are bringing me down."

"You're the one who can't stop crying, Boo." I reminded her.

She semi-chuckled. "I know. I'm hurt right now. I'm so hurt behind this. Of all people to get got, why did it have to be Justus?"

"I know." I seconded.

"I'm sayin'. He was on his way to super-stardom. And now…"

"It's messed up." Chantelle stated.

"It's fucked up!" Bubbles corrected her. She shook her head again. "I gotta go. I'll see y'all later. Chan, I'll call you."

We waved to Bubbles, then watched her leave the church.

Chantelle turned her attention to me. "You wanna leave your car here and ride with me?"

"Nah, I'm leaving the repast early. I don't wanna be there long. Those are Nasir's people and I'm sure he doesn't want me there."

At the repast, I really just wanted to pay my respects to Mrs. Calhoun and Nia, then shake the spot. I found them sitting at the same table with other members of Justus' family.

"Hey Nia." I said giving her hug.

"Hey Joya. Thanks for coming." Her eyes were swollen from crying so many tears.

"You don't have to thank me." I insisted.

"Sweetie, you are really talented." Mrs. Calhoun told me. "The way you sung that song really spoke to my heart. That's my favorite song, and you really sang it well."

I was grateful to receive the compliment. Mrs. Calhoun telling me she liked the song was the highest form of flattery I could receive. "Thank you so much."

"I made sure to give Nasir a little token of my appreciation to pass on to you."

"You didn't have to do that." I said honestly. There was no way I could take money for singing at Justus' funeral.

"I wanted to." She assured me. "You really ministered to my soul with that song. I have to keep telling myself that God is still in control. Even through all this…excruciating pain. God is still on His throne. And the battle is not mine, it's His."

"That's right." One of the other ladies co-signed.

"Well, thank you, Mrs. Calhoun. I'm glad you liked the song." I walked away from their table and over to the table where Chantelle was seated with Israel, Nasir and Patience. "Chan, I'm outta here. I'll call you later."

As I turned to walk away, Nasir got up from the table and started to approach me. "Joya."

I looked over at him. "Yes?"

"Ay, Mrs. Calhoun wanted you to have this." In his outstretched hand was a small white envelope. "It's a little something for singing at the thing. Check it out. I doubled the amount, cuz I thought it was classy of you to look out for my guy, even though me and you ain't…" He let his sentence trail off.

I hit him with the ice grill. "Kick rocks, Shorty." I left him and his envelope of guilt standing right there.

Chapter Fourteen
Now I Gotta Wet 'Cha

Payne

After the repast, a few of us went over to Israel's crib. We chilled downstairs in his finished basement. *Goodfellas* was on the big screen, but I wasn't paying any attention to the movie. My mind was a million miles away. I had a gang of pent-up frustration that I needed to release. I needed to sex. Hard and fast. No talking. No romance. No bullshit. Just sex. I considered stopping through Tashera's spot and putting her through the paces, but I changed my mind right before I texted her. I didn't want to be bothered with her ass.

I was so deep in thought that I raised the beer bottle to my lips without realizing it was empty. I stood up from the leather recliner where I was chilling, and made my way upstairs.

Midori was in the kitchen alone, doing something at the center island. She cut her slanted eyes at me as I entered the room, but she didn't say anything. My eyes moved over her slim frame quickly. She looked good in that little black dress. Testosterone started talking to me.

I walked up behind her, pressed my pelvis into her ass and placed a hand on each of her breasts. "Can I do what I wanna do to you, Midori?" I asked, then kissed her softly on the neck.

"Yes." She responded as I moved my hands from her breasts to the front of her thighs. I hiked up the dress.

"Ooh." She said quietly.

I pulled down her panties, bent her over the island and entered her from the back. I knew I had to be tripping off of losing my guy, because I went in raw. That was something that I never, ever did. I pushed the consequences of hitting a jump-off raw from my mind and allowed myself to get caught up in the juiciness of Midori. I wrapped my hands up in her long, black hair and yanked roughly while I pounded her. She was moaning loud as hell. I fully expected somebody to walk into the kitchen and catch us. But if she didn't care, I definitely didn't give a damn. I kept banging her out. I landed blow after blow in her soft flesh, until finally I felt myself about to erupt. She felt so good that I waited until the last possible second to pull out. Semen splashed down on Israel's terrazzo floor tile.

"Damn. I ain't mean for that to happen" I moved away from her, pulled up my pants, then quickly zipped and buttoned them. I looked down at the sticky puddle on the floor.

Midori adjusted her panties. She pulled her dress down and smoothed it with her hands. She finger-combed her hair, ran her tongue over her lips and spoke with a smile. "I'll get it up."

While she cleaned up the floor, I walked over to the refrigerator and grabbed myself a beer. "Later." I called, as I exited the kitchen.

"Payne." She said throwing the used paper towels in the trash can.

I turned around.

"That's all I get? Later?"

I raised my right eyebrow. "What do you want, Midori?"

"Uhm, can I at least get a kiss?"

"I ain't really into kissin'." I responded with a shake of my head.

"You're not really into kissin'?" She repeated, like she couldn't believe the way I was playing her.

"Nope."

"You do know that you just gave it to me raw-dog, right?" She questioned sarcastically.

"Yeah." I admitted. "It'll never happen again."

"And you won't give me a kiss?"

"Nope."

She rolled her eyes up to the ceiling. "Well, are you into huggin'? Can I at least get a hug?"

I grinned at her. "Yeah, you can get a hug." I walked back over to her and pulled her into my arms. I held her close to me.

"Payne, you shouldn't do me like this. You know it ain't right."

"What're you talking about, Ma?" I fronted.

"You know what I'm talking about. You know how I feel about you."

I was silent.

Israel walked into the kitchen while we were hugging. "The hell y'all doin'? Y'all better not be fuckin' in my crib. The only cat allowed to get ass up in here, is me."

"Ain't nobody havin' sex, Izz." Midori lied as I released her.

"Payne, you ain't out, are you? I need to get at you before you leave."

"What's up?" I asked him. I was ready to go home. Physically, mentally and emotionally, I was exhausted. I needed to chill out and see if I could get my mind to shut down for a few hours. Ever since Justus and Dex had left the earth, it was like I couldn't stop thinking. Twenty-four hours a day, my mind was in overdrive. The shit was starting to wear me out.

Israel turned his gaze to Midori. "Ay Midori, can you go back downstairs?"

"I need to wash my hands."

"There's a bathroom downstairs. Can you wash 'em down there?"

She frowned at him. "Yeah. I guess so." She smirked at me. "Bye Payne. We'll get back."

"No doubt." I assured her. I definitely planned on tapping that again. "Later."

Both Izz and I watched her as she left the kitchen. Izz shook his head and let out a low whistle. "Midori's badder than a motherfucka, but she's too scandalous for me."

She was a scandalous broad. She was the crew's top draft pick when it came to pulling licks. Bubbles was usually the mastermind, but Midori was the hustler. She was the one who was usually responsible for bringing the victims down."

"She's dyin' for you to knock that." He informed me.

"I know."

"Why don't you hit that already?"

"I'm considering it." I changed the subject. "So, what's up?"

"Word finally got back about the cats who popped J and Dex."

"Straight up?"

"Yeah, they belong to the Body Shredders."

I knew the Body Shredders. They were killing the dope game in the Englewood area, while we were killing it in South Shore and Avalon Park.

"Why do they have beef with us?" I was confused. We never had trouble with them while we were in the dope game. Why would we have trouble with them once we were out?

"Elliott. He was a card carryin' member." He sighed.

"Patience never said…"

"Patience's handlin' of the situation wasn't as thorough as it coulda been."

"How did Patience miss the connection between Elliott and The Body Shredders?"

Izz cut his eyes at me. "I ain't quite sure. But I gotta be honest with you, Payne. I don't really know how I'm feelin' about Patience lately."

"What does that mean?" Patience was my man. I couldn't believe that Israel doubted his loyalty to the crew.

"I don't know." He shrugged his broad shoulders. "It's a feelin' I get when I'm around him. I'm wonderin' if somebody got to him."

"Somebody like who?"

"Again, I don't know, Man. It's a gut feelin'." He sighed. "He might be double-agent."

The first thing Unc taught me and Justus when we started balling was to always, always take our gut-instincts about people to heart. Usually whatever vibe I picked up from a person was right on target. So, if Izz was getting a gut-feeling about Patience being double-agent, I had to honor that.

"Patience…dirty?" I mused.

"I know it's crazy, but some crazy thoughts been runnin' through my mind lately about dude. How is it, that him, Justus and Dex all left out the club together and they were gunned down, but he got away clean?"

"I heard you got away clean, too. Nia said that you walked out with them, too."

"I was walkin' out behind Patience, but I saw this cat I knew from juvie. Dude is a bouncer up at the club. I'm choppin' it up with the cat and next thing I know, I hear pap! Pap! Pap! So, I run out the club blastin', as the truck flies down the street. I look around and I see Dex twisted on the street." He shook his head. "I could tell by the angle of his body that he was gone. His neck was like…"

"I got you."

"Yeah. Then, I saw Justus. I went over to him to make sure he was alive. While I was checkin' on J, Chan and Bubbles came outta the club."

"Where was Patience?"

He widened his eyes. "That's what I'm tellin' you, Dog. Chan starts callin' 911, and Patience shows up. I don't know where dude came from. He coulda been around the corner or anything. I don't know. He just *appeared*. He walked up like, 'what's up?' I said, 'Nigga what you think is up? Dex is dead, Motherfucka. That's what's up. Where the hell you been?' He just stood there lookin' at me all stupid."

"You know Patience ain't down to come out blastin', Man."

"That's where you're wrong, Payne. Patience ain't scared of murder. Dude murdered his momma's man when he was eleven. The rest of us was playin' with Hot Wheels, and he was pumpin' four into somebody. He ain't scared. And I know we've babied him, never lettin' him pull licks and shit, but Patience is capable. He's capable of a lot of shit we don't give him credit for. If he wanted to blast back while those cats were murderin' Dex and J, he woulda blasted back. He didn't want to."

I turned that over in my mind. Israel had a good point. The whole situation was suspicious. If Patience had something to do with Justus and Dex getting rocked out, then he had to know that the wages of sin was death. "How are we handling that?"

"Patience is my man, twenty grand. Grew up with that cat. I don't wanna be hasty about layin' him flat. I just want you to know that I'm watchin' dude. And that I don't trust his ass. So, when me and you link up to talk about what we talk about…he don't need to be there."

"You sure you don't wanna handle dude ASAP?" Patience had gone from being my guy for life, to being completely disposable with one conversation.

He nodded slowly. "I'll let him play his hand out. Everything that's done in the dark eventually comes to the light."

"Ay, what's the get back on these cats that touched Justus and Dex? Do we have names or faces yet?" I changed the subject.

"Yeah, they're corner boys. Baby lieutenants for The Body Shredders. They came through the club in the same truck they were in when they blasted *Exit Strategy*."

"Okay." I nodded. At least we knew who blasted the office and why they did it.

"There's three of 'em. One called Trix. One called T-Shaun and one called Dino. They party at The Big Dog's After Hours Strip Club every Thursday night. They kick it hard until Thursday turns into Friday. Spend the little bit of dough they make huggin' the block on the tricks up there."

"You know what they look like?"

"Fo' Sho'."

It was a done deal. "We ride through early Friday morning."

"Friday morning, dude."

"Minus Patience?"

"Hell naw. Dude is ridin' shotgun. He's about to give *his* trigger finger a work-out. He wanna stay crew, then his ass needs to step up his game. I'm through puttin' in work for that cat. If he stutters or hesitates about ridin' with us…his people might as well drop that call to Leak and Sons. Cuz he's done."

Leak & Sons was a successful funeral home on the south side.

"And I mean that shit." Izz continued. "I will lay him flat my damn self. He better be down to handle this business."

***

Early Friday morning, we rode out to Dolton, Illinois to pay a little visit to some of the patrons of Big Dog's After Hours. Izz and Patience were in the bed of the "borrowed" black GMC Sierra, covered by the tarp. I was driving.

Izz had everything under control. He was cool with a dancer at the club, called Dynasti. She was the final act each night. She knew exactly who Izz was talking about when he described the young cats. They spent most of their loot on her and she had even given one of them a $100 dollar blow job a few weeks earlier. She knew they always kicked it in a silver Cutlass Supreme. She told Izz that the club closed at 2:00 and the vics usually left out around 2:20. She promised to keep them inside until at least 3:00. That way the parking lot would be almost empty.

It was 2:25 and men were filing out of the club by the dozens. We waited patiently. By 2:57 there were only three cars left in the parking lot. One was our black GMC Sierra. One was the vics' rusted out, silver Cutlass Supreme. The third car didn't matter.

A minute later, three young cats exited the club. They were talking loudly and laughing. If they knew like I knew, it would be the last time they ever did that. I watched as they got closer to the truck. I turned around in the driver's seat. I was on my knees facing the back of the truck. Slowly I started to roll the darkly tinted window down, just enough for the barrel of my burner to be free. Before they knew what happened, a barrage of bullets began to tear through them. Izz's high powered rifle ripped away skin and flesh as the bullets made contact. They didn't even have time to scream. As quickly as the hail of gun fire had started, it ended. I turned around, threw the truck in drive and exited the parking lot.

Chapter Fifteen
Moving On

Joya

At work, I was back to my post-Monte regiment. I was back to flying six, sometimes seven days a week. I had flown through the Thanksgiving weekend. I had flown through Christmas. I had even managed to fly on both New Year's Eve and New Year's Day. All that flying was an effort to keep my mind off of things like Nasir and our break up. And I finally felt like I was getting over him. I decided that I had shed all of the tears that I planned to shed over dude. He didn't want me. It was time for me to move on.

I was deep in thought as I perused the perfume counter at Macy's on State Street. I was sampling Ralph Lauren's newest fragrance when I felt somebody tap me on the shoulder. I turned around slowly. I was shocked to see KJ Jamison grinning at me.

"Shorty Songbird, check you out. What's good?" He asked.

"Not much." I replied honestly.

"Where've you been? I saw your boy, Trey over at *Freestyle Friday* a couple of weeks ago. I was surprised you weren't with him."

"How'd he do?"

He shook his head, and responded with a smirk. "I murked 'im. He got second. Your boy can't touch me. I told you the only reason he beat me that other day, was because he had you."

"Trey is nice on the mic." I insisted.

"He's nice...but I'm better."

"And so modest." I laughed.

He chuckled, too. "Why weren't you with him? Y'all have a falling out?"

"Quit fishing." I told him. "Nah, we didn't have a falling out. Trey is my guy. I've been working a lot lately. I haven't had time for much else."

"What kinda work do you do, Ma? Super model?"

I laughed out loud at his corniness. "Try again." I teased.

"I don't know." He shrugged his shoulders. "It has to have something to do with having a killer voice or being fine as hell."

I kept laughing, but didn't comment on his compliment.

"You still glued to Payne's hip?"

"Why?" I wasn't about to answer a question like that.

"I'm having a showcase up at *Kacey's,* right before Valentine's Day. It'll be me, this R & B group, and a neo-soul chick. We're being featured as hot talent outta Chicago. Julien Biddleworth and a couple of other industry heavies are supposed to come through."

"Julien Biddleworth who owns Hard Tyme Records?"

"No doubt. And if you didn't have such a strong commitment to Payne Killer Productions, I would ask you to come through the spot and blow the hook on this one track I got." He paused. "You'd be perfect for it."

"If I'd be perfect for it, then you should probably ask me to come through and blow the hook." I told him.

He cocked his head to the side. "Are you serious, Shorty? Cuz I'mma be honest, I ain't good with rejection."

I cracked up. "You think I'm trying to set you up for rejection? Nah, I don't play like that, KJ. If you want me on the track, then you should make me an offer."

"How much does Trey usually give you?"

"Now, you know that's none of your business. Draw up a contract, and I'll have my lawyer look it over."

"You made Trey give you a contract?" He asked in disbelief.

"Again, what I do with Trey is between me and Trey. Just like what I do with you, is between us. Feel me?"

"Yeah." He nodded slowly. "I like your style. Gimme your number. I'll have that contract for you by the day after tomorrow."

I recited my phone number. "Oh yeah, make sure you don't address me as 'Shorty Songbird' on the contract. You do know that's not my real name, don't you?"

"I know your name, *Joya*. I've been asking around about you."

"You've been asking who about me?"

"Don't even worry about all that. Just worry about this offer that I'm about to make you. I'll get back in a few days."

***

I had the only lawyer that I knew (one of my mother's fellow church members) look over the contract that KJ sent me. Once she "okayed" it, I signed the contract for the one track deal. The contract stated that I was committed to practicing and recording at Northern McKinley's studio. Unlike Nasir, Northern had a recording studio in the basement of his house out in Country Club Hills, a southern suburb of Chicago. Since I didn't know Northern or KJ well enough to trust them, I took Chantelle and Bubbles with me out to the studio. I also took 'Thriller Killer', just in case somebody tried to get cute with us.

"You know Payne is pissed that you're recordin' with KJ and Northern." Chantelle told me, as I flew down I57, heading for the Vollmer Road exit.

"How does he know I'm recording with KJ and Northern?"

"Please, you know how these cats are. They talk more than women. I heard Payne tellin' Izz that he ran into KJ at Best Buy. He said KJ couldn't wait to throw it up that he was puttin' you on a track."

"He probably thinks you're sexin' KJ. You know how cats are. Since he was hittin' it, he probably assumes that you're lettin' KJ hit, too." Bubbles commented.

I doubted that was true. Nasir knew how long it took me to give it up to him. He knew good and well that I wasn't blessing KJ.

"Whatever he thinks, he was pissed." Chantelle continued. "He was practically throwin' a temper tantrum." She chuckled. "I was crackin' up. I was thinkin', that's what your ass gets for playin' my girl."

"Right. That's exactly what he gets." I agreed. Deep down inside I was happy to hear that it bothered him that I was working with a different producer and artist.

"And what would be crazy, is if KJ got picked up by Hard Tyme Records and took you with him." Chantelle said.

"Now that, would definitely serve Nasir right." I mumbled.

When I pulled into Northern's over-sized driveway, I took out my cell phone and called KJ. He instructed me to leave my car, and come around to the side door. When we got there, he was waiting on us.

He looked at me quizzically. "I see you brought the crew."

"Yeah. That's not a problem, is it?"

"Pretty women? Hell, nah." He assured me.

"This is Chantelle, and that's Bubbles." I told him, gesturing towards each of my friends as I told him their names.

"Hey." Chantelle said.

"What's up?" Bubbles asked.

"What's good, Ladies? Nice to meet you. The studio's downstairs. Come on."

We followed him into the house, down a short flight of stairs, and into the studio. The studio that I was used to recording in was the studio where Nasir worked. It was in a warehouse building on the north side of the city. It was industrial, without any luxuries or extras. The only things in that studio were a worn couch, a raggedy table, a stark recording booth, and a mix board. Northern's studio was homey and comfortable. The walls were painted a neutral shade, the tile floor was covered with an area rug, and the furniture was over-stuffed and inviting. It was really nice.

There were three guys inside, including Northern. I was glad that I brought Chantelle and Bubbles with me. I would've been pissed if I had shown up alone, and four cats were in the studio.

KJ introduced me around. "You know Northern." He told me.

I nodded. "Hey Northern."

"Shorty Songbird, I've been waiting to get you in my studio for a minute."

"Well, you know they say that the best things in life are worth waitin' for." Bubbles chimed.

Northern's glance moved passed me and landed on Bubbles.

"I'm Bubbles." She stated with a smirk.

He raised his left eyebrow. "Now, you know I'm wondering how you got a nickname like Bubbles."

"My grandmother gave me that nickname."

"Why?"

"Ay North! I need you to run that track back, Man. I need to hear that section, where I'm comin' outta the bridge."

Northern winked at Bubbles. "I'mma definitely get back. Let me take of business."

"You do that." She said.

"Anyway," KJ said.

"Exactly. You were saying?" I prompted.

"That's Young Trotter. Over there," he pointed, "that's Vibe. He's my manager."

"You have a manager?"

"Most definitely." He told me. "This is the hustle that I love. I take everything about this business seriously. I do what it takes to make my name ring bells."

"Okay." I said, with a nod of my head. "So, what are we doing?"

"You ready to work?"

"Definitely."

"Cool. I'mma let you hear this track, then I'mma let you show me what you can do with the hook. Do you write your own bars?"

I twisted my face. "I haven't before. Why, do I need to?"

"Nah, I got your hook for this track. But you might wanna think about making a move into writing your own stuff in the future, Shorty. The money ain't really in spittin' these lyrics. The money's in song writing."

"I'll keep that in mind." I promised.

Thirty minutes later, I was in the booth. KJ and Northern were at the boards, watching me with hopeful anticipation. I was nervous. I adjusted the headphones for the one hundredth time, and moved closer to the microphone.

"I'mma feed you the hook. Sing it back to me, however you feel it. We'll make the adjustments later. Right now, I wanna hear you flow. Get a feel for your style." KJ said.

The fact that KJ was acting so laid back about the situation made me finally relax. When he gave me the words, I sang them back with sassiness.

Promises of romance, tales of love for life;

Promises of sweet talk, kisses down my spine.

That don't do it for me. That don't blow my mind.

You wanna get next to me?

Make my finger shine.

Promises of Bentleys. Platinum filled with ice.

Feet wrapped up in Prada. Seven covered thighs.

That's the stuff that I like.

Let the haters hate me.

You can't play for my team, unless you can upgrade me.

"Damn!" KJ said happily. He was practically bouncing off of the studio walls. He and Northern kept grinning at each other.

"I likes. I likes." Northern said, finally. "I like the little bit of attitude you're showing, but on that second stanza…"

I nodded my head, and urged him to continue.

"I want you to go for a sexier sound."

After four and a half hours in that studio, I understood why Northern and KJ killed it when they worked together. Payne was thorough, but KJ and Northern were both total perfectionists. When Northern finally told me that he had the track done, I wanted to fall out on the floor. My throat was raw. I didn't think I would be able to sing for weeks.

"Shorty Songbird, go home and rest your vocal cords."

KJ told me. "I'll hit you up in a few days so we can rehearse for the showcase."

I didn't even want to think about singing, but it was what it was. "Okay." I mumbled.

***

Two weeks later, the crowd at *Kacey's* was deep. I was in KJ's dressing room with him, Northern, and Vibe. I sipped tea and ran the scales to warm up my vocal cords. KJ was in the cut, getting a massage from a young girl who introduced herself to me as his stylist. Northern was typing into his cell phone, while Vibe talked into his. He was trying to get information on exactly who was in the audience that we needed to impress.

The first act to hit the stage was the neo-soul singer, Sierra Haze. Although I wasn't able to see her perform, I could hear her. She sounded good. Her voice was sweet and clear. The R & B group was okay. I could tell from the tonal quality of their singing that they still needed development. Once the R & B group completed their set, there was a short intermission. After the intermission, KJ and I were up.

I adjusted the straps on my keyhole-neck blouse, smoothed down the creases in my True Religion skinny jeans, and stood up on the four inch heels of the Christian

Louboutin boots that all of the overtime had helped me purchase. I felt confident as I followed KJ out of the dressing room. I knew I looked good in my outfit, and all of my body parts were covered. I was ready to blow up the stage and kill the microphone. My partner in crime turned around and looked at me, as we headed towards the stage entrance.

"You ready to do this?"

I smirked at him. "Definitely."

"So, let's rip it." He suggested.

KJ and I were on fire. The crowd was pumped from the second the first beat of Northern's track dropped. They were on their feet and going crazy. KJ fed off of their excitement. He was maniacal while spitting his lyrics. What I liked most about working with KJ was that he was seasoned. He understood how to work the crowd, and he was able to teach me things right there on the stage without the audience even noticing. When it was time for me to sing the hook, KJ got right in my face and stared directly into my eyes. At first, it kind of knocked me off of my square. I tried to break the eye contact, so I could concentrate on the words and on the notes. But he grabbed my hand, and held me there. While I was singing he watched me like I was the baddest female he had ever laid eyes on. Like the words coming out of my mouth were the emancipation proclamation and I was about to give him his freedom papers or something.

After the showcase, KJ got the word from Vibe. The representative from *Ride or Die Records* liked what he saw. He was setting up a meeting for us with the president and C.E.O. of the label, Bruno Ricci.

Chapter Sixteen
It's So Hard to Say Goodbye to Yesterday

Payne

The months after Justus' death were hell. My head was everywhere, except on what it needed to be on. Houses that needed work were sitting untouched. Buyers that we had on the line were threatening to walk. Our lawyer was asking when we were going to be ready to close on properties. Our real estate broker was calling about setting up showings. *Exit Strategy*'s business was in the damn toilet.

I knew that I needed to get my shit together, but I could never concentrate on one thing long enough to complete it. My mind was always racing. Always. It seemed to me like the only places I could find peace were in the studio, and dipping into some broad. So, that was basically what I did. I recorded hot ass tracks, and got it in.

"It's getting late." I told the naked beauty who was lying next to me in the hotel bed. "I gotta get outta here."

She nodded her pretty head. "I know. I was supposed to pick up my kids from my mom's spot two hours ago."

I threw the sheets off of my nude body, grabbed the used condoms from the floor, and took them to the bathroom to flush them. I walked back into the room retrieved my clothes from the floor and started to get dressed.

She stretched, moaning noisily all the while. I figured that she was just a loud person, because she had screamed bloody murder the entire time I was boning her out. She acted like I was slaughtering her. With every stroke, I waited for the police to bust down the door.

"Ooh Payne." She purred. "Now I see why Tashera couldn't stay away from you."

Scandalous. The naked beauty in the bed was Tashera's next door neighbor and alleged best friend, Tanya. Tashera had introduced me to shorty years ago. I never really felt Tanya, though. Didn't like her style. But somehow, she and I had managed to link up and sex.

"Tashera told me you were a beast in the bedroom, but I never imagined…"

I zoned out. I was thinking that Tashera talked too damn much. She needed a lesson in discretion. That was one of the things I always appreciated about Joya. She kept her mouth shut. I pushed thoughts of Joya from my mind.

After I tied my custom designed Nikes, Tanya hit me with the conversation that I always wanted to avoid.

"You know I'm really diggin' you, Payne." She said. "So, hit me up if you ever wanna link, again."

I didn't. "Cool." I responded.

She wrapped herself up in the bed sheets, and walked me to the door of room 417 at the Hilton on 95th and Cicero Avenue.

"Don't stay too long." I warned, even though I had made sure that she used her credit card to get the room.

"I won't." She promised, with a grin.

Before I made my escape, I bent down and kissed her softly of the forehead. "Later."

***

As soon as I walked through the front door of my spot, my cell phone vibrated alerting me that I had a text message. I was hesitant to check it, because it was after four in the morning. I knew that only bad news and booty calls came at that time of the morning. I wasn't feeling up to either option, so I ignored it.

Instead, I pulled my Chicago Bulls hoodie over my head, and tossed it over the back of the arm chair. My cell vibrated again, then a third time. I finally viewed one of the messages, because somebody was pressed to get at me.

I know ur awake. Hit me back. Can't sleep. ~ Nia.

Since Justus had left the earth, Nia and I had both been having trouble sleeping.

I plopped down on my sofa, kicked my feet up on the coffee table and hit her back. "What's up, Ma?"

"Not a damn thing, Man. I'm telling you, if I'm up to see the sun rise one more time, I'mma get me some prescription sleeping pills. I feel like I'm going crazy." She told me.

She was preaching to the choir. Lack of sleep had me bugging, too. "I feel ya, Shorty."

"I'm so tired, Payne. I don't know what to do with myself. My house is so clean you could eat off the floors. I've reorganized the store so many times that my regular customers don't know where to find anything, and I can't even remember where I put the stuff. You should see me and the customers wandering around the store, looking for nipple-less bras together."

I chuckled at the visual.

"I think I'm losing my mind."

"Well, if you're losing your mind, then I'm losing mine, too."

"What have you been doing with yourself?"

I shook my head, even though I knew she couldn't see the gesture. "You don't even wanna know."

"Running around with any funky slut that'll have you?" She sucked her teeth. "Showing off and acting like your grandmother didn't raise you right?"

"Ay, I gotta do something while I'm wide awake at four o'clock in the morning." I joked.

"You still haven't worked things out with Joya?"

"Fall back, Nia. I don't wanna talk about Joya."

"Well, I do. I think you still love her. I think you miss her." She said quietly.

"Come on, Man. My guy was fighting for his life, and I was out in Vegas, romancing her ass."

"Joya didn't do anything, Payne. All she did was ask to stay an extra day."

"Didn't I tell you to fall back?" I asked harshly. "I ain't trying to talk about her, and I definitely ain't trying to hear you defending her."

"I'm not defending her. I'm being honest with you, Boo. It's not Joya's fault that Justus got shot. You can't hold her responsible for that. If you wanna hold anybody responsible, hold the motherfuckers who pulled the triggers responsible."

I didn't talk business over the telephone line, so I couldn't tell her that the situation had been handled months ago.

Neither of us spoke for a while, both of us lost in our own thoughts.

"Payne, call Joya. You're running around here with this hoe and that hoe. You're screwing that Chinese-looking broad. I know you're not happy. You can't be happy."

"I'm straight."

"I love you. I want you to be happy…again."

"I want you to be happy, too." I told her, and I meant it.

I heard her clock strike five o'clock.

"I'mma try to get a couple of hours of sleep, so I can go to work in the morning." She told me. "I'll talk to you later."

"Later, Nia." I ended the call, pulled my exhausted body off of the couch and dragged myself to the bedroom. I leaned against my dresser for support, and yanked the Nikes from my feet. Then I unfastened my belt, and let my Coogi jeans fall to the floor. I stepped out of them, and tugged my shirt over my head. I was dog-tired, but I needed to holler at the shower. Tanya's scent was all over me, and it was making me straight nauseous. Not that she smelled rotten or nothing, I just wasn't feeling that scent.

I took off both of my rings, my earring, my bracelet, and my watch. I opened up the top drawer of my dresser. That was where I kept all of my jewelry. I had a wall safe, but the truth of the matter was that most of the time, I was too lazy to put my jewels in the safe. I usually threw everything in the top drawer for easy access. When I opened the drawer, for some odd reason my eyes came to rest on the watch I bought for Joya. Even though I never gave it to her, I always thought of it as Joya's watch.

I picked up the timepiece and held it in my hand. Thoughts of my shorty flooded my mind. As much as I hated to admit it, even to myself, I missed the hell out of that girl. I missed the way her smile…her touch, could have me on ten. I missed the feel of her skin. The taste of her kisses. The sound of her moans. I missed basically everything about her.

It had been almost five months since Justus had left the earth. It was getting to the point that I could acknowledge to myself that I messed up big time when I pushed Joya away. Even though it still hurt like hell that my guy was gone, I knew it wasn't really Joya's fault. She took the fall, because at that time…somebody had to. Deep down inside, I still loved her. I wanted her back. But knowing Joya, I couldn't see how that was ever going to happen.

***

A few nights later Midori hit up my cell and begged me to stop through her spot. One thing that I appreciated about Midori was that she wasn't a sweating broad. She was the type who let me fall into her spot whenever I wanted to, and let me leave the same way. So, when she called and requested my presence, I had an ominous feeling about it.

I didn't like the look on her face when she answered the door. The feeling of dread intensified. "What's good?" I asked her.

"That depends." She replied, allowing me to step into her apartment.

I stuttered-stepped as I walked. "On what?"

"We need to talk." She said, making her way into the living room.

I followed her and sat down on the love seat.

"Payne, I'm pregnant." She announced.

"What?" I asked in confusion.

"I'm pregnant." She repeated.

My mind started spinning. I stood up from the love seat. "Midori, please tell me that you *think* you're pregnant. Tell me that your period is late and you might be pregnant. Come on, Ma. Don't do this shit to me."

"I took the test." She pulled something out of the pocket of her jean shorts. "It came out positive."

I focused on the object. It was a little white stick that I immediately recognized as an at-home pregnancy test. She held out the stick, and showed me the two unmistakably pink lines. They were as clear as day.

I knew I had been hitting Midori frequently. Like four to five times a week, but I didn't remember going in raw. How the hell was she pregnant by me? "When..."

She cut on top of me. "It had to be that day at Izz's house…in the kitchen. Right after Justus' funeral. You must've pulled out too late."

I sat back down on the love seat. Images of me going in raw and spilling on the floor ran through my mind. Carelessness had bent me over. Now, I was stuck. "What're you thinking about doing?" I asked, while I silently prayed and tried to cut a deal with God.

"I don't know." She looked like she might cry.

"Damn."

"I've been going back and forth with this for more than a month tryin' to decide what I wanna do. The look you have on your face right now, that's not the look I wanna see when I tell my child's father that I'm pregnant. I guess you're hoping I'mma have an abortion."

I didn't reply.

"I can't have another abortion." She shook her head, as tears started to stream down her face. "The guilt eats me up on the inside. After the last one, I promised myself I wasn't doing it no more."

The dramatics were heartfelt and all, but she was on some bullshit and I was on the bottom line. "Ay, where does this leave us?"

"Payne, do you want this baby?" She asked me straight-up.

"I can't answer that." I said honestly. "If you weren't sitting here telling me that you're pregnant? Hell no! I don't want no kids right now. But you're pregnant, and it could be mine. Do I want you to flush my shorty into Lake Michigan? Not really. So, I don't know how to answer your question."

***

I left Midori's spot about twenty minutes later, thinking that I really needed to talk to Justus. Only he wasn't around for me to talk to anymore. I needed to get my mind right. I jumped in the Denali and sped off. Ten minutes later, I pulled into the parking lot of *Classified*.

Joe must've had the night off, because the back-up bartender Corinne was working. I slid up to the bar.

She grinned at me. "What's up, green eyes? What're you drinking?"

"Grey Goose, and don't stop 'em 'til I tell you."

I couldn't get a shot down, before Unc showed up at the bar. "Nephew, what's going on?" He wrapped his arm around my shoulder.

Damn those security cameras. I thought to myself. I couldn't even sneak in, have a few shots and sneak out. I needed to find a new place to drink. "Nothing." I lied, and threw back the first shot.

Corinne got ready to refill me, but I saw Unc give her the high-sign not to. She nodded her understanding, and went to wait on the next customer.

"Come on, Unc. Why won't you let a brother have a drink? I gotta lot on my mind. I need to decompress."

"In the office, Nephew."

He didn't wait to see if I was gonna follow. He just started walking towards his office. Of course, like anybody with good sense, I did what Unc expected me to do.

The two of us sat in his office in complete silence for about five minutes. Finally, he spoke.

"I know you've probably heard this a lot lately, but I know what you're going through. Trust me. If nobody else knows what kinds of thoughts are running through your mind right about now, I do."

"I know." I told him.

"Not only did I lose my closest road dog, I lost him because he was handling *my* business." He stood up and walked over to his personal liquor cabinet. I watched as he pulled out a bottle of Sea Wynde rum and grabbed two glasses. He filled each glass half way, then carried both back over to his desk. He handed me a glass of the amber colored liquor.

"Even after I had laid over ten members of the Franklin

Street Family to rest, they still wouldn't hand over Little Jimmy." He continued. "You know he's the one I still swear to this day pulled the trigger on my Angel. Well, I was pissed with the fact that they wouldn't hand him over, so I kept getting more and more aggressive. I guess I was a little too careless. Them boys in blue started watching me and my operation after that thirteenth body floated to the top of Lake Michigan, out at Oak Street Beach. It was Khalil who suggested that I lay low in Texas. You know your people are from Texas."

I nodded my head. I had spent practically every summer down there as a kid, visiting my paternal grandparents and other family members from my father's side.

"He had connections down there. Got me a nice house to crib in, found a good private school for Passion. He helped me get set up down there." He took a drink from his glass.

I knew all this. I had heard the stories a million times.

"Khalil promised that he would pick up where I left off. He would kill Little Jimmy for me, if it was the last thing he did. It was the last thing he did, Nephew. The night after they rocked Little Jimmy to sleep, five of my comrades were ambushed at a pool hall. They murdered four of them on the spot, but they kidnapped Khalil and tortured him for three days before they finally killed him."

I knew my father was murdered handling business, but I

never knew that he was actually settling Unc's debt. I couldn't imagine how torn up Unc must've felt, knowing my pops was killed doing him a solid.

"I thought about taking myself outta the game, Nephew." He said, as if he was reading my mind. "I didn't feel fit to live. I had put my closest homey on the path that led to his death. The pain of losing my guy was multiplied to the umpteenth power, because of the fact that he was doing *my* dirty work. I rounded up all of my remaining crew and told them to get their minds right. We were going to war. I couldn't fly up for the funeral; I had to drive from Texas, because I brought enough weapons with me to supply the Crips and Bloods into the next millennium. I spent all day at my Aunt Georgia's house, loading guns, making sure I had enough clips, going over details. I planned to go out in a blaze of glory, and I planned to take every last one of the motherfuckas who killed my guy with me."

I felt him. That was exactly how I felt about the cats who murdered Justus and Dex.

"It was Joe who stopped me from throwing my life away, Nephew. It was Joe who sat me down, and told me that it was too easy to let my pain lead me into certain death. He asked me who would raise Passion if I was gone. Who would look out for you, Justus, Nicki, Dorothy Jane, and those two beautiful sisters of yours? Who would make sure that Khalil was remembered as more than another nameless nigga who got gunned down in the streets? He told me that I didn't have the right to go crazy. I didn't have the right to give up on life. He cared enough to pull me back from the brink of recklessness. Now I'm doing the same for you, Nephew. I know you're hurting. I know it. But you gotta find a way to maintain. You gotta find a reason to keep going."

"Unc, my mind is somewhere rotating around Saturn right now." I sighed heavily. "My guy is dead. He's dead. I pushed the one female who showed me real love away, and now my jump-off is claiming that she's pregnant by me. What the hell reason do I have to maintain? Why can't I take a flying leap off the top of the Sear's Tower? That would have to be less fucked up than what I'm going through right now."

"Is the jump-off's kid really yours?"

"I went in raw." I shrugged my shoulders. "Maybe."

"Dorothy Jane came by here yesterday." He confided.

That shocked me. My grandmother wasn't the type to frequent lounges. She was the type who frequented church services. "Word?"

"Yeah. She's worried about you. She thinks that instead of dealing with Justus' death and coming out of it, you're slipping further and further into depression. She thinks she's losing you to your grief. She says that you don't even come by and check on her anymore."

I didn't respond. I couldn't debate the truth. Besides, I really didn't have an excuse as to why I was playing my grandmother off. I just wasn't up to dealing with family commitments.

"You can't stop loving people, Nephew. I know it's tempting to try to distance yourself from emotional connections. I know it's tempting to build a wall around your heart so you won't have to experience this type of pain again, but you can't do that. You gotta let yourself feel, Man. If you don't let yourself feel the bad, you won't let yourself feel the good, either. And you need to feel the good, Nasir."

"How do I make that happen?" I questioned.

He smiled at me. "Start by going to see your grandmother. She loves you, and she's worried about you."

I nodded weakly.

"As far as your girl...call her and see where her head is. Real men make moves, they don't sit around waiting for things to happen. With the jump-off, be 'cautiously convinced' that this is your kid. Support her as much as is called for, then when the baby comes out...demand a blood test. I raised you myself, so I know if this child is yours, you'll do right by it. If it's not, tell her to kick rocks and continue doing you." He paused. "What's going on with your business, Nephew? Are you letting that slip, too?"

"Nah, I'm in the studio like, every other day."

He eyed me. "I'm talking about your other business."

I couldn't lie to him. "Yeah, I got houses that are ready to be sold that I haven't put on the market. I haven't done anything since…I don't know when." I admitted. "I thought Patience and Izz would pick up the slack, but that ain't happening."

"Nephew, always remember this: the best person to handle your business is *you*. Don't hand off to anybody else, what you should be doing for self. If *Exit Strategy* is not where it should be…get it back on track."

I was quiet.

Unc cocked his head to the side and took a good look at me. "What's the problem? The real problem."

"I never did deals without Justus right there by my side. The thought of doing deals without him, reminds me that he ain't here to do them with me." I knew my thinking was crazy, but I felt like I was going crazy.

Unc nodded like he understood me, though. "I get you. But let me be real, business deals wait for no man. If your buyers find new houses to purchase, they ain't coming back to you when you get your act together. You need to make a decision. Either you're in business, or you're out of business. Which is it?"

"I'm in."

"Then you know what you need to do."

I took a sip of my liquor and nodded my head. Unc was right.

He sighed. "Elizabeth stopped through here a few days after the funeral."

Elizabeth was Justus' mother.

"She had this look on her face...I knew what it was as soon as I saw that look. She reminded me of a couple of favors James had done for me. She didn't have to do all that, though. Justus was my nephew. My family means everything to me. I'll protect them at all cost or I'll avenge them at all cost."

"We got you." I promised him.

"That situation's been handled?"

"Yeah, the damage is done on that one." I assured him. "We took care of that a few months ago. Not long after the funeral."

"Good. Good."

I swallowed the last of my rum, and sat the glass down on Unc's desk. "I'm outta here."

He stood up, and walked over to me. He embraced me and hugged me more tightly than he ever had. "Just remember this, Nephew. Justus is dead. You're not. You're still on earth; that means there's still work for you to do. Don't clock out until all of your work is done."

***

The following afternoon, I stopped by my grandmother's spot. I parked behind her white Volvo S80, and got out of my Denali. Instead of using my key to open her front door, I rang the bell. Dorothy Jane grinned when she saw me at her door.

"Do I know you?" She asked, still grinning.

"I hope so." I responded.

She opened the screen and pulled me into her arms. "Nasir, I know you're a man, so you look at the world differently than I do. I just want to make sure you understand this one thing, Grandson. If you ever disappear like this again, I will break my foot off in your behind. Do I make myself clear?"

"Yes ma'am."

"Get in here, boy." She told me.

Inside the house, I sat down at the kitchen island. Grandma handed me a glass of sweet tea, and a bowl of piping hot seafood gumbo, fresh off of stove.

"Talk to me, Nasir." She said watching me from where she stood at the sink.

I wanted to laugh, because when I was little she would use food to bribe me into telling her my business. I took a spoonful of gumbo into my mouth to buy myself some time. The spicy broth tasted like perfection.

"Why haven't I heard from you? I've been worried sick. Do you know I actually went by Chad's lounge looking for you?"

"Yeah, he told me."

"I'm waiting for an answer."

"Grandma, it's been mad drama." I looked up at her. Our identical green eyes met. "Can you stall me out this time, if I promise never to do it again?"

"Nasir."

"Come on, Grandma. I was on something. I don't know what else to say. I was in my own little world. I needed to get my mind right."

She sighed.

I took another spoonful of gumbo. "You might be a great-grandmother in a coupla months."

"The heavens and the earth." She muttered. "Who's this girl that might make me a great-grandmother?"

"Just some chick."

"Just some chick?" She repeated, looking at me like she was disgusted. "And you might've gotten her pregnant? Does this *chick* have a name?"

"Midori."

"Will I get to meet this Midori soon, or will I have to wait for the baby shower?"

I cracked a smile. "Actually, you probably won't meet her until I get a blood test. Like I said, you *might* be a great-grandmother."

"Nasir Payne, sometimes you remind me too much of Khalil Payne. And sometimes you remind me too much of Nicole Howse. How those two tortured souls ended up getting together and creating life only the good Lord knows. But God is in His holy temple, so I know everything will work out fine."

I stood up, and walked the empty bowl over to the sink.

"Where are you going? You just got here."

"I know." I said, stealing a kiss from her cheek. "But I gotta ride. I got business to handle."

"Nasir, be careful out there. Please. Okay?"

"Okay." I assured her.

"I love you, and you know I'm still dealing with losing my Justus. There's no way I can deal with losing you, too."

"I'm not going anywhere, Grandma."

"You better not."

***

A few days later I went out to breakfast with Patience. I still wasn't sure if dude was dirty or not, but I wanted to keep things as normal as possible with him, to see if I could get a read.

"Dude, I've been trying to be patient, cuz I know you're going through a thing with J and Dex getting murked." He told me as we waited for our food. "But we need to figure out what we're gonna do with these cribs we got. They're sitting around collecting dust and they need to be making us some dough."

I couldn't argue the truth. It was time to get back to business. "Yeah, I know." I assured him. "I hollered at Tommy yesterday about the property on 103rd."

Tommy was our contractor.

"What did he say?"

"They're tied up with a job, so they can't get to it for another few weeks. But it shouldn't take too long for them to get it ready. I talked to the lawyer's office this morning. The closing for the property in Riverdale is set. We're closing on February 4th."

"That's the Monday after next, right?"

I nodded.

"What's my cut looking like?" He asked me.

I raised my eyes, so that they made contact with his. "I don't know off the top of my head, P. I gotta look at the paperwork and see what's what."

"So, you're going into the office today?"

The mention of the office chilled me. I hadn't stepped foot in that office since a few days before we left for Las Vegas. "I don't know. Maybe."

He sighed. "Check it out, Payne. Why don't we hit the real estate broker up and ask her to find us new office space? It's real obvious that going into *Exit Strategy* ain't happening for you right now."

"What makes you say that?"

He cocked his head to the side. "The fact you ain't been in the office since Dex and J died."

"How do you know I haven't been in the office?"

He hit me with the screw face. "Because I've been in the office, and I ain't seen you there. The same papers been sitting on your desk since September."

"Dude, if you been in the office, how come you haven't been making these deals happen? *Exit Strategy* ain't no one man show. If you knew things needed to be handled that weren't getting taken care of, you should've handled it."

"I would've, but Izz told me to fall back and wait on you." He explained.

The waitress showed up with our food. We were quiet as she sat the plates down in front of us.

"I don't know what's wrong with that cat." Patience said,

once the waitress was out of earshot. "But he's been actin' weird as hell lately."

"Who?"

"Izz. I don't know." Patience shook his head. "The vibe he's puttin' down right about now is *real* suspect."

"Straight up?" I asked. I was almost amused. Both of them had come to me with stories of the other one acting strange.

My cell phone rang before I could say more. I checked the screen. I didn't recognize the number that was displayed. 212 area code. New York City. "Hello?" I asked.

"Please hold the line for a call from Alixandra Harlow." The voice told me.

Alixandra Harlow? Who is that? I thought to myself. *Must be a wrong number*. I was about to end the call when a voice I recognized came on the line.

"Green Eyes." Her voice was a moan. "You still the hottest producer in Chicago, Sexy?"

I grinned at her flirtation. "No doubt. What's the deal, Licks? You still the hottest female in all of hip hop?"

"Those other chicks can't fuck wit' me." She paused. "Yo, I was so sorry to hear about J. I can't believe he got killed. He was so freakin' talented."

"I know. I know."

"I was looking forward to doing really big things with

him, but I guess it wasn't meant to be."

"Guess not."

"I didn't call to bring you down, though." She said. "I called to lift you up, Green Eyes. And to raise you up outta your current circumstances. It's time for the label to drop my next single. It's hot as hell…but it could be even hotter if you did the remix."

She caught me off guard with her offer. "Are you serious?"

"Yeah, I'm serious. I already booked the studio time at The Dope Spot."

The Dope Spot was the name of the *Spot Check Records* recording studio.

"Ay, just tell me when and I'm there."

"Wednesday, the 13th of February. 9:30pm, at The Dope Spot."

"February 13th." I repeated.

"That's right. I'mma have my assistant email your plane ticket, and hotel confirmations. What's ya real name, Green Eyes?"

"Nasir Payne. P-A-Y-N-E." I spelled.

"Nasir, like Nas, the rapper?

"Yep."

She took down my contact information. "If you need anything…don't hesitate to holla at my manager, Big Mike or my assistant, Jackie."

"Fo' Sho'."

"Bye Green Eyes."

"One, Licks."

"Licks?" Patience questioned when I ended the call.

I nodded my head.

"The one Justus did the video for?"

"Yep."

"You about to do a track for her?"

"Looks like." I said, and finally allowed myself to grin at the possibility.

Patience smiled at me, then gave me dap across the table. "Dog, I hope you kill it. Justus ain't get his chance to shine, but now it's your turn. Make it happen, my nigga."

Chapter Seventeen
The Light

Joya

Bruno Ricci was obviously a very busy man. KJ and I didn't get our meeting with him until March 10th. He flew us into LaGuardia Airport early on a Monday morning. A chauffeur driven car picked us up and delivered us to the *Ride or Die* offices in Midtown Manhattan.

Ricci's assistant ushered us into a tastefully decorated conference room. KJ and I sat there in silence for about twenty minutes. Finally, about twelve people filed into the room. The last one to enter was Bruno Ricci.

Ricci was, maybe 32 years old, or close to that. My initial impression was that I didn't like dude. Something about him rubbed me the wrong way. Physically, he was semi-handsome. He had that bi-racial look to him. His skin had those peachy undertones, and he had the facial features of an Anglo person. Thin lips, and a sharp nose.

He took a seat at the head of the table, then smiled at KJ. "KJ Jamison, it's good to finally meet you, Son."

"It's good to finally meet you, too." KJ assured him.

"I've watched the DVD of your performance at the

showcase about six times. I gotta be honest, every time I watch it I'm a little more impressed."

"Thank you. I'm glad to hear that."

"You gotta lot of personality and stage presence. You know how to connect with the crowd. I like that. I like that. It can take years for an artist to develop that skill. I'm impressed that you're coming through the door with it."

"Thank you. I work hard at what I do. I love hip hop. Every time my foot touches a stage, I'm in my element. I give it my all...one hundred percent."

"It shows, Playboy. I'm loving your whole style." He turned to me and the happy grin left his face. It was replaced by a stern frown. "Little Mama."

"Joya." I supplied.

He nodded. "My bad, Joya. I've gotta be real with you. I wasn't feeling you nearly as much as I was feeling KJ."

I braced myself for the rest of the critique.

"Your voice is…all right. You carried your notes well, but so do half of the choir members at my grandmother's church."

Chuckles went around the conference room.

"What I'm saying, is that you gotta bring more to the table than an "all right" voice. You've gotta bring the entire package. The vocals; the body; the swagger; the 'look'. I don't see that in you."

"Okay." I said easily. It was hard to hear the criticism, but music was KJ's dream, not mine. I was cool with the idea that Ricci didn't want to use me.

Apparently Ricci didn't appreciate the fact that I wasn't broken up over his words. He frowned even harder. "If I was gonna use you," he continued, "the first thing I would tell you, is to lose forty pounds."

That surprised me. I wasn't skinny or slim. I knew I was a thick chick, but I kept my body tight. I worked out almost daily, to make sure everything that was supposed to be flat was flat, and everything that was supposed to be round, was round. He didn't know what he was talking about. I weighed 153 pounds. If I lost forty, that would put me at a little over 100 pounds. I liked my curves. I wasn't trying to give them up for nobody.

"Interesting." I stated.

"Probably hit you off with some voice lessons, and get you a style makeover." He paused, waiting for my reaction.

I didn't give him one, so he continued the verbal assault. "And even then, the most you could ever do at *Ride or Die Records* would be background work. Maybe, maybe you could do a hook every now and again."

I smirked at him, and kept my tone neutral. "Thank you so much for the feedback, and for taking the time to meet with me." He had to be crazy if he thought I was going to sit there and chill after being insulted like that. I stood up from my chair. "Enjoy the rest of your day."

Everybody in the room watched in silence and disbelief as I picked up my Chloe bag from the table and pranced out of the room. I closed the door softly, even though I really wanted to slam it. As I walked towards the bank of elevators, I heard the conference room door open.

"Shorty Songbird! Shorty Songbird!" KJ called to me.

I stopped and waited for him to catch up.

When he finally got to me, he reached out and wiped away the one tear that was making its way down my face. "Ma, I don't know what the hell dude is talking about. You're the hotness in and outta Chicago. If Ricci can't see that, then he's blind as hell. Your vocals are bananas. That nigga don't know nothing about you. You're the business, Baby. And your body..." he shook his head, and licked his lips, "don't change a damn thing. Niggas *love* the curves you're holding."

His words made me smile. I thought it was cute that he wanted to make sure that I didn't get down on myself. I gave him a hug and kissed his chocolaty cheek. "Thanks KJ."

"You're welcome, but that's real talk. I think dude's real problem is that he wants to knock you, but he doesn't know how to come at a chick like you."

I didn't agree with KJ. Ricci was getting plenty of sex. I

was sure that there were groupie chicks lined up from New York to Miami waiting to let him get it. I doubted he would consider me unapproachable. "You would think he would know that insulting me is not the way to get the panties." I joked.

"You would think."

"I'm going home." I announced.

He looked alarmed. "Don't go home, Shorty. Go to the hotel, and chill out in your room for a little while. When I get through here, we can hang out in NYC together. You probably been here before."

"I have." I confirmed. I remembered I never told him that I was a flight attendant.

He shook his head. "I'm not surprised. You seem like the type that's traveled a lot. You've probably been a lot of places, and done a lot of stuff."

I laughed.

"Stay." He pleaded. "Show me how to do it big in New York. Show me where to party. Kick it with me."

The offer was tempting. KJ was a genuinely nice guy and I really liked him. Under normal circumstances, I would've stayed and partied like a rock star. New York was one of my favorite cities. But at that moment, all I wanted to do was go back to Chicago. "I can't. I took off work for this. If I leave now, I might have a chance of picking those hours back up tomorrow."

He looked disappointed. "You're leaving me here by myself?"

"I'm leaving you here with your new record label. They've got you. They'll look out."

"Gimme a hug, Shorty." He finally conceded. He pulled me into his arms. Before I realized what was happening, he brought his lips down on top of mine. His kiss was gentle and sweet. It was one of those kisses that put butterflies in a girl's stomach. But my butterflies remained in neutral.

Damn, Nasir! I thought to myself. *Am I ever gonna get over you?*

***

Chantelle picked me up from Midway Airport at 6:56 that night. On the way to my house, I told her what happened to me in Manhattan.

"Fake ass Italian Bastard." She muttered. "I saw his parents on television. His momma is black, and his daddy looks Spanish. He knows good and damn well that his real name ain't no Bruno Ricci. Bastard's name is probably MarShawn Perez or something like that."

"I don't care what his real name is. All I know is that he didn't have to show his ass with me like that."

"I know that's right." She agreed.

We were both silent for a while.

"Since you're already pissed and in a bad mood, here's some more messed up news. Payne has a baby on the way."

Now, why would this heifer think that this was the time to tell me that? I asked myself. "Chan, how could you possibly think that I needed to hear that today…of all days? Are you trying to make me go postal?"

"I'm sorry. I thought since you were already upset…"

"What? Pile some more bull on top? Come on, Girl. You know I'm still trying to get over the boy. The last thing I wanna hear is something about him having a baby on the way."

"My bad. Well, don't think about that. Think about our trip to Phoenix."

Chantelle, Bubbles, Nia and I were going to a spa in Phoenix to celebrate Chantelle's 25th birthday.

"It's only three weeks away." She said happily.

I didn't comment. I went back to the subject of Nasir. "It wasn't the chick from the salon that he got pregnant, was it?" I hoped and prayed it wasn't her.

"Who Tashera? Nah, it's not her."

"Is he in a relationship with the girl?"

She shook her head. "Nope, she's a jump-off. I guess the condom broke or something."

I let that sink in.

"And you know he's gettin' a record deal." She continued. "Licks Harlow's usin' him on the remix to her new single. Girl, he's been flyin' back and forth to Miami to record it."

I thought back to when we met her in Las Vegas. I remembered the way she was all on his nuts. She was practically offering him the panties right there in the club. I wondered if he was hitting that.

"We were all in the studio the night before last. Me, Izz, Nia, Patience, and Bubbles. He let us hear a little bit of the track." She took her hands off of the steering wheel and threw them in the air. "It was ridiculous! It was soooo hot. When that song drops…I'm tellin' you right now, Payne is gonna be the new shit…for real."

Nasir was about to realize his dream. Music obviously wasn't the path for me, but I was happy for him. Even though he was a messed up boyfriend, I had to admit that dude had talent as a producer.

"I always knew Payne would be successful. He's the hottest producer ever." I said.

She cut her eyes at me. "Even better than Northern McKinley?"

"Northern's a dope producer, don't get me wrong. He's dope. But Northern works hard at it. The same things that Northern slaves over, come naturally to Payne. Most producers can't even get close to dude."

***

The first Friday in April, I was on Eastern Airlines flight #1031 with Chantelle; Bubbles and Nia. We were headed to Phoenix, Arizona. I was actually looking forward to having a "girls gone wild" vacation at the Copperwynd Resort and Spa.

When we checked into the two bedroom villa, we couldn't help being impressed by the large space. It was so beautifully decorated in warm and inviting neutral colors. I did a quick run-through of the spot, then I was ready to get my massage.

I practically melted as the warm stones, and scent of the aromatherapy relaxed my over-worked muscles. Chantelle was in the massage room with me. She was moaning and groaning as Raul, the massage therapist, kneaded and rubbed her skin. I wanted her to shut up. She was killing my buzz, but I was too relaxed to even open my mouth and fuss at her.

Instead, I squeezed my eyes more tightly shut and blocked her out.

It was the most relaxed I had felt in months. Ever since my break-up with Nasir, it seemed like I was always stressed. I figured I was missing that good loving that used to keep my nerves calm.

Thoughts of Nasir flooded my brain. For the first time in a long time, I didn't fight them. I let them come. Under the influence of the hot stones and the sweet fragrance of jasmine, I admitted to myself that I was still in love with dude. And that I missed him. Not just his kisses or his sex. I missed his friendship. I missed the times that we used to hang out together and chill. I missed the conversations. The companionship.

I sighed to myself. I couldn't understand why love was so freaking unfair. Two different times I had tried to love men and give them my all, and two times they had kicked me in the ass and sent me on my way. The next time, I promised myself that I wouldn't love so easily. The next cat who stepped up to the plate was going to have to put in overtime to convince me that he was worthy of holding my heart.

***

Later that night, after a relaxing day of spa treatments, shopping and dinner, the four of us were on the balcony of the villa drinking Perrier Jouet and talking.

"I've had a one night stand." Bubbles stated.

We were playing Truth and Consequences. It was a drinking game with simple rules. Each player would have an opportunity to make a true statement. If the statement was true for the other players, they could chill. If the statement was untrue for the other players, they had to pay the consequences and take a drink.

I was the only one to take a drink. I wasn't surprised.

"Damn, Joy!" Bubbles said loudly. "How boring are you?"

I giggled.

"You know Joy is too siddity to give up that coochie on a one night stand." Chantelle stated. "Nia, I'm surprised you had a one night stand."

As often as Nia was trying to hock her sex toys and accessories, I wasn't surprised at all.

"Once." Nia clarified. "How many times have you had one?"

"Girl, Izz was a one-night stand."

"What, the night ain't over yet?" Bubbles joked.

"Apparently not. I don't know what happened." Chantelle

continued. "I gave him the candie, and I couldn't shake him after that."

I laughed and took another swallow of liquor. I was overly relaxed from the massage and half-drunk from the champagne.

"Your turn, Chan." Bubbles told her.

"Okay. Uhm, I've had sex in public." She said.

Again, I was the only one to drink.

"We need to stop, because Joy is gonna be drunk and the rest of us are gonna be sober." Bubbles said. "What is wrong with you, Joy? How did you keep Payne interested?"

I shrugged my shoulders. "I guess he really loved me."

"Still does." Nia assured me.

"Yes, he does. Dude is straight twisted without you in his life. He walks around lookin' all pitiful." Chantelle added.

"Nia, it's your turn." I said. I couldn't get caught up in the idea that Nasir still had feelings for me. I had to go by what he showed me, and what he showed me was that he didn't want me. Anything else was a vicious rumor.

"I've never had sex with any of my friends' men." Nia said.

Bubbles drank alone. "What? Please. If a dude gotta big dick, I'm on him. I don't give a damn who he belongs to. I'm like Snoop Dogg, I don't love these hoes."

"Moving on." I said, since it was my turn. "I've had sex

with a professional athlete."

Nia and Chantelle both drank. I fully expected Bubbles to drink, too. Apparently Chantelle did as well.

"Bubbles, you slept with a professional athlete?" Chantelle questioned her sister. "When? Who?"

Bubbles semi-smirked. "I'd rather not say."

"You'd rather not say?" Chantelle repeated. "I don't think so. You're about to tell me. Who was it? Derrick Rose? Dwyane Wade? Kobe?"

"Nah. You're crazy. If I had slept with any of them, I woulda told everybody I know."

I watched her demeanor, and I knew exactly who she had slept with. "It was Monte."

Chantelle's mouth fell open. "It wasn't Monte."

The expression on my face didn't change. I knew it was Monte. Somehow, I just knew.

"It wasn't Monte. You didn't do that? Did you, Bub?" Chantelle looked really upset.

"It was after they broke up." Bubbles turned to me. "It was after y'all broke up, Joy."

Anger washed over me like a quick moving tide. "Sure it was, Bitch." I said, and threw the rest of my champagne in her face. I sat the glass down and stood up from the table.

"Who is Monte?" Nia asked.

Nobody paid her any attention.

I walked into the villa. Chantelle was right behind me. "Joy!"

I turned around and looked at her. "Chan, leave it alone."

"Joy, she's my sister."

Bubbles came bursting into the villa screaming. "Why'd you throw champagne in my face?"

"Shut up talking to me, Bubbles." I said, and walked away again.

Chantelle continued to follow me. So did Bubbles.

"I told you it was after y'all were broke up." Bubbles reiterated.

"If she says another word to me, I swear I'mma fuck her up." I warned Chantelle, and then headed for the bedroom that I was supposed to share with Nia.

Chantelle stopped walking and turned on her younger sister. "Bubbles, you were wrong. You were wrong and you know it. You messed up. You gotta take your lumps on this one. You were screwin' Joy's man. Go sit down somewhere."

I was zipping my luggage by the time Chantelle came into the bedroom.

"Joy, please don't go." She sighed. "I know Bubbles was wrong. I know she was. If you wanna fight her, I'll stay out of it…as long as you don't use your Krav Maga on her. I mean, she is still my sister."

"I don't care about Monte." I said honestly. "So, it's not about that. It's the principle. Bubbles looks in my face day in, day out. She laughs and grins with me. And she knew all along that she had sex with Monte. How grimy is that? I can't honor that, Chan. I can't kick it with her for the rest of the weekend like its all good. I can't do it."

"I get so sick of Bubbles pulling this type of shit. She's forever sleeping with somebody else's man."

I cut my eyes at her. "You better keep your eyes on Izz."

She raised her left eyebrow. "I would beat her ass. She knows better."

"You heard what she said. If a dude has a big dick, she's on him. So, if Izz is holdin'…" I let my sentence trail off.

"Let's call the front desk and see if they have another room. Don't go home. You still have two spa services to get tomorrow." She pleaded. "They're already paid for."

"You and Nia each take one. Get a bikini wax or something." I teased.

"Don't go, Boo. I can't apologize for my sister's actions, but I'm sorry. Please stay."

"You don't have to be sorry. It is what it is. But I gotta go. I can't look at Bubbles right now. I feel like I'mma hurt her. I'll text you when I get to Chicago."

"Tell me what to say so you won't go, Joy. It's my birthday. My best friend and my sister are pissed with each other. Y'all are ruining my entire vacation."

I hugged her. "I'm sorry, Chan. I'm really sorry. Don't let this ruin your vacation. Have fun. Enjoy your massages. Enjoy being pampered. Have a good time."

Nia walked into the room. "So, you're leaving?"

"Yeah, I can't do Bubbles right now."

"I don't blame you." Nia said. "I would've already whipped her ass."

I gave both Nia and Chantelle hugs. "Have fun, ladies."

***

The resort arranged for a car to take me to the airport. By the time I arrived at Sky Harbor International, it was 10:15pm. My flight was scheduled to leave at 11:30. Once I made it through security and got to my boarding gate, I had a few minutes to chill.

I sat down and slipped my headphones into my ears. I couldn't concentrate on the music coming from my phone, though. A single thought kept running through my mind. I couldn't shake it. It was really bothering with me. Finally, I swiped the screen of my cell phone and dialed his number. It was funny how the brain worked. I hadn't dialed his number in about six months, but my fingers automatically went to the digits.

It was after midnight in his time zone, but he sounded wide awake when he answered. "Joya?"

I sighed heavily. "Yeah, it's me. Look Payne, I didn't call you to talk. I need to ask you a question."

"What's up?"

"Did you ever have sex with Bubbles?"

"What?" He was totally confused.

I repeated myself. "Did you ever have sex with Bubbles?"

"Chantelle's sister, Bubbles?"

"Yeah. Chantelle's sister, Bubbles."

"Hell no! Why?"

Relief flooded my very being. "No reason. I just needed to know. Bye" I ended the call. My phone rang right back. I knew it was him. "Yeah?"

"Ma, what's the deal? Why would you call me and ask me something like that?"

Since I had called him and involved him, I figured the least I could do was tell him the biz. "Tonight I found out that Bubbles was screwing Monte while I was with him."

"Damn! Straight up?"

"Yeah."

"That could've gotten her murked." He paused. "You ain't hit her with the Krav Maga, did you?"

I couldn't help chuckling. "Nah, I kept my head."

Neither of us spoke for a few seconds. I got ready to end the call, but his voice came across the line. "You hit me up, cuz you thought I would do you as dirty as dude did you? How many times do I have to tell you that I ain't dude? I would never do the shit he did to hurt you."

"Nah Payne, you hurt me in other ways." I took a deep breath. "I gotta go."

"Beautiful, you gotta know that…"

I cut him off. "I really have to go. I'm about to board my plane."

"Ay Ma."

"Yeah?"

"I'mma call you back."

"Okay." I agreed. "Call me tomorrow."

"Cool."

***

The next morning, the ringing of my cell phone woke me up. "Hello?" I asked groggily.

"Wake up, Shorty Songbird."

I didn't recognize the voice, but only one person insisted on calling me Shorty Songbird. "KJ?"

"That's right. And your presence is required in NYC on Monday."

"My presence is required for what? What are you talking about?"

"You're back on the track."

That news totally woke me up. "How did that happen? I thought Bruno Ricci hated me."

"Apparently the focus groups loved you. Plus, the rep who came to see us at *Kacey's*? He's Ricci's brother, Vic. He loved you." He paused. "Ricci wasn't trying to hear that, though. He brought in like eight different chicks to do the hook. I'm talking people you know, Ma. Big names. And none of them could make it as hot as you made it."

"You gotta be lying." I told him.

"Hell no. I'm straight up. He called me in for a private meetin' yesterday. You shoulda seen how much he hated having to come to me on the humble. His face was all twisted up. He asked me if I knew how to get in touch with you, and if I thought you would still be interested in doing the project."

"What did you tell him?"

"I told him that you were a busy female. That you have projects lined up, so he would probably have to pay outta the ass to get you."

"You told him that, for real?" I asked in disbelief.

"Yeah, I did. You know how I feel about your vocal skills. I ain't appreciate the way he tried to play you."

"What did he say?"

"He told me to let him worry about the money. Said all he needed me to do was get you here on Monday. Can you do it?"

I was hesitant. After the way Ricci had acted with me, I wasn't trying to do him any favors. But screwing him meant screwing KJ, and I wasn't trying to do that, either. "For Ricci? Definitely not. For you, KJ? Yeah, I'll do it. Gimme the info."

After KJ gave me the info, I hung up the phone. I laid in bed and smiled to myself. The previous night had been seriously jacked, but things were already starting to look up for me. My cell phone rang. I picked it up, and looked at the screen. I recognized Nasir's cell number. Butterflies started running around inside my stomach. "Hello?"

Without any type of standard greeting or pleasantries, Nasir started talking. "Ay Beautiful, I wanna link up with you. Talk face to face. Let's grab lunch or something."

"Okay." I said slowly. "Today?"

"I can't do it today. I'm in the office, and it's crazy. I'm thinking next week. Monday."

"I'm in New York on Monday."

"Yeah, congratulations. I heard you were collaborating with KJ and Northern."

"Thanks. Congratulations to you, too. I hear you're doing

big things with Licks Harlow."

"I'm cooling." He was modest. "How long are you in New York?"

"I don't know. Maybe a few days. Wanna try for Thursday?"

"I can't. I'm in Atlanta on Thursday. I'm looking at doing a few things for this group that Cameron Chambers is developing."

"Damn, Superstar." I teased.

"It's not like that. It's not like that." He chuckled. Then he sighed. "I really wanna see you, Joya."

"Well, text me the week after next. Maybe if we're both free we can connect."

"I can't wait that long."

"What do you wanna do, Payne?"

"Why do you keep calling me that?"

"What?" I asked.

"Payne."

"Isn't that your name?"

"You know what I mean." He told me.

"Real talk?"

"Yeah, gimme real talk, Joy."

"Because it helps me to keep things in the right perspective. I let Nasir into my heart. Payne is just an acquaintance."

He didn't speak for a long while. For a second, I wondered if we had lost our connection.

"I guess I deserve that one." He said finally.

I didn't comment one way or the other. "Text me in a week or two. Maybe we can link up."

"Later Joya."

"Hey Payne." I called, before he hung up.

"What's up?"

"Congratulations on the baby. I heard you're about to be a father."

"Thanks." He said dryly. "Which member of the 'big mouth' committee told you about that?"

"One guess."

"Chantelle."

"Bye." I said and hung up laughing.

***

Nasir texted me a couple of times after that. We never could get our schedules to jibe, so we never linked up.

Chapter Eighteen
If I Ruled The World

Payne

Once I got put on in the music industry, my days and nights were not my own. I was always on the run, laying tracks in this studio or that studio. As soon as my name started to blow, I planned to make the artists come to me, instead of the other way around. They would fly into Chicago, and record their tracks at Payne Killer Studios. I already had my real estate broker, Angela looking for a space for me. But until then, I put in work. I flew back and forth between Chicago, New York, Miami, Houston, L.A., Atlanta, wherever. When I wasn't putting in work on the mix boards, I was putting in work at *Exit Strategy*. Israel and Patience still needed to eat. Houses still needed to be bought, flipped and sold for a profit.

The first weekend in June, I made it my business to be in Chicago for a couple of reasons. The most important was that it was Joya's birthday weekend. I was looking forward to seeing her and spending time with her. I hadn't laid eyes on her in almost nine months. The other reason I was in town was because it was the weekend of *Rock the Park*.

Rock the Park was an event sponsored by WKBC, the

hottest urban radio station in Chicago. It featured a free concert in Washington Park that showcased local talent. It was an annual event that was considered the official kick-off of summer vacation for the school kids. Rook, KJ, Joya and Trey were all performing.

***

WKBC had set up trailers for the talent behind the stage. With my VIP badge hanging from my neck, I headed up the stairs of Trey's trailer. When I got to the top stair, I spotted Joya. She was standing outside of KJ's trailer, talking to Chantelle and sipping on a bottle of water. She had on a strapless mini-dress and high heeled sandals. She looked good. She looked like she had lost some weight, too. She was sexy as hell.

I made my way back down the stairs of the trailer and walked over to where she and Chantelle were standing. I didn't wait for them to acknowledge or greet me. I pulled Joya into my arms. "What's up, Ma?" I asked, liking the way she felt pressed up against me. She still smelled the same. Like soft powder and sexiness. I fought the urge to let my hands rest on her phatty.

"What's good, Payne?" She hugged me back with the same intensity.

I ignored the fact that she called me Payne and played it through. "You Little Mama. Check you out. You're getting too skinny."

She was proud that I noticed the weight loss, I could tell by the grin on her face and by the way she ran her hand over her flattened belly. "Yep, I lost fifteen pounds, and seven inches."

I pulled her back into my arms, and whispered in her ear. "Don't lose no more weight. I don't give a shit what these industry dickheads say to you. Brothers like curves. Your body is perfect."

She smiled up at me. "Thanks."

"You're welcome." I released her.

"Hey to you, too, Payne." Chantelle said finally.

I laughed and gave her a brotherly hug. Arm around the shoulder. "What's the deal, Baby Girl? Your boy Rook ready to do this?"

"I guess so." She said, making the gum in her mouth pop loudly.

"He better be ready. He's up first, right?"

"Third." She held up three fingers.

The shine from Joya's wrist caught the sunlight and sparkled brightly in my eyes. I admired the piece of jewelry that blinded me. "Nice watch."

She looked down at the diamond and mother-of-pearl

Concord LaScala watch that I sent her for her birthday and smirked. "Thanks. A friend got it for me."

"Word? Your friend has good taste."

"Yeah, you have good taste, Payne. I really like the watch." She chuckled lightly. "Plus, I know how much you hated my other one."

"It was garbage, Shorty."

"I know. I know. Anyway, thank you for getting me this one."

"You're welcome. I'm glad you like it. I'm glad you're wearing it. I know how you feel about buying your own stuff."

She smiled for me, and then changed the subject. "Where are we partying tonight for my birthday?"

I wanted to tell her at my house in my bedroom, but I didn't think she would go for that. "Wherever. You got someplace in mind?"

"Not really."

"Wherever you say, Beautiful. It's your day."

"I'll think about it. In the meantime, I need to go do my pre-show thing. You know…warm up my vocal cords. I'll see you guys after the show."

Chantelle and I stood there, as Joya disappeared into the trailer. Once she was gone, Chantelle turned to me with a smirk. "Look at you, sweatin' over my girl and stuff."

"I'm all obvious, huh?"

"Pretty much." She assured me. "I knew you were still in love with her."

I didn't respond.

"You broke her heart."

"I know." It fucked me up that I broke Joya's heart. I never meant to go out like that. "You think I gotta chance at getting back in?"

"Truth be told, Joy's bananas over you. She tries to play hard, but I know her too well. If you play your cards right…you can get back in."

***

Rook took the stage around 5:45 that night. I didn't watch his performance, though. I didn't care about dude or his M.C. skills. I was standing on the side of KJ's trailer making conversation with the only female to ever hold my heart in her hands. "How you love *Ride or Die*?" I asked Joya.

She shook her head before she answered. "I don't like it at all. Bruno Ricci? Oh, he can't stand me."

That surprised me. "Why?"

"I don't know. Ever since the first day I met him, he's let it be known that I am not his first choice when it comes to singing."

"He must wanna tap that."

"That's the same thing KJ said."

I didn't respond. The thought that KJ got to be on the road with, and spend major time with my girl pissed me off. I didn't want to hear nothing about what dude thought.

"But I can't see that being it." She continued. "He can pull basically any chick he wants."

"You're not a man, Joy. You don't understand how our minds work."

"I know, right? Cuz sometimes, y'all don't even understand how your minds work." She teased.

"You and your flip-mouth. Damn girl, I've really missed you." I admitted.

"Payne…" She was cut short when the door to the trailer came open with a loud thud.

"Shorty Songbird, thought you were supposed to be saving your vocals cords for the stage." KJ addressed Joya, but the entire time he was talking; his eyes were locked on mine. He walked down the stairs and joined us at the bottom. "What's up, Payne?"

"What's up, KJ?" I gave him dap. "Congratulations on having that number one video."

He cheesed at me, and I fought the urge to give him a mouth shot. "You know it's all about my girl, stuntin' and profilin' in the video."

His girl? I thought to myself.

"Niggas love her, and even the females think she's cool. You can't lose when you're rollin' with a winner. Joya's a winner." He paused. "But I guess you know that from when you *used* to have her on your team."

He was begging to get his shit mushed in, but I kept my composure. "She's definitely a winner." I shot a wink to Joya.

She grinned at me.

"I'll get her back in the studio, again."

"No doubt." She assured me with a nod of her head.

"Don't make promises you can't keep." KJ told her. "I'mma make sure to keep you hemmed up."

"You're so selfish." She joked with him.

Damn, I wanted to murk dude, right there in the park. While I was thinking about not blasting him in the face, I heard shots pop off not too far from us.

"Gun shots." Joya said softly, looking at me.

I wanted to throw it in dude's face that she looked at me when it was time to get gangsta. Not at his whack-ass. I pulled my heat from my back holster and held it down at my side. I started to make my way around the side of the stage, so I could see what was happening.

The music screeched to a halt. Pandemonium. People were screaming, running, knocking each other down, and stepping on one another in an effort to avoid catching a stray bullet. Sirens were wailing loudly in the background. The police were starting to ensue on horseback and on foot.

I didn't know Joya was standing next to me until she spoke. "Oh my God!" She tapped my shoulder and pointed at the same time.

She was pointing to the stage. I looked in that direction. Rook was stretched out. Israel was on his knees leaning over him. I looked at Joya. My eyes were questioning hers. Was Rook shot? After everything we had been through with Justus and Dex, I didn't even want to think that Rook might have caught a slug. I took off running towards the stage. Being the type of female that she was, Joya took off after me. Weak ass KJ laid in the cut and yelled Joya's name, pleading for her to come back.

When I got to the stage, my worse fear was realized. Israel was crouched down, holding Rook's limp body to his. "Come on, Man." He told his younger brother. "Hold on, Dude. Hold on. Come on, Man."

I could hear the siren of the ambulance in the distance. I prayed it got there soon enough. I wasn't sure that our crew could handle another loss.

Half an hour later, Rook was dead. He died in Israel's arms in the ambulance on the way to the hospital.

***

Monday, June 9th was Joya's 25th birthday. After going through the tragedy with Rook, nobody felt much like partying. I took her out to dinner instead.

She dressed up for me. Black and white dress. Black and white sandals. Her long hair cascaded around her shoulders, just the way I liked it. When she climbed into the Denali, she lit it up with the scent that seemed to follow her.

"I swear to God. Ain't no other female on earth that smells as good as you. What the hell is that perfume you be wearing?"

"Maybe it's not perfume. Maybe it's the scent of me."

"Maybe it is." I conceded with a chuckle.

She got serious. "How's Izz doing?"

"Not too good. He's torn up over this."

"Awwww."

"Wipe that look off your face. This is your day. We're not gonna talk about Rook, or Izz, or death, or nothing like that. We'll deal with that later this week. Tonight is all about you."

***

Joya loved seafood, so I took her to Nick's Fishmarket.

"What does your contract with *Ride or Die* look like?" I asked. I sipped Courvoisier while we waited for our food.

"What do you mean?"

"I'm not trying to get in your business." I knew her well enough to know that she was as private as hell.

"Are you sure? Cuz that's what it sounds like."

"I'm saying, I'm trying to figure out when I can get you in the studio over at *Spot Check*."

She eyed me. "What? You wanna put me on a track with your girl, *Licks*?"

I heard the hate, but I played it through. "Why? You wanna do a track with Licks?" I questioned to mess with her. "I'll holla at her for you."

"I'll bet you will."

I cocked my head to the side. "What does that mean?" My ego puffed up at the thought that she was jealous of my relationship with Licks, even though there wasn't a damn thing going on between us. Licks wasn't my type. She could never be more than jump-off material to me.

"Whatever, Payne." She said dismissively.

"When can I get you in the studio?"

"When do you want me in the studio?"

"As soon as possible."

"As long as I'm on tour with KJ, I can't perform with any other artist. You would have to wait until the tour wraps up."

"When is that?"

"Who knows?" She shrugged her shoulders. "Ricci keeps adding dates. But when I know something for sure, I'll get at you. You can make me an offer."

I chuckled. "Oh, I gotta make you an offer, now? You're big time."

"*You're* big time. I'm little. But I am professional about mine. So, you have to make me a *written* offer. I'll present it to my lawyer, and we'll go from there."

"You gotta lawyer now, too? Damn, Money Maker. I can't hang." I joked.

"Whatever."

I changed the subject. "KJ really digs you, huh?"

"KJ's just a friend, Payne. Nothing's going on between us."

"I could tell at the concert that it's killing him. He wants it to be more than a friendly thing." I taunted.

"What about your baby's mom? How's she doing?"

"Aww hell naw! You took it there."

"Stay outta mine, and I'll stay outta yours." She gave me a pretty smile.

"Man Beautiful, you gotta know I missed you, because I even missed your flip ass mouth."

"I missed you, too." She admitted, then sighed. "But don't think that I'm not pissed at you for getting that chick pregnant. I can't believe you did that. What? Did you knock her the day after you told me to kick rocks?"

"Real talk? I know it's not an excuse, but I wasn't myself around that time."

"You're right, that's not an excuse, Payne."

"It was a humble. I made a mistake."

"A HUGE one!" She reminded me.

"Yeah, you're right. It was a big one. I made a lot of bad decisions around that time. I wish I could take most of them back."

We were both lost in our own thoughts for a few moments. Finally, I spoke. "How're you loving being on tour? Different city every night. Partying your ass off."

"I love singing, but honestly I hate being on tour. It's so…boring. It's like…from the bus, to the venue, to the after party, back to the bus. Every day it's the same old same."

"Ay, there's a way to get around everything. Have your lawyer put a clause in the next contract that you'll only do a limited number of shows. It must be bananas for you. Are you still flying five and six days a week?"

"Nah. I only fly on Monday, Tuesday and Wednesday now. Every Wednesday, I fly into whatever city we're performing in. Then it's the tour bus, the venue, the after party, back to the tour bus. Sunday night, I fly back into Chicago and get ready to do it all over again."

I twisted my face. "That's a hectic schedule. I don't wanna hear about you falling out from exhaustion."

"I know." She agreed. "But everybody's schedule is hectic. I can't complain. I have to suck it up and ride. I'm doing what a lot of people would love to do for a living."

"Yeah, a lot of people would love to do it for a living, but it doesn't seem like you love doing it."

"The money's good. The experience is cool." She said. "Once this tour is over, I'm gonna sit back and evaluate things. Decide if I really wanna pursue music seriously, or what."

***

After dinner, I drove Joya back to her house.

"Come upstairs and hang out with me for a minute." She suggested when I double parked in front of her building.

It didn't take much convincing for me to agree to her plan. I let Joya lead the way into her building. I walked behind her up the stairs, and watched every sway of her hips. By the time we made it to the first floor landing, I was on bone. I had to have her. While she was unlocking her door, I moved behind her. I pressed my pelvis into her ass, moved her long hair to the side, and kissed her neck gently. I kissed her neck and grinded her ass about three times before I heard the moan escape her lips that I was waiting for. I turned her around, backed her up against the door, licked her pink lips, and sucked the bottom one before I dipped my tongue inside. I loved that she kissed me back. She wrapped her arms around my neck and kissed me back. We kissed like that, until the keys that were in her hand dropped to the floor with a clank.

I backed up off of her.

"We should go inside." She told me.

I nodded easily. Inside was exactly where I wanted to be.

Once we were inside her condo, she knew what it was. We took it straight to her bedroom. My hands were all over her. I unzipped the sexy black and white dress, and let it fall to the floor. She stood there in her underwear and high heels. My dick was harder than granite. I gently pushed her on to the queen sized bed.

"I still have my shoes on."

I winked at her, as I removed her lacy black panties. "I know."

Once her panties were on the floor, I buried my face between her silky thighs. Joya was the only female on earth who could get me to put my mouth on her pussy. I loved the taste of her. She tasted like peaches and sweet cream. I tried to eat her inside out, while she held me hostage with her hands placed firmly on the back of my head. We went at it like that until she couldn't hold back any longer. She came in my mouth, shuddering and moaning happily.

I climbed up her body. "Where's the condoms?"

"Night stand." She responded, still panting.

Once I strapped up, I entered my baby gently. I remembered what she liked. Every hot spot, every pleasure point, everything…it all came back to me. I put in work. I tagged that ass like she had given me directions on how to operate her.

"Ooh yes." She moaned, holding her own legs up.

I tried not to smirk as I sped up my pace and went deeper with each thrust. She wrapped her legs around my mid-section and moaned my name while I laid in it. Swam in it. Tattooed it.

She was wilding out. Her body was responding to mine in ways it never had before. Her mouth was raw as hell. I couldn't believe Joya was talking dirty to me. Saying stuff I had never heard her say. Encouraging me. Begging me. She held me close. Pulled me to her. I was in deeper than I had ever been before.

"I'm about to cum, Nasir." She moaned.

I liked the sound of that. I increased the intensity of my pumps, but not the force. I pulled the strokes up with an arch in my back, so the dick hit her walls and tickled the bottom. Joya whined and whimpered as her orgasm overtook her.

But my girl wasn't selfish; she still managed to hit me off with enough of the figure eight to make me cum about two minutes after her. I let her rest for about ten minutes, then round two...backshots.

After four rounds, I was worn out. Joya had me busting nuts like a motherfucker.

"Damn." I mumbled. The condom slipped when I went to pull out. I grabbed it by the rim, hoping no sperm got left inside her.

Joya sat straight up. "Okay, that is not what I want to hear when I finish having sex. What's the matter?"

"Nothing." I assured her, and I tied the top of the condom.

"Please tell me the condom didn't break."

"Nah, the condom didn't break. It slipped when I was pulling out."

She looked panicked. "Did any sperm get inside of me?"

"Doubtful, Beautiful." I promised, then kissed her lips.

The panicked look remained plastered on her pretty face. "Are you sure, Nasir? I mean, seriously. Are you sure?"

I hated her facial expression. I hated to see her so pressed. "Ma, I caught it. I promise...I caught it." I got up from the bed and went to the bathroom to flush the sperm-filled condom.

***

Saturday dawned overcast and gloomy. The last thing on earth that I wanted to be doing was attending a funeral. Even though Rook and I hadn't been friends since we were shorties, I still hated to see him stretched out in a casket. The whole situation was crazy. It was the third funeral I had been to for one of my comrades in less than a year. I hoped and prayed that it would be the last one.

I got to the church about fifteen minutes into the wake. I sat down towards the back of New Beginning Covenant Fellowship. About ten minutes later, I knew I was going to have to step outside. Sitting in the church with that slow music playing, all those floral arrangements, and that casket took me right back to the place of pain and despair I felt when Justus was killed. I stood up and left the building. I walked out to the parking lot.

I watched a blue Lexus RX with tinted windows, sitting on chromed out 20s pull up. Surprisingly, Joya stepped out of it. She looked majorly delicious in a black dress that accented her every curve, and strappy stilettos. Her eyes were covered by dark glasses, but I could tell by her body language that she had either been crying or was on the verge of it.

I met her halfway between where she parked and the front door of the church. She came into my open arms and let me hold her. "What's the deal, Beautiful?"

Her body started to rack with sobs. "I'm getting so sick of this, Payne. I don't wanna sing at no more funerals for people I know. I don't know why Chan keeps volunteering me."

"I know. I know." I said, caressing her back. While I was holding her, my cell phone started to vibrate in my pants pocket. I took it out and checked the screen quickly. Midori's number was displayed. Typically, I would've blown her off, and continued to give all of my attention to Joya. But Midori was nine months pregnant and due any day. I had to take her call. "I gotta take this." I released Joya and took two steps away from her. "What's up, Midori?"

"Payne, my water broke. I'm on my way to the hospital." She sounded relatively calm.

"When did your water break?"

"About thirty minutes ago. My parents are takin' me to the hospital." She paused. "Are you gonna come through?"

"Yeah, I'm coming through." I didn't know for sure if the baby was mine or not, but I knew that I needed to get a paternity test. The way I looked at it, the sooner I had the test, the better. "What hospital are you going to?"

"Emmanuel. On 65th Street."

"Ay, I'm at Rook's…thing. I'll be through there as soon as I can."

"Okay."

When I ended the call, I noticed Joya watching me. "Is your girl in labor?" She asked with concern. She had stopped crying and fixed her face.

"Nah, my girl ain't in labor. My girl's standing right here."

"I'm not your girl, Payne." She shook her head.

"Yeah, you are."

"How do you figure?"

"You called me Nasir the other night."

"The other night, when?"

"When I was making your eyes roll back." I reminded her.

"Oh. Well, I'm liable to say anything when my eyes are rolling back. You should hear what I say to the other cats when I let them hit it."

I got real serious, real fast. "That shit ain't funny."

She hit me on the arm. "Stop cursing in front of the church."

"Stop lying in front of the church."

"I wasn't lying." She insisted. "I was playing."

"That wasn't funny."

She rolled her pretty brown eyes. "You know I ain't let nobody else hit it."

I couldn't help grinning at the memory of her behavior a

few nights earlier. "I know. That's why you were all crying and begging when I was in it."

"Shut up."

I changed the subject. "When did you get new wheels? A truck, too? Look at you, big baller. The recession ain't breaking your pockets, huh?"

"I got that truck as soon as my first check from *Ride or Die* cleared. I had a BMW before I got that little Civic. I was ready to get back to the luxurious side of life."

"KJ go with you to buy it?" I questioned.

"Yep. Northern, too."

I felt my blood start to boil. I hated them cats. "Why?"

"Stop tripping. They're my friends. They were doing me a favor."

I wanted to press the issue, but I didn't want it to turn into an argument. I dropped it. "How long are you in town? How long can I have you?" I asked instead.

"Not long. I'm flying out tonight."

"Damn."

"You've got enough stuff on your plate. If old girl is in labor, you're about to have to deal with that. You don't need me distracting you. You need to focus."

"You can't tell me what I need, Beautiful. I know what I need. It's standing right here in front of me."

"You always say the exact right thing, Payne." She told

me with a shake of her head. "If you could manage to *do* the right thing, you would have me…and you wouldn't be in this predicament with the pregnant jump-off."

***

After Rook's burial, I left the cemetery and rushed the hospital. When I walked into the room, Midori was in the bed, propped up on pillows, looking like she was in pain. She still smiled when she spotted me, though. "Payne."

"What's the deal, Little Mama?" I returned the smile.

"Nothin'. Ready to get this baby out."

"Well, do ya thing." I taunted.

She chuckled through the pain. "I wish."

"You straight? You look like you're hurtin'. Did they give you anything for the pain?"

"Yeah, they gave me something, but it didn't help. So, they gave me something else, and that only helped a little. I'm waiting on the anesthesiologist to give me an epidural. Until then, I'm just tryin' to maintain."

I nodded my head.

"Anyway, these are my parents, Mr. and Mrs. Anderson. Mom and Dad, this is Payne."

Midori's mother was a beautiful, petite, and delicate looking Japanese woman. She nodded and gave me a small smile as she shook my hand.

"Nasir." I told her.

"Nasir?" She repeated in confusion.

"Yes, that's my name."

"I thought your name was Payne." Boomed her father. He was a large, tall, dark skinned cat with the demeanor of a drill sergeant. "What is that, your street name? Your drug dealing name?"

He probably figured that his appearance, the questions and the big voice would intimidate me. They didn't.

"Payne is actually my last name. My first name is Nasir." I responded.

I caught the look of annoyance that Mrs. Anderson shot her daughter. She probably wondered why Midori was out in the world sexing somebody whose real name she didn't even know.

"Well Nasir," her father stated, "I hope you've got your check book ready...if you have one. Because once this blood test proves you're the father, Midori will be seeking financial assistance from you."

"If this blood test proves I'm the father, trust me, she won't have to *seek* it. I'll give it freely."

The next few hours went pretty much the same. Mrs. Anderson never spoke to me. She spoke in whispered tones to Midori. Mr. Anderson spent his time mean-mugging me, and trying to spook me. Finally around 7:00pm, the doctor came in to check Midori's progress.

"As you can see, Dr. Hampton, the child's father has finally arrived. We'll be needing a blood test ASAP to establish paternity." Mr. Anderson said.

The doctor looked over at me. She was a middle-aged black woman, with graying hair that touched her shoulders. She had a full face, and warm dark eyes. "Mr…"

"Payne." I supplied.

"Mr. Payne, why don't I send in somebody to get your blood drawn? Get things moving along with that." She turned to Midori and grinned. "Miss Anderson, you're ten centimeters dilated and 90% effaced. We're gonna get you prepped to start pushing."

I went out of the delivery room with a lab tech to have my blood drawn. When I stepped back into the room about twenty minutes later, all I saw was Midori's ass in the air. Her parents were front and center, encouraging her to "bear down", and "push the baby out." I laid in the cut and watched from a distance.

After about an hour of pushing, I heard Dr. Hampton say that Midori needed to give one more big push. That was when I went closer to the bed. Midori made an ugly face, grunted loudly, pushed hard, and out slid the little red baby. I stood there amazed.

The doctor was all smiles. So were Midori's parents. Midori looked like she had just gone ten rounds with Floyd Mayweather.

"It's a boy." Dr. Hampton announced, over the sound of the baby's loud wails. She plopped the mucky baby down right on Midori's chest. "Mr. Payne, did you want to cut the umbilical cord?"

I was hesitant. I really didn't want to be doing fatherly stuff, until I found out if I was the kid's father.

Mr. Anderson jumped on my hesitancy. "I'll do it."

That pissed me off. He wanted to hit me with the fee schedule for (possibly) getting his daughter pregnant, but he ain't wanna let me cut the damn umbilical cord. He had to be outta his mind. "I got it." I said. "I mean, it is my kid. Ain't that right, Mr. Anderson?"

If looks could kill, he would've murked me right in that delivery room. He stepped out of the way with attitude written all over his stance. At that point, I ain't even care if the baby was mine or not. I just didn't want him to get to cut the umbilical cord. I took the surgical scissors in my hand and separated the baby from Midori with one snip. Shorty looked into my eyes after I disconnected him and stopped crying. We stared at each other, while time stood still.

"Okay." Dr. Hampton said, taking the scissors from my hand and bringing me out of my trance. "We're going to get him cleaned up, and we'll bring him right to you, Mom."

Midori looked over at me. "You have a son, Payne."

I didn't know how to respond to that. The honest side of me wanted to tell her that *maybe* I had a son. I had to wait for the results of the paternity test. Instead, I kept quiet.

"What do you wanna name him?" She asked me. "Nasir Jr.?"

"Maybe." I shrugged my shoulders. "I gotta see."

"Payne." She sighed deeply. "He's your son. I put it on my momma."

I wanted to chuckle when Mrs. Anderson looked alarmed that Midori was putting it on her.

"He's your son." She insisted.

"You don't have to convince him, Dori." Mr. Anderson told his daughter. "That's what the blood test was for."

I hung around for a few more hours and watched Midori interact with the baby. She offered to let me hold him, but I decided against it. I didn't want to catch feelings for shorty if he wasn't mine. I needed to be able to walk away, if it turned out that some other cat had gotten her pregnant. I left the hospital around 2:00 in the morning. Midori was exhausted. She kept complaining that she didn't feel good and that she needed to get some sleep.

∗∗∗

Two days later, Israel hit my phone as I was leaving the crib to head to the hospital. He asked me to stop through the spot, so he could holler at me.

"What did Midori have?" He asked, as we each took seats on the sofa in his family room.

"A little boy."

He cut his eyes at me. "You think it's yours?"

"On the real?" I remembered how little man looked into my eyes when I cut the umbilical cord. It was like, he knew me. "Yeah, I think he's mine. I'm still waiting to see the results of that blood test, though."

He nodded. "I don't blame you. Hoes are scandalous."

We were both quiet for a few seconds.

"I got this text yesterday." He handed me his cell phone.

I read the words that were displayed on the screen. One sentence. *Your brother for my brother, Bitch!*

I shook my head. "Elliott's brother?"

"Gotta be."

"You got a name or anything on this cat?"

"Not yet, but I'll have it in a day or two."

"How do you think dude got your cell number?"

"I think that somebody on our team's probably double-agent. And when I find out who it is…I'mma kill 'em so slow. And this motherfucka right here, the one who texted

343

my phone…he's as good as dead."

"Gimme a week. Let me take care of this thing with Midori and the baby, and I got you."

"Nah." He shook his head. "This right here is personal. I got this one. You take care of your family business."

"You sure?" I was surprised.

"I'm positive. No disrespect, Son. You ain't focused right now. Your mind is probably in a hundred different places. And if this test comes back showin' that this kid is yours? Man, you're gonna have ya hands full."

He wasn't lying about that. I drank a beer with Izz and chilled out for a minute. I blew his spot around 4:00. I needed to get to the hospital. I was expecting to get the results from the paternity test back.

***

I got to Emmanuel Hospital around 4:40. I went up to the front desk and asked for a visitor's pass to see Midori Anderson. The clerk checked her book, then told me to have a seat, she would be with me in a minute. That minute turned into almost an hour. I went back up to the desk. While I was waiting for the clerk to acknowledge me, I spotted Dr. Hampton.

"Dr. Hampton." I said, stepping in front of her path to

keep her from walking passed me.

She looked at me. "Mr…"

"Payne." I reminded her. "I'm here to get the results of my paternity test and to see Midori Anderson."

"Mr. Payne, give me about ten minutes, and I'll talk to you about your results."

About thirty minutes later, I met with Dr. Hampton in a small room, off the waiting room area. She sat down and opened the chart she was holding. I sat down, and waited for her to tell me if I was a father or not.

"Okay Mr. Payne, the results from your blood work show," she read from the chart, "that with less than a one percent margin for error, you are the father of Midori Anderson's son."

She handed me the results, so that I could read them for myself. I didn't know how to feel. Relieved or shook. "I bet Midori can't wait to rub that in my face." I mumbled.

"About Miss Anderson."

Something about the tone in her voice made me look up from the test results.

"Early Sunday morning, Miss Anderson began experiencing complications that may either have been the result of an allergic reaction or the result of a severe bacterial infection. Her lungs collapsed. She went into heart failure three times and was resuscitated."

I felt like I couldn't grasp what the doctor was telling me. "Is she dead?" With all of the death that had seemed to surround me lately, that was all I needed to know.

"She's not dead, Mr. Payne."

I exhaled slowly.

"She is however, in a coma. And we do know that she has suffered brain damage, although we aren't certain how severe."

"So, basically you're telling me that Midori came in here a healthy and normal individual, and now she's a fuckin' vegetable? My son won't have a mother, because this hospital fucked up somewhere? Is that what you're telling me?" I asked, the anger apparent in my voice.

Dr. Hampton sat the clip board she was holding down. "Look, Mr. Payne. You need to calm down. I don't want to have to call security on you, but I will do it. Now, I know this is a lot to take in, but you're gonna have to get a hold of your emotions."

I wasn't trying to hear what she was talking about. "Where's Midori? I wanna see her." Although I considered Midori a jump-off, we still had a friendship thing happening. I respected her. She was a thorough hustler, and I liked her style. I didn't want to think of the chick that had pulled so many cold licks as a vegetable. She was the type of female whose mind was always working. Always plotting. How the hell could her mind be gone? In a matter of days? That didn't make sense.

"She has been moved from the maternity ward, down to intensive care. I will get you in to see her, but just for a few minutes." She paused. "And while I know you're concerned about your son's mother, let me let you in on something else you need to focus on. Your son is being released from this hospital tomorrow. Miss Anderson's parents fully plan on taking him home with them. Have a strategy, Mr. Payne."

***

I sat in Midori's hospital room for almost an hour, watching lines float across screens, and listening to machinery beep and buzz. I stared at her laid out in the bed looking so innocent, and pretty. She looked like she was asleep. I remembered the countless number of times she had looked the exact same way, right before I spanked her on the ass and told her to roll over and give me some.

I walked over to the bed, and picked up her hand. "Damn Midori. Damn! Come on, Shorty Gangsta. Don't do this to me. Little man needs his mother. He needs you." I pleaded with her for about ten minutes. She remained motionless and silent. Finally, I decided that I needed to blow the spot. I needed to head up to maternity ward, and check on my shorty.

Mr. and Mrs. Anderson were coming towards Midori's room as I was leaving it.

"What're you doing here?" Mr. Anderson asked me.

"I came to check on Midori."

At the mention of her daughter's name, Mrs. Anderson began to tear up.

"Well now that you've seen her, I expect that we won't see you here again."

"Expect this, Mr. Anderson. I got the results back from the blood test today, and shorty is my son. I'll be back tomorrow to take him home, until his mother is in a position to take care of him."

"You're not taking my grandson anywhere."

"Yeah, we'll see."

***

The next day, I was at the mall when it opened. I picked up an outfit for my son to wear home from the hospital. When I got to the hospital, the Andersons were already there. They were standing outside of the nursery.

"Why are you here?" Mr. Anderson asked me. "Didn't I tell you that you weren't taking my grandson anywhere?"

I ignored dude. A nurse came out of the nursery. "The

doctor needs to talk to the parents of Baby Boy Anderson."
She said.

"That would be us." Mr. Anderson insisted.

The nurse looked confused.

"I'm his father." I said. "His mother is down on the
second floor in intensive care."

She nodded her head. "Oh yes, we know. So, you're Mr.
Anderson?"

"I'm Mr. Anderson." Midori's father said quickly.

I was about three seconds from getting gangster with Mr.
Anderson. "I'm Mr. Payne." I told the nurse.

"Okay Mr. Payne, follow me."

"Uhm, can you tell me how I can go about naming my
son? I'm not cool with the thought of him being called
'Baby Boy Anderson'." I told the nurse as we walked down
the long hallway.

"Sure, Mr. Payne. Once you meet with the pediatrician,
I'll get that information from you."

"Thanks. Why am I meeting with the pediatrician?"

"Standard procedure." She assured me. She led me into
an empty room. "Dr. Kayler will be right in." She closed the
door.

I looked around the room. I had an ominous feeling about
the whole situation. The room they had me in, reminded me
of the rooms they took you in to tell you that your loved one

had died. I started getting nervous. I was pacing the floor. After about ten minutes, I was ready to get out of there. I grabbed the doorknob to exit, just as the doctor grabbed the doorknob to enter.

He was an older white guy. Looked like a former hippie, with long gray hair, wire rimmed glasses, tan Dockers pants and Reebox on his feet. "Mr. Payne?"

"Yeah. Just cut to the chase, is something wrong with my son?" I wouldn't have been surprised. They had turned Midori into a vegetable, maybe my son was suffering from the same damn thing. Maybe he was messed up, too.

"Hours after your son was born, we noticed that his skin was somewhat ashen, and he was having trouble feeding. We thought maybe he was having problems with his digestive track, so we ran some tests and…nothing. We ran more tests, and heard a little something funny with his heart."

"With his heart?"

He nodded. "We thought it was maybe a pronounced heart murmur. We did an x-ray and discovered that your son has what is known as Hypoplastic Left Heart Syndrome."

That was some scary shit to hear. "What does that mean?" The bottom line for me was life or death.

Dr. Kayler went on to explain the condition where the left side of my son's heart was under-developed in comparison to the right side of his heart. The condition was rare, about 1 in every 1000 babies, but not so rare that they didn't have the medical know how to work with the condition.

"This condition is effectively uncorrectable, but treatment options are available ranging from a heart transplant to surgery."

A heart transplant sounded far-fetched to me. As far as I knew, there wasn't a supply of baby's hearts sitting around waiting for somebody to need one. I asked him to tell me more about the surgery. He described a complex series of events that went completely over my head.

"Okay." I stopped him, because I felt like I was about to wild out. "I need like, a minute to get my mind right."

"Sure." He nodded. "We're going to be taking your son…"

"Justus." I provided. "His name is Justus."

"We'll be getting Justus set up in the neo-natal intensive care unit. But first, I'm going to have one of the nurses set you up in a family room, so you can spend some time with your son. It's my understanding that you haven't spent much time with him."

"I haven't spent any time with him." I admitted.

"I'll give you guys a few hours together, then I'll come and find you, and we'll discuss Justus' future."

The family room that the nurse set me up in was large,

about the size of a hotel room. She told me that it was usually reserved for mothers of multiples, but since they hadn't had any twin or triplet births, I could use it. Once I was alone, I dialed Dorothy Jane's number. I needed to talk to somebody who could keep a calm head. She was the first person that came to mind. I was surprised when Nicki answered her telephone. "Nicki?"

"Yeah."

"This is Nasir. I'm looking for Grandma."

"Your grandmother isn't here right now. She had a hair appointment." She paused. "What's wrong? You sound upset."

"I am kinda upset." I confessed. "I'm at the hospital, and I just found out that my son has a life threatening heart condition."

"So, the baby is yours?"

"Yeah."

"And he's not healthy? Oh no. What hospital are you at?"

"Emmanuel."

"Nasir, I'm gonna hang up and call the hair salon. Me and your grandmother will be there as soon as possible."

***

Not twenty minutes later, the door to the family room

opened. I assumed it was the nurse finally bringing my son in, but it was actually Nicki.

"Hey." I said.

She rushed over to me, and pulled me into her arms. She held me more tightly than I could ever remember her holding me. She showered my left cheek with kisses. "Nasir, everything's gonna be fine. The baby's gonna be fine. Please don't worry."

I hugged her back, because I appreciated her words. It was the first time I could ever remember her speaking words of encouragement over my life, and it meant a lot to me.

While we were hugging, the nurse pushed the hospital bassinette containing my son into the room. "Is somebody looking for Baby Boy Payne?" She asked with a smile.

"Yes. His grandmother is waiting to hold him." Nicki picked him up and cradled him to her chest. Then she looked over at me. "Oh my goodness, Nasir. How did you not know this baby was yours? Outside of the Chinese eyes, he looks exactly like you looked when you were born. This baby is a Payne."

"No doubt. I got the DNA test results to prove it." I joked.

"I should've been here. I wouldn't have needed no DNA test results. Where's his mother?"

I took a deep breath and told her that Midori was in the

intensive care unit. I explained that she had fallen into a coma and the doctors didn't seem to know what caused it.

"And they think that I'm about to let them operate on my grandson? They gotta be crazy. We're gettin' him outta this hospital. We're taking him to Children's. Wait until your grandmother gets here."

"Where is Grandma?"

"When I called the salon, they had just finished shampooing her. Her hair was wet and she had to wait for them to dry it. I didn't know how long that was gonna take, and I didn't want you up here by yourself. You need your family with you."

I semi-smiled. "Thanks."

"Nasir," she said, rocking my son gently. "I know I made some mistakes with you and your sisters. I know I did. But that didn't stop me from loving y'all. Even when I wasn't with you all, you all were always on my mind. I love you and your sisters. And now, I love Little Nasir, too."

"Justus." I corrected.

She looked over at me. "His name is Justus?"

I nodded. "Yep. Even though my guy never got to have shorties, his name will live on."

"But he looks just like you. His name should be Nasir."

"His middle name is Nasir."

"I think everybody should call him Nasir."

"Everybody doesn't even call me Nasir." I reminded her, then took my son from her arms and held him for the very first time. I looked down at him, while he looked up at me. "What's up, Little Payne?" I kissed his forehead. "It's me and you against the world, Shorty."

He stared at me like he knew what I was saying to him. I kissed his forehead again. I was a father. That was mind blowing as hell. I made a silent promise to myself that I would be the best father possible.

An hour later, Dorothy Jane came into the room, followed closely by Yasmeen and Torri.

"You know this is not my first choice for a hospital." Were the first words out of Dorothy Jane's mouth. As a retired nurse, she had an opinion about anything and everything dealing with the medical field.

"Hey Grandma." I said.

"Hey Baby." She gave me a quick hug and a kiss. "Let me wash my hands, then I'll be taking my great-grandson."

I looked around the room and realized that I was the only male in a family filled with females. I looked down at my son and shook my head. I hoped having so many women around him, would help him to understand them more than it had helped me.

When Dr. Kayler came into the room, Dorothy Jane grilled him. Having been a pediatric nurse for more than thirty years, she was familiar with Hypoplastic Left Heart Syndrome. She went over every aspect of the diagnosis, the treatment options, and the prognosis with him. And finally she asked him if there was another hospital where he operated, because there was no way on God's green earth that she was leaving her sickly great-grandson at Emmanuel Hospital. Two days later, my son was transferred to The Children's Hospital via ambulance. The cost to me was $3,300.00. I had to get back on the grind.

Chapter Nineteen
Crazy In Love

Joya

The last week of August rolled around, and the tour was finally winding down. I was happier than words could express. I was exhausted from keeping up my schedule of flying and performing. Plus, for the last three and a half weeks, I had been fighting a major summer cold.

"You ready to do this?" KJ asked walking into my dressing room.

I was balled up in the arm chair; covered by a blanket; patting my running nose with a tissue and sipping warm tea. It was the same position he had found me in before every show for the last week and a half. "What time do we go on?"

"11:45."

"I'll be ready." I promised, even though I felt like crap. Every muscle inn my body hurt, and I was so sleepy that I could barely keep my eyes opened.

"I hope you go to the doctor when this tour ends." He told me. "Something is wrong with you. You've been sick like this for a minute."

On the one hand I agreed with him. I had been sick for a minute. But on the other hand, when had I given my body time to get well? I was always on the move, never getting enough rest, never eating properly. "Yeah, I'm going to the doctor."

He sat down across from me on the sofa. "Ay, I heard that Ricci is gonna offer you a contract with *Ride or Die* after the tour. I heard he wants to make you a solo artist."

"Really?" I asked, not exactly sure how I felt about that.

"Yeah, but you didn't hear that from me."

I nodded.

"You think you might accept an offer from *Ride or Die*? I heard your guy Payne is doing major things at *Spot Check*. Think you might try to get on over there?"

"I don't know." I was honest. "At least Cameron Chambers has never insulted my singing, or told me that I needed to lose forty pounds."

"Yeah, Ricci fucked up with you when he insulted you at that first meeting. I wouldn't be surprised if you turned him down."

"I don't know." I repeated. "I would really have to think about it before I signed anything from Ricci."

He changed the subject. "Tomorrow's our last show. New York City, Baby. You partying with me after the show?"

"If I'm feeling any better? Yeah, I'm partying with you tomorrow."

"Good, cuz I'm gonna miss you when this tour ends, Ma. I'm used to looking into your pretty face almost every day, now."

I smiled slightly, but didn't respond verbally.

"I don't know, Joy. I'm feeling like when we get back to Chicago, me and you might need to spend some time together." He paused. "Outside of the craziness of the music industry thing. Just us two. One on one."

"KJ…" I began.

There were two quick taps at my door, then it opened. "Ay KJ, we need you, Man." Vibe said.

"In a minute." KJ told him.

"This can't wait, Playboy. We need you, now."

He sighed heavily. "Let me see what the problem is. I'll be right back."

Don't hurry! I thought to myself. While I liked KJ as a friend, and I had love for him, I wasn't feeling him romantically. As often as I had tried to tell my heart to get over Nasir, it hadn't listened to me. My heart still wanted him. And the truth of the matter was that there was very little for room for the next brother to slide in and change that.

***

We rolled into Manhattan a little after 5:00 in the

morning. I checked into my hotel room right at 6:00am. The ringing of the telephone woke me up around 10:00.

"Hello?" I asked groggily. I couldn't help thinking that early morning phone calls were one of the reasons that I couldn't shake the cold I was dealing with.

"Good morning, Joya. This is Susan." Susan was Bruno Ricci's assistant. She sounded too damn perky for it to be so early. "Mr. Ricci asked me to give you a call. He's expecting you in his office today at 1:15 sharp."

Thanks to the 'heads-up' from KJ, I knew that Ricci wanted to talk to me about joining the *Ride or Die* label. "Okay Susan. I'll see him then." I promised.

Three hours later, I waited for Ricci in Conference Room D. He strolled in around 1:35pm.

"Shorty Songbird." He said grinning at me.

It seemed like everyone on the label had taken to calling me that.

"How are you this afternoon?" He asked. "I hear you've been dealing with a cold."

"Yeah. But I'm going home in a few days. I'll go to the doctor and hopefully get this taken care of."

"Good, I want you at one hundred percent and healthy. I asked you here today to talk to you about your future with *Ride or Die Records.*"

"Okay." I nodded.

"You know, when I first saw you on the DVD, I wasn't too impressed with your skills."

"I remember."

"But watching you handle yourself on this tour with KJ has shown me a lot about you. The way you've been able to handle the grind of the tour schedule and work your full time job is bananas. You're gangsta for real. I love it. I like your style, Ma. I've always had major respect for hustle, and you've got more hustle than most of the people succeeding in this industry. I need you on my team. I wanna offer you a recording contract. I wanna sign you to *Ride or Die*."

"Wow." I pretended to be amazed. "You gotta be lying."

He was all smiles, believing that I was really surprised. "I'm dead serious, Shorty. You're the future of my label. I'm ready to put major stacks and major support staff behind you to blow you up."

"Wow." I repeated. "I'm trippin'. Give me a few minutes to take it all in."

"You can have more than a few minutes. You can have a few weeks. I'm sending you home after tonight's show. I want you to get well. Take some medicine, sleep late, rest your body, rest your voice. Do whatever you gotta do to get better. When you come back to New York, you're in the studio. I'm in the process of lining up some of the hottest producers and song writers for you."

I held up my hand. "Before you do all that, don't you think my lawyer should accept the contract?"

He shrugged his shoulders. "The contract is a done deal. It's a standard industry contract. There's nothing in it that your lawyer should object to."

"Okay." I said slowly. "But there are certain things that I need to make sure are included in any contract I sign."

"Like what?"

"Like, I want the opportunity to choose to work with certain producers. I wanna write some of my own material. I want writing credits listed on anything I pen. I don't wanna do anymore 800 city tours. I haven't been home in almost two months, and all I do now is sing the hook on a song. I don't wanna look up and realize that I haven't been home in over a *year*. I don't wanna be owned by a record label. I wanna be in control of my own life."

"Let me ask you this, do you wanna be in the music industry? Cuz you gotta long ass wish-list for somebody whose vocals ain't sold one single yet."

I could tell I had offended him, but it was whatever. I needed to be honest with him and with myself. "Yeah, I do wanna be in the music industry, but I don't wanna be a slave to it."

"Slaves didn't get paid. And I pay my artists well at *Ride or Die*. They don't want for anything."

I didn't respond.

"Look, should I send the contract or not, Joya? Make it funky."

I sighed and humbled myself. "Yes, please send it. I will have my lawyer look over it and we'll get back to you."

He slid an envelope across the table towards me. "Those are your plane tickets. Your flight home leaves at 9:25 tomorrow morning, so don't party too late tonight. Five weeks from tomorrow, I'll expect you back in New York, ready to work."

I nodded and picked up the envelope.

"Oh yeah, you might wanna contact your employer while you're at home. Give them your two week notice. You can't be in the studio and in the air. One job has to go."

***

Later that night, KJ and I had our final performance. He killed the microphone at *The Liquid Lounge* and brought everybody in the spot to their feet. After the show, everybody on the tour partied. I left them early, because I knew I had to be at LaGuardia to make my plane.

I climbed into the hotel bed and fell into a deep sleep

before my head hit the pillow. Four hours later, I awoke from a nightmare and sat straight up in the bed. My heart was pounding, as I reached for my cell phone on the nightstand. Once again, my fingers went straight to his number without me even thinking about it.

"Hello?" He sounded like I woke him up.

"Payne, its Joya."

"Ma, its 5:00 in the morning. Are you straight? What's the deal?"

"I had a nightmare." I confessed.

"You had a nightmare?" He repeated.

"Yeah, about you. I needed to hear your voice."

"I needed to hear your voice, too. Where the hell you been for the last two months? You went and changed your cell phone number and didn't tell a brother? What part of the game is that?" He was mad at me. I could tell by his tone.

"I didn't change my cell phone number. I lost my phone somewhere in Philly during a show. I had to get a new one, and a new number."

"Why the hell you ain't call me and give me the new number?"

"I'm sorry. Every time I thought about calling to give it you, I would think about your situation with the new baby, and I didn't wanna be in your space. I wanted you to have time to bond with your shorty."

He sighed heavily. "I wish you woulda called me, Beautiful. I needed you…on the real. You don't even know what I've been going through since you left."

I listened while he told me the story of how after his son was born, the baby's mother went into a coma. He told me how she was still in a coma more than eight weeks later. He told me about his son's heart condition and how his son had already endured two surgeries. He told me that the baby had never left the hospital in eight weeks of life. He told me how the baby's other grandparents were giving him major drama on every issue concerning the baby. After hearing his story, I felt real selfish for not calling him in two months.

And at the same time, warm feelings for him flooded my heart. I was impressed by the way he had stepped up and accepted responsibility for his son against all the challenges that had presented themselves. I shook my head at the thought of how much I loved that man. "I am so sorry, Nah. I'm so sorry."

"It's cool, Ma. I'm not trying to be mad at you. I miss you. When am I seeing you? I need to see you."

"I'm coming home today."

"I'm at the hospital with my shorty today. Come through. I want you to see him."

"I would, but I'm fighting a cold. I can't put your son at risk like that."

"Then put on a surgical mask or some shit. I need to see you. Come through the hospital."

"I'm sick, Nasir. True story. I think I have the flu. I can't bring these types of germs around your son."

"Okay." He finally relented. "Then you need to come through my spot. I ain't playing with you. When I pull up, I wanna see you sitting outside my building waiting for me."

"Ill, when did you get so bossy?" I asked him

"When you decided to get ghost for two months."

I chuckled. "Yeah, I'll be out there waiting for you."

"You better be."

"I said I would."

"What was the dream about that made you call me at 5:00 in the morning, Beautiful?"

"It was crazy. Somebody was trying to kill you, and you didn't get your gun out fast enough. I know you think you're too good for the gun range, but you might need to go a few times and practice pulling out. That dream was vivid. It felt real."

"Between taking care of my son; dropping these beats; and flipping these houses, I don't really have time to rush the gun range. But I will keep your dream in mind...especially since it has you so spooked."

"It does." I mumbled.

"What time does your plane get in? You need a ride from

the airport?"

"Nah, *Ride or Die* arranged a car for me."

"Damn, Miss Got-Rocks, check you out."

"Forget you." I laughed.

"I thought you had."

Never that. I thought to myself. "Nah." I said out loud.

"So, I'll see you at my spot…at 8:30."

"8:30. I'll be there." I promised. "Hey Nasir."

"What's up, Gorgeous?"

"It's so sexy to see a cat step up and take care of the business. You're gangsta as hell for the way you've been handling yours with your son and everything."

"Ay, am I gangsta enough that you'll show up at my spot with no panties on?"

I laughed out loud. "Bye Nasir."

***

I fell asleep in my truck waiting for Nasir to show up. He nearly scared me to death when he tapped on the window to get my attention. I woke up with a jolt.

"How long you been here?" He was concerned.

I looked at my watch. "Five minutes."

He cocked his head to the side. "And you fell asleep?"

"I told you that I don't feel good." I reminded him

"Come on." He beckoned with his hand. "Let's go upstairs."

Once we were inside his apartment, he pulled me into his arms. "Don't kiss me, Nasir. I'm sick. I don't want you taking nothing back to your son."

"How am I supposed to not kiss you?"

"I don't know, but you're gonna have to work it out. You do not want whatever this is I have. I feel like a piece of doo-doo."

"When are you going to the doctor?"

"I have an appointment for tomorrow." I changed the subject. "How's your son?"

He smiled at me. Showed me his pretty dimples. "He's straight. Little man is a fighter. He gotta lot of his daddy in him."

"What's Little Man's name?"

"Justus."

"Awww, that's so sweet. Nia must love that."

"Yeah, she does. Nia's crazy about him. She's the only one who calls him Justus. Everybody else calls him LP…Little Payne. They say he looks just like me." He yawned and stretched.

"You're sleepy. I'm sleepy. Let's go get in the bed." I

suggested.

He gave me the eye. "Now, you know what's gonna happen if we get in the bed together, Joy. You down?"

"Come on, Boo." I whined. "I'm sick. I'm exhausted. I really don't have the energy to get it in. Unless you wanna just take it, while I lay there."

"Hell no." He shook his head. "You know I'm not havin' that. And I'm horny, too? I ain't got it in since the last time you and me…"

"Stop your lying!" I cut on top of him.

"Real talk."

I twisted my lips, so he would know that I still didn't believe him.

"I'm dead serious. I ain't gettin' it in with nobody else but you, Joy. You're like…my heart, Girl. You got my mind messed up. I don't want nobody but you."

"You haven't seen me or heard from me in two months." I reminded him.

"That doesn't matter. You're the only one I want."

"And you're sure that you're not just coochie-whipped?" I teased, barely able to control my laughter. "You're sure Gangsta Kitty doesn't have you in a choke hold?"

"I'm saying, Gangsta Kitty is a bad motherfucka, but no. This ain't about that. I love you."

After the way he had broken my heart, I wasn't ready to

verbalize my feelings for him. I wasn't ready to tell him that I loved him, too. "Let me find out fatherhood has made you soft." I joked instead.

"I won't say it made me soft, but it has made me appreciate what's important." He beckoned to me. "Come here."

I moved across the sofa and went into his arms. He kissed me on the cheek and held me close.

***

The next day I sat in the doctor's office and waited for the doctor to prescribe something for my illness. He seemed concerned when I told him of all of my symptoms. He was particularly troubled by the fact that I had been suffering from the same symptoms for such a long period of time. He had the nurse take some blood, to rule out a few things. It took forever.

Finally, nursey entered the examination room. "Okay. Dr. Bermudez told me to set you up to see your gynecologist. Is Wednesday, the 10th good for you?"

"Why?" I asked. "Why would I need to see my gynecologist?"

"You're pregnant."

I chuckled. "They're overworking you, Girl. You're in the wrong room. I'm Joya Bingham." I said my name slowly, so she could really catch it.

She smirked at me. "I know who you are, Miss Bingham. You're my patient who thought she had the flu, but is really pregnant. Congratulations."

I jumped down from the examination table. "How could I be pregnant? I never have unprotected sex. Never! Plus, I had my period last month. I'm not pregnant."

"Calm down, Miss Bingham. We did your blood work, Sugar. Your HCG levels indicate that you're pregnant. Blood doesn't lie."

Tears started flowing from my eyes. I was confused. How could I be pregnant? I hadn't even had sex since my birthday in June. Nasir and I always used condoms. Always. I thought back to the last time we had sex, and remembered him asking me where they were. I remembered telling him to look in the nightstand. I remembered watching him tie it up after we finished.

"Dammit." I mumbled as I remembered him telling me it slipped. He *said he caught it*! I thought to myself.

The nurse attempted to hand me some facial tissue. I declined and wiped my tears with my fingers.

"You okay?" She asked sympathetically.

"Yeah. I wasn't expecting to hear that. I really wasn't expecting to hear that."

"When you meet with your gynecologist, he or she can schedule an ultrasound to determine how far along you are. And, the two of you can discuss *options*." She stressed the word options, like she thought I wanted to get an abortion. "Now, is Wednesday, September 10th good for you?"

"That's fine." I responded. I was pregnant. I couldn't believe it. There was no way that Ricci was going to spend money to promote a pregnant artist. And how could I tour with a baby? I wasn't Beyonce or Jennifer Lopez. There was no way on earth I could see myself rocking the stage with a big, fat pregnant belly.

Besides, Nasir already had a baby. And that baby had major health problems, which were costing him major dough. How could I go to him and tell him I was pregnant, like it was a good thing? Another kid was probably the last thing he wanted.

Yeah. I thought to myself. *I definitely need to talk to somebody about my options.*

***

After three days of taking prenatal vitamins, the cold symptoms dissipated and I started to feel like my old self. Finally, I went with Nasir to the hospital to see the baby and to meet his family. When the nurse brought the baby in, I couldn't help noticing how gorgeous he was. He was a sweet little, light brown angel with wavy hair, chubby cheeks, slanted eyes, and a happy disposition. He started laughing the second Nasir picked him up.

"What's so funny, Dude?" Nasir asked him, then kissed his cheek. "You're having a good day, huh? I brought somebody new for you to meet. This is Joya. She's your future step-mother."

I rolled my eyes. "Whatever."

"He loves women."

"Just like his daddy." I retorted.

"Right, so hold him up against them big..."

"Nasir." I cut him off.

"My bad. Hold him to your chest. He likes...pillows. And as soft and fluffy as yours are, I'm sure he'll love them."

I took the baby from his arms. "I can't stand you."

"That's a lie. You love me. You're just scared to say it."

I cut my eyes at him. "If somebody broke your heart into a million pieces, would you be so willing to give them another chance at it?"

He was honest. "Nope. That's why I'm not stressing

you."

"He's gorgeous, Nasir. His mother must be really pretty." I changed the subject.

"She's decent."

"Uhm huh." I said sarcastically. "Is she Chinese, too? You told me to kick rocks and got loose with some Chinese heifer?"

"Stop bringing up old shit, Joya. His momma is black…"

I cut him off. "Most black people do not have slanted eyes."

"And Japanese. She's black and Japanese."

"Ooh, I could really beat on you right about now."

"You wanna hit me with the Krav Maga?" He joked.

"I wanna hit you with the left hook. Getting some random chick pregnant, days after you treated me like a sideline hoe."

"Ma, come on. Forgive me already. I don't know how many ways to tell you that I know I fucked up. Whatchu want me to do?"

"I don't know what I want you to do." I held Nasir's son close to me. He was so sweet. He looked into my eyes. I thought about the baby growing inside me and wondered why the timing had to be so off.

While I was cuddling the baby, four women walked into the room. The first lady was older. She was tall, and heavy set. Her skin was a beautiful chocolate brown. Her long gray hair was neatly styled, and she was dressed to the nines in a soft blue pants suit and matching pumps. But the main thing that caught my attention was her striking green eyes. I knew right away that she was Nasir's grandmother.

The second lady was younger than the first. She was a pretty woman, whose face showed signs that she had lived a hard and difficult life. She had the same peanut-butter colored skin as Nasir, but her eyes weren't green. She was dressed in a t-shirt, denim shorts and gym shoes.

The next two women were younger than me. Both were medium height, slim, and beautiful in different ways. One had the exact same creamy, peanut butter colored skin as Nasir's. She actually looked like a female version of him, but her eyes were dark brown. The final young lady was cocoa colored like his grandmother, and her eyes were as green as Nasir's. He couldn't deny his family. They all looked alike.

"Hello." His grandmother said to me.

"Hello." I replied.

"Ay family, I want y'all to meet Joy. She's wifey."

I tried not to sigh at him telling his family members that I was wifey. He was so ghetto. Why couldn't he tell them that I was a friend? "Hello." I said, again.

"Wifey?" One of the younger girls repeated. "Thought

you didn't believe in wifeys."

"Ay, this is wifey. What can I say? People change."

"Oh my goodness. Let me shake your hand, Sister." She said.

I chuckled at how dramatic she was being.

"I'm his sister, Yasmeen. It's nice to meet you."

"It's nice to meet you, too." I adjusted the baby so I could shake her hand. "You're the event planner, right?"

Her mouth dropped. "And he told you about me? Dig that. What did you do to my brother?"

I was sure that she didn't want to know that I was hitting her brother off with the figure eight every chance I got. Instead, I smiled, shrugged a little bit and lied. "I don't know."

She cut her eyes from me to him. "Yeah, okay."

"I'm Nasir's mother, Nicki. It's nice to meet you."

"It's nice to meet you, too."

"Thanks Sweetie, but you're gonna have to give up my grandson." She told me.

"Oh, okay." I handed the baby to her.

"How're you gonna come in gangsterin' the baby?" Nasir asked her.

"I'm his grandmother. Certain privileges come with that."

"Joy. That's a pretty name." His grandmother said.

"Thank you."

"It's nice to meet you. Nasir doesn't bring too many of his lady friends around. In fact, I think you're the first one I've met in quite a while. How long have you known him?"

"A little more than a year." I replied.

I could see his grandmother doing the calculations.

"Ay Dorothy Jane, don't start. Joy knows I got Midori pregnant on a humble."

"Yes, and we're not a couple." I explained quickly. "We're friends."

"For now." Nasir said.

"I'm Mrs. Howse."

"It's nice to meet you, Mrs. Howse." I looked over at the final young woman. "You must be Torri. I love the way you decorated Nasir's apartment. I told him to ask you how I can get you to design one of those rugs for me that you got for him."

While I was speaking, I noticed that the room had gotten so quiet, that you could hear a pin drop. I looked at Nasir, so he could give me a clue as to what I said wrong. He gave me a blank stare in return.

Finally, Yasmeen spoke. "You've been to his condo? The Bat-Cave? He never takes females there. Who are you? Neo, from The Matrix? Are you the *one*?" She asked dramatically.

I could tell that Yasmeen thought she was a comedienne.

"Shut up, Yas." Nasir told her.

"Yeah, I'm Torri." The dark skinned sister told me. "I create the design for the rugs, and this place on Pershing Road makes them for me. If you really want one, we'll get together to discuss your color scheme and your taste. I'll get your number from Nasir, then we'll talk." She offered.

"Thanks."

"Look at LP trying to sit up and join the conversation." Nicki said. "This boy is growing up too fast."

Mrs. Howse cut her eyes at Nasir. "Yeah, he acts like he's trying to get out of the way for the next one. You don't have another baby on the way, do you Nasir?"

"Hell...heck no." He assured her. "Definitely not."

I glanced out of the window, and pretended like I didn't hear them talking.

Chapter Twenty
Can't Truss It

Payne

The morning of September 16th, I woke up early. Pent up anxiety had me on ten, because I was bringing my son home for the first time. I turned on the television, then I went around the house and made sure that I had everything I needed.

Joya, Nia, Torri and I had spent the last two weeks picking out furniture and turning my former office into LP's room. Once it was painted and outfitted with a circular crib, a chest of drawers, a changing table, multiple pictures of Sesame Street characters, an Elmo lamp, a rocking chair, and a rug featuring race cars and tug boats, you couldn't even tell that it used to be an office.

The three women made sure that it was supplied with everything a baby could ever need. The only thing my son lacked was a mother. I knew the women in my family, and even Nia would give him love in the way only a female could, but it killed me that Midori wasn't there to take an active part in his life.

I walked back into my bedroom, and pulled out the outfit LP was wearing home from the hospital. He had outgrown the first one I bought, before he ever got to wear it. I looked up at the television just in time to catch the story that was headlining the news that day.

"Chicago's gang world took a hit this morning, as one of the top members of the north side gang, which calls itself 'The Body Shredders' was found dead in this south side apartment building. Twenty seven year old Orville "Big Dog" Pettigrew was found murdered, along with an unidentified female companion around six this morning, after neighbors reported hearing what sounded like muffled screaming. Inside the apartment, police found the body of Orville Pettigrew in the bedroom. He had been shot more than ten times. The female companion, whose identity has not yet been released, was found in the living room of the apartment. She was shot once, in the face. There were no signs of forced entry, and the police have no suspects. Judy and Hosea, back to you."

I shook my head. The deed was done. Israel had made good on his promise to murder Elliott's brother.

***

It took forever for the hospital to release LP. By the time he, Joya and I made it to my crib, it was after 6:00pm. Joya did the mommy-thing with him. That took a lot of pressure off of me. Truth be told, I wasn't too confident about taking care of Little Man all by myself.

Joya gave him a bath, lotioned him up, powdered him down, put him in his pajamas and rocked him while she gave him a bottle. I watched her chilling in the rocking chair she had convinced me to buy. She looked perfect holding my shorty, and singing to him while he sucked on his bottle.

"I can already tell that he's gonna have you wrapped around his finger." I joked from the doorway.

She looked over at me and winked. "Probably. He's real easy to love, Nasir."

"Just like his father."

"Honestly? Yes, just like his father."

"Look at him, all curled up on you. In my spot."

"I can't believe you're jealous of your own son." She told me.0

"I won't be, if you promise to hold me like that when you finish with him."

She shook her head, and grinned. "Yeah, I promise."

***

After Joya put the baby to sleep, she met me in the bedroom. I put down three shots of loving, before I couldn't keep my eyes open any longer. I fell asleep with my girl wrapped up in my arms. A few hours later I woke up alone in the bed.

I found Joya in the baby's room. She was leaning over the crib, singing to him as she changed his diaper.

"Hey. He straight?" I asked.

"He's hungry. Can you get his bottle together, while I finish changing him?"

I warmed up his bottle then brought it back to the room. I held it out to Joya. Before she could take it, we heard a cell phone ringing.

"That's your phone, Ma." I told her.

She handed LP to me. "I'll be right back."

I followed her into the living room. On the real, I wanted to know who was calling her so late. Joya wasn't the grimy type to be sexing me, while she belonged to the next man. But still, I was curious.

I watched as she checked to see who was calling, then swiped the screen. "What's up, Chan?" Loud screaming came across the line. It was so loud, that Joya pulled the phone away from her ear. "What?" She asked.

More loud screaming.

"Chan, I can't understand you, Boo. What happened?

Where is Bubbles?" Joya listened intently. "Chan, no! Please don't tell me that. What happened?"

"What's the matter, Ma?" I asked crossing the room to stand by her side.

She handed me the phone as she left the room.

"Chantelle? What's the deal?" I asked.

"My sister is gone. She's gone." She cried hysterically.

"What?"

"The police found her dead this morning." She was crying so hard, that I had to struggle to make out the words. "Somebody shot her…"

Nah, it couldn't be. I thought to myself. *It couldn't be.*

Chantelle was speaking gibberish as she tried to give me more details. The only word I could make out was "Pettigrew." I didn't hear another word she said.

I ended the call and walked into my bedroom. Joya was sprawled out on the bed, crying into my pillow. It hurt my heart to see her so upset.

"Joy, baby." I said. I couldn't pull her to me the way I wanted to, because Little Man was in my arms, and he was sucking hungrily on the bottle. I sat down next to her and rubbed my hand across her exposed thigh. "Damn, Girl. I can't believe this."

She sat up, still crying. "I gotta go over Chan's. She needs me right now."

I nodded my understanding. "Cool. We'll drop the baby off at Dorothy Jane's, and we'll roll through."

"Nasir, it's his first night home. He needs his daddy. Stay here with your son."

I shook my head. "Right now, he's cool. And he'll be cool with Dorothy Jane. You need me more. So, let me make a call, then we're outta here."

***

I dropped my son off at my grandmother's house, then Joya and I headed for Israel's. I was bugging the hell out. On one hand, I couldn't believe that Izz had iced Bubbles. On the other hand, if she was laid up with Orville Pettigrew, that meant she was double-agent. There was only one way to deal with dirty comrades.

At Israel's house, the two of us went in the basement while the females stayed upstairs.

"I hated to do her, Man." He told me as he poured himself a glass of Ciroc vodka. He offered me one, but I declined. "I hated to murk her, but she ain't leave me no choice. She was dirty. She was in cahoots with the enemy."

"What happened?"

He sighed. "It's a long story."

"You were knockin' her, right?"

He looked over at me, surprised. "How'd you know?"

I shrugged my shoulders. "I don't know. After the hit on Elliott, I saw her at Dex's crib. She asked me if I had ever been in love with somebody who didn't love me back. At first I thought she was talking about Dex, but she was talking about you."

"I loved her. I did. But she was too needy…and too fuckin' greedy. She wanted more of me than I could give her."

She sounded like Tashera.

"So, I cut her off. I stopped dealin' with her. That's when she tried to make me jealous by hollerin' at Dex. But Dex knew what it was between me and Bubbles. He wasn't gonna put his hands on her. That pissed her off, too." He downed the entire contents of his glass and poured himself another drink. "Asking her to pull that lick was the beginning of the end. Once she saw how connected Elliott was, she went double-agent. She went to dude and told him that she knew who murked his brother. She gave me and Dex to him. She set us up to get killed…except Justus ate my bullets."

"What?" I asked. "How do you know this?"

"She told me…right before I did her."

"So, J died over a case of mistaken identity?"

He nodded. "I know this don't make it no better, but she was really hurt over the fact that Justus caught those bullets."

Hell no, it didn't make it better.

"She got spooked after that. She didn't want to see you or Patience catch no bullets that were meant for me. So, she stopped dropping dime on me and dropped dime on Rook at the *Rock the Park* concert. She knew when he would be on stage." He shook his head. "He was a sitting duck, and he never even knew it."

I shook my head. The stuff Israel was telling me was hard to believe. I couldn't reconcile it with the Bubbles that I thought I knew. "I can't believe she was this scandalous. All this because you didn't wanna be with her?"

"Pretty much." He said, then stood up and poured himself a third glass of vodka.

I knew he was lying. There was no way in hell Bubbles set him, Rook and Dex up to get murked over some 'scorned woman' bullshit. Bubbles was one of the most calculating chicks I had ever met. She was grimy, but she wasn't petty. I knew there was more to the story than what Izz was telling me. But I also knew that dude wasn't about to make it funky with me. He wasn't about to tell me the whole truth.

"Chantelle is fucked up over this." I commented.

"Yeah, I gotta try to be there for her. I know how it feels to lose your only sibling. It hurts like hell."

"How did you put it together? How'd you know it was Bubbles who was feeding the information to Elliott's brother?"

"That text I got from dude, that was some female shit. Bubbles was the only chick that came to mind who was scandalous enough to give dude my number. I started following her. She led me right to him. Then, it was what it was."

"Damn."

"Ay, it's the life we chose, Son."

I stood up from the recliner. "Take care of your wifey, Dude. I'm about to get outta here. I'm about to grab my girl, pick up my shorty from Grandma's and head back to the crib."

He stood up after me. "Ay Payne, this conversation goes no further than this basement."

I hit him with the screw face. "Do you really think you need to tell me that?"

"I'm sayin'. I know you're trying to get your thing back on track with Joya and everything. I don't want none of this coming out during pillow-talk or something."

"I know you got a lot on your mind. So, I'mma pretend like you didn't just say that, cuz otherwise I'mma be real offended. You know me better than that, Dog."

After that conversation, I started thinking that Patience was right. Israel was suspect as hell. I didn't trust either one of their asses.

Chapter Twenty-One
Mind Blowing Decisions

Joya

Once the police had finished their investigation of Bubbles' apartment as a crime scene, Chantelle and her family members were allowed to go inside for the first time. I was working, so I hadn't spoken to Chantelle. I was surprised to find her parked in front of my building when the taxi dropped me off at home that night.

She rolled down the window of her truck and called out to me. "Hey Joy."

I walked over to the vehicle. I could tell she had been crying. "Hey Chan. Come on upstairs."

After I changed out of my uniform, Chantelle and I sat together on my couch. I could tell she was really upset, although she wasn't saying much. Every now and again, she would start to cry.

"My sister was fucking Izz." She announced finally.

"What?" I asked, because I knew I had heard her wrong. "What?"

"She was messing around with Izz."

"What makes you think that?"

"Her cell phone was sitting on her dresser. I went through it, trying to see if there was anything on it that would tell me who would do that to her. She had text messages on her phone to and from Izz." She told me. "Nasty messages. Messages talking about how she loved riding his dick. Messages about how much she loved sucking him off. Stuff like that."

Yuck!!! I thought to myself. Israel wasn't a good looking cat by any stretch of the imagination. I couldn't imagine kissing dude, let alone getting freaky with him. "Are you serious?"

She nodded slowly.

I tried not to vomit at the thought of Izz with Bubbles. "I can't believe that." I stated, but even as I said it, I knew that was a lie. I could believe it. But it was still heinous that Bubbles would do that to Chan.

"Believe it."

"Were these recent messages?"

"Recent enough. They were in a relationship, Joy. This wasn't random sex. They were basically dating. He was spending money on that girl like crazy. He was taking her on weekend trips. He was even making her car payments and paying her rent." She paused and blew her nose. "I wait on that nigga hand and foot, and he fucks my little sister? I don't even know how to process that shit."

"Dang." My heart went out to Chantelle.

"They ended up having a falling out about me." She

continued. "Bubbles felt like Izz was giving me more time than he was giving her. She was pressing him to give her more time. So, he stopped messing with her. That was when she started throwing herself at Dex."

"Does Izz know that you know all of this?"

"Yeah, I called his trife ass from Bubbles' apartment. What could he say? He was all tongue twisted. Stutterin' and tellin' me that we need to talk in person. Fuck him! He needs to talk to my ass."

"If I was him, I would be scared to face you."

"He oughtta be scared to face me. I wanna kill his ass. I hate him." She shook her head. "Sitting at my sister's funeral acting all torn up, when he knew he was tappin' both of us. I oughtta have my cousins break both of his fuckin' legs." She sighed heavily. "I gotta find someplace to stay. I'm not goin' back to that scandalous ass bastard's crib."

I nodded my understanding. I couldn't say that I blamed her. I wouldn't have gone back to his crib, either.

"I need to figure things out. I'll move back in with my momma and daddy before I stay at that motherfucker's house another day."

"You can stay here, Chan." I offered. "Between flying, and the time I spend at Nasir's, I'm hardly ever here anyway. Plus, I'm supposed to be going back to New York in two weeks."

"Thanks for the offer, but I already have an idea about where I'm staying."

Chantelle left my house at 10:45. I really didn't want her to leave with the mindset she was in. I was worried about her.

Nasir noticed that something was bothering me when he opened the door for me at his place an hour later. "What's the matter, Ma? Why is your face all twisted up?"

"Long story." I gave him a hug. "I have a lot on my mind."

"Ay, I just fed and changed Little Man, so you got at least…fifteen minutes to speak on it." He joked.

I laughed. "I gotta decide if I'm signing with *Ride or Die* or not." I plopped down on his sofa.

"What would stop you from signing with them?"

"I don't know. A gut feeling. I don't get a positive vibe from *Ride or Die*. I mean, the people are all really nice. They're friendly and everything, but there's something about Ricci that I can't stand."

"Trust ya instincts. God gave 'em to you for a reason."

I sighed. "I don't know. Ricci wants me to quit my job, and everything. Eventually, he's gonna want me to move to New York. Then what?"

"You move."

"Just like that?"

"If it's your dream? Yeah, just like that." He sat down on the opposite end of the couch.

"What if it's not my dream?"

"See, that's the problem. I don't think it is your dream, Joy. If it was, you wouldn't be having so much trouble deciding what to do. If you don't wanna do music, why not be honest about it?"

"It's not that I don't wanna do music…"

"Listen," he interrupted me, "just because you're musically talented, doesn't mean you have to be in the industry."

"I know that. But some people would kill to have this opportunity. I don't wanna piss on it. What if I choose not to do music now, then next year, I'm wishing that I would've done it?"

"Then you start over from the beginning. If you walk away now, and decide later that you wanna come back to music, I got you. I'll put you on. I'll introduce you to Cameron Chambers, and you can be the new business at *Spot Check Records*." He winked at me.

I sighed.

"What else is wrong? Your face is still twisted."

"The police let Chantelle and her family to go into Bubbles' apartment today. She found Bubbles' cell phone and it had texts on it from Israel." I paused and waited for his reaction, but he didn't give me one. "She knows that Izz was messing with Bubbles."

"Damn."

"I take it that you knew that."

"Yeah." He admitted. "I knew."

"Why would Izz do that? Why would he mess around on Chan with her sister?"

"You gotta ask that man why he would do that. I have no idea."

"Chan is so hurt."

"I'm sure."

I needed a hug. I slid over to him and wrapped my arms around his waist. He held me tightly. We stayed like that for a few minutes. "Let me check on the baby." I said finally breaking the embrace.

He pulled me back into his arms. "He's straight. I laid him down right before you came."

"I still wanna check on him. I haven't seen him all day. I miss him."

He shook his head. "Keep being such a good mother to him. I'mma petition the courts and have you adopt him."

***

Three days later Chantelle asked me to meet her at Israel's house. She wanted to move her stuff out of his place and she needed help. She was sitting on the front stairs when I pulled up. I parked my truck and got out.

"Hey Chan." I said stopping a few stairs down from where she was sitting.

"Hey, Girl. Come on, let's get this over with before Israel brings his fat ass home."

I wanted to laugh that after Chantelle found out about Izz's betrayal, he became "fat ass." Before then, she never seemed to have a problem with his large size.

"I asked him not to have his bastard ass here while I moved out. I told him that the least he could do is not make me have to look at him."

"He agreed?"

"Yeah, but he had the nerve to tell me that if I took anything that didn't belong to me, he was gonna fuck me up."

I shook my head. Israel was forever cocky. He was messing around with Bubbles, and he had the audacity to threaten Chantelle about taking something out of his place. "Ain't that nothing?"

"Yeah, it is. I oughtta ransack this motherfucka and let him deal with puttin' it back together."

We walked into the house together. "What are we taking?" I asked her.

"My clothes, my shoes and my purses. The rest of this crap is his."

We walked upstairs to the master bedroom.

"My luggage is in the closet. I know it won't hold everything, but we can get most of my stuff. I'll have to come back for the rest next week or something." She went into the walk-in closet and brought out about four pieces of luggage to be filled.

I started with the dresser drawers. She started in the walk-in closet.

"Where have you been staying, Chan?" I asked, as we packed.

"You don't even wanna know."

I stopped packing and looked towards the closet. "Chan."

She came out of the closet. "I've been at Patience's. And yes, I had sex with him."

I stared at her.

"I did it on purpose." She confided. "To get back at Izz for sleepin' with my sister."

"And Patience was down for the get-down, huh? He let you use him like that?"

"Patience wanted the coochie, Girl. He thought he was Usher while he was in it. He thought it was his opportunity to give me his *confessions*." She sighed heavily. "He was tellin' me how much he digs me, and how he's been wantin' to get at me for so long."

"You gotta be lying." I insisted.

"I am so serious. Remember the day that I beat up that chick at the club? The day Rook was in that contest, '*Blaze The Mic*'? Remember Bubbles kept tellin' me that Patience was feelin' me?"

I nodded. I remembered Bubbles saying that Patience had a crush on Chantelle.

"I didn't think she knew what she was talkin' about. But I guess she was right all along."

"I don't even know what to say."

"Me either. All I know is that when I start thinkin' about my sister, or about how Izz played me, I can call up Patience. He's like Johnny-on-the-spot. He stops whatever he's doin' to get at me. I need that right now. I need somebody to be down for *me*, for once."

"Wow."

"Yeah."

I stood there silently. I couldn't believe that Chantelle slept with Patience. That was as crazy as Bubbles messing with Izz.

"I don't know what's goin' on with me, Joy." She said, as if she read my mind. She dropped to the closet floor and put her face in her hands while she cried softly.

I went over, and sat next to her. I put my arm around her shoulder.

"My sister is dead. I'm fuckin' one of Izz's men. This is not me. I'm actin' like somebody I don't even know." She continued to cry. "Why am I fuckin' this nigga? To get back at Izz? Why do I even care about Izz? He don't care about me."

I continued to hold her.

"Sometimes, I miss my sister so much. I lie in bed and cry all day. Other times, I'm so pissed at her that I wanna hurt her. Then, I feel guilty about being mad at her. Do I sound crazy? Cuz I think I'm goin' crazy."

"You don't sound crazy." I promised her.

"I'm messin' up so bad, though." She told me. "I never even made Patience use a condom. I gotta be crazy."

"Oh Chan, please tell me you didn't slip like that."

"I did. What if I'm pregnant?"

The mention of pregnancy made me subconsciously run my hand across my own stomach. I needed to make a decision about the situation I was in. The measurements from the sonogram put me at eleven weeks pregnant. Abortion was still a viable option for me, but I only had one week to make the decision. My gynecologist had given me a list of referrals. Places that took my insurance. But I was crossed up over the thought of getting rid of the baby. Having an abortion without at least telling Nasir that I was pregnant was grimy as hell. I didn't think I could go out like that. Besides, the more deeply I fell in love with Little Payne and watched his fight for life, the more having an abortion seemed unlikely. Not to mention that it had been three weeks since my doctor told me that I had one week to make my decision.

I couldn't lie, though. The thought of having the baby seemed even more unlikely. Bruno Ricci expected me in the studio. Eastern Airlines expected me in the sky. Nasir expected to have one child, not two. I didn't know how I had gotten myself into such a ridiculous predicament.

I sighed before I spoke. I was probably the last person who needed to be giving advice about pregnancy, but I knew I had to say something. "An unwanted pregnancy is something we can take care of." I assured her. "But AIDS is real, Boo. You can't be sleeping with cats raw. It's too dangerous. Black women are running up the number of new AIDS cases. You gotta be careful."

She cried some more. I comforted her.

"Chan, why don't you move out of Patience's crib and come stay at my spot?" I suggested.

She cut her eyes at me. "I know this is gonna make me sound like a gold digger, but if I move outta Patience's crib, what am I gonna do for money? I'm ass-out, Joya. For two years, I've been eatin' off of Izz's table. I ain't got no job. I don't have no money of my own. The only loot I have in my wallet is from the five hundred dollars Patience gave me a couple of days ago."

"He gave you five hundred dollars? Damn, what're you working with, Chan?" I teased looking her up and down. "Kryptonite?"

She laughed through the tears. "Shut up! You're crazy."

"Patience is the crazy one…to be giving you five hundred dollars for the same coochie old boy in high school used to get for free." I joked.

"Stop tryin' to make me laugh." She admonished. "Patience is tryin' to buy my affection. He thinks if he hits me off with constant dough, he'll be able to hang on to me. He knows I'm not into him. He knows that I still have feelings for Izz."

"I'll look out. I'mma write you a check. I can at least match what Patience let you hold…and you don't have to give me *none* of what you're giving him."

"Joy, shut up! I can't stand you." She chuckled. "Anyway, I can't take money from you. I mean, you and Payne have the baby and everything."

I froze. *How does she know about the baby?* I thought to myself. Then I realized that she was talking about LP.

"Please. LP is not my son. I don't take care of him financially. That's Nasir's responsibility."

"Are you sure? I can't tell, with the way you're over Payne's crib everyday playing house. What's up with that?"

"I don't know." I shrugged my shoulders. "I really love that baby. He's too sweet."

"Yeah, and what about his daddy?"

"Unfortunately, I love him, too."

"Why is that unfortunate? You love him, he loves you. Do you know how many people in this world are searchin' for that? You could have my fucked-up life. You could live with a cat for two years, give up everything for him, wait on him hand and foot, then find out that he's been sexin' your little sister. Payne ain't perfect. I'll be the first to admit that, but hell...he loves your dirty drawers."

"I'm helping Payne raise the son that he had with a jump-off." I reminded her. "A baby that it seems like was conceived the day after he told me to 'kick rocks.' Payne's idea of love and my idea of love are totally different, Chan. Payne's love hurts."

"Whose doesn't?" She asked. "I'm not tryin' to take up for Payne..."

"Yes, you are." I disagreed. "You're always trying to take up for Payne, because you gotta soft spot for him."

"Nah, I'm givin' you real talk. Payne loves you. He more

than loves you. Dude adores you. It's written all over his face when he looks at you. The day we were at *Rock the Park*, I watched the way he looked at you. He looked at you exactly the same way Justus used to look at Nia." She cocked her head to the side. "And you know dude worshiped the ground Nia walked on."

We both chuckled lightly at the memory of the love Nia and Justus shared.

"And on the real," she continued, "I was kinda jealous. I don't think Izz ever looked at me that way."

I didn't respond.

She kept talking. "And you love Payne, too."

"I do."

"I know. Because I know how particular you are about havin' sex with people. If you didn't love Payne, you wouldn't still be lettin' him hit it. Plus, you be lookin' at him like he's the captain of the football team or somethin'…all star-struck like he's Nas or somebody. You act like everything outta dude's mouth is the word of God."

"Shut up, Chan." I told her, but I could help grinning, because there was truth in her words.

"You do. Y'all are some sickenin' bastards." She teased.

"Forget you."

"For real, Joy. I think you'll be a lot happier if you forgive Payne for his mistakes. Especially for the things that happened after Justus died. Cuz I can tell you honestly, if he was feelin' the way I feel, he really didn't know what he was doin'. He was probably tryin' to manage the pain the best way he knew how."

"I don't know, Chan. He broke my heart. I can't see myself giving him another chance to do it again."

"Psshhhttt." She said sucking her teeth dismissively. "Dude's been sick as hell since he lost you, Girl. When he gets you back, he ain't lettin' you go, again."

I cut my eyes at her. "Don't think I didn't catch the fact that you said, '*when*' he gets me back."

"I know I did." She said with a smirk. "Payne's gonna win you back. I don't know why you're tryin' to play hard to get."

***

Chantelle's words stayed with me for the rest of the day. I ate dinner with Nasir that night. After dinner I bathed the baby, put pajamas on him, and rocked him while he had his last bottle of the day. I took the empty bottle from LP's mouth, burped him, kissed him, and then laid him down on his Sesame Street linens. I watched silently as he drifted off into a peaceful sleep. Nasir came into the room, as I was about to walk out.

He stopped me by LP's changing table. "Ma, what's going on with you? You're being too quiet. You got something on your mind?"

"I'm thinking about my life."

"What about it?"

"I've got a lot of decisions to make, and instead of making them, I'm messing around. Ricci expects me in New York by next Monday. That's a week away, and I haven't even decided if I'm signing this contract. He told me to give Eastern Airlines my two week notice, and here I am, still flying three days a week. Plus, I got this…other decision hanging over my head."

"What other decision?"

"Nothing." I said, waving my hand dismissively. "I just have a lot going on."

"You wanna talk about it?"

"I don't know."

He cocked his head to the side. "You want me to take ya mind off ya problems for a while?"

I giggled. "All you think about is sex."

"Ay, I'm trying to help *you* out."

I giggled again. "You are so silly. You're gonna make me wake up the baby."

"Come on." He took my hand and led me out of the nursery. We sat down on the sofa together. "I don't think you should sign the contract." He said, with no sugar-coating.

"Why would you say that? You haven't even seen the contract."

"True, but I have seen you. You've been running around here stressed out wondering whether or not you should sign this contract. My feeling about the whole shit is that if it takes this much contemplation, you shouldn't sign it. I'm not positive that you really wanna make music for a living, but it's obvious that you don't wanna make music for *Ride or Die*." He took a breath. "I'm not trying to tell you how to do you. This is *my* opinion. Whatever you decide…I got you."

"You got me?" I teased, pushing him lightly on the shoulder.

"True story. I always got you."

"Why are you so sweet to me?" I asked, stretching out on the couch and resting my head in his lap.

"I don't know. I must like you or something." He ran his fingers through my hair.

"I like you, too."

"Word?"

"Yep."

"Maybe I love you."

"I love you, too."

"Straight up?" He was shocked by my confession. I wasn't surprised. I hadn't told him that I loved him since we were in Las Vegas, a year earlier.

"Yep."

"Maybe I trust you."

I hesitated momentarily. "Maybe I'm starting to rebuild my trust in you."

"You don't expect me to wait forever for you to trust me again, right?"

"Nah, I don't expect you to wait forever."

"Then, we're cool."

"Yeah, we're cool." I agreed. I sat up on the couch. "Come on. I want you to take my mind off my problems for a little while."

"You're lucky you told me that you love me. Cuz I was starting to feel like your jump-off."

"Are you serious?" I asked as I led the way to his bedroom.

"Hell yeah. I thought I was gonna have to cut you off from the dick."

"Wow." I teased. "Imagine that."

We undressed and got in the bed. Nasir kissed me tenderly a few times, then stopped abruptly. My eyes flew open. "What?"

"I meant to ask you something."

"What's up?"

"Did you get your period?"

Where did that come from? I thought to myself. I didn't want to lie to him, so I avoided answering him directly. "Why?"

"I don't know. I was with my grandmother today, and she told me that she keeps dreaming about fish. Then she came right out and asked me if you were pregnant."

"What did you tell her?"

"I told her, no." He paused. "You ain't pregnant, are you?"

"How would I be pregnant? We always use protection. Anyway, don't you have your hands full with LP?"

"This ain't about LP. This is about you."

"Come on, Nah Nah. I don't wanna talk about pregnancy right before it's going down. I'm trying to get blessed, please don't kill the mood."

He watched me in silence for a few seconds, then swallowed the garbage that I was feeding him. He grabbed a condom from the nightstand.

"And make sure you put that joint on *extra tight*." I fronted.

Nasir pulled my body to his. His fingers explored the center of my goodness and I opened my legs wider to his touch, allowing him to pleasure me that way for a while. When it was time, Nasir positioned himself between my legs. I pushed my pelvis up towards him, so that he would know I was ready for him to take me.

He entered me slowly. Letting me feel him inch by wonderful inch. Penetration with Nasir was like the Fourth of July. He made me see stars and fireworks behind my closed eyelids. He drove me insane kissing me, pulling my hair and stroking me deeply all at the same time.

"Uhm, Nasir." My moan was barely above a whisper.

"Yeah baby, just like that." He encouraged.

I gave him back every stroke he gave me, with the same amount of force. He positioned my feet, so they were flat on his chest. Everything I owned was exposed to that man. His wish was my body's command. He explored me more deeply. My moans became a foreign language. I called his name over and over. Screams of ecstasy filled the apartment. My body began to quiver. Nasir's legs started to shake. A few minutes later, I felt him start to throb deep inside me. I was right there with him. Breathing hard, and tingling like crazy.

After round two, I drifted off into a peaceful sleep. Thoughts of the pregnancy and of me being dishonest with Nasir were a distant memory.

***

Chantelle called me on Wednesday afternoon. She caught me right before I boarded my plane. "Your timing's perfect. I was just about to get on the plane. What's up?"

"Are you on your way back to Chicago?"

"Yep."

"Where are you comin' from? How long is it gonna take you to get home?"

"I'm leaving Dallas. I should be home in about two and a half, three hours. Why?"

"My mom's church is havin' a prayer service tonight. A guest preacher is comin' in to do a sermon and they're gonna pray for families who've lost loved ones to gun violence this year. You wanna go with me?"

I was exhausted. I really didn't want to go, but maybe some Jesus was exactly what I needed in my life. Maybe He could show me what I was supposed to do about the *Ride or Die* contract, Nasir and the pregnancy. "Yeah, I'll go. Gimme the details."

***

The church service was excellent. The visiting minister's word spoke to my heart and made me feel one hundred pounds lighter. I still didn't know exactly what I was supposed to do, but I knew that everything would work out in the way that it was supposed to work out.

Chantelle and I decided to grab dinner before we called it a night. We rode over to Dixie Kitchen in Hyde Park. Halfway through our blackened chicken breasts, Chantelle's cell jingled. I watched while she checked the screen.

"It's a text from Izz." She told me.

"What does he want?"

"Who knows?" She shrugged.

I tuned out while she read the message, and thought about how weird it was that I was eating fried green tomatoes. I didn't usually eat fried foods at all, let alone fried tomatoes. *This baby has me tripping.* I thought to myself.

Chantelle tossed her phone to the table with a thud. "He said I left some stuff at his house. If I don't come and get it tonight, he's tossing it."

I knew that Chantelle had left a little less than half of her things at dude's house. It wasn't more than she could pack up by herself, but I knew that would take her a couple of hours. "I'll go with you." I offered.

"Thanks, Girl. I hope his ass isn't there. I really don't wanna be bothered with him. The last few times I've spoken to him, we got into it."

"You've been talking to Izz?"

"Yeah, I talked to him the other night. We ended up gettin' into it. He cursed me out, and called me outta my name."

"Why is he showing you shade?" I was shocked that Israel would go out like that, when he was the one who had been messing around on Chantelle.

"Cuz he found out about me and Patience."

"How did he find out? Who told him?"

"Me." She admitted.

My jaw dropped. "Why?"

"I wanted him to know how it felt to get cheated on. I wanted him to feel the pain of knowin' that I let one of his guys hit it."

"I can't believe you did that."

"I wasn't in my right mind. I was pissed…and thinking about my sister. Thinkin' about how he played me. So, I called him up and told him."

"Girl, I'm surprised he didn't kill you."

"He wanted to. He was mad as hell. He was threatenin' me and stuff. Asking me where I was, so he could come beat my ass. Like I was gonna tell him. I kept tellin' him that I was with Patience."

"Were you trying to get Patience killed?"

"I wasn't thinkin' straight. I was tryin' to hurt Izz. I wanted him to feel the way I was feelin'."

"Chan, I really don't think you should go over there. I think you should let him throw the clothes away. Hell, he can burn 'em if he wants to."

She waved her hand dismissively. "I'm not about to let him throw my clothes away. Anyway, he should've calmed down by now. That was Monday night."

"I don't know." I said slowly. "And I didn't bring 'Thriller Killer' with me."

"You got your Krav Maga if dude tries to get cute."

"Girl, Krav Maga cannot stop a bullet."

"Pssshhttt! Izz is not about to shoot me. Trust. He ain't crazy."

We left the restaurant and walked to our respective wheels.

"I'mma follow you over there." I said, before I climbed into my truck.

"Okay."

Once I was alone in my Lexus, I dialed Nasir. "Hey Nah Nah. You busy?"

"I'm chilling at Dorothy Jane's with her, Nicki and LP.

You just got back in town?"

"Nah, I've been back for a minute. Chan asked me to go to church with her."

"Church?"

"Yeah, we went to a prayer service. But I didn't call for that. I need a favor."

"What's the deal?"

"I need you to meet me at Izz's house."

"Izz's house?" He repeated. "Why?"

"I'm going over there with Chan to get the last of her stuff, and I don't trust Israel right now. I gotta nasty feeling about the whole thing. I would feel better if I had 'Thriller Killer' with me, but I left her at home."

"You think you might need ya heat?" He was concerned. "Ma, what kinda situation are you walking into? Why don't you and Chan chill? I'll link up with y'all and the three of us will go over there together."

"We're already on the way. Can you meet us there?"

"Yeah. No doubt. I'm on my way."

"Nasir, please hurry up. Izz found out that Chan had sex with Patience. I gotta feeling that we're walking into a set-up."

"What the hell is Chan doing having sex with Patience?"

"It's a long story. Are you coming?"

"I'm about to tell Dorothy Jane to keep an eye on LP,

then I'm walking to my wheels."

***

Once we got to Izz's house, Chantelle and I met up on the front porch. "Uhm, Izz is here." She gestured to the red Chrysler that was Israel's pride and joy.

"Girl, we do not have to go in here. You can let him have the clothes, or we can sit on this porch and wait for Nasir to pull up."

"Nasir?"

"Yeah, I called him while I was in my truck. I told him to meet us over here, because I don't know about you, but I don't trust Izz."

"Izz ain't gone do shit." She assured me. "Come on."

I couldn't help remembering the last time she said the exact same thing. If my memory served me correctly, Israel choked her and smacked her up at *Kacey's*. "Let me call Nasir and see where he is."

"Meet me inside." She said, then used her key to unlock the door and let herself in.

I pulled out my cell phone and dialed Nasir. He answered on the first ring. "Ay, what's up?"

"How far away are you?"

"I'm on 75th and Cottage Grove. Stay in your wheels, Joy. I'll be there in ten minutes."

"Chan already went inside. I can't leave her in there by herself." I walked into the house. The foyer was empty. I peeked around the corner into the living room. It was empty, too. Then I heard voices coming from down the hall. "They're either in the kitchen or the family room." I whispered into the phone. "What if Izz is choking her or something?"

"Joy, be careful."

"Hurry up! I'm leaving the door open for you. Hurry up."

"Leave your phone on, so I can hear what's happening." He told me.

I placed my cell phone inside my purse, and left my purse opened, so Nasir could hear. Then I walked down the long hallway as quietly as I could.

I peeked around the doorway of the family room. I wasn't smooth enough, Patience saw me. He grinned, then beckoned to me with the gun that was in his hand. "Ay Joya. I see you came with ya girl."

I stood in the doorway of the room. Chantelle was standing about five feet away from me, looking scared. I was lost as to what was going on. I expected to find Israel trying to murder Chantelle. Instead, Patience was in the house, he was holding heat, and Israel was nowhere to be found. I let my eyes move around the large room quickly. Finally, I spotted Israel. He was laid out on the floor by Patience's feet. He looked dead. "What's going on?" I asked.

Chantelle bugged her eyes, like that was the dumbest question she had ever heard.

Patience grinned at me, again. I didn't like the vibe I was getting from him. A pit started to settle in the middle of my stomach.

"We're about to get to the bottom of this shit, today."

"What shit?"

"Izz is gonna make some true confessions in a minute." Patience told me.

"So, you sent the text to get Chan here?" I asked.

"Yeah, I wasn't expecting her to bring you. I was expecting her to be by herself."

That was my cue. "Well, if y'all got this, I'm outta here." I started backing out of the room.

Patience wasn't amused. He shook his head. "I ain't Payne. That cute shit won't work. Get ya ass in here."

I stepped into the room a little more.

"Why'd you text me?" Chantelle asked him.

"I told you, I wanna get to the bottom of this for once and for all. Chan, you know how I feel about you. I've loved you ever since the first time I saw you." Patience confessed.

"And I wanted to step to you. I planned to step to you, but Izz's fat ass got in my way. He was already fuckin' Bubbles, so I couldn't understand why he had to have you, too. Guess he can't help being a greedy bitch."

"I already know he was messin' around with Bubbles." Chantelle said, her voice shaking.

"He didn't deserve you. You're a queen, Chan." He stared at her with lovesick eyes. "I wouldn't do you like that, Shorty. I'd put you on a pedestal. Anything you could ever want…I'd make it happen for you."

"I know you would, Patience." She assured him. She looked over at Israel. "What'd you do to him? Is he dead?"

"Nah, his fat ass ain't dead." He gave Israel a hard kick.

Israel groaned.

"I pumped his ass up with dope. Do you know how much dope it takes to bring a fat motherfucka like him down? I had to use the whole needle full of shit. When I finish with this," he gestured around the family room, "we're gonna bounce out. I'mma take you somewhere beautiful…like Hawaii or the Bahamas. I'mma spend the rest of my life making you happy."

This motherfucker really is crazy! I thought to myself. *I knew it! I knew it! I told Chan his ass was weird!*

"I shoulda killed ya ass a long time ago." Israel said. He sounded like his tongue was the size of a football.

"Too late now." Patience gloated. "Ain't it, you fat bitch?"

"Patience, you don't have to do all this. We can go somewhere right now and talk about our future together."

I was tripping at the thought of Chantelle trying to fast-talk Patience.

He smiled at her. "We'll talk. But business first. This nigga gotta die for what he did to you."

"Fuck him." She cooed. "He ain't worth you facin' jail time over."

"Tell her what you did to Bubbles." Patience told Israel.

Israel winced, but remained silent.

"Tell her, before I shoot your ass."

"Nigga, just kill me, cuz I ain't sayin' shit." Israel sounded like he was getting his swagger back.

Patience aimed his heat and pulled the trigger. The silencer muffled the sound of the bullet, but nothing could muffle Israel's groans as the bullet tore through his right leg.

"Sit down, Baby." Patience told Chantelle. He gestured to the couch with his gun. "I wanna talk to you."

"I don't wanna sit down."

Patience took a few steps towards Chantelle. She pressed up against the wall like she was trying to go through it.

"What's the matter?" He asked. His voice was filled with concern.

"You're scarin' me, Patience. What are you doin'?"

"I'm handling all my unfinished business. Fat-Ass is problem numero uno."

She sighed. "Okay, you can handle Izz. Let Joya go, though. She ain't got nothin' to do with this. This is between us, Boo."

I appreciated my girl trying to get me sprung. I hoped and prayed that Patience would listen to her.

He shook his head. "Joya's straight. She ain't goin' nowhere. She's already seen too much."

What does that mean? I thought to myself.

"Baby, Joya's scared and the way you're actin' is scaring me, too." Chantelle was still trying her best to talk slick enough to get us out of there.

"Don't be scared, now." Israel taunted. "You wasn't scared while you was fuckin' dude."

He was definitely getting his swag back. Whatever Patience had in that syringe wasn't strong enough to lay Israel completely flat.

"Shut the fuck up!" Chantelle told him. "Your fat ass shouldn't say nothing about who I'm fuckin'."

"Shut the fuck up, before I blast your dumb ass." Patience seconded.

"Do it. I dare you." Israel pressed, like he wasn't afraid to die.

Patience politely lifted the gun, aimed at Israel's left leg and let off a shot.

Even though the gun had a silencer, I couldn't help jumping. "Uh!" I said, reflexively turning my head away from the scene.

Patience ignored both Israel and me. He was all about Chantelle. "Chan, there was a lot of shit going on between Izz and Bubbles that you didn't know about."

"I went through my sister's cell phone." She admitted. "I read the text messages. I know all about the weekend trips, and the shopping sprees."

"Did you know that Izz, Dex and Rook set your sister up?"

"Set her up for what?"

"Set her up to get your man's brother a spot on the '*Rock the Park*' show."

"What are you talkin' about?" The scared expression had left her face. She wanted answers.

"Izz gave a little party for the heavy hitters at WKBC. He wanted them to give one of the slots on the show to Rook. To give Rook an edge, Izz, and Dex slipped some shit in Bubbles' drinks."

"What kind of shit?"

"X and meth, I don't know. Plus, they had her blowing trees all night, and it's no telling what was mixed up in that shit. All I know, is that once Bubbles was high enough, everybody at the party who wanted to hit, got a chance to hit. They let more than eight different cats run up in your sister that night. They taped it. Dex showed me the DVD. Bubbles was barely conscious, while dude after dude ran up in her."

I wanted to believe that Patience was standing there lying. I didn't want to believe that Izz, Dex and Rook were really that grimy.

Chantelle started to cry. "Is that true? Is that true?" She asked Israel through the tears. "Why would you do that? Why would you do that to my sister?" She ran over to where Israel was laid out on the floor and started pounding and kicking him.

Neither Patience nor I tried to stop her. I didn't know about Patience, but I was in shock. I couldn't believe that dudes I had chilled with so easily had been sinister enough to orchestrate something like that against Bubbles. It wasn't like she was a stranger. They kicked it with her practically every day. They knew her.

Izz didn't say a word as Chantelle beat the hell out of him. He took the beating like he knew he had it coming.

"That's why she set them up to get murked." Patience continued.

Chantelle stopped beating Israel momentarily. "She set who up to get murked?"

"Dex, Rook, and Fat Ass, over here." He responded.

"She set them up to get killed?" Chantelle looked like she might faint.

I wanted Patience to shut up and not tell her anything else. I didn't think she could take it.

But Patience was too intent on getting his story out. He had to tell it. "After Bubbles helped Izz and Dex kill Elliott, she decided to flip sides. She went to Elliott's brother with the info."

"Who is Elliott and what does his brother have to do with this?" Chantelle was getting confused.

"Elliott was the dude who blazed three of our spots." Patience explained. "His brother, Orville, was the cat they found dead at your sister's apartment. Orville offered your sister dough to get him info about Izz and Dex. She put me on for a cut of the money."

"I knew you was dirty, Bitch! I told Payne your ass was dirty." Israel said.

"Shut! The! Fuck! Up!" Patience gave Israel a vicious kick to the head.

I was trying to keep my mind focused. I wanted to keep up with what they were saying, but I also wanted to look for an opportunity to escape.

"Why would you agree to help her?" Chantelle questioned.

I had been wondering the same thing.

He shrugged his shoulders. "Because they were wrong for what they did to her...and because she was your sister. I love you, Chan. I would do anything for you."

"Oh my God." She dropped down to the couch. "Oh my God. Bubbles had Dex and Rook killed?"

"Justus, too." He added quickly. "They were supposed to kill fat ass, but J ate those bullets."

It was too much information to take in at once. I shook my head back and forth to try to clear my mind. That explained why Bubbles was so upset at Justus' funeral. She knew that she was responsible for him being killed.

Patience wouldn't stop talking. "When ya man found out that Bubbles set him up, he went to her apartment and killed her and Orville."

That was the straw that broke the camel's back. Chantelle looked like she was demon possessed. Her eyes actually rolled up to the back of her head. She started swaying slightly from side to side. She was making sounds like she was somewhere between crying, and screaming. She jumped up from the couch and turned to Israel with nothing but hate in her eyes. "Kill his ass!" She told Patience, as her foot made contact with Israel's ribs. "Kill him! Kill his ass! Kill him!" She was hysterical. She threw her body on top of Israel's and began to pound him again.

Patience stood there watching her like he was shook.

I started easing towards the door of the room.

Chantelle got off of Israel, and moved towards Patience. "I'll shoot him! Gimme the fuckin' gun." She tried to take the gun from Patience's hand.

That was when Patience came back to himself. He batted her hand away. "Stop Chan."

Chantelle wasn't trying to go. She was determined to shoot Izz. While they were fighting over the gun, I decided to make my move. I started moving towards the door, fast as hell. Patience spotted me, and let off a bullet over my head. "Where you going, Joya?" He asked calmly. "The party ain't over."

"This is between you, Chan and Izz. This doesn't have anything to do with me." I told him.

I watched as he emptied five shots in Israel. "Uhm, now you're an accomplice." He grinned at me, looking as psychotic as I always knew he was. "Or a witness. You can't go nowhere. You know too much."

"I don't know nothing." I insisted, wishing like hell that I had 'Thriller Killer' with me.

Nasir chose that moment to step into the doorway. I was relieved to see him, but I did notice that he wasn't holding.

Where is his gun? He needs his gun! I thought to myself.

"Damn, what the fuck is going on?" Nasir asked Patience.

"I'm handling my business. What does it look like?" He responded sarcastically. "And I ain't finished." Before any of us knew what was happening, Patience pointed the gun and fired.

Chapter Twenty-Two
Life We Chose

Payne

I knew the situation that I was walking into before I even got there. With Joya's cell phone line open, I could hear everything that was being said. I parked the Denali on the next block; went through the gangway; crossed the alley; jumped Izz's back fence; and journeyed around the front of the house. I took the steps three at a time. When I got to the door, it was wide opened just like Joya had promised it would be.

As soon as I stepped into the foyer, a chill went down my spine. The feeling of death enveloped me. My mind went to Joya's dream of me being in a shoot-out, and not pulling out fast enough. I let my hand gently graze my burner and my back holster.

I walked towards the back of the house as quietly as possible. I could hear Patience's voice and Chantelle screaming for him to kill Israel. I heard a shot go off. I started trying to formulate a quick plan. But thoughts of putting something together went out of my mind when I heard five shots pop off. I didn't know who was shot. I was nervous as hell that my girl had caught a bullet. I picked up my pace.

I stepped into the doorway. I was about three feet away from Joya. I let my eyes move around the room as quickly as possible. Chantelle was by the sofa. Israel was stretched out on the floor.

"Damn, what the fuck is going on?" I directed my question to Patience.

He sneered at me. "I'm handling my business. What does it look like?"

I knew Izz shoulda took him out way back when. I thought to myself.

"And I ain't finished." His punk ass continued.

Then, he pointed the burner at me. It was Joya's dream playing itself out. I pulled out as quickly as I could and pointed back at him, but he got his shot off faster. His aim was all fucked up, though. I watched helplessly as his shot tore into Joya, knocking her to the hardwood floor with a thud. Chantelle's breath caught loudly in her throat. Time stood still. I was paralyzed. The only female I had ever loved was sprawled out on the floor in front of me.

Patience brought me back to the present. "You next, Payne." He pointed his gun again.

I didn't even have to think about it. Reflex took over. I lit my trigger. Three quick shots blasted him. Two to the chest. One to the head. "You now, Motherfucker!" I told his crumpled body. Then, fell down next to my wifey, who was pouring blood on to the floor. "Chan, call 911!"

She just stood there staring at me with blank eyes.

"Chan! Call 911! Hurry up. Chan, hurry up! Call 911."

Chantelle was in shock. I reluctantly released Joya, grabbed my cell phone and called for an ambulance. Once the call was made, I pulled my wifey into my arms and held her while we waited.

***

The cops arrested me for the murder of Patience Black. It didn't matter to them that Chantelle insisted it was self-defense. It didn't matter that Patience had shot both Joya and Israel. It didn't matter that I never wanted to have to kill Patience. He was my guy. We had grown up together. It didn't matter that I had done the one thing I had been spooked about doing my entire life. I had killed behind the woman I loved.

All that mattered was that I had murdered another man with an unregistered weapon. Standard procedure was what they called it. They handcuffed me and read me my rights. As they put me in the back of the squad car, I yelled for Chantelle to call Unc and let him know the deal.

I sat in the police station on 71st and South Chicago and prayed that Unc could get me out before they processed me, and sent me to the county. I knew if I got sent to the county, I was going to be down for a minute. And I was too stressed to be locked down like that. I needed to know what the hell was going on with my wifey. It was eating me up on the inside.

Finally, around eight o'clock in the morning, Unc showed up and got me sprung. He had connections all over the city, so I knew that if anybody could get me out, it would be him. While we walked to his Maybach 62, I whipped out my phone. I needed to make some calls and find out where Joya was.

"Put that away, Nephew." Unc told me. "I need to get at you for a second."

"Come on, Man. Dude shot my wifey. I need to check on her."

"Your girl is cool. I've got all the info on her that you need. She's in good condition. She's stable and she's at Christ Hospital. She was shot in the right shoulder. Lost a lot of blood, but other than that, she's good. Your guy is alive, too."

"My guy, who?"

"Survived five shots to stomach and a bullet to each leg."

"Izz?" I asked in disbelief. I couldn't believe dude had survived. Patience shot him at point blank range. I figured those years of Patience laying in the cut while we did his dirty work had hurt him. The cat couldn't even murk somebody when he was standing right next to them. That was a damn shame. I sighed. "What's up? What do you need to holler at me about?"

We slipped into the luxuriousness of his car. "The gun, Nephew. I got my guy to spring you on my word that you were a clean cat. Be real with me, are there any hot ones on that gun they took from the scene?"

I twisted my face. "Hell no. You raised me yourself. You know what I do. I don't keep no dirty guns. That gun was clean. I just got it."

He nodded slowly. "Well done, Nephew. Well done. Cuz any murders on that heat, and they were coming to lock you up. Plus, I was gonna lose my connect at the station."

I noticed that Unc was headed towards my house. "Come on, Man." I told him. "Can you take me to the hospital? I told you I wanna see my girl."

"I understand that. But what you don't understand is that

you stink, Nephew. You've been in jail all night. Go home, wash your ass, throw on a fresh 'fit and check on your son. Then, you can head to the hospital."

***

I didn't get to the hospital until after three o'clock that afternoon. Once Unc dropped me at the crib, I called myself chilling on the couch for a minute after I talked to my grandmother and checked on my son. I woke up two hours later. I showered, dressed, and made my way over to Christ Hospital.

Once I had my visitor's pass, I took the elevator up to Joya's floor. I was moving so fast that I almost bumped into Chantelle. She was a blur to me. Luckily she wasn't so pressed.

"Payne." She threw her arms around my neck. "Payne."

I hugged her back. I had nothing but love for Chantelle right about then. After everything she had been through, she was standing like a straight soldier. "Ma, how're you doing?" I asked looking into her tired eyes.

"I'm cool. I don't allow myself to think about too much, except what's happenin' right now. I'm supposed to be gettin' Joy some juice from the cafeteria. So, that's what my mind is on."

I nodded my understanding. "Ay, whatever you gotta do to maintain, Baby. Whatever you gotta do."

She looked at me for a second, then sucker-punched me in the stomach.

"What?" I asked.

"Do you get somebody pregnant every time you have sex or what?"

I was lost. "What do you mean?"

"You ain't gotta play dumb. The doctor let the cat outta the bag. He told us Joy is pregnant. Her mother was trippin' behind that, too. She was hot. She couldn't believe that her baby girl is pregnant by some cat she's never even met."

"Joy is pregnant?" I repeated, ignoring everything else she said.

The expression on Chantelle's face changed. "Oh hell. You didn't know?"

"Hell nah, I didn't know. Joy's pregnant? And Patience shot her?"

"Calm down, Payne. Everything's fine. The baby's fine. Joy lost a lot of blood, but both of them are fine."

I walked away from Chantelle. She followed hot on my heels. I burst into Joya's room.

She was posted up in the bed, flipping through the

television channels. When the door flew open, she looked over at me and grinned. My face remained frowned up.

"Nasir." She said happily. "Hey."

We looked into each other's eyes. I noticed that her right shoulder was covered with huge bandages. The thought of her being pregnant and getting shot made me go soft. My anger started to subside. "He shot your shoulder, huh?" I walked over to the bed.

"Yeah, and it hurts so bad, too." She whined.

"Damn, I'm sorry to hear that." I hugged her gently, and kissed her lips.

"Chan told me that the police arrested you. Are you okay?"

"I'm coolin'…but I'm pissed with you."

"Why?" She asked. "Because I walked into an obvious set-up?"

"No. Because you didn't tell me that you're pregnant?"

"Oh."

"Yeah…oh. I asked you straight up. I asked you. Why the hell you lie to me?"

"I didn't lie." She clarified. "I avoided answering the question."

"You lied. And the thing that pisses me off is that I knew you were lying. Deep down inside, I knew you were lying. But you gave me that bullshit and I chose not to press you."

"I'm sorry." She hit me with the pouty face.

"Hell no. That ain't riding. There's no reason on earth why I shoulda had to hear that from Chan."

"I am so sorry, Girl." Chantelle stated quickly. "I had no idea that Payne didn't know."

Joya gave her the evil eye.

"I'm about to go get your juice, so y'all can finish talkin'. Bye." Chantelle disappeared from the room.

"Why couldn't you tell me?"

"I don't know, Nasir. I was trying to decide what I was gonna do. You know Ricci is expecting me back in New York. I haven't quit my job." She paused. "I was weighing my options."

I hit her with the screw face. "What options did you have? You weren't about to get rid of my seed. What options did you have?"

She sighed heavily. "As much as I wanna pop off at the mouth and say something flip, I can't. You're right. I really didn't have any options. I couldn't have an abortion. I didn't know what to do. It was...too much. I got overwhelmed and I started tripping. I don't know what else to say."

"How far along are you...or is that big secret, too?"

She rolled her eyes at me. "No, it's not a secret. I'm about 14 or 15 weeks."

"Damn, Ma. And how long have you known?"

"I've only known for like…four weeks, Nah Nah."

"That's a month. You knew for an entire month."

"I said I was sorry. I don't know what else you want me to say."

We were both silent.

After a minute or so, she popped me lightly. "I'm pissed with you, too." She announced.

"What're you pissed with me for?"

"Why you tell me you caught the condom, when you knew you didn't?"

I was busted. I had to chuckle. "I thought I caught it. Real talk."

"That's not funny, Nasir. Do you know how embarrassed I was when the doctor announced in front of my mother that I'm pregnant? My mother doesn't even know you."

"That's your fault. My family knows you."

"Nasir."

"I'm sorry, Beautiful. But I guess you need to stop treating me like a jump-off and introduce me to ya moms."

"You know she's never gonna like you now." She told me. "You're always gonna be the cat she never met, who got her daughter pregnant."

"She'll like me. I'm good with moms." I promised. "Where is she?"

"She went to my house to get me some clothes. They're

supposed to be releasing me today."

"Good. How're you gonna take care of yourself? I know you can't lift that arm."

"Nah, I'm gonna stay at my mom's house."

"You know you could always stay at my pad."

She rolled her eyes at me. "I don't think so, Playboy. When I stay at your pad, I tend to end up pregnant."

"Uh, that ain't happen at my pad. That happened at your spot." I said to mess with her.

She punched me lightly with her good arm, then sighed heavily. "I can't believe I'm pregnant. This is not how I would have chosen this to happen."

"Do you know how much shit has happened to me in the last year that I wouldn't have chosen to happen? Sometimes things happen to you, and you have to ride. I got you pregnant. My bad. I wasn't trying to. But I ain't gonna pretend like I'm upset about it, either. Because I'm not."

"Uhm, I'm sure Ricci will be upset about it."

"Fuck Ricci. When you get ready to do music again, I'll put you on the hook of whoever's shit is hottest at that time. Record execs from everywhere are gonna want you." I raised her hospital gown, exposed her stomach and kissed her there. "You're the hottest thing to come outta Chicago since Kanye, Shorty." I kissed her again, then rested my head on her stomach. "You too, Little Mama."

"Little Mama?" She repeated.

"Yeah. That's my little princess in there."

"Whatever." She chuckled.

"I love you so much, Man." I admitted. "I was worried as hell about you, sitting in that jail cell."

She rubbed her hand over my hair. "I love you too, Nah Nah. I probably love you too much."

"There's no such thing." I laid there with my head still resting on her stomach. "You're pregnant with my shorty. This whole thing is crazy, because I'm actually happy."

"Really?"

"Yeah. It's messing me up, cuz when Midori told me that she was pregnant, happy is not the emotion I was feeling."

"I'm glad you're happy, because I'm totally scared."

I pulled her hospital gown down, moved up the bed and kissed her soft lips. "Don't be scared. I got you. From here on out…it's me and you against the world."

In that moment, I decided that I wanted to commit to Joya. Nobody on earth made me feel the way she did. No other female challenged me like her. No other female could make me smile, or laugh like she did. No other female frustrated me in the ways that she did. Joya made me want to love her. The only other female to ever do that was Dorothy Jane. That meant something to me. That meant that I had finally found my wife.

Epilogue
Same Old Love

Joya

Two years later…

I brushed my hair repeatedly, caught it with my hands and wrestled it into a neat ponytail. I adjusted the four carat diamond ring that adorned my swollen finger and prepared to finally leave my bedroom. The ringing of the phone stopped me. I walked back over to the dresser and picked up my cell. Nasir's number was displayed on the screen. "Yes, Nah Nah."

"Mrs. Payne," he said to me, "what's taking you so long? You were supposed to be in the studio fifteen minutes ago. Time is money, Ma."

"I'm coming. I'm coming." I promised. "I'm leaving the house now."

"Hurry up."

I walked down the stairs, stopped to grab my house keys from the table beside the door, then exited the house. I crossed the driveway, and made my way into Nasir's studio. "I'm here." I announced. "I told you I was coming."

"Mommy!" My two year old son, Justus yelled, delighted to see me. He ran over, looking like the spitting image of his father, with the exception of the slanted eyes that confirmed his Asian heritage.

I bent down and pulled him close, in spite of the largeness of my seven-month pregnant belly. I kissed him sloppily on his peanut-butter colored cheek. "Hey, handsome boy."

"Ma-ma!" My one year old daughter, Charity cooed as she toddled over.

"Hey Doll-face." I scooped her into my arms, hugged her tightly and kissed her cheek loudly, before placing her back down.

I looked up just in time to see Nasir grinning at me. I still got butterflies looking into those green eyes, and staring at those ridiculous dimples. I smiled back at him.

"Ay dude, this is my wife, Joya." Nasir said to one of his guests. "Joya, this is Tahkim Steele and you already know Trey."

"Hey Trey." I greeted him with a quick hug. He had finally gotten the record deal that he was after, and was an artist on *Spot Check Records'* roster.

"What's good, Joya? Look at you." He touched my stomach lightly. "Payne's ass loves to keep you swolled up, huh?"

I chuckled. "So, you noticed that, too?"

"Can't believe y'all on baby number three already. Real talk, congratulations."

"Thank you." I waddled over to Tahkim Steele. Nasir didn't need to introduce him. I knew who Tahkim Steele was. He was the godfather of hip hop. He had been making music for almost as long as I could remember. His first single, *Hot Chocolate* was the first rap song that I ever learned the lyrics to. Now, because Nasir's company, Payne Killer Productions was majorly successful and killing the industry, I was about to blow the hook on the song Tahkim was doing with Trey. "It's nice to meet you." I shook his large hand.

"You, too. Any day now, huh?" He asked gesturing to my protruding stomach.

"Not really." I confessed. "I just seem to be extra big with this one for some reason."

"It's not affectin' your voice, though." He told me. "From what Payne played for me, you sound good as hell, Shorty."

"It's not affecting her voice or her hustle." Nasir assured him. "You wanna go in the booth, while I run the track back?"

Tahkim nodded, then went into the state-of-the-art recording booth. Nasir walked over to me and pulled me into his arms. He sucked my bottom lip hungrily, then kissed me deeply. "Damn, you're sexy pregnant."

"I do not feel sexy." My hands and feet were swollen, and I was as big as a house.

"You are, though."

"You're sweet." I kissed his lips.

After the shooting and my hospital stay, everything went to the left for a while.

Chantelle spent about eleven months acting out with self-destructive behavior. She couldn't deal with everything that had gone down. Knowing that Israel was not only having a relationship with, but had killed Bubbles left my best friend's world spinning. Nia and I watched helplessly as she lived recklessly and put her own life in danger. For a while she gave up on men and started to date women. She dabbled in drugs, and she had even done a short stint as a stripper. Finally, she was convinced to try grief counseling. The therapy helped Chantelle deal with the emotions that were eating her up, and she had gotten her life back on track. After Nasir's name started ringing bells in the industry, he invested some money into Chantelle's dream. She was finally able to open a dance academy. It was a successful business that managed to begin operating in the black before the end of its first year in existence.

Israel survived being shot repeatedly by Patience, but his life was never the same. Two of the bullets that Patience had pumped into him had traveled through his body and damaged his spinal cord. He was paralyzed from the waist down and wheel chair bound. He was also arrested for the double murders of Orville Pettigrew and Keena "Bubbles" Price. He was tried, convicted and sentenced to two consecutive life sentences which he was serving at Ely State Prison in Ely, Nevada. He was appealing the ruling, but by most accounts things didn't look good for Israel.

Nia opened a second *Pleasure Principle* store. She was moving passed the death of Justus and had started dating, again.

Midori never came out of the coma, but she did begin responding mildly to stimuli. That gave her parents enough hope to keep her on the machines and to believe that one day she would open her eyes and come back into the land of the living. Nasir took LP by the hospital once a month to see her. LP didn't understand what was going on. He didn't know why he had to go to the hospital to see a lady that he didn't know, but Nasir believed that it was the right thing to do. Eventually, we were able to build up a cordial rapport with Midori's parents. The Andersons would visit our home from time to time to spend time with LP.

The District Attorney's office brought charges against Nasir for Patience's murder. He was never indicted, though. With Chantelle's, Israel's and my testimony about the events that led up to the shooting, they knew they probably weren't going to get a guilty verdict. The charges were later dropped, and Patience's murder was ruled self-defense.

I married Nasir right after the charges were dropped. We were wed at The Sanctuary at Kiawah Island, right outside of Charleston, South Carolina. He married me on the Grand

Lawn, overlooking the resort's private beach and the Atlantic Ocean.

After the shooting, Bruno Ricci withdrew his offer for me to join *Ride or Die Records*. He basically told me that he wasn't looking to bring any unnecessary drama into his record label. I knew it was more about me being pregnant, than it was about me getting shot, but it didn't matter. I was ready to take a break from music and concentrate on my family, anyway. I took a leave of absence from Eastern Airlines as well, to begin the process of legally adopting Justus, and to prepare for the impending arrival of Charity.

Nasir was true to his word, though. As soon as I felt like singing again, he made it happen for me. Anytime he had a hot track that needed a female on the hook, he threw my name out there. So, even though I never got that solo deal, I was still able to make money and have a career in the industry. When I wasn't doing music, I helped Nasir run *Exit Strategy LLC*. We decided to keep the business as a legacy for our children.

Two years later, Nasir was outwardly maintaining, but still silently dealing with shooting Patience. Even though he never admitted it out loud, I knew that having to kill his guy had done something to Nasir on the inside. The nightmares had finally started to subside, but my husband had been changed.

Nasir rubbed his hand across my stomach. "Ay, how's my baby girl doing?"

"This one's a girl, too, huh?" I teased.

"Yeah, Beautiful. I gotta feeling that you won't give me nothing but little girls. I think you're too damn feminine to make me another son."

I laughed. "You're probably right."

"Just make sure this one looks more like you, though."

"I know, right?" I agreed. Both Justus and Charity sported Nasir's peanut butter complexion, his deep dimples and his green eyes.

"Yo Payne, let's do this!" Tahkim called from the booth.

Nasir nodded, never releasing his hold on me. "I got you, Dude."

"Go do your thing." I told him.

"One second. Have I told you how much I love you, Joy?"

"You tell me every day, Nah Nah. And I love you back."

"Thanks for marrying me."

"Thank you for asking me." I replied.

While we were hugging, Justus and Charity got up from where they were playing and came over to get in on the action. They wrapped their little bodies around our legs and held on tight. Even the baby started bouncing in my stomach. I smiled to myself and thanked God for His goodness. I was blessed, in love and happy. And I was wise enough to appreciate it.

The End

About the Author

Tracy Gray was born and raised on the south side of Chicago, Illinois. At the age of 9, she began writing plays that included characters based on the children who lived on her block. Creative expression became a way of life for Tracy, and has continued throughout the years.

She enjoys traveling, spending time with her family and reading. She is currently working on her next novel.

www.ingramcontent.com/pod-product-compliance
Lightning Source LLC
Chambersburg PA
CBHW051511250626
47156CB00001B/45